THE
SIXTH PILLAR

Alan Reynolds

Fisher King Publishing

The Sixth Pillar
Copyright © Alan Reynolds 2013
ISBN 978-1-906377-95-3

Cover design based on an original work by
Leon Reynolds Design

Photograph of the author by
Karen Ross Photography

Published by
Fisher King Publishing
The Studio
Arthington Lane
Pool-in-Wharfedale
LS21 1JZ
England

"What is the final destination of hatred when you look at the enemy and see yourself?"

Anon

Chapter One

Southern Iraq, January 1991.

Sergeant Rory Calderwood turned from his vantage point and made a hand signal to his number two behind him indicating, 'contact ahead'.

Corporal Lennie 'the Loon' Arthur acknowledged with the 'ok' sign.

At his command, the rest of the eight-man platoon dropped to their haunches against the friable brick of what was possibly a barn or some sort of small storage facility.

The village had not been on their original itinerary.

Their orders were to seek and destroy the launchers which deployed the deadly Scud missiles which were already creating havoc in Israel, potentially threatening to bring the Israelis into the war. Saddam Hussein was gambling that this strategy would cause a rift between the coalition partners, thus jeopardising cooperation between the Arab members. There had also been credible intelligence that Scuds were about to be launched from Southern Iraq directed at Saudi Arabia, which, both politically and militarily, would prove more than an embarrassment; such was the importance of this mission.

The population of this part of Iraq was mainly Shiite and considered sympathetic to the overthrow of Saddam Hussein, but squads of Republican Guards were in evidence across the region as they prepared for the expected invasion by coalition forces. It was an extremely hostile place.

Calderwood had been given orders to investigate reports of sightings of possible launchers along a main road west of Basra. Iraqis were quick and clever in hiding their weaponry; wadis and culverts were regularly used to conceal them. The team was tasked with a 'seek and destroy' remit.

This small village, close to the road, was of interest, and he had chosen to take a closer look.

A whirl of dust was kicked up by a squall. Calderwood pulled up the edge of his shemagh to protect his eyes and once again peered through the site of his NVD and the green triangle which was now his field of vision. Anyone associating the desert with blistering heat should be here now, he thought - it was bitterly cold, but his focus was total, and he shrugged off the temperature as an inconvenience.

The object of his interest appeared again; then, as quickly, disappeared from sight.

It had been a three-hour hike since they had been dropped off by their Chinook transport. From their helicopter landing-zone their first objective was to locate the tarmac road.

That part of the journey had been comparatively easy, but, having followed the deserted road for several miles, they had now stumbled across the village; although that description was euphemistic. It was a small collection of, what appeared to be, farm buildings and a scattering of around ten or twelve houses situated down a track about two hundred yards from the road. It was a comparable size to some of the hamlets Calderwood was familiar with back in his native Herefordshire. There was no other similarity. The environment was hostile, and not just because of the proximity of enemy forces. There was no evidence of water, just dust and scrub. He wondered how anyone could survive in this place never mind eke out any sort of living. The cold was dry and penetrating, not like a winter's day back in England.

Spotting the buildings, the platoon had crept up the track to their present locale, overlooking a courtyard. There was no cover and a stealth approach had been required. Directly ahead of them was a larger structure on two floors. A dim flickering light was visible from the windows, probably hurricane lamps. There was no sign of electricity that Calderwood could see; no power lines, nor the tell-tale noise of a generator. There was also no evidence of a telephone connection.

Although Calderwood had taken up a recce position, their observation post was not ideal; they were stretched out along the side of the first building and only the sergeant had a proper view of proceedings.

Calderwood ducked back from the corner of the building and, shielded by the wall, the team gathered around him. He briefed his men in faint whispers.

"Two trucks covered in netting parked against the wall of the building opposite, could be carrying Scuds, certainly big enough, and someone's gone to a lot of trouble to hide them. One rag-head, heavily armed, came out for a smoke; there'll be more inside. Lennie, you take Stan and Digger, scout around the back of the main building and see what you can find. I'm going to take a peek at the trucks. Rendezvous back here in seven... go."

The three men set off. A tinkling of bells from a herd of goats could be heard, disturbed by the intrusion. The remaining squad dropped lower.

Calderwood spoke to lance corporal Steve Swanson. "Swannie, take the NVD and cover me."

Calderwood handed him his night vision device and checked his M16 before silently and swiftly moving to the first vehicle, fifty feet or so across the square. Swanson looked on closely, his assault rifle at the ready.

The sergeant was totally in the zone, adrenaline taking him

to a high, senses on alert. He stooped behind the nearest truck, unseen from the house. He lifted the loose netting to check its cargo; then moved quickly to the leading truck and did the same before heading back to his team.

He dropped down behind the wall of the barn and briefed his men again.

"Bingo!" he whispered. "Two missile launchers... Right, time to announce our presence. As soon as Lennie gets back, I'll outline the plan."

Two minutes later, the corporal returned with his two buddies and dropped down next to the sergeant.

"What have we got?" asked Calderwood.

"Ok, one exit, three rag-heads having a smoke, looked very relaxed, don't think they're going anywhere soon. No other vehicles or weaponry visible," he replied.

Lennie took a stick and drew a rough outline of the complex in the dirt. It was ten-thirteen p.m. and pitch-black, but with their eyesight attuned to the lack of light, they could clearly make out the corporal's map of the target.

"This is the main building... this is us. Around the back there's another piece of ground about fifty feet, then a couple of houses, civvy I think. There're two houses here, and two here."

He drew two blocks, north and south of the target and two blocks immediately behind, forming a shape of a horse shoe. The team watched on.

Calderwood summarised. "Right, priority one will be the launchers... Swannie, be ready to come with me with the PE4 and detonators. Lennie, around the back with Stan and Digger and take Phillips with you... So that's four here and four at the back. When the trucks go the shit's gonna hit the fan. We'll take out as many rag-heads as we can. Rendezvous back at the main road, here."

He drew a mark in the sand at the top of the track where it met the tarmac.

"Then we'll exfil and tab parallel to the road until we break off to the pick-up point."

Calderwood made gestures with his hands to emphasise the point.

"Everybody clear?" There were nods of agreement. "Bernie, let HQ know... Get them to meet us at zero two hundred. Should give us enough time in case we have to make a detour or two."

"Roger that," said the wireless operator, who was immediately surrounded by three of his team to absorb any possible sounds.

"Alpha-two-bravo to kingfisher, this is Highlight, be advised we have two, repeat two runners in sight and are pursuing with vigour, lift home zero two hundred from DOP... over."

"Roger that, alpha-two-bravo... out."

Calderwood deployed his men and waited five minutes for Lennie and his team to get into position. It was at times like this that he appreciated the value of the training which had brought him to this lonely piece of the Iraqi desert. Trust in his men was total.

"Right Swannie, here we go."

The two men moved across the open ground to the first truck; the two remaining squad members covering their backs. A gust of wind blew some dead scrub across their path.

Swanson crawled under the nearest lorry and took out the plastic explosive from its container. He shaped the putty-like substance and molded it to the underside of the vehicle then inserted the LPD detonator. Within seconds he was out and making his way to the next truck; Calderwood acting look-out and cover. Same process, and the two men returned to their comrades.

"How long, Swannie?" asked Calderwood.

"Three minutes, number one; two minutes, number two." Calderwood checked his watch and waited.

"Right lads take cover," and the men scrummed down, bracing themselves against the wall safely away from any blast wave and flying debris.

Suddenly a loud boom disturbed the silence, followed by the clattering of metal and other objects. A few seconds later a second explosion echoed around the compound.

The sound of machine gun fire rattled from the back of the building. Calderwood and his team appeared from behind the barn and opened up on the front of the building as Iraqi soldiers appeared.

At the rear it was a killing field, as Lennie and his team took out the exiting Iraqis with withering fire. The corporal had taken cover behind the low wall in front of the house immediately behind the target building.

Suddenly, Digger cried out. "Incoming!!"

An RPG launched from an upstairs window arrowed towards Lennie. He dropped to the floor and the missile went over his head, through the window of the house behind him and exploded with such ferocity that the front wall disintegrated. Lennie, momentarily deafened by the compression, was showered by brick dust and rubble. A second missile followed, again too high, but completing the demolition of the dwelling. Screams could be heard from inside. Lennie watched as he cleared his head. A fire had taken hold and he could see flames dancing around the remains, growing in intensity.

Digger was about twenty metres away from the main

building. He loaded a grenade into his M16 and fired at the window where the Iraqi had appeared. The window blew outwards showering debris and body parts across the open ground. The firing stopped; Lennie joined Digger and the rest of his team. They slowly headed for the back door; then entered the building.

Inside it was total devastation, the walls pock-marked with shell holes. The team slowly went from room to room ensuring no threat remained; Lennie counted five bodies. Worryingly, there was a radio in one of the downstairs rooms. Although now completely inoperable, there was no way of knowing whether a message had been relayed; they had to assume one had.

The front door was suddenly kicked in. Lennie instinctively swung around to confront the intrusion, but relaxed as Calderwood appeared with Swanson. The team continued clearing the building, looking for anything that might provide future intel.

"Building secure," called Lennie, as he came down the stairs. "Two rag-heads dead, first floor... another with the RPG is spread across the open ground at the back; five more in the back room."

Calderwood looked at the nearest body, a lad of no more than seventeen, clearly a conscript.

"Right, let's get out of here," said Calderwood, and led the assault squad back to the covering team at the barn before making their getaway.

Half an hour later, as the platoon was making their escape; two trucks laden with troops entered the compound. The officer in charge, a major, sporting the ubiquitous Saddam Hussein moustache, got out of the leading vehicle and surveyed the carnage. Both Scud missile launchers were scattered across the courtyard, twisted metal and pieces of machinery littered the area. He barked orders to his men; one truck was directed back to the main road to search for the perpetrators.

Around the back of the building, the fire blazed on in the demolished house. It would be allowed to burn itself out. Without water, there was no alternative.

The major went through the building and exited at the rear. He noticed a spent round on the floor, bent down and picked it up. He examined it carefully.

His aide, and body guard, never more than a few feet away from him, looked at the commander. "What is it?"

"M16, probably British," the major replied, looking closely at the cartridge case.

"SAS?" asked the junior officer.

"Almost certainly. We must find them before they are picked up," spat the major.

One of the men who had been scouting around the rest of the compound approached the officer holding the hand of a small boy about five years old.

"Who is this?" asked the major.

"I don't know. We found him wandering at the back of the buildings," said the trooper.

The young boy was completely covered with white dust which gave him a ghostly appearance. He was clearly traumatised and incoherent, sobbing dry sobs, as if his whole body was convulsing.

The major bent down and put his hand on the young lad's shoulder and spoke softly to him. The boy reminded him of his own son back in Baghdad. His mind wandered momentarily as he thought about him and wondered how he was coping during the air strikes. He would be frightened just like the young boy who stood in front of him, hair matted, his face streaked with tears; he was shaking from shock and cold.

"Get him inside and keep him warm... Any other survivors?"

"No, I don't know how anyone could have survived that," said the squaddie, looking at the smouldering remnants of what was somebody's home.

Back inside the main building, the major spoke to his aide who had now taken over custody of the lad.

"Get him some water... and ask him if he saw anything," said the major.

The aide took a plastic bottle of water from his kit bag and helped the boy take in some liquid. Then he gently asked him a few questions.

Meanwhile the major was on the walkie-talkie to the searching truck.

"No, go west, you fools... They won't be heading to Basra, they'll be heading into the desert to be picked up," he said, with an air of exasperation.

The aide approached. The major looked in anticipation. "Anything?"

"Says his name is Tariq, lives in that house," pointing to the burning ruin. "Mother, three sisters, grandparents... he appears to have escaped with no injuries; says he was in the back bedroom, seems the wall blew out."

"Did he see anything?" asked the major.

"No, he's been wandering about, he's still in shock. We need to get him to a hospital."

"There's no time for that," said the major. "What about neighbours?"

"The rest of the houses are deserted... Looks like everyone has fled."

"Ah yes, the invasion," said the major, mockingly. "We can't just leave him, sir."

The major thought for a moment.

"No, no, of course, you're right; we'll take him back to base, but first we must find the bastards that did this."

He punched his fist into the palm of his hand in frustration.

The major called his men together.

"Right let's get back on the truck… there's nothing more we can do here."

The eight conscripts climbed into the vehicle, the aide joining the major in the front with the driver. The child sat on the aide's lap whimpering for his mother.

Further west, Calderwood and his team had made good time, moving parallel to the road as planned; the regular draining culverts had provided ideal cover from the occasional passing car. Concealment was far less hazardous than confrontation.

He checked his GPS to confirm his course courtesy of the US who had made the new tracking system available to all coalition forces. He was able to pin-point his position to the accuracy of a few feet.

"Five clicks to the pick-up point," said Calderwood as the team took on liquid.

The group had been marching for over an hour and a brief stop was necessary. They were about to set off again for the pick-up point when a shout went up.

"Vehicle approaching!" called Digger, who was on watch.

The road was dead straight for mile upon mile and visibility was good. The truck was just using sidelights, but even with its restricted lighting, it could clearly be seen a good half a mile away, enough time for the squad to take up defensive positions.

"It's military... What do you want to do sarge?" said Digger, who had joined his leader.

Calderwood used his binoculars. "Yeah, search party... Ok, we'll let them go by, but be ready just in case... You know what to do."

Calderwood gave the orders and the team spread out along each side of the tarmac. Digger was in front with the grenade launcher, behind him Lennie, hidden in the culvert. There was no other cover.

The truck's progress was inexorable, closer, closer, a searchlight scanning the immediate area as it approached. The squad readied themselves as the vehicle slowly trundled past at little more than walking pace, then it suddenly ground to a halt. Someone on the back swung the searchlight around and scanned the highway ahead of them; then out into the desert, left, then right. Calderwood and his team hunkered down flat to the side of the road.

The beam turned slowly a hundred and eighty degrees scanning the tarmac behind. From that angle there was no hiding place and an excited shout went out as the stream of light picked up the shape of a crouching SAS soldier.

Wild automatic fire went out from the back of the truck and ricocheted off the road a good twenty feet in front of him. Digger took aim with the Grenade launcher and fired. There was a whooshing noise as the missile left the rifle followed by an explosion as it landed in the back of the truck. Those that could attempted to flee from the vehicle, but the squad had closed in putting down a lethal barrage of fire. The screams of the wounded echoed around the still night air. There was another explosion as the fuel tank blew up sending debris in all directions; the truck now well ablaze.

Calderwood and Swanson reached the vehicle checking for any survivors; the remainder of the squad covering their back. A pitiful moaning noise could be heard from the drainage ditch at the side of the road where an injured Iraqi lay. Lennie went over to the prostrate soldier and dispatched him with a double tap to the head; there would be nobody to reveal their presence or be able to describe the direction in which they would travel. The body count was ten.

Calderwood led his team off the road and into the desert travelling at a ninety-degree angle to the tarmac until they came to a dry wadi which they had traversed on their way in. The squad slithered down the dusty bank. It was about a five-feet drop to the arid river bed which would at least provide them with a semblance of cover. It took less than half an hour to reach the drop-off point three miles away; now the wait. The terrain was flat, and in the far distance the fire-engulfed truck lit up the horizon.

Meanwhile, the major's truck was some way behind the burning vehicle, and it had taken almost half an hour before they reached their luckless comrades. Once again, the commander got down from his cab to a scene of devastation. He could smell the unmistakable aroma of burning flesh mixed in with the heady scent of fuel oil and metal. He looked down at the first body with sadness and vowed revenge. He realised it was probably a forlorn hope finding the perpetrators, but he would drive ahead for a few miles; he might just be lucky.

Back in the desert the wait continued. Then, just a few minutes after the appointed time, Calderwood and his team heard the unmistakable sound of a Chinook. A long droning noise echoed across the desert floor. This was a dangerous time, when they were at their most vulnerable. A low flying helicopter, particularly the lumbering Chinook would be an easy target for any surface-to-air missile. The team huddled together in the cold night air as the helicopter closed in on the given co-ordinates. Swanson flashed a beam from his torch to guide in the pilot. Louder and louder the noise, the shape, not thirty feet from the ground, now visible against the desolate terrain. It hovered for a moment before touching down and the men scrambled on board. The evac took a matter of seconds and the Chinook made height and turned until it was well out of range of any artillery.

Despite their training and expertise, the team felt a degree of elation at a job well done. The banter was positive, before the adrenaline dissipated and they were enveloped by tiredness.

Later, as Calderwood and his team relaxed in the belly of the Chinook each with his own thoughts, the sergeant took stock and reflected on the mission. He recalled once being asked if he was a soldier or a man, as if the two were somehow incompatible and right now he understood the relevance of the question. He had seen sights that no human being should witness; done things which were against the very fabric of human behaviour... it was his job; he had to live with the consequences.

Rory Calderwood was eventually awarded the Military Medal for the mission and was to lead subsequent forays into enemy territory; each time he felt the same.

Back in Iraq the major never got his revenge. It was a long and difficult journey back to their base in Basra after the incident and it was made in complete silence interrupted only by the pitiful crying of the young Tariq. The following day the boy was handed over to the local Red Crescent who would take responsibility for him. A few days later, shortly before the start of Operation Desert Sabre, the major was called back to Baghdad ostensibly to assist in the protection of the City and the President. A full report of the incident had been dispatched to his superiors and on his return to the capital, the unsuspecting major was arrested and tried at a military tribunal for dereliction of duty, carrying the can for the raid. He was shot three days later.

Tariq Siddique on the face of it would enjoy a better fate.

Chapter Two

Following his tour of duty in Iraq, Rory Calderwood left the Regiment in 1993 at the age of thirty, having completed seven years' service. Despite representations from his Commanding Officer, it had been an easy decision to leave; the missions had taken their toll mentally. The nightly flashbacks still haunted him.

As so many of his former colleagues had done, he used his contacts to secure a place working in a security firm, but he found it difficult to settle. It was like an old school reunion, a job that paid well but provided little in the way of job satisfaction, whatever that was. Same old, same old; same blokey banter, same personalities, same nightmares; he needed something different.

The opportunity came by chance.

It was three years later, in June 1996; he was working at Petronix Headquarters in London giving the Operations Director and his team the latest thinking on security. The company is one of the world's largest producers of oil and petroleum products with global assets and a significant interest in the North Sea gas industry.

It was a full day's training course which had proved popular in the sector; and very lucrative for the security consultancy that provided them. Over lunch Calderwood, whilst balancing a plate of sandwiches in one hand and a beaker of water in the other, was examining one of the several stunning pictures of oil rigs which decorated the walls of the room. There was something foreboding about them, intimidating almost, but at the same time, as pieces of engineering, they were things of beauty. Calderwood was drawn to the images.

The Operations Director noticed his interest and approached him.

"I see you like the picture," observed the man.

"Yeah," replied Calderwood.

"Do you have any background in engineering?" asked the director.

"Yeah, you could say that," replied Calderwood, without elaboration. The director's eyes lit up.

"Tell me more," said the director,

"I've got a BSc in engineering from Birmingham University."

"Now that's interesting… What grade?"

"Two-one," said Calderwood.

"Excellent," said the director.

The academic background, together with his ability to adapt to new situations and think on his feet, as well as his proven leadership skills, meant he would be an ideal candidate for almost any organisation. A point not lost on his inquisitor who had been impressed with Calderwood. There was an air of confidence about him that people seemed to respect, someone with potential.

"Have you ever considered working offshore?" asked the man.

"Not until today," Calderwood replied.

Six weeks later he was removing his worldly goods, such as they were, from his rented flat in Holloway, piling them into the back of his ten-year-old Volkswagen and heading north, to Aberdeen, the oil capital of the UK.

In fact, it hadn't taken long to make the decision. The thought of the challenge appealed, and he had convinced himself he wouldn't mind the isolation. Calderwood was not one for crowds; he rarely socialised, and, like many in the Regiment, he had found it hard to form relationships. The job also paid very well; a few years and he would be set up for life, he reasoned.

After settling into his new company flat, he reported to the Aberdeen office of Petronix at the start of September.

It had given him a few days to have a look around the area. He made a point of visiting the memorial sculpture in Hazlehead Park and the Kirk of St Nicholas on Union Street which has dedicated a chapel in memory of the men who perished on the Piper Alpha rig in1988. It brought some clarity to the potential dangers that lay ahead.

Following the standard induction, which included the infamous three-day Survival course - "if you survive, you've passed," was a familiar jibe, on a cold Monday in early October, Calderwood found himself at the airport at six forty-five preparing for his flight to the rig.

Aberdeen is the world's largest heliport and despite the early hour, it was a hive of activity with taxi's dropping off oil workers every couple of minutes ready for the start of their next shift.

For his first trip Calderwood was allocated a 'buddy' whose responsibility it was to look after him and show him the ropes. There was the usual fire safety video which included evacuation instruction and details of the helicopter they would be using – a Super Puma, with which he was very familiar from his military days.

He made little conversation; his new colleagues would remain completely unaware of Calderwood's background.

He sat in the waiting room along with seven other men waiting to start their shift, each decked out in their Personal Protection Equipment. The kit consisted of a yellow flame- resistant hi-visibility suit, ear protectors and life-jacket complete with re-breather equipment – a sort of oxygen mask that allows you to breathe for a short time under water by re-cycling the unused seventy per cent of oxygen that is exhaled. His buddy introduced himself in a broad Scottish accent.

"Hi, I'm Glen, Glen Stoddard," he said, offering his hand.

"Calderwood, they call me 'Woody'," said Calderwood.

This was not strictly true; nobody had ever called him 'Woody', not to his face anyway. At University he had always been 'Rory', and in the Army, it was 'Calderwood' or 'Sarge'. It was a deliberate attempt to draw a line under his military life and move on.

"Where are you from?" asked the buddy.

"London."

"What did you do in London?"

"In Security," replied Calderwood.

Losing interest, the buddy returned to his newspaper. Outside the whirring of a helicopter's rotors could be heard as the waiting Puma on the helipad started its engines while the captain did his final checks.

The men waited as the meagre allowance of luggage was loaded onto the small baggage compartment at the rear of the aircraft, not much bigger than the boot of a large car; before the go-ahead by the flight supervisor was given to enter the helicopter.

"Stick with me," said Glen, shouting above the noise of the rotors. Calderwood nodded.

There was not a lot of room, two banks of four seats behind the pilot and as a rookie; Calderwood was ushered into the middle so that more experienced team members familiar with exit procedures, were by the windows. The pilot eased the chopper towards the runway and gathered speed before rising vertically. Momentarily Calderwood was back in the desert on a Chinook; part of him would always react that way in a helicopter; he had been conditioned. He watched as the airport and the environs of the town disappeared below and replaced by a grey mass that was the North Sea; there was nothing blue about these waters. Deep down he felt some natural apprehension at what lay in front of him, but his mind was totally focused.

Much of the journey was spent dodging cloud and it took the Puma over an hour at its optimum speed of one hundred and fifty mph to reach the platform. With the noise of the rotors and the protective ear plugs, conversation during the flight was limited and the men were mostly locked in their own thoughts.

A two week shift away from their family did nothing to lift the rather sombre atmosphere. The new recruit peered through the window across his buddy but there was little to see apart from the uncompromising waves below. The rig eventually appeared on the horizon and through the pilot's window Calderwood watched the shape in the distance grow as the Puma moved towards its destination. He wondered what this change of career direction would bring him.

Delta Bravo Oil and Gas Platform, to give it its official name, is an early construction dating from the mid 1970's, and sits isolated in the North Sea about one hundred and fifty miles north east of Aberdeen. It is a semi-submersible structure, technically known as a 'tension leg platform' and designed for use in deep water. It is held in place over the location by several enormous wire cables attached to weights piled into the sea bed.

Following the tragedy of the Piper Alpha disaster, it had been completely renovated with all the latest safety features. The accommodation block had been protected with a blast-proof housing away from the main drilling area.

The helicopter hovered over the platform ensuring the correct wind direction before gently descending onto the helipad. Adjacent to the landing area, two teams of fire fighters in, what looked like, space suits, manned hoses in case of emergencies.

Calderwood exited the aircraft behind his buddy, bending forward away from the downdraft of the rotors and into the biting wind which whipped across his face, made more uncomfortable by splashes of rain. The luggage had been unloaded by the landing team and placed on a trolley; Calderwood retrieved his gear and slung it over his shoulder before following the rest of the men down three floors to the accommodation deck. The walkways around the outside of the rig were open and only a scaffold guardrail and a wire mesh shroud protected them from a three-hundred-feet drop to the icy waters below.

Once inside the accommodation block, Calderwood was shown the locker room where he removed and stored his PPE and, as instructed, he reported to the Offshore Installation Manager.

The OIM, another Scot by the name of Bill McCredie, has overall responsibility for the rig, like that of a ship's captain at sea, and has significant authority, including the ability to shut down production if circumstances dictate. Calderwood was ushered into his office which bore all the hallmarks of a command centre, with radio and computer equipment perched on desks and charts and maps around the walls. There was information in a league-table format depicting flow-rates and tonnage shipped. It seemed all very haphazard with little semblance of any order, Calderwood noticed.

"Hello, welcome to Delta Bravo," said the OIM, and held out his hand in greeting. "Calderwood, right?"

"Yes," Calderwood replied, and responded accordingly.

The OIM looked at the sheet of paper in front of him. "Rory, now that's a good Celtic name," added McCredie.

"Yeah," said Calderwood. "But they call me Woody."

"Woody, it is then. Here, let me introduce you to the team," said McCredie. "Do you take coffee?"

"Thanks," said Calderwood, and McCredie poured out a measure into a mug from a filter jug and handed it to him.

"Watch out with that stuff, it's got a government health warning," shouted one of the team. There were smiles from the OIM and the others.

"Got to find some way of keeping you bastards awake," said McCredie.

There were four others around the table all eying up the new arrival as Calderwood was introduced to them individually; Frank Cameron, Operations Manager, Dave Brewster, Head of Production, and instigator of the humour; and finally, Keith Jameson, Chief Technician.

"You'll report to Dave for the time being," said McCredie.

There were a few minutes of interrogation as Calderwood answered questions about his background and experience before McCredie called a halt to the inquisition.

"Come on I'll give you a quick tour of the accommodation area."

He dismissed the team who dispersed to their respective duties.

"There're just over two-hundred people working on the rig,"

he explained, as they walked down the corridor towards the canteen. "That includes maintenance, catering staff… we even have our own doctor on board."

They reached the eating area and McCredie introduced the new-comer to the catering manager who was cleaning down the serving space.

"This is Jim Pike. You need to keep on the good side of Jim… he controls the food."

Jim acknowledged Calderwood.

They continued the tour with the OIM providing a running commentary.

"As you know shift patterns whilst on board are twelve hours off and twelve hours on," said McCredie.

"Yeah, they told me… What about down time?" asked Calderwood.

"We have the canteen, as you've seen, and there's the communal room, games room, gym and cinema… oh, and there's satellite TV, including channel eighteen."

"Channel eighteen?" queried Calderwood, with a quizzical look.

"I'll let you find out," replied McCredie.

After a few minutes, they returned to the command centre where two other guys were waiting.

"I'll get someone to show you to your quarters, so you can settle in; then report back here in an hour and we can discuss your duties. Doug, here'll do the honours," said McCredie.

A lean looking forty-something with receding hair nodded to him.

After more introductions, Calderwood left the OIM's office accompanied by the rig's safety representative, Doug Smallbrook. He led Calderwood to the staff quarters on the floor above.

The safety representative plays an important part on the rig and is elected by the men with authority to discuss safety issues with the OIM. His early introduction to Calderwood was in keeping with the safety philosophy on the platform. As Calderwood climbed the stairs, the similarity with the inside of a ship was striking. The decor, such as it was, was harsh, cold - certainly no sign of any soft fabrics, everything functional, and fire resistant. The cabins were similarly functional and austere, one bunk bed, a storage space, a toilet and a small shower; the swinging cat analogy was apposite. There was a small television on his bedside cabinet.

Calderwood stowed his gear - toiletries, three pairs of jeans, four work-shirts and two sweaters plus underwear, socks and trainers. There was little need for anything else, or room for that matter.

He looked around at his Spartan quarters; not unlike his time in the army; luckily home comforts were not high on his list of priorities. This was to be his life until he decided otherwise and after a few minutes, as instructed, Calderwood made his way back down to the Operations room.

"Bill's doing the rounds," said a new face who was seated at the table. "I'm Derek Tinsdale, deputy OIM, pleased to meet you."

He stood up and shook Calderwood's hand. "I was about to go for a brew, why don't you tag along."

Calderwood followed him out of the office.

Back in the canteen there were ten or twelve others enjoying a break. The safety representative made more introductions. Calderwood. If he was honest, was starting to feel overwhelmed.

After yet more questions over another coffee Doug turned

to Calderwood. "You'll need your safety induction before you can work outside. You can do that after we have had a drink."

"Do you smoke, bonny lad?" asked one of the crew in a North-East accent.

"No," replied Calderwood.

"Probably just as well," said Smallbrook. "It's restricted to a special room for obvious reasons."

In fact, nothing remotely combustible was allowed, even batteries, and those with mobile phones had to leave them at the airport; they were banned from the rig.

The induction took over an hour and there was another new recruit Calderwood noticed who introduced himself as Paddy, "from Belfast," he explained.

The briefing included alarms, musters, working practices, emergency drills and so on, all designed to make the rig as safe a working environment as possible.

After an enormous lunch, it was time to move outside and as with the helicopter trip, Calderwood was allocated a buddy to show him the routines and give him an idea of his duties. Initially, he was told, he would be on routine maintenance and supervised, until he had been signed off as 'competent'.

Before venturing outside the accommodation block onto the business-end of the rig, he was introduced to Pete Wilding, his buddy, who would supervise him whilst outside. There were more procedures and instructions.

"Full PPE is compulsory," said Pete, as Calderwood was given his kit comprising of his helicopter gear plus hard hat, goggles and boots. Once fully compliant, Pete led the way to one of the external doors.

He shouted to be heard as he opened the door. "You need to watch the wind." He struggled against the force to push the door wide enough for them to exit. There was a large notice on the door confirming this warning.

Outside the noise from the sea was unbelievable and it easily drowned the mechanical sounds of the rig. A gust of wind tugged at the men trying to rip them from the open walk-way as Pete led Calderwood to one of the work areas. He looked down at the rolling waves and tried to take it all in; the metal pipes, which snaked in every direction; the enormous piles which anchored the gigantic structure to the sea bed; the cacophony. It was, by any standards, awe-inspiring.

Calderwood noticed a vessel quite close to the rig about the size of a large tug.

"What's that ship?"' asked Calderwood.

"That's the stand-by vessel, the Pericles. It stays close to the rig as a safety ship. It's even got fire-fighting equipment… not that it would be much use if this lot were ever to go up. It would be like pissing on a bonfire."

Pete was still having to shout to be heard above the noise. Calderwood nodded in acknowledgement.

Pete led his protégé into a maintenance area where the noise from the sea was less intrusive.

"What do you know about the 'permit to work' process?" he asked.

"Only what they told me onshore," said Calderwood, and his buddy explained the workings of the permit arrangement which requires all work in progress to have a central monitoring system.

"This is one of the things that went wrong on Piper Alpha… Someone'd removed a pressure valve for repair and didn't tell anyone. When the next shift opened up the pipe, condensate just poured through and ignited… whoosh. A right fuck up."

He made a dramatic gesture with his arms to highlight an explosion.

"Condensate?" said Calderwood.

"The raw stuff that comes out of the ground," replied Pete.

He had very much simplified the cause of the disaster on that stricken rig but the point was well made, and Calderwood listened intently to the instruction.

The time went by quickly and at seven o'clock Calderwood signed off for the day as the next shift took over. The buddy explained the hand-over system, another safety factor which ensured continuity of any work in progress in line with the permit process.

Pete accompanied Calderwood who was now getting used to being called 'Woody', to the canteen. He was amazed at the quality, and quantity, of the food.

"They do look after us," said Pete, as he tucked into one of his four pork chops that balanced on top of a pile of chips and vegetables.

After dinner, Calderwood went back to his room to change and explore further. He decided to try out the gym; fitness had always been important to him and he was in pretty good shape, but he would have to forego his usual three mile run around the common. The fitness centre was small but contained a couple of running machines, cross trainers and a selection of weights enough to keep the enthusiast occupied. He managed to borrow some kit, provided he washed it afterwards.

Following a reasonable workout, he made his way to the common room where twenty or thirty men were occupied watching the re-run of an earlier football match, reading newspapers or playing snooker. There was no alcohol allowed he had been warned; there were random breath-tests, so those who were drinking were into fruit juices or non-alcoholic lager.

He returned to his quarters early weary from the day, and as he lay on his bed contemplating everything the low hum of a generator permeated the room becoming intrusive like a dripping tap, then he remembered... channel 18! What was that all about?

He switched on the TV and scrolled down with the remote control until he got to the appropriate channel and then he understood the OIM's levity – a French porn channel!

Over the next two weeks Calderwood soon got used to the work schedule and he managed to drop into a workable routine which would stem any thoughts of isolation. As the count-down to his demarcation commenced, he noticed that his mood changed, and he was beginning to feel like he had as a child at end of term. Others who were on the same rota behaved in a similar fashion, cracking jokes and almost giggly, a strange and unexpected phenomenon.

He had been warned about getting 'demob-happy', as many times weather had intervened preventing helicopters from landing. The feeling of deflation was quite marked. Some men had got violent at the frustration. The worst case lasted four days he was told, but the prospect of such a scenario was nothing new to Calderwood. His SAS training had conditioned him to cope with such situations.

Nevertheless, when his home-bound flight landed on the deck of the platform and he climbed aboard the Puma to return to 'civilisation', he felt a sense of elation and couldn't wait to get back to his new flat.

The Puma landed at six-thirty and Rory chose to take a taxi; his trusty VW would remain in the garage during his off- shore shift saving on parking charges which were extortionate. He bid farewell to the other men on his shift.

"See you in two weeks," he said, as they shook hands.

He got back to his flat and stowed his gear before changing out of his rig uniform into some clean clothes. With no food in he made a call to a local take-away for a Chinese; he would do some shopping tomorrow, and visit a launderette. As he sat at his table eating his Chicken stir fry in front of his TV, he pondered his recent career move, and thought about those he had met on the rig who had families; how did they cope with the absences, he wondered.

It was Monday night, and, although it was almost nine o'clock by the time he had finished his meal, he decided to get some fresh air. After being cooped up for two weeks he needed to feel space again.

He walked down toward the old harbour, past the Maritime Museum, and took deep gulps of the night air trying to cleanse his system from the smells of oil and sweat of the past two weeks. It was cold, but dry, as he made his way along the rather drab streets.

It was surprisingly busy for a Monday and as a lone male it wasn't long before he became the interest of certain 'ladies'. It was well-known that Monday was a shift- change day and men would be on the look-out for services that hadn't been available off-shore. Some of the working girls were quite insistent but Rory just ignored them, much to their annoyance.

Instead, he found a wine bar which looked presentable and not too crowded, and went inside. Rory was not a big drinker, his time in the military had given him little opportunity. His present employ would continue this fairly monastic existence.

There was a vacant high seat at the bar and he sat down and

looked around, taking in the ambience. It was modern with glass and chrome prominent in the decor. The clientele was mainly couples but there were one or two other single men supping bottles of lager. The bar tender walked across to Calderwood.

"Bottle of lager."

The barman walked away and retrieved a suitable brand from one of the shelves. Rory watched him pour the drink into a glass, taking in the ambience. Prices were at least fifty-per-cent higher than the local pubs, but he was happy with that.

He made polite chat with the barman, confirming he was 'off-shore' to the enquiry.

Suddenly, as he was taking a sip of his beer, he felt a sharp push in his back which caused him to jolt forward and almost choke, spilling lager down the front of his jacket.

He turned around to see the cause of this disruption, ready to remonstrate with the assailant.

Rory did a double take; there was a profuse apology.

"I'm so sorry," said an attractive girl in an expensive looking leather jacket and designer jeans.

"That's ok," he managed to say, trying to reclaim his breath from a near-drowning experience.

"Let me buy you another," said the girl.

"That's ok, no need, no harm one," said Rory.

"I insist… I'm so sorry about that. My heel caught in the carpet... You broke my fall."

"Glad I could be of service," said Rory with a smile. "Ok, if you insist, just a lager then, thank you."

She ordered another bottle for him and a large glass of red wine.

"Would you like to join me?" asked Rory, getting down from his bar stool and dabbing the remains of the spilt lager from his jacket and chinos with his handkerchief.

"Aye, ok... we can sit over there."

She pointed to a vacant table by the window. They retrieved their drinks and walked across the bar to the empty seats.

"I'm Janie."

"Rory," he said, reverting to his given name. He would keep 'Woody' for the rig.

"I've been stood up," she said in a smooth Scots lilt, not the harsh grating accent of a Glaswegian. "I was supposed to be meeting a girlfriend, but she wasn't able to get away."

"Her loss is my gain," said Rory.

It was not a normal response; he didn't usually do compliments. She smiled.

"Thank you, kind sir."

She looked at him while taking a sip from her glass.

Rory was not comfortable in chatting up girls; he found small talk difficult. The few relationships he'd experienced had been short-lived, due primarily to his line of work. He'd learned to live without the need of the physical presence of a woman, but looking at the girl in front of him, well, it seemed different.

"You work off-shore?" she asked.

"Is it that obvious?"

"Well you're not from round here with that accent, so it was a reasonable guess... Where are you from... originally I mean?"

"Originally? Herefordshire, but recently I lived in London," Rory replied.

"I don't think I've ever met anyone from Herefordshire."

"Not many escape," said Rory, smiling again.

Rory couldn't remember smiling this much in such a brief period of time. During his thirty years, certainly in recent times, there had not been much to smile about.

"What do you do...? For a living, I mean," asked Rory.

"I work in a solicitor's, conveyancing," she added.

"Sounds interesting," said Rory.

"It's not," said Janie. "It's just shifting paper, but it pays the bills."

She took a sip of her drink and looked at him. "How long have you worked off-shore?"

"This was my first tour... two weeks, early days."

"Do you enjoy it?" she asked.

"As you say, it pays the bills," he replied, and smiled once again.

For an hour they kept up the small talk in an easy and relaxed way. There was an attraction, Rory was in her thrall; not an experience he could remember having before.

"Is there anyone in your life?" Janie asked at an appropriate moment.

"I have a sister in Worcester," Rory replied, knowing that was not what she meant.

"Anyone else?"

"No, no-one else. My work hasn't been very conducive to relationships."

He stared into his lager, momentarily, as if it was something of which he should be ashamed.

"What about you?" Rory asked, believing it to be the polite thing to do.

"No, a few scars along the way, but no-one special."

She drained her glass.

"Refill?" he asked.

She checked her watch; it was ten-thirty.

"I would love to, but I've got to work tomorrow... another time, perhaps."

"Ok… would you like to meet up again, I don't know a... a bite to eat or something, perhaps."

She looked at him.

"Aye, ok, why not. Friday, I won't have to play the Cinderella card."

"What time?" he asked.

"Eight-ish ok? We can meet here and go on to the Bistro on the corner.".

"Yeah, ok… I'll book a table for nine o'clock. How does that sound?"

"Aye, sounds fine."

She got up from the table. Rory finished his drink and followed her out of the bar.

"Which way? I'll walk you," he said.

"It's ok, I'll get a cab. There'll be one at the rank just around the corner."

"I'll walk you there, see you're ok."

"Aye, ok, thanks."

He walked alongside her and turned the corner where three taxis were lined up waiting for customers. Janie made her way to the first car, Rory walking beside her.

She gave the driver an address and opened the door, but before getting in she leaned to Rory and kissed him on the cheek which took him aback.

"I enjoyed tonight," she said.

"So did I," he replied, and she got into the back of the cab and closed the door.

Rory watched as it made a right turn and disappeared from view. He turned and walked back to the flat contemplating the events of the evening. He suddenly found himself looking forward to Friday.

Chapter Three

As Rory made his way back to the flat, he couldn't get the thought of his recent acquaintance out of his head. He felt on a high as he walked through the drab streets. It was drizzling, but the slight rain did nothing to dampen his mood.

He reached his apartment and went inside. It was dark and empty. Rory switched on the light which did little to change the atmosphere. He went to the table in the corner; there was a bottle of scotch and a glass next to it. He poured himself a drink and sat down on the rather worn armchair, head on his chest, his glass of scotch in his hand. The drink was from his duty-free stash which had returned with him on his last overseas tour. That was three years ago; he rarely felt the urge to imbibe, but tonight was different.

He sat in silence looking around the room, one settee - a marginal two-seater, one standard lamp, a rather ancient TV, a carpet which was almost threadbare where the footfall was most frequent, but underneath the sofa it looked brand new. The kitchen was functional, certainly no frills.

The bedroom was in a similar condition, well used. The decor looked tired, but the bed was clean and comfortable and would sleep two albeit cosily. It was, however, a lot better than his quarters on the rig. The bathroom was small with a washbasin, toilet and bath with a shower above. The spare bedroom had become a storage area for the rest of his personal possessions such as they were. Not much to show for his ten year's labour.

Still restless he turned on the TV and flicked through a few channels before eventually turning in around one o'clock. He ambled into his bedroom and, as he stowed his clothes in the wardrobe, he rattled a number of empty coat-hangers and something else struck him; it was decidedly barren. A couple of shirts, two pairs of trousers, which were not at the cutting edge of present trends, some jeans and his trusty leather jacket were the sum total of years of sartorial neglect. He made a mental note to remedy that.

He switched off the light, but sleep did not come easily and, when it did, the nightmares returned. He could see a village ravaged by war, feel the heat from the burning buildings as if he were there. He could make out the rotting remains of innocent people; the simple clothing, mostly shawls and sandals scattered, lying around waiting for their owners to claim them.

Then there were the children. Twisted little bodies, some dressed in their favourite football kit; he remembered one in a Liverpool Football Club shirt. He could see toys and other paraphernalia of an unfulfilled childhood; were they that different from us, he would question.

At just turned four o'clock he woke again with a start and went to the bathroom for a drink of water. He splashed his face and wondered if the thoughts would ever leave him. The counselling on offer, as with many combatants, had been declined; a question of pride, or machismo.

He eventually got up around seven-thirty and, slightly heady, made himself a reviving coffee. As he sipped his drink, he reflected again on the events of the previous evening. He took another look around the flat. He had a six-month lease from Petronix and, up until now, had no other thoughts than to use it as a base for his off-shore endeavours. Today, however, he felt differently and had an urge to do something to make the flat homelier. He didn't normally do 'homely' and wondered if it was the subliminal influence of his meeting with Janie. He wouldn't admit it, but deep down, he hoped that one day she would return to his flat, and he needed it to look decent. Suddenly he had a new mission and felt motivated at the thought.

Finance was not an issue; with the bounty he received from the Army and his accumulated savings of many years frugal living, he had quite a nest egg sitting in a high interest account. Now he needed to spend some.

After a couple of slices of toast, he headed out of the flat.

The apartment was in a converted late-nineteenth century stone terrace which, from the outside, had a lot of character. In Edinburgh or London, it would cost a fortune to rent and outside his means.

He turned right at the end of the block and right again following the access road to the rear of the building where there were some residents-only parking places. His trusty VW was stationed next to a Ford Escort of similar vintage. The rest of the bays were vacant. As he was about to start the car there was something else he hadn't noticed before; it was a tip. Empty sweet wrappers, CD cases, bits of paper, were liberally scattered around the inside. He couldn't remember the last time he had cleaned it, but it must have been at least a year ago. A valet was definitely needed, not a word with which the car was associated.

It took no more than ten minutes to get to the Academy Shopping Centre where Rory spent some time stocking up on new clothes and a few furnishings, nothing too fancy; some cushions, mugs, glasses and a new stereo system. He also bought a mobile phone. Without a landline at the flat, he thought it would come in handy; particularly if things with Janie progressed the way he hoped.

By early afternoon he was heading back to the flat feeling a strange sense of excitement that he hadn't experienced for a long time; conditioned by the army, emotional attachment had always been something of a luxury. Just before the road leading to the flat he called into the supermarket on the corner to stock up on food and essentials and it took two journeys to get his purchases from the car into the flat.

As Friday approached Rory became more apprehensive. He had no means of contacting Janie; he didn't even know her second name, and started to wonder if she would turn up at all. He had booked a table for two, at nine o'clock at Bistro 30; the restaurant she had recommended.

On the appointed day, by six-thirty he had showered and changed into a smart pair of light-brown slacks, casual shirt and loafers topped by a new leather jacket. He couldn't remember ever dressing for a woman before. He was an attractive guy, with rugged features, and mature for his age, reflecting the life experiences that had conditioned his present persona. There was something 'dangerous' about him that did attract women, which would occasionally end in a one-night stand. His record relationship was three months. The endless days apart made bonding very hard and, to some degree, he had accepted this life choice.

Before leaving the flat, he poured a glass of scotch to ward off the cold he convinced himself. He downed it in one gulp. Checking his new phone was fully-charged, he placed it in his pocket and headed out of the flat around seven-thirty to give himself plenty of time to reach the bar. A brisk twenty-minute walk would see him at his rendezvous.

The walk helped clear his head and he felt quite relaxed as he ran the gauntlet of prostitutes before reaching Cherutti's wine bar.

It was the same barman as Monday, and he recognised Rory straightaway as he walked towards the bar.

"Lager?" said the barman.

"Yeah, thanks," he replied, making himself comfortable on a stool. "You've got a good memory."

"Rarely forget faces," said Dan, the name on his badge, as he poured the drink.

Rory handed him a ten-pound note. "Take one for yourself," he said, as Dan went to the till.

"Cheers," said Dan, as he handed Rory his change.

Rory scanned the room. "Not many in tonight."

There were fifteen or so punters scattered throughout the bar, mostly stragglers from the after-work, five o'clock crowd.

"Aye, it was packed earlier, but it'll be quiet until around nine, then it'll pick up again," said Dan.

Rory checked his watch, five-past eight, and he started to wonder whether his fears of being stood up would be realised. Then a couple of minutes later, as he sipped his beer, he felt a tap on his shoulder.

"Is this seat taken?"

His immediate response was to react as if under threat, but luckily his natural instincts were quickly suppressed by the sight of Janie, looking absolutely stunning.

"Hi, good to see you again," said Rory, which was about the limit of his small-talk. "What can I get you?"

"A dry white wine, please," she replied.

"Chablis, ok?" asked Dan, hearing the request.

"Great," replied Janie.

"Hope I haven't kept you waiting," said Janie, perching on the empty seat next to Rory.

"No, just a few minutes... You look terrific."

Rory couldn't believe his own words, which seemed to just pour from his mouth, another compliment; it was like someone else speaking.

It had been a question of conditioning. In his male- dominated world, it never happened; you got bollocked for screwing up and that was it. A job accomplished was acknowledged, but not congratulated. Even his medal receiving ceremony was a very stiff-upper-lip affair. A 'well- done' from his commanding officer as he walked down the line pinning the award to the recipient's chest, before moving to the next.

"Thank you," she said.

Rory was trying not to stare as she undid her short leather coat, revealing a low-cut, white blouse, and short black skirt with stockings. Her outfit was completed by a pair of black, elegant shoes with three-inch heels. Her blonde hair looked as though it had recently received some serious attention from a stylist.

Rory was again under her spell. 'Wow' was what he was thinking, but the words came out, "how was your week?" which did not exactly resonate with originality.

She saw the funny side. "Not bad," she replied, which killed that part of the conversation.

"How about you?"

She took taking a slip of her wine. "Ooh I needed that," she said before Rory could answer.

"Yeah, good, just trying to sort myself out... Only moved in a couple of months' ago, still unpacking boxes," he exaggerated.

There was a pause as he took a drink; he looked at her. "I wasn't sure whether you would show or not."

"Why was that?"

"Don't know, but glad you did. Dan's a nice bloke, but it's not the same," he joked.

"Well, I was intrigued, if I'm honest."

"Really?" said Rory.

"Mmm…"

She did not expand further. "Shall we move over there?" she said, pointing to a vacant table at the back of the bar. "It'll be easier to talk."

As Dan had predicted, it was starting to get busier and any semblance of dialogue around the bar area was becoming increasingly difficult.

They moved seats, and after the somewhat strained start, the exchange gradually became more relaxed as the alcohol worked its customary magic.

At eight forty-five Rory looked at his watch. "I've ordered a table for nine, would you like another before we go?"

"No, I'm fine," said Janie. "I'll just pop to the little girls' room to freshen up."

Rory watched as she got up from her seat and headed to the other side of the bar area. He found it difficult to keep his eyes off her. He also noticed other wolf-like males doing the same and felt a strange sensation. Perhaps it was some primitive territorial response, but, more likely, jealousy.

She reappeared and took her jacket from the chair; Rory helped her with it over her shoulders.

"Thank you, you're a gentleman."

As they made their way from the bar, Rory waived to Dan who acknowledged.

"Have a good evening," he shouted to them.

It was a cool night and Janie grabbed Rory's arm and hooked hers around it bringing them closer as they walked. There were no complaints.

Five minutes later they were in Bistro No 30 and, as they entered, the smell of garlic attacked their senses. Rory was beginning to feel hungry.

A waiter of indeterminable nationality approached them.

"You have a reservation?" he said in a strange accent.

Rory stifled a laugh as his mind switched back momentarily to a night out in Hereford when his great buddy, Lennie 'The Loon' Arthur reposted to a similar question from a waiter. "Do I look like a fucking Red-Indian?"

He still thought of Lennie and some of the times they had enjoyed off-barracks. One of the low points of his life had been to write the letter to his widow informing her that Lennie had been killed in action. Rory learned later that he had been another victim of friendly fire, the blue-on-blue call made when an American jet fired on his jeep mistaking them for insurgents.

"Yes, Calderwood," Rory replied politely to the request.

'Luigi' ushered them to a small table neatly set out in the corner with a 'Reserved' notice in the middle. It was dark and candle-lit, and the ambience could not have been better. The maître d' took their coats and once again Rory couldn't help staring.

"You're beautiful," he said again.

"Thank you," she replied, her eyes fixed on his.

The spell was temporarily broken by the wine waiter. Rory looked down the list.

"Red ok?"

"Fine," said Janie and Rory requested a bottle of Australian Cabinet Sauvignon.

They ordered food; Rory a peppered steak, Janie, chicken in white wine sauce and linguine pasta.

"So, what did you do in Herefordshire?" asked Janie, after the wine-waiter had poured the red.

Rory looked at her.

"My parents owned a farm in a tiny village called Tedstone Wafre. Not large, but enough to scrape a living. Unfortunately, they split up when I was fifteen and my mother and me moved to a cottage just outside Ledbury."

The names meant nothing to Janie.

"Then what?" she said.

"After Hereford Grammar, I got a place at Birmingham University, did mechanical engineering... When I graduated, I joined the army."

Janie was listening intently.

"Why the army?"

"Seemed a good idea at the time, plus we have family history."

"So, when did you leave?"

"Three years ago," he replied.

"So, you were in the Gulf?" she asked as a statement.

"Ha, you could say that."

His voice tailed off and he finished his glass of wine. Somehow Janie sensed it was not an area for discussion. There was a short intermission as she contemplated the revelations.

"What about you?" asked Rory.

"Oh, nothing as glamorous," she replied.

The word 'glamorous' was not something with which he had associated his time in the SAS.

"Grew up in Peterhead, my father was a fisherman and owned a trawler, but he sold out in 1986, and started his own wholesale business... Did well. I've been very lucky. Went to Edinburgh to study law and moved here three years ago. I've been with Simpson and Giddins... they're the biggest law firm in town, ever since."

She took another sip of her wine.

"So, do you live in town?" asked Rory.

"Just off Deemount Drive." Rory was none the wiser.

"It's on the south side, not far from the river, couple of miles out… What about you?" asked Janie.

"Company flat, a mile or so from here, near Victoria Park," he replied.

"Sounds nice," she said.

"Ah, don't be fooled by my description, 'functional' is the word," he replied.

Her eyes caught his and she raised her glass to her lips. She took a sip without moving her gaze. Rory was transfixed; suddenly he no longer felt hungry, a more burning need was beginning to surface.

They continued their discovery over dinner engrossed in each other's stories and by ten-thirty the food was more or less consumed. The waiter looked at the left-overs and thought about asking if the food wasn't up to standard, but let it pass after Rory declared, "really nice," as the plates were cleared away.

"Coffee?" asked Rory.

"Great… cappuccino please."

The waiter arrived with the dessert menu.

"Just two cappuccinos please," said Rory, and the waiter looked crestfallen as he walked away to prepare the coffees.

By eleven, Janie sipped the last of her coffee and pushed the cup forward indicating its completion. She looked at Rory.

"Would you like to come back to mine?"

Rory looked at her. "Yes, I'd like that very much," he said, and attracted the waiter's attention for the bill.

"I'll get this," said Rory.

"Mine next time," said Janie, without thinking.

After settling the bill on his card, Rory helped Janie with her coat and they left the Bistro.

Despite the hour, it was busy, and customers were still arriving. The cold air hit them as they left the restaurant and Janie grabbed Rory's arm again; this time she leaned up and kissed him passionately.

"Hope there's plenty of taxis," said Rory, as they walked towards the rank around the corner.

There were three traditional black cabs parked up, waiting for a fare. The two got inside the back of the first one and Janie gave the driver the address. She moved closer to him and held his arm.

After about ten minutes the taxi pulled up alongside a smart detached bungalow in a row of similar houses. She got out and Rory followed. Janie paid the driver.

"My shout... I insist," she said, before Rory could offer payment and led her escort to the front door.

The porch light had been left on and Rory could see it was a fairly new property with a small, lawned front garden surrounded by flower beds. Evidence of much loving care was all around.

She opened the front door. There was a small entrance hall and Janie slipped off her shoes. Taking the hint, Rory did the same and he followed her into the living room. He looked around; the furniture was tasteful and modern with cushions and nick-knacks. It wasn't a large room, but comfortably housed a sofa, dining table, book case and a small bureau against the wall with family photographs in frames on the top. She switched on the lights and three table lamps sprung into life creating a warm ambience. Here was someone well organised.

"Make yourself at home," she said, and Rory sat down on the three-seater settee.

He looked down at his feet and noticed his big toe was visible in his right sock. He tried to hide the digit under his foot to avoid any embarrassment.

Janie took off her coat.

"Drink?" she asked. "I've only got wine."

"Wine will be fine," replied Rory, and she left him on the sofa while she went into the kitchen.

"Just white, I'm afraid," she shouted from the adjacent room.

"That's fine," he replied, loud enough for her to hear.

Janie returned with two glasses, she pulled over a small table and placed their drinks on coasters. Then she went over to the hi-fi system on the book case and put on a CD... Sadé - music for connoisseurs, and lovers.

She lit the faux-coal gas fire. "Soon warm up," she said, as the flames danced behind the glass frontage.

Rory took off his jacket and placed it on one of the two armchairs and watched as she approached him undoing the buttons on her blouse. He was captivated, mesmerized as his eyes took in the vision. She dropped her top on the floor and unclipped her bra.Then she was on him, hungrily devouring him, lips, mouths, bodies. She almost ripped Rory's shirt off him. He responded in kind and was soon feasting on her breasts. She moaned gently.

"Please Rory, now."

The first time was rushed, urgent, but incredibly satisfying.

"God, I wanted you so badly," said Janie as they lay in front of the gas fire surrounded by discarded clothes.

Rory was still recovering, his breathing deep and measured.

"Me too," he said, totally understating his emotions.

He held her close trying to remember feeling this way about anyone, but he hadn't. It was as though all the frustrations of his life had exploded in one crescendo leaving him with a contentment he had never known before.

Janie held his hand and drew them to her breasts again. She responded to his touch. Now she was breathing deeply.

"Let's go to bed, it will be more comfortable," she said, and kissed him. They got up from the floor and Janie led him to the bedroom.

Once more the lovemaking was passionate and fulfilling. There was silence for a long time, sleep was beckoning; then Janie leant up on one elbow to look into his eyes and asked a question.

"What was it like, the war I mean?"

The question surprised Rory; it was almost incongruous given the moment, and, initially, he did not know how to answer it. The topic had never been raised as directly as that before. In social gatherings the subject had generally been avoided or skirted around and Rory would head it off with some dismissive deflecting comment, but this time he felt differently. Maybe it was time to unburden himself.

Rory began cryptically. He spoke slowly staring at the ceiling in the soothing light of the bedside lamp. She watched as he appeared to wrestle with the words.

"July 1st 1916, was the first day of the battle of the Somme, my great-grandfather was one of Kitchener's men that went over the top. Within hours over 19,000 men had died including Lieutenant Arthur Calderwood. I often think about him. He was the same age as me."

He turned his head and looked across at her. "They say when the guns stopped you could hear skylarks singing..."

Rory paused, before continuing. "On the first day of Desert Storm, we were in enemy territory searching for Scud missile launchers ahead of the main attack. We had already completed a dozen missions without any real problems, but this time, on the way back to base, we were shelled by an American F-15. They thought we were insurgents. It was just me and my best mate, Lennie. We were in a jeep, and it flipped over... I was thrown clear, but Lennie was killed... That's what it was like, confusion, fuck-ups, mayhem, death, certainly no glory... just like the Somme. All wars are the same. My grandfather was in Normandy, but he would never talk about it."

He turned his gaze back to the ceiling. She watched as a tear trickled down the side of his face. She leant over and kissed his cheek trying to remove the pain. They both lay in silence; he closed his eyes and then he was asleep.

Janie carefully got out of bed so as not to disturb Rory, went downstairs to the kitchen, and poured herself a glass of water from the tap. As she put the drink to her lips, she thought about her new lover and wondered about his troubled soul.

She left the kitchen, turned out the lights in the lounge and went back to the bedroom. Rory was in a deep slumber; she hoped his demons were at rest. She climbed slowly back into bed, then she too was soon asleep.

It was nearly eight o'clock before Rory stirred and for a moment he couldn't get his bearings, then gradually he came around. He turned over and Janie was laying there facing him, her eyes starting to focus.

"Hello," he said.

"Hello," she replied and leaned across and kissed him.

He responded immediately and wrapped his arms around her

naked body. The proximity of her flesh soon had its effect and they made love once more.

Janie could have stayed there all day, but she had commitments. "Would you like some breakfast?" she said, indicating it was time to get up.

"Thanks, yeah, that would be great, then I better get going and let you get on."

"There's no rush. I've got to go into town. I can drop you off at your flat if you like."

"I was going to get a cab," said Rory.

"It's no problem, honest," she replied, and leaned over and kissed him again.

So, while Rory grabbed a shower, Janie made some tea and toast. Then, he read the paper while Janie got ready. After half an hour she reappeared from the bedroom, wearing a sweater and jeans. Rory was again under her spell.

"You look good," he said.

"Thank you," Janie replied.

Chapter Four

Basra, Iraq, January 1991.

Abu Hanifa, the aging but powerful mullah, would always remember that day at the end of January 1991, when a Red Crescent ambulance turned up at his mosque. Not the large Ali Bin Abi Talib mosque, but a smaller church on the outskirts of the city which served a largely working class and farming community not far from Sa'ad Al Ibn Abi Waqas square.

It was a warm day, he would recall, although the streets were layered in mud from a recent shower of rain. Freed from their Morning Prayer ritual, his flock jostled their way to the busy market place close by. The Imam watched them disappear around the corner with no more than a passing interest as the vehicle drew up alongside him.

He recognised the driver immediately and went to the open window to get the latest news.

"As-salam alaykum." The cleric still dressed in his white prayer robes, greeted the man.

"Wa alaykum e-salam," responded the driver. "I have someone for you. A patrol picked him up last night from a village about fifty kilometres away."

He pointed to a bedraggled and terrified figure beside him on the front seat.

"Family are all dead, killed by the British… says his name is Tariq, Tariq Siddique. Need a home for him and I thought of you after your recent loss," said the man.

Abu Hanifa looked at the floor in great despair, his care-worn features twisted in the pain of grief at the memory of his beloved sons, taken from him so brutally only two weeks earlier. They were killed by an American air attack while trying to escape from Kuwait; it was an open wound. He raised his hands to his face momentarily, as if hiding his eyes, then dragged them down his cheeks and grey beard; he murmured a quiet prayer.

The cleric looked at the boy, totally lost and almost rigid with fear and shock.

"Of course, leave him with me. I will look after him," replied Abu Hanifa, but without much emotion.

The driver got out of the truck, lifted the lad out of his seat and handed him to the mullah. The boy was as light as a feather, not starving but severely undernourished, and Abu Hanifa could feel his body shaking as he held him in his arms. The cleric was immediately moved by the boy's plight.

"As-salamu alaykum, Tariq," he said to the boy, trying to reassure him. Tariq buried his head in the man's shoulder as if trying to hide.

The cleric turned to the driver, thanked him and bid him farewell, "shukran, ma'a as-salaama."

"Alla ysalmak," replied the driver, before moving slowly away through the narrow streets.

Abu Hanifa looked at the boy with an air of despair. "What have we done to deserve this," he said under his breath, and walked towards his house.

The mullah lived a modest life, as befitting someone of his status within the Muslim community, with his family, wife Raheem and his two teenage daughters Badia and Na'eema. The house, just across the street from the mosque, was a two-story white-washed building with four rooms downstairs and the same above. The two girls shared a bedroom as had his sons before their untimely deaths. Their room had since become a shrine to their memory.

There were religious symbols dotted around the house and

simple furnishings, but there was a TV set; everyone had a TV set; it was a necessity in understanding what was happening in the outside world. Most evenings after prayers the family would sit and, on those occasions when the electricity allowed, watch news reports of the war.

There was some excitement as Abu Hanifa walked in and presented young Tariq to Raheem. The two girls came running in from the garden when they heard the arrival of their father wanting to see what all the fuss was about. Immediately the girls took over Tariq's well-being as they would a favoured pet.

Basra used to be a beautiful city. In the 1930's it was known as the Venice of Iraq due to its myriad canals and channels and the gondolier-looking craft which flitted about like water-boatmen across the waterways. Now it was different; they say that if you were to fall in one of the rivers you would die of toxic poisoning before you would drown. Oil, carcasses of all description, rusting hulks, even unexploded ordinance lay in the waters where once annual swimming events took place. Being a border city Basra had taken the brunt of recent conflicts right from the late 1960s, through the Iran-Iraq war of the 1980's to the present altercation. Its waterways bore witness to the city's decaying infrastructure and, to some extent, its spirit.

In 1991 it was a particularly dangerous place. With its predominantly Shiite population, the city was at odds with the Saddam Hussein regime. The end of the fighting was a mixed blessing for the people of Basra. The capitulation to the coalition was a humiliation, but Saddam Hussein was still in power and the mullah's family regularly debated what the future might bring in the wake of the cease fire. They would soon find out.

The day after the cessation of hostilities by the coalition at the end of February 1991, a T-72 tank gunner, returning home after Iraq's defeat in Kuwait, fired a shell into a portrait of Saddam and watching soldiers applauded. Taking this as a cue, a spontaneous uprising followed, buoyed in no small part by a tacit promise of support from the West who dearly wanted rid of Saddam, but lacked the conviction to complete the task. The insurrection continued until the end of March when the opposition was mercilessly put down by Saddam's forces with much death and destruction.

The mullah was one of several ulama in Basra, the educated class of Muslim legal scholars engaged in several fields of the hadith. They are best known as the arbiters of Shari'a law and, as head of the church locally, wielded a great deal of power. In this respect Abu Hanifa was potentially a target for the Republican Guard, Saddam's elite squad, who were largely responsible for the atrocities. The mullah escaped any retribution; the local military recognising that the authority of the cleric was vital in keeping some sort of order in the community.

During this time the noise of explosions and small arms in the city made it hard for the family to form any bonds with the traumatised Tariq Siddique. He would sit in silence, incommunicative, shaking with fear and shock like a pet dog might do during a firework display. Once the fighting had stopped, however, they slowly managed to nurture the boy back to health with kindness and providing him with a sense of belonging.

Over the coming weeks, as Tariq acclimatised to his new surroundings, he became more responsive. Daily the mullah would take him with him to the mosque and talk to him, not as a father would to a child, but as a teacher would to a pupil. The cleric would explain the function and purpose of the mosque and the teachings of the holy Quran.

The indoctrination of young Tariq started almost immediately. The bitterness that the mullah felt towards the regime of Saddam Hussein was nothing compared with the hatred he felt for the West, driven not by any religious ideology, but by the blame he attached for the deaths of his beloved sons and the perfidy in not coming to the support of his community when they needed it.

Abu Hanifa saw the boy not so much as an adopted son but as a potential vehicle for his own retribution, a šahīd of the future. Each day, the boy's studies of the Holy Scriptures were embellished by stories from the Crusades of Jihad and the glory of martyrdom, proclaimed by the cleric as the sixth pillar of Islam.

It became clear early on that the young Tariq was an intelligent boy. Always inquisitive, he soon showed an appreciation of the teachings of his mentor. He also developed a keen interest in mechanics and had a natural fascination for how things worked. Recognising this, the cleric, who had a brother who owned a small garage about a mile away from the mosque, one day after prayers, took Tariq to visit his workshop.

"How would you like to spend some time with Uncle Hanif?" he said, as he walked through the dusty streets.

"I would like that very much," said the ten-year-old Tariq.

So, from the age of ten, when he wasn't studying, Tariq would spend many hours holding spanners and maintenance lamps for the mechanic; watching him in wonderment as he used his acetylene torch like a magician, welding together distressed bodywork that frequented the roads of Basra. New cars were a luxury few locals could afford, and every ounce of life was cajoled out of the wrecks that were sent to Uncle Hanif's repair shop.

"I want to be a mechanic when I am older," he told the mullah excitedly, as Abu Hanifa collected him from the garage one afternoon. The cleric smiled; he had other plans for Tariq; God's work.

Violence was never far away from the city and three years later, in early 1999, Tariq Siddique was on his way to the mosque when a loud explosion shook the city. Terrified, he ran for the cover of the building. His adopted father had just finished morning prayers and was at the door and ushered him inside. Others soon congregated seeking shelter, solace or news.

With memories of past horrors still firmly etched into his psyche, Tariq stood there shaking. A paternal arm wrapped around him. Other comforting voices joined in. Word went out that it was a missile fired by a U.S. warplane. The mullah and some of his followers made their way to the locale of the carnage. It was in a small market place, less than two kilometres away; a scene of total devastation greeted them. The injured lay among the broken bodies, their cries of pain echoing around the narrow streets. The debris - bricks, boulders, dust, broken vehicles of every kind, twisted metal and dismembered limbs were scattered everywhere. The cleric watched helplessly and cursed the infidel.

Later that year, further trials fell on Basra when another revolt against the regime of Saddam Hussein occurred, which went the same way as the first. It was brutally put down with mass executions in and around the area. As a punishment for the insurrection, the Iraqi government made the decision to deliberately exclude Basra in an attempt to kill the City economically. As a result, most of the trade on which it relied for its prosperity was diverted to Umm Qasr, the coastal port fifty miles to the south.

In chronicling the events that would shape young Tariq, 9/11 2001 played a significant role. Radicalised Muslims feted the perpetrators as martyrs; the '19' would never be forgotten. Abu Hanifa was aware of Al-Qaeda of course, but more in the terms of idealism rather than a physical group or army to which someone with a common belief could sign up. It was a disparate organisation, a brand almost, with Osama Bin Laden as the figurehead. There was no obvious command structure, merely a collection of cells, but with a deadly aim. It was clear where the Mullah's sympathy lay.

The Iraq 'branch' of al-Qaeda was known as Jama'at al-Tawhid wal-Jihad or 'JTJ' for short. It was started by Abu Musab al-Zarqawi in Afghanistan, but he decamped to Iraq after the US declaration of war on terror and subsequent action in that country. Zarqawi, a Jordanian by birth, and his organisation were instrumental in promoting terrorist activity against the coalition. His main activity was in Baghdad and areas to the north in the Kurdish homelands. The network did however, extend as far south as Basra and, due to the Shiite ethnicity of the area, there was growing support for the aims of establishing a devout Islamic Iraq.

The 2003 conflict would change the dynamics considerably, and once again, Basra found itself in the vanguard of yet another conflict, which became known as the second Gulf War.

During the spring of 2003, the outskirts of the city were the scene of some of the heaviest fighting before British forces took control on April 6th. The lengthy period of occupation started, and, once again, Abu Hanifa would play a major part in helping to maintain order in the local population.

The overthrow of Saddam was a mixed blessing for the people of Basra. Particularly after the economic isolation the regime had imposed on the city, the local populous were glad to see the back of the tyrant. However, they were now faced with an army of occupation.

The remit of 'peace-keeper' by the British forces would prove to be a major challenge. With so much destruction, and no government to speak of, a power vacuum emerged, creating an ideal climate for extremism to thrive.

The Multi-National Division (South-East) was a British commanded section and assumed responsibility for security in the south-east of Iraq at the end of the war. It included the Basra area, and, initially, had its headquarters at the local Airport. It would face an uphill task in keeping law and order.

Abu Hanifa found himself to be an influential person, acting as a point of liaison for the occupying powers in his area of the city. The mullah cursed the invaders with every breath, but it was a question of expediency. To achieve his aims, he would drink with the devil himself.

His first meeting with the British commander took place in the late spring when Major Tim Howard called by way of introduction. The British tactic was to work with the local population in a so-called 'hearts and minds' campaign rather than subjugate them, and the meeting was set up as part of this objective.

This was to be an uncomfortable meeting for both sides, and   not just because of the oppressive heat and humidity. The British were understandably, and rightly, nervous about their safety, and a significant armed presence accompanied the major. The followers of the cleric on the other hand were astonished at his apparent collusion with the 'enemy' given his normal rhetoric against the occupying powers. The cleric recognised the dilemma and, through trusted worshippers, he spread the word about the true intent. "Keep your enemies close at hand," he had said.

The mullah, although now into his seventieth year, had lost none of his fire, and still struck an imposing figure. Resplendent in his white robes, he exuded an air of authority as he greeted his guests in an annex adjoining the mosque. He bowed respectfully. "As-salam alaykum."

The cleric, flanked by two of his most trusted people, invited the major, two lieutenants and an interpreter to sit at a large round table. The room was small and stuffy, and the glass-less windows provided only a modicum of the necessary air to feel comfortable. In no-time the army officers were sweating profusely.

"Wa alaykum e-salam," replied the major, much to the surprise and delight of his hosts.

"Thank you for your courtesy," replied the cleric, recognising the attempt by the Major to address his host in his native language, "I speak good English."

The interpreter looked relieved, but he was clearly nervous in the presence of the mullah. His involvement with the army of occupation would make him a target for the anti-British factions.

Major Howard was not a product of Sandhurst or Cranfield, but someone who had earned his promotion through the ranks and spoke in a straightforward manner without the 'plumminess' associated with some officers. He outlined his brief as he saw it for the local community.

"We are here not with any aggressive intentions. Primarily, our role is to preserve the peace and support the local population."

"I am pleased to hear it," said the cleric. "Then we have mutual objectives."

The British officers looked at each other and a wry smile was exchanged. There was a long way to go before any thought of mutuality would be applied to the situation. Trust would need to be earned.

As part of his long-term aims, Abu Hanifa was keen for, the now seventeen-year-old, Tariq Siddique to meet his first British soldier and right on cue his son entered the room carrying a tray of tea and water for the guests.

"Major Howard, let me introduce you to my son, Tariq," said the cleric.

"Tariq, this is Major Howard, who is going to look after us." He spoke in Arabic and grinned. The interpreter translated for the major.

"Pleased to meet you, sir," said Tariq confidently, finally able to practice the results of his English lessons for the first time outside the classroom.

"Pleased to meet you, too" said the major. "You speak very good English."

"Thank you, sir," replied the young man.

"Would you like to join us, Tariq? If you have no objections, major."

"No, of course not, in fact he would be very helpful in spreading the word among the younger people that we are not here with any ulterior motives, merely trying to maintain law and order."

The cleric translated the last sentence for Tariq who smiled. Tariq sat alongside his adopted father and the two other elders. The group continued to debate various issues relating to security, water distribution and communication. Before leaving, the major turned to the cleric.

"Would you consider helping set up a local government here in Basra?"

He asked in a way that almost expected a positive response.

The mullah felt cornered. On the one hand, it would extend his power-base significantly, but on the other, it threatened to alienate him from his followers.

Abu Hanifa turned to the major and again bowed. "That is a most kind offer, but I am a humble servant of God and my place is here with my people."

The major accepted his response with regret.

"That is a pity. You have a great deal to offer the people of Basra, and the peace process, but I do of course respect your position. Shukran, ilaa al-liqaa."

The major bid farewell in Arabic and bowed his head in customary fashion.

"Ilaa al-liqaa," replied the cleric, and, despite their differences, some mutual respect had been established. It would not of course deflect the cleric from his mission.

There were huge obstacles for the British forces. After such a conflict, there were huge logistical issues. Much of the infrastructure had been destroyed, which made practical communication - just getting around, a real problem. There was only spasmodic electricity and TV and radio had been cut off. Clean water was in limited supply, and sewage facilities virtually non-existent.

In the event, after an initial period of looting and general disorder, within a week some sort of social cohesion emerged. This was driven by the local population's determination to forge their own destiny with as little outside help as possible.

The local power station was a case in point, where the workers dismissed US support.

"Actually, we'd like to do it ourselves." said, Adel Hussein al-Shati, the station's planning manager at a meeting with American engineers. He then explained how long it would take and how many men he would need. The Americans were more than happy with this arrangement.

Someone had even written on a wall: "Farewell bad dictator. Thank you for your help, British."

These sentiments would not last.

Abu Hanifa was not impressed with the coalition's political agenda, he had no interest in a people's democracy; his main aim was to secure an Islamic Iraqi State, and a stable regime would not help him achieve this goal. What he wanted was a population living in fear and uncertainty which would be malleable to more extreme influences. The Taliban regime in Afghanistan after the Russian invasion of the 1980's was the template.

At Friday prayers he would emphasise this message but was careful to fall short of advocating any civil disobedience. He had other, more direct ways of bringing about change.

The mullah had gathered a pool of about twenty trusted, like-minded followers who between them had formed a committee bent on fulfilling the cleric's ideals. Acting as an informal Islamic council, they met every week in the same annex that had afforded the recent hospitality to Major Howard.

After Friday prayers, following the meeting with the major, the cleric addressed his group and explained his position of candid co-operation and tacit disruption. His adopted son Tariq would attend these meetings anxious to forward his father's cause, and having witnessed at first hand the suffering of the local population by the invaders, he was, if anything, becoming even more extreme.

"There is only one thing the infidel understands and that is might of the sword of Allah," he said to much applause from the gathering. The cleric ruffled his hair playfully as a gesture of acknowledgement.

Back at Uncle Hanif's repair shop Tariq had mastered many of the skills of his mentor and was now an accomplished engineer, often staying-on late into the evening well after Hanif had closed for the day. Unbeknown to the cleric and his uncle, Tariq had been perfecting a new skill.

At school his interest in physics had come to the attention of the science teacher, Mohammed Meki, who, as well as being considered an intellectual by the local population, was also sympathetic to the broader ideals of an Islamic Iraqi State. Following a lesson on electrical circuits, after the class had gone, Tariq confronted the teacher and came straight out with a dangerous request. "Sir," he said anxiously. "Do you know how to make a bomb?"

The teacher eyed the youth. His initial reaction was to remonstrate with him, but something held the teacher back.

"Of course, it is not difficult," said Mohammed.

"Will you show me?" asked Tariq.

Chapter Five

By May 2003, a month after the end of formal hostilities, there some were positive signs in Basra, a new motivation among the people to mend the city. Shops were open for business, and some commerce at least was boosting the local economy. This was not necessarily good news for the cleric.

In the western press, however, a new word was beginning to gain prominence, 'insurgency'.

Daily, the reports of terrorist activities, particularly around the capital, were headline news. The death toll was appalling, mostly civilian, but coalition forces were also suffering casualties. Suicide bombers were targeting markets as well as military bases as the ethnic, tribal, and religious schisms were exposed, threatening to turn Iraq toward civil war.

For the British, Iraq was becoming a political 'hot potato', with growing criticism of the policy at home. It was essential that the military forces hand over responsibilities to the civilian agencies as soon as practicable, not only to appease the powers in Whitehall, but to reduce the amount of local resentment to the occupation.

It was a key strategy.

In Basra, Major Howard was concentrating his efforts on maintaining law and order and training the local police force, including soldiers of the former Republican Guard who, generally, had divided loyalties. Although it was still dangerous, security was much better than in Baghdad. However, with the restoration of the electricity supply to most of the population, together with the gradual recovery of basic utilities, the situation across the country as a whole started to improve.

Abu Hanifa continued his daily duties at the mosque

expressing his doctrine to willing followers, however, in August 2003 an event occurred which would have a significant effect on the mullah's future.

Word of his work had reached the ears of Zarqawi in Baghdad and arrangements were made, in strictest secrecy, for the head of Al-Qaeda in Iraq to visit the cleric in Basra to discuss the escalation of direct action in the south.

The meeting took place at the beginning of September when a truck carrying fruit pulled up outside the mosque. The cleric was waiting anxiously. It was another hot and humid day; the air almost visibly damp with the moisture that rose from the swamps surrounding the city; it made standing outside for any length of time was impossible. The cleric was relieved when the truck pulled up at the appointed time.

Zarqawi and his body guard were dressed simply, disguised as common farmers; Zarqawi, resplendent in full beard and moustache disguising his plump, oval face which would soon become essential notice-board material in Army HQs across the country as one of the coalition's 'most-wanted'. Their ruse had enabled them to pass through numerous road blocks unhindered.

The Jordanian got down from the truck and embraced the cleric genially.

"As-salam alaykum."

"Wa alaykum e-salam," responded the mullah with equal warmth.

The pair had not met previously but there was an immediate affinity through the bond of a common cause. After the introductions, Abu Hanifa led the two men into the annex where Tariq was waiting with tea and refreshments.

"Shukran, Abu Hanifa." Zarqawi thanked his host.

The cleric and his adopted son sat opposite their two guests as they refreshed from their long journey.

Zarqawi raised his drink to his lips and took a sip of his tea, then stared deep into the cup before slowly putting it down on the table. He wiped his mouth with the back of his hand and looked at the cleric; his eyes were wide as if assessing his guest.

"We have many volunteers willing to give their lives to the defeat of the infidels… We have money and weapons from our brothers in Palestine and Iran. There is much support in the country from our people wanting rid of the foreign invaders. In Baghdad we have had many successes."

"I have seen the fruits of our struggle, Alhamdulillah," said the cleric, praising God for His guidance. "How can we help?"

"Here in Basra things are different," said Zarqawi. "If we are going to fulfill our dream of a Muslim State of Iraq we need our Shiite cousins to be engaged in the struggle."

"We do what we can," interjected the cleric.

"But words are not sufficient when they fall on deaf ears," replied the guest.

Abu Hanifa was a wily character and not about to be intimidated by the new arrival. He stood and looked directly at the Jordanian.

"Abu Musab al-Zarqawi, you are a man of great deeds, but you know nothing of the spirit of people. Fear is not the way to win the hearts of Iraqi's, the devil Saddam found that out. It is only by capturing their souls will you sway them to follow the cause; without that we will not endure. It could even, God forbid, drive them into the hands of the infidels."

"Wise words and truly acknowledged, but our enemy is at our door and we must strike at the heart of Satan and its serpents that despoil our country and suck out its wealth. For, mark my words, America and its puppets are raping our country... If we do not act quickly, they will bleed it dry of the wealth that comes from its soil, which rightly belongs to the Iraqi people."

"What can I do?" asked the cleric, not wishing to be drawn into an ideological argument on which he was in broad agreement.

"As I have said, I have many brave warriors, but if we are to mount a campaign here in Basra, I will need a base from which they can work and safe houses where they can live before they complete their missions. Can you help us?" replied Zarqawi.

"Of course, I have many followers only too willing to help our cause," replied the cleric.

"That is good, but there is much to discuss... Security will be our main threat; you cannot trust anyone; the infidels have eyes and ears everywhere. They even watch us from the skies."

Zarqawi turned to his companion.

"Mohammed here is my most trusted associate, and he will stay with you for a day or two to arrange communication. He is an expert in such things, and will ensure that you are not compromised... It is easy to leave a path that leads right to your door."

The dialogue was 'business-like', and a strategy on how Abu Hanifa could assist Al-Qaeda in practical terms was agreed. The cleric would arrange for facilities to be available to accommodate the jihadists in the form of safe houses. To facilitate this, Zarqawi agreed to set up a logistics network that would enable vehicles to be used in a bombing campaign. A communication web would be established, guided by Mohammed, who would supply computers and set up phone protocols and secure Internet connections, everything that would be necessary to provide backup for the proposed campaign.

Tariq listened intently to the discussions desperate to be involved but, much to his frustration, the cleric insisted he continued with his studies; there would be more important work for him in the future.

Later that month, an incident took place which played into the hands of Abu Hanifa.

Working on a tip-off, British forces entered the Haitham Hotel in Basra and a number of suspected terrorists were detained. The detainees were taken to a three-room building in the city where they were questioned for thirty-six hours. Among the detainees was a twenty-six-year-old employee of the hotel, who died during interrogation. The subsequent post-mortem found ninety-three injuries, including fractured ribs and a broken nose. Other detainees claimed that the British soldiers had held kicking competitions, competing to see who could kick the prisoners the furthest. Prisoners were also made to assume stress positions and were beaten and kicked if they failed to maintain these. Pictures of Baha Mousa, the victim of the incident, was paraded on local television and caused an outrage which led to a number of anti-British protests.

Major Howard, in a later meeting with the cleric, was forced to apologise for the behaviour of the troops, but the damage was done, and the reputation of the occupying forces would be tainted forever. The hearts and minds campaign had taken an irretrievable step backwards.

Abu Hanifa of course couldn't have been happier. His mosque had become a hot-bed of unrest, fuelled in no small part by the cleric's continued rhetoric against the occupation.

Given the logistics, it would take several months before the terror campaign could begin in earnest. Some locals were impatient at the lack of activity against the military, and would take the occasional pot-shot at patrols, but with only limited success. Unfortunately, as a result of this action, security checks and arrests increased, which made moving around more hazardous, ultimately working against the wider objectives.

Naturally, Tariq was anxious to contribute to the cause in some direct way and had many heated discussions with his adopted father. The cleric appreciated Tariq's impatience and put it down to the impetuosity of youth, but recognised he would soon need to give the young man his head.

In January 2004, on his eighteenth birthday, Abu Hanifa presented Tariq with a laptop which had been provided by Mohammed as a gift for the cleric's support. After prayers the cleric sat Tariq down and for the first time outlined his plans for him.

"Tariq, my son, for that is how I look at you, a precious gift from Allah to assuage my grief for my beloved boys." He looked at the heavens and uttered a prayer before continuing.

"For you my thoughts lie in a different direction. You have been blessed by Allah with many gifts and you are capable of greatness, I am certain of this... but your destiny my son is in God's hands... You must take the path that He has laid before you."

Tariq looked intrigued and excited.

"But not yet." Tariq's face dropped in disappointment.

"I want to arrange for you to go to England after you have completed your studies here. You will go to University there, become an engineer and learn about life and the ways of the infidel, then you will be ready," said the cleric.

Tariq was lost for words.

"Everything I have done for you has been to this goal; I

dream that one day you will rise to achieve great things. You will become a leader of men and inspire others to follow you… It will require much hard work and you will need to gain the skills which will enable you to reach your destiny."

Tariq wanted to know more but the cleric would not go further. "It is important you do well in your studies to be accepted into the University. I have spoken to Major Howard about it."

Tariq grimaced which the Mullah ignored. "He has said that there may be opportunities to provide a sponsor for your education in England, but they will only select the best students."

Tariq could see the logic and the love that his adopted father had for him. He got up and hugged the old man. "I will work hard father, I will. Allah will give me the strength."

So, while Tariq concentrated on his studies, in Basra the strategy of direct action was gaining momentum. Anyone working for the coalition forces, the police, judiciary, as well as military patrols were targets. There were also sectarian killings against Shia civilians and other non-Muslim groups. An early victim was Major Howard's interpreter who was paraded before a camera on an internet link and, kneeling in front of a Tawhid and Jihad banner, beheaded slowly with a knife. It was a particularly brutal murder and designed as part of the terror tactics used by Zarqawi to deter fraternisation.

Tariq continued to work diligently at school, and in his spare time continued his work at the garage where he was now a fully proficient mechanic. However, his frustration at not being able to contribute directly to the cause was not dissipating.

Unbeknown to the cleric, Tariq had been using Uncle Hanif's garage to indulge in a new passion, constructing remote controlled detonators. With the information given to him by his tutor and his circuitry knowledge he had made several prototypes, although not connected to any real explosives, yet.

His closest friend at school, who of course shared Tariq's idea of jihad, was Ahmed Younis who had specialised in chemistry at school and between them they were to form a lethal partnership.

Having perfected his firing mechanism, Tariq's next step was to obtain explosive material, and this is where Ahmed came in. Tariq would probably be able to get hold of military ordinance - shells, grenades and so on, but word would almost certainly get back to his father, and he was keen to do this on his own to make a statement in retribution for the murder of his parents and relatives.

One night, at the end of February, Tariq arranged to meet Ahmed at his uncle's workshop. It was around nine o'clock, and quite dark.

The garage, from the outside, looked run-down and shabby; there was no money for any cosmetic attention. It had a large roll-down frontage where cars would be driven in for repair. There was no hydraulic hoist, and all service work was carried out in the claustrophobic confines of the two service pits. In the corner stood five gas canisters used for welding, and around the walls various tools - spanners, socket sets, and so on; everything which Uncle Hanif needed to repair the vehicles. Inside, everything appeared to be covered in grease and oil, evidence of the many years' toil endured by the master mechanic.

There was a side door next to the frontage. Tariq answered the knock and, checking there was no-one following, let Ahmed in.

"Is everything ok, Tariq?" asked Ahmed. "You sounded quite mysterious when you phoned."

Tariq placed the bottom of a cardboard box on one of the upturned oil drums and invited Ahmed to sit. He outlined his plan.

"You must swear by Allah not to reveal anything I tell you, Ahmed."

"Of course," replied his friend.

Tariq continued, "I could not say anything in school, but I have perfected a simple detonating device for exploding a bomb which can be triggered remotely. I have tested it and it works well but I need your help with the explosive itself. Will you help me?"

"You want to make a bomb?" exclaimed Ahmed louder than he had intended.

"Sshhh," whispered Tariq, holding his index finger to his mouth. "With your help."

Ahmed looked down in thought.

"It is very dangerous, and I don't just mean the possibility of getting caught."

"I know, and I would not ask if I did not think you were by my side," said Tariq.

"What do you need to know?" asked Ahmed somewhat reluctantly.

"Everything," replied Tariq.

Ahmed paused in thought for a moment and then spoke. "Unless you can get hold of any plastic explosive your options are limited. The brothers tend to use Acetone peroxide mixed with sulfuric acid, but this combination is extremely dangerous. They call it 'mother of Satan' because of the many faithful it has taken... a better way is to mix it with nitrocellulose."

Tariq listened intently in fascination, and admiration.

Ahmed was in his stride now even surprising himself at his

knowledge. He looked at Tariq and explained in more detail.

"Ok, now if you dissolve the nitrocellulose in acetone and then mix in the acetone peroxide and let it dry, it will result in a mixture that is both more stable and more powerful than acetone peroxide by itself."

"Can you do that?" asked Tariq.

"Of course," said Ahmed. "If you can get hold of the chemicals. That is the difficult part."

"What about Mr. Meki? Do you think he would help?" asked Tariq.

"I will ask him," Ahmed said.

"But we must be very careful," said Tariq. "Don't mention this over the phone under any circumstances. My father says they listen to us all the time."

Tariq embraced his friend and agreed to meet again in a week which would give Ahmed time to explore possibilities.

As arranged, the pair met the following week at the garage. It was about the same time and the two sat together on the oil drums as Ahmed spoke quietly but excitedly.

"I have some good news. I have been able to get the chemicals you will need."

"That's great. How did you manage that?"

"I told Meki I wanted it for research purposes," said Ahmed.

"And he believed you?"

"I don't know, I don't think so. He smiled when I asked him. He wanted to know if I had spoken to you."

"What did you say?" asked Tariq inquisitively.

"I just said I wanted to examine the chemical reaction for myself. He warned me that it would be very dangerous and to be extremely careful. He wouldn't be able to get much without causing suspicion… He will let me have the stuff in the morning; he says he knows someone. I will bring it around tomorrow night."

"How will you get past the checkpoints?" asked Tariq.

"I will have my cycle; they don't tend to bother me… I can hide the material in my drinks bottle and saddle bags. I don't think we will be able to make very much, but it might be enough to hurt a small patrol or even an armoured car if we plant it in the right place."

Tariq felt an adrenaline rush as the thought of direct action, at last, took hold.

"That is excellent, excellent." said Tariq and hugged his friend.

The next evening was a Friday, the holy day. Ahmed arrived as arranged and wheeled his cycle into the garage. The pair of them removed the ingredients and Ahmed went to work. After an hour it was done and the crystallisation was complete. He carefully tipped the drying crystals from the bowl he had used to mix the ingredients into an old thermos flask to keep them cool.

"When will it be ready?" asked Tariq, anxious to try out his handy work.

"Tomorrow it will be properly dry… We will need to find a container," said Ahmed. "How will you detonate it?"

"By phone. I will attach a phone to the bomb and telephone the number, then when it connects, it will trigger the bomb."

"But that's brilliant," said Ahmed. "What about a target?"

"There's an alley not far from here where patrols cut through to get to the canal. I will try it there."

"I will join you," said Ahmed.

"No, this is for my parents. It is something I must do for

them," replied Tariq.

"But I will need to be here. To load the container and show you where to attach the detonator," countered Ahmed.

"Very well, but as soon as that is done you must return home. This is my revenge," said Tariq firmly.

"One thing," said Ahmed, almost as an afterthought. "You will need to store it somewhere cool. If it gets too hot it might still explode."

Tariq looked concerned.

"Hmm, well, there's always the refrigerator; we only keep water in it, but there is a problem, the power cuts… we can't always rely on it."

"It will have to do. How will you explain it to your Uncle?" asked Ahmed.

"I will put the container at the back with some cans of drink. He never uses it much anyway."

Tariq walked to the corner and examined the rusting container that hardly lived up to the definition of a fridge. He cleared a layer of dust and dead insects off the top, opened the door with a sharp tug and looked inside. There were some plastic water containers in the rack at the front, otherwise it was empty. Tariq switched on the plug, nothing. He stood back and aimed a kick on the side and the fridge stuttered into life. The light had come on and, at the back, Tariq could see some decaying fruit; what variety though was difficult to tell past the furry coating of mould. He took the offending article out and dropped it in the rubbish bin among the empty cans of oil and other garage residue.

Ahmed gently picked the thermos holding the crystals from the workbench and moved slowly and carefully to the fridge, as if carrying a tray of eggs. Tariq moved one of the shelves to accommodate it, then stood back and watched as Ahmed put the container at the back.

"We will have to hide it," said Ahmed.

"Don't worry I will get some cans of drink. I am working tomorrow. It will be quite safe," replied Tariq.

Ahmed wheeled his bike out of the garage and Tariq locked up. It was almost ten o'clock, and the noise of military vehicles disturbed the stillness of the night. The evening was clammy, still twenty-five degrees, and the mosquitoes were out in force. Around every light source moths bounced backwards and forwards. There was no official curfew, but everyone was indoors, which meant moving about was potentially dangerous. The security forces took the view that anyone out and about at this time of night was up to no good, which was, by and large, a correct assumption.

"Watch out for patrols," shout/whispered Tariq, as he watched Ahmed get on his bicycle and ride away.

Tariq walked the kilometer to his house in the opposite direction. He had no concerns about being stopped by a patrol; his father's position meant he would be immune from any interrogation. He also knew several of the local soldiers through their visits to the Imam. He felt a sense of excitement and nervousness as he headed from the garage.

Back home, the Imam waited for Tariq's return, as any loving father would do. Both his daughters were now married and living in other parts of the city, so it was just the three of them. Before leaving, Tariq had told his father he was studying with Ahmed, which to some extent was accurate, and the cleric had no reason to suspect otherwise.

On his return there was no inquisition, just genuine interest in Tariq's activities.

"Have you had a good evening…? How is Ahmed?" his father enquired on his arrival

Tariq sat and chatted with him for a while before going to bed, but sleep did not come. He lay awake for hours wondering what the coming day would bring and the excitement that he was now at last able to play his part in the Jihad.

All day at the garage Tariq was unable to concentrate. He checked the fridge regularly to ensure it was still working. As planned, he had bought three cans of soft drinks and placed them on the shelf in front of the thermos, which, if not completely hiding it, at least drew attention away from the container.

Although it was officially winter, the temperature outside was still over twenty degrees and in the confines of the cramped garage, considerably more. About midday the electricity did fail for about half an hour, and Tariq paced anxiously around the workshop until it resumed, to much relief.

Uncle Hanif had many of the traits of his brother but did not have Abu Hanif's communication skills and could be gruff with people. He had a take-it-or-leave-it attitude when it came to negotiating prices for his work, but he had a good reputation and people trusted him. He had shown great patience with Tariq and his encouragement and support had contributed significantly to Tariq's development as an individual.

On that Saturday he watched Tariq with interest and could tell straight away something was not right. He seemed distracted and on a couple of occasions he confronted him. "Is everything ok Tariq, you seem very anxious?".

"Of course," replied Tariq. "I have an exam next week that is all," and Hanif let it drop.

By six o'clock, Hanif had closed the garage and pulled down

the roller door.

"Well that's enough for today," he said to Tariq, wiping his hands on an oily rag. "Are you heading back for your dinner?"

"Soon," replied Tariq. "Is it ok if I stay a while? I want to work on Ashim's old Mercedes. He needs it back on Monday for his taxi service."

"Well don't stay too late. You need to have a life away from here and your studies," he counselled.

"No, I won't," said Tariq, and he watched his uncle leave the workshop.

Hanif shared the living-quarters above the garage with his wife and three children, and, work-worn, he trudged up the outside steps leading to the entrance of the flat feeling a degree of satisfaction at the completion of another hard day's labour. He couldn't wait to clean himself up and have something to eat with his family. He thought again about Tariq, who clearly hadn't been himself, and hoped there was nothing troubling the lad.

Ahmed arrived early around six-thirty and parked his bike against the wall of the garage. Tariq let him in and, before his friend could speak, put his index finger to his lips again in a conspiratorial manner.

"Sshhh... We don't want to disturb Uncle Hanif," he whispered.

"Is everything ok?" whispered Ahmed in response.

"Yes, I wasn't expecting you until eight. I will need to go back home for a few minutes to get something to eat. My mother will be expecting me."

"That's ok," replied Ahmed. "I wasn't doing anything, so I thought I would come around to see if everything was still ok for tonight... I can prepare the material while you are away so that it will be ready to go when you get back."

"Yes, ok, wait a second," and Tariq crawled under one of the work benches and retrieved a metal container about the size of a child's lunch box. He opened the lid and inside was a mobile phone and circuit board.

"This is the firing mechanism. We just need to connect it to the explosive and we are in business," said Tariq.

"What about the container for the bomb?" asked Ahmed.

"I thought we could use this container," said Tariq handing Ahmed the box.

"Not big enough... and we need to put in nails or ball bearings, bits of metal, anything that will fly through the air. That's what does the damage," replied Ahmed.

"What about this?" said Tariq, picking up an empty five-litre oil can.

"That could work, but we will need to open it up. We can't pour the crystals through that small opening," said Ahmed.

Tariq went to work on the can with a metal cutter and soon had made a large opening on the side of the can which he prized open.

"Yes, that will do... Then you can lay your device on top of the crystals and surround it with some nails and seal it up with some tape. That should work very well," said Ahmed.

Tariq opened the fridge door and carefully removed the thermos flask containing the, now dried, explosive. Ahmed peered at the contents and carefully revolved the container. The crystals rolled with the turn.

"Yes, they look fine."

Tariq went to the workbench and picked up a large bag of nails. "We have plenty of these."

"They will be ideal," replied Ahmed.

"Are you sure you will be alright till I get back? I won't be long."

"Sure, borrow my bike; it will save some time," said Ahmed.

"Thanks," said Tariq. "I'll be back very soon," and he cycled away.

It took only ten minutes on Ahmed's bike for Tariq to return to his house; his mother was waiting for him.

"Your father is out, some business with Mohammed."

Tariq's ears pricked up; the communications expert from Baghdad was back. He looked forward to meeting him again. They had forged a good relationship during his previous visit and he thought he would be impressed by his bomb-making initiative.

His mother went into the kitchen and returned with Tariq's evening meal.

"I'm going out again after my dinner... I'm meeting up with Ahmed," Tariq explained. His mother acknowledged and returned to the kitchen.

A few minutes later Tariq called to his mother who was still washing dishes.

"I'm going now."

His mother came in from the kitchen and looked at his plate; his meal had hardly been touched.

"Are you ok, Tariq? You've hardly eaten anything," she observed.

"I'm fine. I'll be back in a couple of hours, I won't be late," and he kissed his mother's forehead, then left the house.

Tariq crossed the main bridge over the canal that led to the Shat Al Arab waterway. His mind was elsewhere, racing, planning what he would need to do. Then suddenly, as he reached the other side, his worse fears. There was a check point ahead.

He slammed on his breaks and stopped dead. His heart flew to his mouth. All vehicles were being searched and pedestrians were having their bags examined. Even though he had nothing to hide, Tariq felt nauseous, but it was too late to turn around; it would look suspicious.

He anxiously awaited his turn in the small line that had built up. There were three armed-soldiers checking vehicles and another searching the rest of the foot traffic. After five minutes Tariq was next in line, and the soldier approached him.

"Name?" asked the soldier, who was taking a close look at the bike as he spoke.

"Tariq Siddique," he replied.

"Where are you going?" he asked authoritatively.

"My uncle's garage on Al-Kamiah Street," Tariq replied.

The soldier had another look at the bike and then waved him through. Tariq breathed a sigh of relief and headed on to his destination.

He turned the final corner and his uncle's garage was directly in front of him when everything seemed to happen in slow motion. He saw the roof of the garage lift from its fastenings, the wall of the flat behind collapsing outwards revealing Uncle Hanif's lounge; the roller door blew open as if it was being pushed by a giant's hand. Then the flames... ten metres, twenty metres, fifty... a hundred; then the blast wave that knocked Tariq off the bike and flung him head first against a wall of a house momentarily rendering him unconscious.

Two parked cars were tossed in the air like children's toys before crashing down on their roofs. Debris descended like pumice from a volcano. A large boulder landed a metre or so from Tariq's feet, crushing Ahmed's bike. Tariq was dazed and in shock; he began shaking violently, suddenly transported back to a bygone time that he had locked from his mind.

His eyes focused on the garage, or where it once was. There was just a hole. Then, another enormous explosion as the acetylene cylinders ignited, bringing down the side walls. Overturned trucks were strewn immediately in front of the shell that once housed Uncle Hanif's business. Bricks, mortar, machinery, parts of cars, furniture were strewn across the street as far as you could see. The apartment had disappeared; in fact, everything within fifty metres of the building was flattened. Flames started to lick at what little remained, just a few girders, twisted, contorted out of shape, as if God himself had wrung them with His own hand.

Movement, movement everywhere... a patrol vehicle, another, an armoured car, then an ambulance. Tariq drifted back into unconsciousness and a paramedic in a military uniform raised his head.

"Can you hear me, son...? What's your name?" An English voice.

"Tariq," he managed to utter in a whisper. "Tariq Siddique."

"Stay with me Tariq. You'll be fine," and he lost consciousness again.

Chapter Six

February 28th 2004, Al Zubir General Hospital, Basra.

It was several hours before Tariq was able to focus coherently. He looked around the crowded hospital ward. It was total chaos; with only two nurses and one doctor the place was overwhelmed. It was swelteringly hot. Confused people were rushing around everywhere and still they were bringing in injured that had been dug out from the rubble on anything they could find. Chairs, tables, even a door, were being used as makeshift stretchers. There were screams from people in pain; medicines were still in very short supply. He could hear a mother calling desperately for her children, a man praying for Allah to save him, and men in military uniform asking questions. Then there was the smell, a pungent pine which irritated the sinuses to mask the odour of death.

He heard a voice closer to him.

"Tariq, Tariq can you hear me?" It was the cleric.

"Thank God you are alright; we thought we had lost you. I heard the explosion and came looking for you. Mother said you would be at Uncle Hanif's, but when I got there..." He lowered his head in despair. "Who would do such a thing? I have spoken to Major Howard and he thinks it was a bomb. But who would kill Hanif? He is a gentle man, a man who mends things not destroys them."

The cleric looked down and wiped a tear from his eye. Tariq looked at the desolation in his face and wanted to cry but tears would not come; he was beyond that.

"Major Howard says that Shia militia may have been behind it; they are active in Baghdad. Whoever did this I curse with every part of my being," he said, and raised his head to the heavens and uttered a prayer.

His attention turned back to Tariq.

"How are you feeling, my son? Are you in any pain?"

Tariq managed to respond in a guttural wheezing voice. "No, I'm ok I think, just my head."

"I thank Allah," he said and lifted his head in prayer once again.

"You had good fortune, my son. Allah was clearly watching over you. Any closer…" he paused. "And, well, you would have been killed."

The cleric mopped his son's brow with his hand.

"What were you doing going to Hanif's? I thought you had finished for the day," he asked, not in a judgmental way, just an enquiry.

Tariq repeated the story he had told his mother.

"It was Ashim's Mercedes. I wanted to finish it so he could use it on Monday. It is his only way of making money; he is a taxi driver," he managed to stammer his voice picking up timbre.

"Praise be to Allah," said the cleric. "Hanif was surely lucky to have such dedication."

Tariq looked at his father bent over him; his eyes red and filled with tears. Tariq had picked up on the past tense.

"Was, father? What do you mean 'was'?" he whispered, then swallowed to clear the mucus from his throat.

Abu Hanifa looked at his son with a pitiful expression; he could hardly get the words out.

"They are all dead. Hanif, Basha'ir and the children. They were having dinner. They found them next to the table, food still in the dishes, burned beyond recognition the major said.

They have found another body, or what was left of one, a boy about your age."

"Ahmed!" said Tariq still in shock, "Oh no!"

Tariq's face distorted again wanting cry, but nothing was there.

"He was waiting for me to return… He wanted to help me. Then we were going back to his house to study for a while."

A doctor approached and looked at Tariq. He shone a small torch into his eyes. "Look straight ahead."

"How is he?" asked the concerned cleric.

"He'll be ok, concussion and some cuts and bruises, nothing broken that we can see. Any pain anywhere?" the doctor asked Tariq.

There was a pause while he checked his body. "My chest is sore, and my legs feel like they have been kicked."

"Let me see," said the doctor and he examined both legs and took a stethoscope to his chest.

"Just bruising. It will be painful for a couple of days, but you'll be ok."

The conversation was interrupted by a long scream from the other side of the room, and the doctor rushed off.

"Praise be to Allah; that is good news, Tariq," said the cleric. "I will leave you now, so you can get some rest. I will be back in the morning," and the cleric kissed his son on the forehead and said a prayer.

The following day the cleric returned to the hospital, driven by Mohammed in the fruit lorry. He had bought clean clothes. The night had proved a watershed for Tariq, with the pain and the psychological impact of the explosion, sleep had been impossible. The sight of the bodies, young children, old men, indiscriminate victims of the blast. This was not what Tariq intended. His quarrel was against the infidels who had killed his family and occupied his country; not Hanif, Ahmed and the other innocents that had been inadvertently been caught up in his ambition. Trauma from earlier times had resurfaced and he had had vivid flashbacks of falling walls and burning buildings; he wanted to die.

He barely acknowledged the arrival of his father, just moved his head in the direction of the voice.

"How are you this morning?" asked the cleric, placing his hand on Tariq's forehead. No reply. Tariq looked up at his father and squinted as if trying to focus his eyes. They were joyless, blank, as if in a trance. A long pause and then slowly he whispered, "I am so sorry."

His lips were dry and cracked. The cleric took a bottle of water from his bag and opened it and gently tilted it to his son's mouth, the words had not registered. Tariq sipped slowly.

"We are taking you home. Your mother and sisters are waiting for you; they have been so worried."

The cleric opened the bag and put the fresh set of clothes on the bed. Tariq just stared.

"Come on my son, let's get you out of here; we will look after you."

He raised Tariq into a sitting position and removed his shirt which was still covered in dust and dried blood. There was a purplish mark on his chest the size of a potato, a bruise from a flying rock. Tariq winced as he raised his arms to let his father remove his shirt. The cleric pulled back the bed clothes. His jeans had been removed by the nurse the previous evening, so they could stitch the cuts to his legs. There were angry welts on both legs and two long gashes on his right shin where the bike had been torn from under him, which had been roughly stitched. More bruises were starting to form around the clotting wounds.

"Can you stand up?" asked the cleric and Mohammed grabbed Tariq under the arm and helped him to his feet. His legs gave way and he sat back on the bed still staring blankly ahead.

"Mohammed will carry you. You will die here if you stay."

Mohammed knelt down with his back to Tariq and gently lifted him off the bed, piggy-back style. Tariq was skinny for his age and as light as a feather. The cleric picked up the discarded clothes and followed Mohammed and his passenger through the ward. The remaining patients who had survived the night were being attended by their families, but the cleric noticed there were two military doctors supporting the team. One of them approached Abu Hanifa before they reached the door.

"Where are you taking him? He shouldn't be moved. He's still in a bad way," said the man.

"We will take care of him. He needs his family," replied the cleric and they headed out of the hospital past a line of patients queuing for drugs to the waiting truck.

It was ten o'clock and the temperature was already in the 20's, average for the end of February in Basra. As they made their way to the vehicle with Mohammed carrying Tariq on his back, the brightness of the sun reflecting on the white buildings caused the young man to close his eyes in pain. The cleric opened the door of the truck and Mohammed lifted Tariq into the seat. The cab was hot and the seat uncomfortable. Tariq winced as his body took his weight as he sat down.

Slowly, the lorry headed back towards the mosque where other followers, who were anxious to hear of Tariq's well-being, were gathered. Word had quickly got around the community that Tariq had been injured in the explosion and prayers were being said for his safe recovery.

Also waiting for the party to return was Abu Hanifa's personal doctor, who had promised to provide what medical help he could. The group gathered around the truck when it pulled up outside the mosque, jostling to see the stricken Tariq and offering their prayers. The cleric thanked them for their kindness, then pushed his way through the small crowd and crossed the road to his house. The Imam was quickly joined by Mohammed carrying Tariq on his back, the doctor following behind.

Raheem Hanifa was waiting anxiously with Tariq's sisters. Badia was holding her baby daughter and Na'eema was sat down; her first-born was due in a few weeks. Tariq was greeted with much love and concern, which did nothing to ease his conscience. He was taken upstairs to his bed, Mohammed still providing the carriage duties.

The doctor immediately began a further check of Tariq's condition and confirmed the hospital diagnosis. There were no major injuries and, with a period of rest and care, in a few weeks his body would heal. Unfortunately, he was unable to see the turmoil and despair coursing around Tariq's brain.

With Tariq safely in the hands of his family and the doctor, Abu Hanifa left the house; he had other, important work to discuss with Mohammed.

They were back in the annex of the mosque. "What are we going to do, Mohammed?" asked the cleric, "The brothers are in place and just waiting for the word."

Mohammed was deep in thought. "I will speak with Zarqawi, but we will need to postpone the attack."

"But for how long? They will need feeding, and all the time they are hiding here, the risk of discovery is great."

"I will see that you have the money, and, if necessary, we can move them from time to time. What about bringing them here? There are only six of them and there is plenty of room."

The cleric was aghast. "What...? No, you cannot bring them here; that would be madness. The military visit all the time... No, no, it would not be safe."

Mohammed riposted. "But, that's my point. You have a good... ahem, 'understanding', with the infidels. They would not suspect."

"No, no. I cannot take the chance. No, out of the question; we will leave them where they are for the moment. I will ensure that they are looked after until they are called..." He paused for a moment. "What about the... equipment?"

"I will bring the vests to you the day before the mujahedeen are called to duty," said Mohammed.

He looked at the cleric. "I can see you are concerned, my friend, but do not fear everything will be in place. I will talk with Zarqawi and I will be staying here in Basra to take charge of things."

Mohammed bid farewell to the cleric promising to call again once he had spoken to Baghdad.

Abu Hanifa had another sad, but necessary, duty to perform today. As is custom in Moslem culture, he needed to arrange the funeral of Hanif and his family to be performed before sunset; a bitter task which he would undertake with a heavy heart.

Monday morning saw the cleric back at the Mosque. Tariq was recovering slowly from his wounds, but, mentally, he was suffering greatly from the trauma; he was incommunicative and depressed. The doctor visited him regularly to check his well-being and was happy that the external wounds were healing, but was becoming extremely concerned at the young man's mental health. Although expensive and hard to come by, the doctor had managed to supply some Fluoxetine, a powerful anti-depressant, more familiarly known in the West as Prozac. He was hopeful that, with time, Tariq would return to full health.

The cleric continued to use his position in the community to good effect. He was never bothered by the military, usually waved through check-points. This this comparative freedom gave him the opportunity to move around the streets with impunity. Visiting his 'guests' therefore would be straightforward.

The six jihadists were being hidden at the house of one of his closest confidants, Ibn Hajar Al-asqulani, known by everyone as Hajar.

Arriving at the house, a twenty-minute walk away from the mosque, the mullah knocked on the door and was greeted by Hajar, a fifty-year-old veteran of life's struggles, his face lined with years of hardship and toil.

"As-salam alaykum."

The cleric dressed in his usual white prayer robes, greeted his friend as the door was opened.

"Wa alaykum e-salam," the man responded, and they embraced warmly.

Abu Hanifa was led inside, through to a room at the back of the house. Hajar opened the door and the cleric was greeted by the presence of six youths, about thirteen or fourteen years-of-age. The smell of sweat was overpowering.

They were sat on blankets on the floor which had obviously doubled as beds. There was a bucket in the corner of the room used as a toilet and, at first glance, looked more like a prison than a 'safe-house'.

Wide eyes stared back at the visitor in the gloom. It was a pitiful sight, and the cleric felt uneasy at their plight, but he was assured that they were being well-looked after.

He addressed the group and explained that there had been a delay in their trip to paradise. There was little acknowledgement. The cleric invited them to prayer and they dutifully lined up with their mats and knelt down in submission to their Creator.

Having given the chosen ones further assurance of their place in paradise, he left them and sat in conversation with Hajar.

"You are doing great work, Hajar, but in the light of recent events I will need to presume on your generous hospitality for a while longer."

The cleric outlined the conversation with Mohammed and confirmed that the date of the action would need to be revised. He reassured Hajar that the extended stay would be properly funded and gave him some money to cover the cost of food for the next week.

Later that day, Abu Hanifa heard the familiar sound of military trucks approaching the mosque. He went to the door of the annex where he had been at work, and saw Major Howard approaching with two other officers. The cleric invited them in and again formal greetings were exchanged.

The major made the introductions.

"This is Lieutenant Chambers, and this is Lieutenant Gibbons, they're investigating the explosion at the garage on Saturday."

They took off their helmets and shook hands with the cleric. The major continued. "I wanted to keep you informed of our findings as I understand that one of the victims was a relative."

"Thank you for your courtesy," replied the cleric and he

bowed his head in acknowledgement. "You are well informed. My brother owned the garage. He and his family were all killed in the disaster."

The cleric lowered his head again and uttered a prayer.

"I am very sorry to hear that, my condolences for your loss," said the major. The cleric did not reply.

"Lieutenant, tell the mullah what you have found," instructed the major.

Chambers outlined what they knew. He was a tall man, with dark hair and stern features, a product of the Guards, and he spoke in typically military officer parlance, formal and with copious use of jargon.

"We have made a thorough investigation of the scene and can confirm that it was an explosive device that caused the initial blast. We found remnants of a possible detonation mechanism, but there was a secondary explosion which, we believe, was the result of oxy-acetylene gas canisters igniting, which was responsible for the worst of the damage."

The cleric listened in silence, trying to translate the words and consider the implications. The lieutenant continued.

"From the information we have, we conclude there are two possibilities. One, the garage was targeted by extremists for some reason or, two; someone was in there engaged in bomb making activity."

The cleric stifled a reaction.

"But that is very worrying on both accounts. I can't imagine why anybody would target Hanif. He was a man of peace just mending cars… and the thought of anyone in there making bombs, you say? No, not possible."

Inside however, the penny had dropped, and the cleric was in no doubt what had happened.

"We are of course still carrying out our investigations, it is early days," said the major, who nodded to the lieutenant in acknowledgement of his contribution.

After a few minutes further discussions, the officers left with a promise from the cleric to get in touch if he had any more information.

Abu Hanifa had much to consider.

That evening on his return from the mosque, the cleric went to Tariq's room to check on his condition. He found him sitting up in his bed reading the Quran and then closing his eyes and repeating verses. At first, he was reluctant to disturb him, but matters needed resolving.

"Tariq."

Tariq opened his eyes and focussed on his father's presence. The cleric spoke slowly not wishing to cause his son any undue stress.

"How are you, my son?" he asked.

Tariq looked at his father, but seemed unable to speak.

"It is alright my son; there is nothing to worry about. I know that you are much troubled, but remember this; Allah is all-seeing and all-forgiving to those in pursuance of His work."

Tariq looked at his father and his face contorted, overcome with grief and for the first time tears flowed down his cheeks. He cried bitterly, and the cleric put his arms round him to provide comfort.

"It is going to be alright, my son," said the cleric in a paternal, caring way. "We will work through this. Allah will give you the strength for the trials ahead."

Once his son was calmer the cleric spoke again. "What happened my son? Can you tell me?"

Tariq took a deep breath and explained how he wanted to

contribute to the cause, undertake God's work. He explained about his detonation device and his collaboration with Ahmed and his plan to explode the bomb.

"I wanted to prove to you I was ready," he sobbed. "Ahmed must have set off the explosives. He said they were dangerous, but he seemed to know what he was doing. If only..."

"Life is full of if onlys, my son, but you must not take the burden of guilt on your shoulders. It is the will of Allah."

Tariq looked down unable to face his father despite his wise words, riddled with the guilt and shame of his misguided, but well-meant, action.

There was a long reflective pause. "What is going to happen?" asked Tariq.

"I am going to arrange for you to go away for a while to recuperate. There is a special place where our brothers study and learn about the Holy Scriptures and the jihad. You will derive great solace from such a place and return refreshed and reinvigorated and your spirit will be cleansed from this tragedy."

"When will I have to leave?" asked Tariq

"As soon as you are well enough," replied the cleric.

Abu Hanifa's connections had grown significantly following his introduction to Zarqawi, and he had been made aware of training camps in Iran specifically designed to train and radicalise vulnerable young men. Recruits came from all over the Middle East - Palestine, Syria, Lebanon and Iran itself. There was no shortage of volunteers willing to become martyrs.

The camps and the training centres were under the control of former Republican Guard elite, many of whom had fled to Iran after the war to continue the conflict. Known as Qods Force, they had an extensive network, using the facilities of Iranian embassies or cultural and economic missions, and a number of religious institutions, such as the Islamic Communications and Culture Organisation, to recruit radical Islamists in Muslim countries or among the Muslims living in the West. After going through preliminary training and security checks in those countries, the recruits were sent to Iran via third countries and would end up in one of the Qods Force training camps.

One such camp was outside the small town of Saiyid Tamul in Western Iran, lying on the banks of the Karun River, about 200 miles from Basra.

The cleric had arranged, through Mohammed, for Tariq to attend the camp for three months. The objective was twofold; to help Tariq recover from the trauma of recent events, but also to get him out of Basra. Not that the cleric was overly concerned, merely a precaution. If the investigation into the explosion established that Tariq worked at the garage, further questions might be asked. No-one in the local community was likely to divulge that information, but the cleric was not prepared to take that risk.

Then there was the question of the Mujahedeen who were waiting in Hajar's house to carry out their mission; the cleric was anxious to ensure that there was no chance of compromising the planned action.

With Tariq almost recovered from the physical effects of the explosion, he still had a slight limp; it was in the first week in April, and another hot day in Basra, that he said farewell to his family. There had been no rain for several weeks and the streets were dusty. The glare of the sun reflected off the white buildings, making Tariq squint as he left the house. His mother and sisters were in tears as he carried his small suitcase to the waiting Mercedes and the waiting driver who had been provided by Mohammed.

The cleric hugged his son and wished him well on his voyage of renewal and discovery and watched in sadness as the car pulled away.

Chapter Seven

April 4th 2004, Main Border Crossing, Highway 96, Iraq-Iran Border near Abadan.

Crossing the border into Iran would normally be a very difficult proposition, with detailed checks carried out. However, with the right connections, any problems could be overcome; and of course, Mohammed had the right contacts. A note of the vehicle's details and sufficient dollars would see the car waved through with little formality. Even the military Iraqi checkpoints were negotiated without too much delay.

It would be a long and tedious journey for Tariq; after an initial stop at Abadan, the first large town across the border, there would be the trek up Highway 39, following the course of the river Karun to Ahvaz. The driver, who was introduced as Abdul, was Iranian and spoke little Arabic which meant that Tariq spent much of the time locked in his own thoughts and staring at the bleak, desolate landscape.

Despite it being early April, temperatures were now well into the thirties and the frequent dust storms forced the Mercedes to stop at regular intervals. The road surface was shiny, reflecting the incessant flow of traffic. There were no verges or curb stones, and the tarmac just petered out at the edges where rough gravel then scrub would welcome any straying vehicle. There was also no drainage, but rain was unlikely for several months. Tariq noticed shredded rubber littering the carriageway. In desert conditions the extreme temperatures meant tyres would regularly burst due to the heat. The carcasses of failed vehicles were everywhere, waiting to be swallowed by the desert.

It had taken most of the day to reach the camp. They had

stopped to take on water along the way and had food in Ahvaz, a large city with over a million people and the provincial capital. Straddling the river, it is a bustling place and the Mercedes made slow progress getting through the streets.

The small town of Saiyid Tamul is about twenty miles north of the city, situated on the Karun, and, being close to the river, the area is relatively fertile. Agriculture is its main industry.

The camp was, as one would expect, in an isolated position along a cart track off the main road, some five miles from the town. It was different to what Tariq had imagined. Due to the satellite surveillance by the Americans, from the outside it looked like a working farm. There were cattle, chickens and goats in the fields around the outside of the buildings trying to extract what sustenance they could from the arid earth. A herdsman appeared to be watching them but the AK47 hidden underneath his tunic away from any prying eyes, suggested his presence was more than just to keep the animals in line.

The only entry to the 'farm' compound was by way of an archway in the main building, rather like a western horse-riding establishment, and was protected by a pair of heavy wooden gates, which were open. That in turn led to the central courtyard.

The surrounding area was completely flat, with no trees or any other cover for over a mile in all directions giving perfect visibility from the camp. Two guards, armed with machine guns, hid in the shadows of the portal, and only appeared as the Mercedes slowly approached the gate.

Tariq could see about ten white buildings in a rough horseshoe shape, protected by razor wire, which would not be visible from the all-seeing eyes in the sky. The main building, containing the only access point, was situated laterally across the open end. It was Spartan by any standards, but importantly it was unremarkable, which would help it retain its anonymity.

At the camp entrance, the guards moved to one side and stood to attention as the Mercedes, now stationary, was approached by another man in a military uniform and side arm. Tariq was expected, and the man welcomed him warmly.

"You must be Tariq," he said. "As-salam alaykum."

"Wa alaykum e-salam," replied Tariq.

News of Tariq's prowess in electronics and engineering had preceded him, and his arrival was greeted with a degree of anticipation. He took his suitcase from the boot of the car and the driver bid farewell and set off on the long journey back to Basra.

The military man introduced himself as Ardashir al-Muqaddasi. "You can call me Ardash, but everyone else calls me El Faqih."

The man would be in his early thirties very dark hair and a Saddam moustache. He spoke Arabic suggesting he was not from the local area where Farsi was the common language.

El Faqih, literally 'the commander', led Tariq through the covered way which opened up to a courtyard. The man described the small complex to his new arrival. Accommodation was basic, the white buildings were actually disguised wooden constructs, no more than huts, and close up looked much flimsier than from a distance.

The main building appeared more substantial, almost certainly the original structure, the outhouses added later. Next to the inner entrance to the covered way was a door and the commander led Tariq up a small steep flight of wooden steps to the second floor which was the nerve centre of the complex.

"You will be based in here when you are not studying. We

have some very sophisticated equipment which Zarqawi has provided," said the commander.

Tariq gasped in amazement at the banks of computers, radios, satellite systems, TV monitors being attended by three civilians. They paid no attention to their visitor, engrossed in their work.

The man continued. "We are only a small facility, but we have some of the best equipment. Our satellite feed is hidden in the animal shed... Look, you can see it." The commander went to the window which overlooked the courtyard and pointed.

Tariq looked across to the building directly opposite. On the roof was a sophisticated selection of antennae under white netting which would not be invisible from the air.

El Faqih continued his briefing.

"There are thirty šahīds here at the moment and they live in three huts in the far corner next to the animals. There is a school with our own cleric and most of the time the martyrs are with him studying. The other buildings..." he swept his hands around the area, "are for study, and that one there..." He pointed to the third block from the main building, "is the cook house where we eat. Toilet facilities for the martyrs are over there." A smaller hut, which he explained contained a slit latrine. "Punishment duties include emptying and cleaning the latrines on a daily basis," he clarified; "Discipline is paramount."

"But, you must be tired after your long journey. I will show you to your quarters and you can get some food."

Tariq's right leg had stiffened from the long journey and was causing him some pain. The commander noticed he was dragging it. "How is your leg?" enquired the man. "You have suffered a great deal to the cause, I understand," he added. "Here let me take your case."

"I am fine now," said Tariq. "Alhamdulillah."

He passed his valise to the man.

The commander led Tariq down a corridor passing several closed doors.

"These rooms are occupied by the technicians and myself, oh, and the cleric," he said. "Mine is the end room."

Half way down the building, the commander opened a door to reveal a small but tidy room with bed, table, two chairs and a small wardrobe. The window looked outward across the plain towards the river. They went inside.

"This one will be yours while you are here. The washing and toilet facilities are just down the corridor on the right,"

"Thank you," said Tariq as he looked around his new residence.

The man left the newcomer to settle in.

Half an hour later, more refreshed, Tariq returned to the control room where the commander was on the satellite phone to a caller in Baghdad. One of the technicians got up and approached Tariq and spoke in Arabic.

"My name is Yasir, the Faqih has asked me to look after you while you are here. Would you like a coffee?"

"Just some water, please," replied Tariq, and his new acquaintance went to a water cooler in the corner of the room and dispensed a measure in a plastic cup. "Thank you," he replied, as Yasir passed him the drink. Tariq looked at him; he would not be much older than himself dressed in an AC Milan football shirt and a faded pair of jeans which would have been fashionable on the streets of London or New York, but here they were just well-worn.

"Come over here, and I will show you what we do," and Yasir led Tariq to the bank of monitors.

"Security is very tight, it has to be, the Americans watch

everywhere by satellite and would send in missiles to destroy us if we were ever discovered. We have cameras and security lighting on all sides of the compound."

He pointed to grainy images of the outside terrain showing on four TV monitors.

"There are trip wires around the complex linked to this equipment here."

He showed Tariq a board with a row lights. "They light up if a wire is disturbed." Tariq looked with keen interest.

Yasir continued. "We have the latest encrypted internet feed, which is bounced around the world... nobody can trace it. We use it to co-ordinate our action. It is Zarqawi who controls everything from Baghdad."

Tariq was wide-eyed; he had never seen anything like it.

After the briefing, Tariq was inquisitive. "Where are you from?"

"Baghdad... I left the University six months ago. Zarqawi enlisted me. He has several students studying there who will join us as soon when they are qualified. One of the professors keeps him informed. That's how I was spotted," he said. "He is always on the look-out for engineers, chemists, and of course computer technicians. He pays well but that is not the motivation. We are here to follow our destiny and rid our homeland of the infidels."

He looked at Tariq.

"What about you? The Faqih says that you are a brilliant engineer."

"I don't know about that," said Tariq modestly. "But I do what I can... What about the others, the martyrs?"

"There are about thirty šahīds, there are so many wanting to come, but the Faqih is very clever; he will only bring a few in at a time, usually on the weekly supply truck. They stay for one month, sometimes two, depending on when they are called."

"Where do they come from?" asked Tariq.

"All over the Middle East," replied his new friend.

"Yes, Ardash told me that... No, I meant here in Iran. There must be somewhere where they are kept before coming here?"

"Ardash eh? You must be very special; no-one calls him Ardash," said Yasir.

"That's what he told me to call him," said Tariq, feeling embarrassed at the possible breach of etiquette.

Yasir smiled. "That's ok... To answer your question, there is another camp in Eastern Iran near the border with Afghanistan. Two, maybe three hundred martyrs are there. They wait their turn, and then get moved here or to other camps near the Iraqi border."

"So, there are more like this one?" asked Tariq.

"Yes, there are several," he said, without going into too much detail.

"You are very well informed," observed Tariq.

"It's my job... I look after communication," he replied.

The Faqih joined them having finished his satellite call.

"We are moving six brothers tonight. Can you let the adjutant know? Transport in one hour."

"Yes, El Faqih," replied Yasir and left the room. Tariq heard him descend the staircase.

"I better explain," said the Faqih. "When there is a need for our martyrs, we arrange to take them to the border. They have to cross on foot at special points; it is too well patrolled."

"What about the mines?" asked Tariq.

"Ah yes, the mines," said the Faqih. "Let us say that some of the brothers reach paradise early." He looked at the floor. "We send them ahead and the guides follow in their footsteps; it is very dangerous."

Tariq had worked out the rest.

"So, they are used to clear the mines."

"Yes, some are," said the Faqih. "But it is all in the cause. They will surely reach paradise, Alhamdulillah,' he added.

"Amen," replied Tariq.

An hour later, as arranged, a truck was heard approaching the camp. Tariq looked through the window and could see the lorry loaded with all kinds of vegetable produce on the back. It was dusk and the orange glow in the west was fast being replaced by the blackness of the coming night. Tariq watched in fascination as six boys were escorted from the compound and stood beside the truck. The driver got out and lifted the tailgate where there was a space underneath the crates of vegetables. The boys crawled under, one-by-one, and the tailgate was lowered again so the boys could not be seen. The truck pulled away.

The Faqih returned. "It's only an hour to the border," he said anticipating a question. "The truck will drop them at a small village about half a kilometre away and the guides will take them across. There are more guides on the other side and transport will be waiting to take them to the destination."

"Baghdad?" enquired Tariq.

"Sometimes, but not always," replied the Faqih.

The man walked to the control desk and talked to Yasir who had returned and was sat at one of the computers. He turned to Tariq.

"Yasir will take you to get some food and then I suggest you get some sleep, we start early here."

The hut where food was eaten was slightly larger than the accommodation blocks and consisted of benches and tables, with a longer table at the front where meals were served. The place was empty.

"The martyrs have eaten earlier, but I can get something for you from the kitchen," and Yasir disappeared into an adjoining room.

After a few minutes he returned with some soup, bread and fruit. Despite the long day, Tariq wasn't very hungry, but managed to finish the food on offer.

Back in his room, Tariq took out his Quran and started to read. The book belonged to Abu Hanifa's eldest son and Tariq treasured it. Later, in the darkness, Tariq reflected on the day and realised that things had started to change, and he found himself strangely excited at the prospect of what lay ahead. His motivation was returning.

The following day, Tariq was given details of his duties. Study would take a lot of his time, but, given his value to the camp, the Faqih was keen to use and develop his skills. Zarqawi had insisted on it. Mohammed had told the Faqih about the detonation device Tariq had developed and he was particularly keen to learn more about it. "It could save the lives of many brave martyrs for more interesting projects," he said.

Tariq listened intently to the Faqih. After the instructions the Faqih asked Tariq if he had any questions. Tariq did have something on his mind which had troubled him for some time and decided that the Faqih could provide an answer.

"I do have a question which I have been wrestling with for many years, but I have not been able to ask my father."

"Go on," said the Faqih.

"I have studied the Holy Scriptures, and in all my teachings I understand it is against the will of Allah to take one's own life. Only He can decide when it is time. How can we encourage the martyrs? Surely that is against the will of God."

"You are wise beyond your years, young Tariq. Many scholars have wrestled with this, but it is quite clear in my mind. The martyrs are not taking their own life in the sense described in the Holy Quran. They are weapons of Allah in a Holy Jihad and, for this sacrifice, they will enter paradise and claim the everlasting peace."

Tariq pondered this answer and nodded.

"Thank you for explaining that to me. I can see the difference as you describe. The brothers are surely doing God's work and bound for paradise. I have such desires myself, but my father forbids it. He has more work for me."

"And we will make sure that you are given every chance to do God's work while you are here," said the commander.

So, Tariq spent the next three months learning communications techniques and became an expert in covert internet usage. He also had further training in weaponry and explosives at a small quarry, three miles away. This was a regularly used training area, and secure.

Or so they thought...

7th June 2004, CIA Headquarters, Langley, Virginia.

Communications expert, Darryl Lazenby, was viewing the latest satellite feed from Iran.

He called to his boss. "Hey, Perry, you wanna take a look at this?"

Perry Kasich, the balding paunchy, fifty-something, head of section, looked at the monitor.

"What am I looking at?" he drawled.

"There... above the river... three, four miles... looks like a compound," replied the agent.

"Looks like a farm to me," replied the chief.

"Yeah, that's what I thought, but I've been monitoring some of the movements, and there's more going on there than just a goat herd. Look..." He flicked to a still picture from a previous day.

"See..."

"Yeah, what is that?" asked the chief.

"It's a quarry, we think, about three miles away. Trucks have been going there from the farm, not regularly, and usually when it's getting dark. About ten, twelve guys get out and then there are explosions. I reckon it's a training camp," said Lazenby.

"Lemmy see," replied Kasich and he squinted at the image.

"Yeah, you could be right. Keep it under close observation for a few days and see if we can get some intel. Tap up any of our contacts in the area, see if they can find out anything."

"We've got a couple of guys in Ahvaz, about thirty miles away. Could get them to have a look," said Lazenby.

"Yeah, do that," replied the controller.

10th June 2004, Ahvaz, Khuzestan Province, Iran.

CIA agents, Moralez and Asabi, were drinking coffee in a riverside bar. Both were Iranian nationals; at least that's what it said on their passports. They spoke in Farsi. Moralez raised his local newspaper and addressed his colleague.

"So, what say we pay a visit to the farm tonight?" he said. It was suitably vague so as not to alert any possible eavesdropper.

"Yeah, suits me I was only going to wash my hair," replied Asabi and they both laughed as he rubbed his shaved pate.

June in Ahvaz was stifling, the air humid, due to the proximity of the river. It was nine o'clock and dark as Moralez backed out the battered five-year-old Toyota Land Cruiser from the garage. The two men shared an apartment in the predominantly working-class area of the city and were disguised, dressed as farmers, for tonight's recce. As the headlights illuminated the back of the garage, a million bugs came into view, awakened by the sudden illumination. Asabi closed the pull-down garage door, locked it and got in beside his buddy.

"What do we know about this place?" asked Moralez in English.

"Not much, the geeks want us to drive by and check. Supposed to be a farm, but they're not convinced. Lot of activity going down apparently… They reckon it could be another training camp.'

"Got the coordinates?" asked Moralez.

"Yeah, GPS will get us to the front door," replied Asabi.

It took the Toyota half an hour to get out of the city and onto the back road to Saiyid Tamul. It was pitch black as the headlights picked out the road ahead, a mix of tarmac and gravel. The river appeared again to their left, dark and foreboding, but at the same time wide and majestic as it rolled onwards towards Ahvaz behind them. Then in the distance they could see a few twinkling lights spread out across the horizon. Moralez slowed the car down to around thirty miles an hour and went through the village at a sedate pace. The land Cruiser rattled and bounced as it struck the regular pot-holes in the road.

"Jeez, I wonder when they're gonna do something about these roads?" Moralez complained.

"Yeah, take it up with the mayor next time you see him," replied Asabi.

"Shouldn't be far now," he said.

Asabi was following the route with a pen-torch in the passenger seat.

"About half a mile on the right we should see a track."

Five minutes later he called out. "What's that?" pointing to a right-hand turn beyond a tree.

The Toyota braked to a stop, Moralez killed the lights. "Looks pretty open here. We'll carry on a piece and find some cover, it's too exposed here," said Moralez.

"Copy that," said Asabi.

The Land Cruiser moved forward slowly in total darkness. After a minute or so their eyes adjusted to the visibility and moving at a crawl was relatively straightforward.

"There," shouted Asabi.

"Yeah, I see it," said Moralez. It was a scrub bush about six feet tall and ten wide and tilting at a crazy angle, bent by the wind.

"We can get behind that, nobody will see it," said Asabi.

"Copy that," replied Moralez, and he negotiated the Toyota under the bush.

Asabi got out and tilted the seat forward to reveal a handle in the floor. He turned it and a panel lifted out. He felt inside and pulled out a large hold-all from the hide-away and replaced and locked the panel. He dropped the seat back in its place.

Moralez was already in the hold-all. Camouflage clothing, night-goggles, GPS tracker and rifles; the two men geared up and smeared blacking over their faces. They locked the Toyota, pulled up their balaclavas and headed back along the road to the tree at the entrance to the track.

"Jeez, it's so open here," said Moralez, walking in a crouching position with Asabi following.

"Yeah, you can say that again," said Asabi.

It was a warm, but moonless night; the sky was a myriad of stars, blinking overhead like tiny fragments of glass.

They could see the complex in the distance silhouetted against the dark skyline. About two hundred metres away Moralez dropped to the floor into a crawling position; Asabi did the same and drew up alongside him. Moralez pointed at the main entrance, which, with its gate closed, looked more like a fortress. He used hand signals indicating he was going to take a closer look and for Asabi to wait for him. Asabi nodded agreement and watched his buddy through his night goggles as he snaked towards the compound.

It was about twenty minutes before Moralez returned.

"Back to the wagon," he whispered, and the pair retraced their steps.

Once back on the tarmac they quickly reached the hidden Land Cruiser, changed and stowed their gear back under the seat. Moralez started the vehicle and made a one-eighty.

"So, what did you find?" said Asabi, as the Toyota gathered speed.

"Langley's right. It's a training camp, no doubt about it... Trip alarms everywhere, razor wire round the perimeter and what looked like a comms tower under netting at the back of the complex. We'll call it in when we get back."

Chapter Eight

Back in Basra, after the departure of Tariq to the camp, Abu Hanifa had much on his mind. The delay of the direct action which had been planned for early March had been a set-back.

A new date had been decided but not until the end of April to let the clamour of the garage blast settle down. Road-blocks and increased security had made moving around very difficult even for the cleric.

The well-being of the Mujahedeen was giving him serious concern. Being cooped up in such a small place was causing problems. Anxious to fulfill their destiny, the six were understandably growing impatient. This was leading to strife among the martyrs with fights regularly breaking out. The cleric had to visit them often to maintain their focus and motivation; he could not afford to have one hesitate in their purpose. Any dissenters now would have to be dealt with, which would leave them short of volunteers for the mission; so much to think about. Despite the problems, the cleric was reluctant to move them from their present safe house which had at least proved to be secure. Any transfers at this late stage could jeopardise everything; it was too much of a risk.

Three days after Tariq had left for Iran, Abu Hanifa received a visit from Mohammed who had come to brief the cleric on the revised plan. The cleric ushered him into a backroom in the annex of the Mosque where they would not be disturbed.

After exchanging pleasantries, Mohammed spoke.

"Zarqawi has decided it will be a car bomb attack, five in Basra and one in Az Zubayr. I have a special team from Baghdad here who will support the operation."

The cleric was momentarily taken aback.

"Cars! Cars you say, but you said they were going to have vests."

"Change of plan, we have more experience in Baghdad now. Vests aren't as, how can I put it? Effective. Trucks are far more destructive."

Mohammed continued. "We have decided the date will be April 24th, which will give us enough time for preparations. It will be in the morning, about eight o'clock. I will need you to have the chosen ones ready the night before. They will be taken to my base where the team will be waiting to give them their final instructions."

"But they are not old enough to drive." the cleric interjected as an afterthought.

"But they are. They've been trained for this eventuality and have had many hours learning to drive," said Mohammed.

"Won't they look suspicious, driving so young... and a truck. What if they get stopped?"

"If they get stopped they will be told to detonate the bomb at the checkpoint which will at least kill soldiers," replied Mohammed.

The cleric did not respond but Mohammed could see the reservation on his face.

"Don't worry, my friend, the plan has been well worked out. My men will drive the šuhadā close to their targets, then they will have only a short journey before they complete their mission."

The cleric was still uneasy, but nodded in acquiescence.

"And afterwards?" asked the cleric.

"I will take the team back to Baghdad."

This did nothing to assuage the cleric's concern.

Later, the cleric visited the six martyrs, who were still closeted in his friend Hajar's house. The cleric briefed his friend.

"I have just spoken with Mohammed. We will need them ready for the twenty-third, someone will call for them."

"Alhamdulillah. Praise be to Allah," said Hajar. "It has been very difficult."

"Can I see them?" asked the cleric.

"Of course," and the man led Abu Hanifa to the room where the jihadists were held.

Concerned at being implicated in any insurrection, he was not a frequent visitor to Hajar's house and had not been for over a week. He was dismayed at how the conditions had deteriorated. Their clothes were lank and lice-ridden, the smell unbearable, and the overall demeanour, one of abject depression.

The cleric attempted to give them a pep talk, but the six were incommunicative and just looked at him blankly. They dutifully joined him in prayers, but it was clear that in their present condition there was some doubt whether they would be fit enough to carry out the mission.

The cleric thanked his friend and went back to the mosque where he immediately contacted Mohammed. He explained his concern at the condition of the šuhadā and the possibility that they would be in no state to carry out the operation. This registered with Mohammed and he promised to make enquiries and report back.

Later that day, Mohammed called with some good news. He had found another safe house for them, a farm outside the city where the Mujahedeen could get some fresh produce and, importantly, fresh air. They would also be able to practice their driving which would give the martyrs some welcome activity. The cleric thanked him and breathed a sigh of relief.

The following day, the cleric was at Hajar's house as the

familiar gaily-coloured fruit lorry pulled up outside. Mohammed was driving, and, ensuring there was no-one around, raised the tail-gate and ushered the six boys into the void under the pallets of produce.

"We use this method a lot," he said. "It is very effective."

He completed the loading and returned to the two men who were watching the activity with interest.

Mohammed walked up to the two men. "Thank you for everything," he said, then kissed them in turn on both cheeks as old friends.

"It may be some time before I am in touch again," he said through the open window as the truck pulled away.

"Come inside," said Hajar, "I think this calls for a celebration."

Abu Hanifa was a relieved man.

Wednesday April 24th 2004 turned out to be a tragedy for Basra.

As a relatively secure and stable place, the carnage unleashed on that day came totally unexpected. However, it also proved to be a disaster for Abu Hanifa and the Islamist cause.

Included in the death toll of seventy-four, were sixteen school children who were in a school bus passing as one of the bombs detonated. They were incinerated.

The swell of anger among the local population was unimaginable and riots against the occupying forces took place, people believing, not unreasonably, that they had not been protected. Anyone caught responsible for the bombings would literally be torn limb from limb.

It had affected Abu Hanifa deeply; he was a troubled man. His hands, he knew, were tainted with blood. He spent many hours in prayer trying to find a way of mentally freeing himself from any guilt, but absolution would not come.

He also felt a sense of betrayal by Mohammed and Zarqawi. He assumed the targets would be army barracks and troop concentrations; his enemy was the occupying forces, not innocent Iraqis.

It got worse. Two days later, the cleric was reading the local newspaper in the Mosque annex; the news was bleak. The police had arrested five men in connection with the suicide bombings. As he read the words, he retched. There was a stinging sensation in the back of his throat as the reflux reached his oesophagus. He read further, according to the report, the chief of police intelligence confirmed that they had three suspects in custody with links with Al Qaeda, and, knowing the brutality of the local police, the captives would certainly talk. He was now growing concerned for his own safety. The police were still searching for at least one more car bomb somewhere in the city.

After Friday prayers, the cleric was talking to some of his followers. There was a disturbing rumour going around, which seemed to confirm the earlier news. Two men, presumably those employed by Zarqawi through Mohammed, and one of the martyrs, had been captured in a truck on its way to a designated target. According to reports, the lorry was carrying three and a half tons of explosives. It was still not known why it had not exploded as Mohammed had instructed. Perhaps it had failed to detonate, but, under interrogation, the men had led police to the farm where the brothers had been sent from Hajar's house and found the rest of the explosives. The cleric listened intently to the gossip. This time the cleric was sick; the captured martyr could, of course, recognise the mullah.

This had been a massive setback. Mohammed had disappeared;

the cleric had not heard from him since the atrocity. Abu Hanifa felt very alone, unable to confide in anyone. He missed Tariq.

June 16th 2004, CIA Operations Centre, Langley, Virginia.

Operations Director, Lewis Kent 3rd, was in his office chewing the fat with Perry Kasich regarding the discovery of the new camp in Iran.

"I've been reading the latest intel from our people in Iran, and it's quite clear in my mind we're dealing with a major Al Qaeda asset here, Chief. According to the latest surveillance pictures, there're probably around twenty-five, thirty suicide bombers in training plus a number of technicians."

Kasich passed over three still photographs of the compound to Kent, then moved around the other side of the desk, so he could view the pictures with the Director over his shoulder.

"That building there..." Kasich, quite animated, pointed to the main block. "Is the control centre. These other buildings are accommodation and we believe there's a comms tower... here. We have pictures of trucks taking people from the compound, presumably to the border, and to another area about three miles away, a quarry, it looks like, where they practice. Here you can see explosions on this one." He pointed to the third picture.

The director looked at the pictures sagely.

"What's your recommendation, Perry?"

"We gotta take it out, ASAP." He pronounced the acronym as a word.

"Hmm, the chiefs will take some persuading. What's your M.O?" asked Kent.

"Tomahawk, best option," said Kasich.

The Director inhaled sharply almost whistling through his teeth.

"You know how much those mothers cost? Over $600k a piece."

"Yeah, I know the cost, but I've done a rough assessment and compared with a ground hit, it's gotta be the best bet... and of course it'll send a message to Al Qaeda - they can't hide."

"Yeah, it'd certainly be one up Bin Laden's ass and no mistake."

Kent paused. "Ok, look, put me a strategy plan together and I'll give it to the Chiefs with my backing."

"Thanks Chief," said Kasich and he picked up his papers and photographs and left the office in buoyant mood.

June was another blistering month in Basra. Temperatures by early afternoon regularly reached fifty degrees centigrade. It was energy sapping, not that the cleric had any. The last two months had been the worst of Abu Hanifa's life. When he wasn't at the mosque he had spent the time in prayer or quiet reflection, he had eaten infrequently and consequently had lost weight. He was now looking frail and every one of his seventy years; his wife and family were concerned.

He still received the occasional visit from the major, and each time it had brought more worries; the sound of a military truck approaching or even passing the mosque was purgative.

As events were unfolding in another part of the world, the cleric had a surprise visitor. He too looked different; a beard which was showing specs of grey and a pair of glasses, not the most original of disguises but effective enough. It was Mohammed, not in his vegetable lorry but in a ten-year-old Mercedes taxi.

Despite the cleric's anger at the way he had been misled, there was some relief in seeing the visitor; at least they shared the same guilt. Mohammed too seemed troubled.

"It is good to see you, my friend," said Mohammed solemnly.

The cleric couldn't extend the same sentiment and his gaze dropped to the floor.

"I can see you have been deeply troubled."

The cleric didn't comment; he went to the kitchen and returned with some water. Mohammed was still standing, despite available seats.

"You better sit down," said the cleric.

"We have much to discuss," said Mohammed.

"I don't think so," replied Abu Hanifa sharply.

"I know the outcome of our action did not go well."

"Not go well!?" the cleric interjected. "Not go well!" he repeated, angry at the meiosis. "Seventy-four innocent Iraqis killed, for what? Sixteen schoolchildren burned to death, for what?" he paused. "Is this what Zarqawi views as a blow against the infidels?"

Ignoring the venting, Mohammed continued. "There is more than one way to achieve our goal."

He paused and sipped some water careful not to be drawn into a verbal battle with the cleric.

"Basra was becoming… how can I phrase this? Complicit."

"Complicit…? What do you mean complicit?" countered the cleric.

"It was complacent, flabby. People were accepting the infidels. Dare I say it, helping them. We needed to strike a blow, shake a few feathers."

"But I thought our enemy was the Americans and the British who occupy our land, not innocent children," retorted the cleric.

"That was regrettable," said Mohammed. "But sometimes in war… and make no mistake, this is a war, innocent people get hurt."

The cleric was seated looking at the floor again. The air in the stark room was oppressive; the heat almost unbearable, and the cleric, a beaten man, had no energy for a battle of words.

"The will of Allah," was all he could muster.

"Yes," said Mohammed. "The will of Allah," and he took another drink of his water.

"But I have come with better news," said Mohammed. "Your son, Tariq."

"What about Tariq?" asked the cleric anxiously, his gaze now firmly fixed on his visitor, his face more animated.

"I crossed the border after the attack and reached the camp in Iran where Tariq is based. I have just returned from there, in fact, and he is very well. Completely recovered, if anything even more dedicated to the cause. He prays regularly with the mullah and works in the control room. The commander is very pleased with him."

The old man looked down again and screwed his eyes up as if giving thanks.

Mohammed continued. "I came to ask if you are ready for him to return. He is anxious to see you again and to join the struggle."

Hearing those words sent shockwaves through the cleric's body. He thought of the poor wretches in Hajar's house, and could not countenance that same fate for his beloved son. He had no desire for Tariq to be used as a šahīd. No, he had other plans for his son. He would become a leader, like Zarqawi, inspire others to the cause.

"When will you be returning to the camp?" asked the cleric.

"Not until next month. I must go to Baghdad to speak with Zarqawi and set up a new team. A great deal of damage was done to our operation in April; we have had to be very cautious."

"Can you bring Tariq back here with you?" asked the cleric. "Next time you visit."

"Yes of course, but as I said, it will not be for a few weeks. I will be in touch. I have a new number where you can reach me. It is not traceable."

Mohammed wrote down a mobile phone number on a slip of paper and handed it to the cleric.

After a few more minutes clarifying the details of Tariq's return, Mohammed left and Abu Hanifa went back to the annex to pray, not just for divine guidance but to give thanks. Hearing about Tariq had given him new impetus, he felt energised as if a weight had been lifted off his shoulders.

July 12th CIA Operations Centre, Langley, Virginia.

Operations Director, Lewis Kent 3rd calls in his number two, Perry Kasich.

"Perry, you got a minute? News on that camp in Iran."

In a flash, Kasich was in his boss's office; it was news he had been waiting for.

"Take a seat, Perry," said the Director.

Kasich pulled up one of the two leather-bound seats parked against the wall and placed it directly opposite his boss.

He looked at Kent across the walnut table; he was reading, or at least appeared to be reading, some papers in an open manila folder. He raised his eyes as his colleague sat down.

"Just got off the phone with Washington... we've gotten the green light for the hit on the training camp. They've gone for your Tomahawk option. The Enterprise is on manoeuvres with the Brits in the Gulf. We'll launch from a B52."

"When?"

"Five days, the 17th 06.00, code name, operation Black Sabre," replied Kent.

"Operation Black Sabre?" repeated Kasich.

"Yeah," replied the Director. "We'll need your guys to follow the action and brief our agents over there as well."

"Yeah, no problem, we'll get right on it," replied Kasich, still trying to take in the news. "What about the Iranians?"

"It won't be a problem," said the Director. "They can't admit to an Al Qaeda training camp on their soil." He looked at Kasich. "There'll be a report of an explosion at a farm, something like that. But we'll be keeping an eye on the media traffic from Tehran just in case we need to draft a response."

July 14th 2004, Sa'ad Al Ibn Abi Waqas Mosque, Basra.

Abu Hanifa was in the annex when he heard a familiar sound, one he had begun to dread; a small convoy of military vehicles.

Since the bombings it was rare to see individual army trucks or jeeps; security was still on high alert and they tended to move in packs for protection.

The cleric waited, hoping they would pass by, but the squealing of breaks and urgent shouts as the column pulled up announced their arrival outside the mosque. He began to shake. He went to the window to see what was happening and saw officers exiting the vehicles and walk towards the entrance.

It was Major Howard, he recognised, accompanied by his two intelligence officers, Chambers and Gibbons.

After the charade of a greeting, the cleric invited the officers inside and a drink of tea which they politely declined.

"We're here on official business," said the major with appropriate gravitas.

He put his hand inside his blouson and pulled out a rather dog-eared photograph.

"Do you know this man?" asked the major.

The cleric focused his eyes and knew straight away the identity. His heart pounded, and he was desperately trying to hide his anxiety. He lifted his glasses from his nose and squinted giving the impression of a detailed inspection. The delay gave him sufficient time to compose himself.

"I don't think I know him... it is difficult to say. It's not a very clear picture," the cleric said after what appeared to be careful consideration.

"His name is Ibn Hajar Al-asqulani. We want to speak to him urgently in connection with the April bombings."

The major looked at the cleric, his features were gaunt, and his face drawn; his hands were shaking.

"I understand that he is an acquaintance of yours," said the major, not threatening but assertive, giving no room for misunderstanding. The cleric looked at the photo again.

"Hmmm, it could be him... My eyes are not as good as they were." His voice was hesitant, raspish and weak.

The major looked at the man, bent and feeble in his simple robes which appeared dirty and ill-kempt; he couldn't believe it was the same man who had previously engaged him in a verbal battle on their first meeting only a year ago.

"Have you seen him at all?" asked the major.

"If it is the man you say, then not for some time. He has not been to Friday prayers for many weeks... I don't know him on a personal level, you understand; he is a member of my mosque, that is all."

"We have reason to believe his house was used to shelter the bombers," said the major.

"No, no, that cannot be right. He is a man of peace," said the cleric.

"Do you know where he lives?"

"I'm not sure," said the cleric who was now in a dilemma.

The major looked at the cleric as if trying to weigh him up, and then his demeanour changed.

"How is young Tariq?" he suddenly asked. "I haven't seen him around for a while."

"He is well, thank you. He has been away completing his studies."

The cleric wondered if there was a threat coming.

"I've been thinking about our earlier discussion, a bright lad; I could make some enquiries. There maybe people willing to sponsor him at a university in England. I can ask around, see if I can get a place allocated for him... An English University degree, as you said, could set him up for life."

The major let the words ring.

The joy on the cleric's face was palpable. His joy was however short lived.

"I just need your co-operation on this small matter, an address perhaps?"

"Just one minute," said the cleric, and he disappeared into an adjoining room.

He wanted it to look like he was checking his records but of course he knew the address by heart being a regular visitor until the bombings. He also wanted time to think this through. He did not want to compromise himself, but knew that his friend Hajar would eventually succumb to any interrogation, despite his loyalty. He also did not know how much the major and his colleagues knew about his involvement; it could be a test. He felt the adrenaline pumping round his body.

He returned to the three officers who were still standing in the annex.

"I have found an address... but it is quite old, he may have moved," he said in a whisper, as if to lessen the impact of his treachery.

He gave the major the information. They thanked him and walked to the door.

"I'll be in touch soon about Tariq, see if we can make some arrangements," the major shouted as he was about to leave.

The officers exited the mosque and went back to their vehicles. It was stiflingly hot.

The cleric waited for the vehicles to pull away, then rushed into his office and grabbed his phone. He started to dial, his shaking fingers having difficulty in making the numbers.

"Hajar?" he asked, as the phone was answered.

"Yes," said the voice.

"It is Abu, the British are on their way. You must leave now. Get out; they must not catch you alive."

Ten minutes later the convoy arrived at the house of Ibn Hajar Al-asqulani. Three officers and a local man acting as interpreter, walked to the door.

"Open up," shouted the major. The interpreter translated into Arabic, although given the urgency of the knock it was hardly warranted.

Gun at the ready, Chambers aimed a kick at the door. It was a flimsy construction and soon gave way. The officers rushed inside. Two shots rang out. Chambers was on the floor with a chest wound. Ibn Hajar Al-asqulani was dead, a head shot from Gibbons. He went to aid his comrade. The major went over to Hajar.

"Damn, we needed him alive," said the major.

He raised his walkie-talkie and spoke. "Ambulance, quick."

July 16th 2004, Al Qaeda training camp, Saiyid Tamul, Iran, late afternoon.

A ten-year-old Mercedes pulled up outside the gates of the compound. It had been expected. The Faqih walked past the two guards at the entrance and greeted the new arrival warmly.

"As-salam alaykum," said the Faqih, with a reverential nod of the head.

"Wa alaykum e-salam," replied the man with a similar gesture in response. The two embraced.

"Mohammed, it is good to see you again. Come in and tell me all the news from Baghdad."

The two men walked through the archway to the parade ground and up the flight of stairs to the control room. Mohammed noticed Tariq who was engrossed in a computer screen.

"Tariq?" enquired the Faqih, "You have a visitor."

Tariq jumped as if disturbed from a dream, broke his gaze from the monitor, refocused, then recognised Mohammed.

"Mohammed!" he exclaimed, and got up from the seat and embraced his visitor.

"How are you Tariq?" enquired Mohammed.

"I am well, thank you," replied Tariq.

"I have some news… We leave tomorrow."

"Tomorrow!?" exclaimed Tariq.

"Yes, I have spoken to your father and it is time for you to return to Basra," replied Mohammed.

Tariq couldn't hide his excitement his eyes widened as he spoke. "How is my father?"

"He's ok, but old. I think he needs you," said Mohammed.

"We leave first thing, if that is ok, Faqih?"

"Of course," said the commander. "His work here is finished. He is ready for the trials ahead."

The Faqih looked at Tariq and smiled, then addressed Mohammed.

"Come, my friend, join us for dinner you must be weary from your journey."

"You are most kind," replied Mohammed.

Tariq went back to the monitor he had been attending and logged off. The three of them left the control centre and headed towards the eating area.

July 17th 2004, Persian Gulf.

A dog day, USS Enterprise was on exercises with the Royal Navy in the Persian Gulf. It had recently returned from offensive action against the Taliban in Afghanistan. Three B52's were on deck, engine's running, the lead plane was equipped with two Raytheon/McDonnell Douglas BGM-109 Tomahawks strapped beneath its wings. The deck commander gave the signal and the aircraft left the ancient carrier for yet another mission. Two hundred miles out, and well away from Iranian airspace, the Tomahawks were released, sixth-thirty local time.

The average speed of a Cruise Missile is around 550 mph; using its sophisticated Inertial Guidance System and Terrain Contour Matching programme the Tomahawk was unstoppable and in just over an hour it would reach its target.

July 17th 2004, Al Qaeda training camp, Saiyid Tamul, Iran.

It was just turned six-thirty and Tariq was slowly making his way from his room in the annex of the control room to the dining area in the next block, Mohammed was already there.

"I was about to come and get you," he said, as Tariq approached the adjoining seat and sat down.

"I couldn't sleep. I was thinking about my father. I am so looking forward to seeing him again, and of course my mother and my sisters... What time do you want to leave?" he asked, as he helped himself to a small bread roll and some butter.

"As soon as we have eaten. We have a long way to go," replied Mohammed.

"But I must pray with the brothers first."

"Very well, but we must not delay; it might be difficult crossing the border," replied Mohammed.

"I thought everything was arranged," said Tariq.

"It is, but my contact will go off-duty at six o'clock and we must be there before then."

Seven-thirty, and Mohammed was waiting at the car by the front gate, engine running, anxiously tapping the steering wheel; he checked his watch again. He could see Tariq coming through the covered way accompanied by the Faqih and two of the technicians he had worked alongside during his stay. They embraced warmly and said their farewells.

"Come on, Tariq, come on," shouted Mohammed. "We must leave now."

The Faqih escorted Tariq to the car carrying a small valise; Tariq was also carrying a case and a bag of local produce given to him by the cook. He opened the boot and stashed the various pieces of luggage inside.

"Thank you for everything," said Tariq to the Faqih as he climbed into the passenger seat. "I shall never forget my time here... I can never repay you for what you have done for me."

He got into the Mercedes, the window was open; it was already twenty-five degrees, and more inside, despite the air conditioning. He waved to the small gathering as the car slowly drew away from the camp and down the dusty track towards the road. They reached the tree and turned left towards the village.

Then it happened. It was a strange sensation, not unlike the one Tariq had experienced that day as he approached the garage. This time, however, he was safely out of range. He was looking back fondly at the camp, one last look as it disappeared over the horizon when the sky lit up. The retort took a second or two before it was heard and then the shockwave rocked the car. A fireball went skywards, then another explosion as the second missile hit.

Mohammed was driving and looking at the road ahead, but his senses caused him to glance behind him, to his left. There was no mistaking the scene. He braked sharply and stopped the car. They looked toward the camp.

"We must go back! We must go back!" shouted Tariq.

"We cannot," said Mohammed. "There will be nothing we can do. The place will be swarming with troops very soon. We cannot afford to wait; we will not be able to cross the border."

Tariq knew he was right, but he was gripped with more pain knowing that many, if not all, his former comrades, many of whom were now friends, would be dead.

Chapter Nine

Mohammed started the car and pulled away. Tariq continued looking back at the conflagration that once was the training camp. A huge plume of smoke rose skywards from the spot in the distance.

As they approached Ahvaz, several military vehicles passed them heading in the opposite direction.

Mohammed negotiated the Mercedes through the city and down Highway 39, but he had little recollection; it had been a blur, his mind totally in another place.

Tariq was asking questions he could not answer satisfactorily.

"What do you think caused the explosions?"

"Probably cruise missiles."

"How did they find out about the camp?"

"Probably satellite surveillance."

He was asking himself the same questions.

On the main highway, trucks trundled backwards and forwards carrying all manner of goods; life going on as normal. This was far from normal. The loss of the camp was a serious blow, no mistake.

Mohammed was trying to work out the implications and possible remedies. Set up a new one? But where? Afghanistan? Possibly, but it was a long way to Baghdad, and the further from Iraq, the more chances of detection. No, it would need to be Iran. At least the regime tended to turn a blind eye to such matters.

Then there was the cost. Replacing the equipment and the expertise would not be cheap; computer engineers of the calibre of those at Saiyid Tamul who shared the same ideals would be difficult to find. He needed to speak to Zarqawi, but didn't trust using the mobile phone it could be being tracked. Suddenly he felt vulnerable.

Tariq was still trying to take it all in, the explosions, the loss of his friends; it brought back past nightmares. He shut his eyes but could only see falling buildings and broken bodies.

He stared out across the flat landscape of the Karun Valley, mid-July and the sun was high, the temperatures well into the forties. He sipped from a bottle of water, but it was warm and failed to quench his dry mouth. His mind turned to anger and revenge; his appetite for Jihad renewed by his time at the camp.

By mid-day, they were over half way to the border, and making reasonable time. Mohammed kept the speed down to fifty miles an hour, not just to preserve petrol, but, most importantly, not to overheat the engine.

The Mercedes gradually ate up the miles. Ahead in the distance they spotted a sign indicating a service area. Mohammed took the turn onto a gravel track and pulled up outside the petrol pumps. The diner was set back from the gas-station and was surrounded by twenty or thirty wagons of various descriptions parked in the large car park.

Tariq got out to stretch his legs. Gazing across the flat landscape towards the distant hills he could see what looked like pools of water, dancing mirages created by the fierce sun. There was no water, nor would there be for several months, apart from the lumbering Karun River, five kilometers away. Many of the truck drivers had placed reflective silver cardboard across the inside of their windscreens to keep their cabs free from the sun's blaze. A metal seatbelt buckle could burn the flesh and leave a blister.

A patch of dead couch grass lifted off the ground in front of him, tossed by the arid wind and dropped again three feet away. A gecko deprived of its hiding placed scurried across the ground searching new cover.

"I will get some water and some food," said Tariq. Mohammed gave him a fifty thousand Iranian Rial note, the equivalent of about six dollars or twelve Iraqi Dinar.

"Here, you better take your passport; you never know, you might need them," said Mohammed, and he took out Tariq's papers from the glove compartment and handed them to him. Mohammed examined the price on the pump and waited for the attendant.

Tariq went inside and looked around for his requirements. It was like an American Truck-Stop with a long food counter with preparation being carried out by several women behind it. There was a smell of frying intermingled with the stench of smoke from numerous cigarettes. A large fridge stood in one of the corners containing cold drinks. A couple of waiters of dubious nationality were flitting about clearing tables with filthy cloths. One or two truckers who were eating at wooden tables looked up at the interloper.

Tariq felt the whole place was staring at him. He opened the fridge door and took out a litre of cool water and continued to the sandwich counter. All the signs were in Farsi and Tariq had difficulty in making out the labels but eventually he chose what appeared to be a salad sandwich. He walked towards the counter to pay, but stopped as he noticed several customers had moved to the window and were looking intently to events happening outside.

Tariq, out of curiosity, joined them and reeled back in horror. There was a Toyota Land Cruiser parked directly behind the Mercedes and three armed men were talking to Mohammed. After a few moments two of them drew their weapons then grabbed him, and after a struggle another, the third man, put hand-cuffs around Mohammed's wrists.

A trucker stood next to Tariq whistled through his teeth and looked at Tariq.

"VEVAK," he said, and raised his eyebrows in an ominous way.

Tariq had heard of the Iranian Secret Police whilst at the camp; they had a fearsome reputation for brutality. He could only watch as Mohammed was bundled into the Land Cruiser. Another got into the Mercedes and moved it away from the pumps, then went back to the Toyota. There appeared to be some discussion and then two of the occupants left the vehicle and moved towards the cafe.

Tariq's blood ran cold. The man standing next to him was dressed casually in typical trucker's style, weathered face, in his fifties with three days stubble spiking from his chin. He saw Tariq's reaction and spoke to him in Arabic.

"Iraqi?" he asked.

Tariq looked at him and nodded.

"Come and sit with me, say nothing," said the trucker.

They sat opposite each other at a table where there was an empty plate.

The trucker moved the plate so it was in front of Tariq. The door of the cafe opened, and the two men entered and started moving around the tables looking at the clientele. Tariq froze as one of the men approached their area. The trucker acted quite nonchalantly and handed Tariq a cigarette. He had never smoked, but took one anyway. The trucker pulled out a lighter and lit it for Tariq, then lit his own. Tariq stifled a cough as the unfamiliar fumes hit his throat.

The trucker started a conversation making it look like they

were driving buddies. The Iranian looked at them and moved on. One of them went through the door with the word TOILET stencilled on it in English; then returned. One final check round and they left the building. Tariq breathed a sigh of relief.

"Your friend is in trouble, I think," said the trucker.

Tariq nodded.

"Where are you headed?" the man asked.

"Basra," replied Tariq.

The trucker looked at him.

"You need a lift, I think… You are lucky I am headed there. I can give you a ride if you like, he said.

"Alhamdulillah, " said Tariq.

Tariq and his new companion waited for twenty minutes; Tariq declining another cigarette, before the man got up and looked towards the petrol pumps. The Land Cruiser and Mohammed's Mercedes had gone. There was no way of knowing where they had taken him.

"Get some food and come with me," said the trucker and Tariq went to the counter and paid for his sandwich and water; that was the last of his money. All his belongings were in the boot of the Mercedes. They headed out of the diner and around the back, where several more large trucks were parked. The third one from the pathway was a Scania about five-years-old.

"This one," said the man.

As he opened the driver's door, he shouted above the noise of passing traffic.

"My name is Younis, Younis al- Ahmed al-Muwali."

"Tariq... my name is Tariq," was the reply and he went around to the passenger side and climbed up to the cab.

It was steaming inside; Younis had not put up a sunshield having parked the truck facing away from the direct sunlight.

133

The trucker opened the cab windows and eased the Scania out of the service area and onto the highway. There was a breeze, but it was not cool.

"Next stop Abadan, then the border, about three hours, I think. Do you have your papers?"

"Yes, they are in my pocket. But everything else was in the car," he added. "Clothes, my Quran, my laptop..."

Tariq looked down, recognising that he was unlikely to see his treasured possessions ever again.

The journey was as long as Younis had predicted and included a brief stop for a cigarette and coffee in Abadan. Younis was glad of the company and anxious to talk. He explained he had been delivering some machinery to a factory just outside Tehran, and the truck was now empty. He and his family lived on the other side of Basra. Tariq explained he was the son of the Mullah of the Sa'ad Al Ibn Abi Waqas Mosque.

"Abu Hanifa?" asked Younis.

"Yes, do you know him?" asked Tariq.

"Yes, he is a good man. He says many good things; many share his views."

"Do you?" asked Tariq.

"Of course," said the driver.

"The sooner we rid ourselves of the vultures that pick the bones of our country the better."

Tariq had found a kindred spirit.

It was around four-thirty when they reached the border checkpoint, and, as expected, two heavily armed guards approached the truck and told Younis to turn off the engine.

"Papers," said the first one, as the second looked around the vehicle.

Younis opened the cab door and handed the guard a folder of documents which he proceeded to scour with some interest. He looked across at Tariq.

"Who is this?" he asked.

"My nephew," said Younis.

"Your papers," said the guard and Tariq leant across Younis and passed them to the man. He opened up the passport, checked the name and picture and looked at Tariq inquisitively.

"You are Tariq?" asked the guard with some surprise.

"Yes," said Tariq.

"Where is Mohammed?" asked the guard, and Tariq realised that this must be one of the men that Mohammed had paid to get them through.

"VEVAK," said Younis, and the guard looked concerned.

"You go... now!" said the guard with some urgency

He handed back the documents to Tariq and slammed the driver's door shut.

Younis started the engine and pulled away into the gap between the border crossings and through the Iraq gates. As they headed out towards the main road towards Basra they both let out a sigh of relief.

"Next stop Basra," said Younis.

It took another two hours to get the mosque having been stopped twice at checkpoints.

The truck drew up outside the annex, Tariq recognising that his father would not have returned to the house yet.

He thanked the driver.

"I shall always remember your kindness," said Tariq.

"Good luck young Tariq, may Allah be with you," he said, and drove away through the narrow side streets; the noise of the six-cylinder diesel engine reverberating against the white walls of the houses.

Abu Hanifa had heard the truck and, thinking it might be military, had come outside to check. The lorry pulled away in a cloud of impenetrable fog-like dust and as it cleared the cleric could make out the shape of someone standing on the roadside.

"Tariq? Is that you?" he said, and hobbled across the road as fast as his aching limbs could take him.

"Father," said Tariq, and the two embraced.

"But what has happened?" asked the cleric as they broke from their greeting. "Where is Mohammed?"

"He was taken by the Iranians," and Tariq explained about the incident at the truck stop and Mohammed's capture.

He held his son at arms' length and looked at him up and down.

"You look so different my son. You have grown up, and the beard, it suits you," he said, looking at Tariq's unshaven face, a by-product of the camp.

The cleric looked at the sky and said a prayer before wrapping his arm around his son's shoulder and escorting him back to the house.

"Come, we have so much to talk about."

Tariq's mother and sisters, both now with children, were waiting for his return. They embraced him warmly as his father had done. Tariq made a fuss of the most recent arrival.

"Another girl in the house," said the cleric and the family laughed for the first time in a long while.

Over dinner the conversation was upbeat, and excited chatter emanated from the women at the return of Tariq. He told his family about life in the camp and the mood change when he described the explosion and Mohammed's capture.

"Why would they arrest him?" asked Tariq. No-one of course

could answer that question.

Back at Langley, Operation Black Sabre was being heralded as a great result. The compound had been entirely obliterated and recent satellite pictures showed a few troops around the devastated compound but little else. Two days later a short paragraph in the official Tehran newspaper stated that an explosion had occurred at a farm near the village of Saiyid Tamul. Investigations were being carried out to find the cause but it was thought to be the result of a store of explosives being used at a nearby quarry. Some workers had been killed but numbers were not mentioned.

Kasich and Kent were overjoyed.

"Well that's one bazooka up Bin Laden's ass,' said the director, as they toasted their success in a local bar later that day.

The reuniting with Tariq had come at an appropriate time for Abu Hanifa; he felt at peace with himself again. The bombings and his perfidy in giving up his friend Hajar to the military, had weighed heavily on him.

After dinner Tariq commented to his mother about the cleric's physical state. "He looks so old," Tariq had remarked.

His mother just nodded without comment, then added quickly changed the subject.

"We must get you some new clothes for you to replace those you have lost. We will go to the market tomorrow."

Later that evening father and son talked together for the first time in several months. The cleric described what had happened in the April bombings and how much it had affected him. Tariq had of course heard of the car bombings from Mohammed, but not the detail.

"This cannot be the way, my son. There has to be a better

means of achieving our aims; so many innocents have been killed."

"But this is the will of Allah, father, surely?" replied Tariq. "In as' Allāh, in šā' Allāh," repeated the cleric. "If God wills, then so be it, but I cannot be a part of it; the burden is too heavy."

He put his hands to his head and drew them down his face as he had done many times in despair.

"But what about the Jihad? The Imam at the camp told us that it is every believer's duty to take holy war to the infidels, it is written," said Tariq.

"That is some people's view, but not all. Opinion is divided," replied the cleric. "I have thought long and hard about this and my mind is clear, martyrdom will never achieve our goals, whatever the interpretations of the scholars. The end does not necessarily justify the means."

Tariq pondered his father's words, but kept his council; he respected his father deeply, but something had happened to him; he had changed. It was obvious the bombings had had a profound effect on the cleric; he was not the same man that he had left in the spring.

Tariq would excuse his father; he, however, was as committed as ever and had his own thoughts about how he might take the struggle to the infidels.

"I do have some other news for you, my son," the cleric said, looking at him across the table. Tariq was anxious to hear.

"Major Howard, you remember him?" Tariq scowled; the cleric ignored the body language and continued. "He is making enquiries to get you a place at University in England."

Tariq looked at his father in disbelief. "England?" he queried.

"We did discuss the possibility," replied the cleric.

"I know but..."

The cleric cut him off. "Yes, I know you have only just returned, but going to university in England will open many doors for you; it is very important."

Tariq was speechless and tried to take in the consequences. "When will I have to go?"' asked Tariq.

"In September, God willing, but there is much to do and arrange," replied the cleric.

Tariq considered this for a moment then said, "If it is the will of Allah, then I will, father."

His father looked at him.

"It will be, my son, it will be," he said, and he left his son to his deliberations.

Tariq could not concentrate; the thought of leaving his family again after just being reunited was bad enough, but to go to England, the viper's nest, was unimaginable. He had much to consider. But then he reconciled with himself, maybe this was the way; perhaps Allah was showing him a different path to take up Jihad. He pondered at the possibilities.

A few days later the cleric had another visit from the major. This time, he did accept the offer of some refreshment and the atmosphere was much more convivial than his last visit, although the cleric remained anxious. The major had entered the mosque on his own, although there were two armed guards stationed outside.

After the usual formalities the major described the reason for the visit.

"First, I would like to thank you for your help in the other matter, which unfortunately did not end well."

"I had heard," replied the cleric.

"I had no doubt you had," replied the major with a wry smile.

"How is the officer?" asked the cleric.

"He's back in England now, but he'll be ok," said the major.

"Alhamdulillah," said the cleric.

"Indeed," replied the major. He continued. "I wanted to let you know that I have managed to get a sponsor for Tariq... It's a multi-national company, Petronix, you might know it."

The cleric tried to avoid any adverse reactions but deep down he wanted to howl in derision. This global conglomerate was commercially raping his country extracting its oil and reaping the profits without any thought for the local populace. That was the view held by most Iraqis he knew. He nodded, but was non-committal.

The major continued. "As part of their involvement in the future of Iraq, they have agreed to sponsor several students, including your son. They will fund his college fees for the duration of his course, and they've arranged for Leeds University to take him... subject, of course, to a full assessment of Tariq's qualifications."

"Leeds University?" queried the cleric.

"Yes, it's one of the best in the UK offering engineering," replied the major. "That is what Tariq wanted, I understood."

Despite his bitterness toward the company, the cleric played the game.

"Yes, yes... that is wonderful news, thank you."

"You mentioned that he has completed his studies here in Iraq," said the major.

"Yes, he was an exceptional student and he had many, how do you say? Distinctions, in his subjects."

"I will need to send his certificates and paperwork to the University," said the major.

"I have them at home, I will let you have them... but they are in Arabic," queried the cleric.

"Don't worry about that, I'm sure they'll manage... He will need to find his own accommodation, though."

"Hmm, that may not be a problem... There is an uncle on my wife's side who lives in the north of England somewhere... let me think."

The cleric paused and searched his memory.

"Yes, I remember... Batley, I think it is called, Batley. Not a big place I think."

The major thought for a moment.

"Hmm, yes, I know of it, Batley... I've never been. They used to have a variety club there, if I remember correctly." The meaning was lost on the cleric.

"It's in Yorkshire, though... not sure how far from Leeds, but it sounds as if it could be ideal... As I understand it, the engineering course is for four years, two years study then working with the company for a year, followed by a final year at Leeds... He can read and write English, I take it?"

"Yes, of course, he has been studying for many years..." The cleric paused. "Four years, you say... a long time."

The magnitude of what was in front of Tariq was now beginning to register. After more discussion about the security situation, the major left and the cleric went back to the house to see his son. He was in his room reading a copy of the Quran which he had borrowed from the mosque.

The cleric gave Tariq the news which was received with little enthusiasm, and, after a brief acknowledgement, Tariq returned to his book. The cleric went to search for the certificates.

Fortunately for Tariq, he had acquired his grades at High School the previous year and was doing an extra year to top up his qualifications, which included English, before the garage bomb and his subsequent move to Iran, intervened.

As well as his skill in engineering, Tariq also had an ear for languages and had picked up English without too much difficulty, even being able to read and write the unfamiliar script. Abu Hanifa was confident his son would have sufficient academic achievement to warrant the university place.

Eventually by the end of August the confirmation had come through that Tariq Siddique had been granted a place at Leeds University and was to report there on Monday Oct 4th.

There was much to do.

Abdul Hussein lived in a typical three-bedroomed terraced house in Batley; a small, former mill town in West Yorkshire, close to Bradford and Leeds, with his wife, Sabeen, and their two sons, aged nineteen and twenty. Abdul had moved to the UK as a student in the 1970's and stayed; he had little contact with his former homeland. The boys were born in Yorkshire, attended school there, and did not speak Arabic, even acquiring a strong local accent. He had set up a small grocery business in 1979 and it had expanded to become a large cash and carry emporium employing over twenty staff. His two sons were already part of the business and were being groomed to take over when Abdul retired.

It was a surprise therefore when, in early August, Abdul received a phone call from his sister. He had to retune his hearing to Arabic; Raheem Hanifa did not speak English.

She outlined Tariq's plight and the need for accommodation to enable him to take up his university place in Leeds. Despite the limited contact, the family ties remained strong and Abdul was only too pleased to help. The cleric's wife promised further contact when they had more details.

In the intervening time, Tariq was starting to warm to the challenge of his pending career move. His radicalisation had not waned in the slightest and he was already starting to formulate ideas to take Jihad straight to the heart of the infidel. An attack on Parliament, mayhem in the transport system, the Underground in London perhaps, a nuclear installation, the possibilities were mouth-watering, but working for Petronix, now that could open all manner of possibilities. It was the will of Allah; Tariq was being shown the way.

In preparation for his departure, Tariq had replaced his old laptop which was languishing somewhere in Mohammed's car, with a new English version. In a subsequent phone call with his Aunt in England, he had obtained his cousins' email addresses and started contacting them. He was interested to get to know his new relatives. He quickly established that they were around the same age. He had been told their names were Yusuf and Jamal, but was disappointed when he discovered that they had adopted English names and were known at school as Freddie and Jake.

They too seemed curious about Tariq and seemed pleased that he was going to 'visit' them; it seemed they had not been told that the visit was likely to be protracted. He read the first email from the elder cousin.

'Hi Tariq cool that you are coming to visit us in UK. Freddie is clearing out his room and you will be sleeping there. Do you watch football? We luv Leeds United – they're cool. How are things in Iraq – it don't look good on TV. Do you have a girlfriend? I do she is called Jasmine she's proper fit. We've got a new Play Station 2 it's well good I always beat Freddie on Grand Theft Auto also got FIFA Soccer which is great. We will

teach you how to play. See you soon, Jake.'

The letter stretched Tariq's English skills and he realised he had a great deal of catching up to do. He drafted a brief reply. *'Dear Jamal, thank you for your kind letter. It sounds very interesting. I look forward to meeting you and Yusuf. Tariq.'*

The exchange of correspondence continued for the next few weeks, but the gap in culture was clear, the dialogue emanating from Batley typical of teenager interest, conditioned by peer groups and school - sport, particularly football, computer games and girls. There was no mention of any religious references, Friday prayers, nothing. This was a total anathema to Tariq whose interests were purely spiritual and ideological.

Eventually, with final preparations completed, on the twenty-second of September 2004, Tariq said his final goodbyes to his family. All the paperwork had been completed, including a new passport and visa, which had all been facilitated by Major Howard and his team at the British compound. They even provided transportation for the trip to the airport and a place on a military plane to Baghdad.

Basra airport had only been re-opened for a few weeks, but, as yet, there were no non-military flights, and he would need to travel to the capital to catch a connecting flight to London.

It was five-thirty, the temperature already over twenty degrees; the red shimmering sun now visible low over the rooftops, highlighting the myriad television aerials on top of the whitewashed houses. He stood with his family and waited for the truck which was to take him to the airport. He was dressed for the long journey casually, in a short-sleeved shirt, battered leather jacket, which for the moment he carried over his arm, jeans and trainers, a universal student look.

By his side a small suitcase which contained a change of

clothes and some essential toiletries. His laptop was stowed in his hand-luggage, an old briefcase, a farewell present from one of his father's congregation. He had few other possessions. Tariq was unusually anxious; no second thoughts, just the uncertainty of what lay ahead.

Five minutes later the truck pulled up outside the house where Tariq had lived for most of his life. The cleric hugged his adopted son and, as they broke away, Abu Hanifa produced a package from his pocket, a gift to help Tariq in his endeavours, to give him strength on his way. It was his own personal copy of the Quran, a leather-bound edition which had been in the family for three generations. Tariq was emotional as he held the battered family heirloom.

"I won't let you down father," he said, as he turned and walked towards the vehicle.

His mother and two sisters were both wiping tears as they said goodbye with promises of keeping in touch ringing in his ears. A new chapter in the life of Tariq Siddique was about to start.

Chapter Ten

22nd September 2004, Basra Airport.

Tariq looked around the arrivals area and headed for passport control. This was a military flight; it would be another nine months before public-scheduled flights between Basra and Baghdad would resume, but security, as one would expect, was still strict. It took an hour for all the necessary checks to be completed.

This was Tariq's first trip in an aircraft and he felt uneasy as the plane took off. He closed his eyes and placed himself in the hands of Allah. As he relaxed he looked around at his fellow passengers, most were dressed in military uniform. He cursed them under his breath. The fifty-minute flight to Baghdad, however, passed off without incident.

Before landing, the plane circled Baghdad and Tariq was able to see firsthand the devastation that had been caused by the American and allied bombing. He felt angry at the violation of his country.

He left the plane and followed the group into the arrivals hall. The airport was in a similar state of alert to Basra, and it seemed total chaos from an outsider's perspective. It was a confusing place and Tariq wandered around for a while in bemusement before a fellow passenger, who had noticed his uncertainty, explained the routine. Soldiers and police were everywhere, outnumbering passengers; but again, with security completed, the flight to London departed less than an hour late, and Tariq sat back to endure the five and a half-hour journey with nothing more to occupy him than the copy of his father's Quran. Prayers would be said quietly from his seat.

He checked his itinerary again. The plane left Iraq at just after two o'clock and, allowing for the three hours' time difference, would be landing at Heathrow at around five-thirty. There was a train from London Kings Cross station at around eight-thirty which would get into Leeds at eleven o'clock where his uncle had arranged to meet him.

The journey was uneventful. The plane was less than half full and he had a row of seats to himself. He was pleased he did not have to make conversation. Looking around the aircraft his fellow travellers were again mostly military. Through sheer boredom his mind wandered, and he started playing mind games, thinking of the possibilities of jihad - a suicide bomb perhaps. Detonate it as it was descending over London; he would be remembered as the nineteen 9/11 martyrs were. The idea buoyed him for a while, but logistically, he recognised, the high level of security at all airports meant that this was probably not a viable option.

Tariq recognised that this was not the destiny that his father had set out for him; a leader of men he had said; an inspiration, like Zarqawi or Bin Laden, but he did not share this view. He had different ideas and a different path to follow, something more direct.

Landing at Heathrow, Tariq was wishing he was back home on familiar ground surrounded by people that cared for him. All his teachings and beliefs had convinced him he was entering the gates of hell and he was experiencing a range of emotions; anxiety, loathing and a degree of uncertainty of what he might find. He was on new territory, enemy territory.

He stared out of the cabin window as the plane taxied to a halt and watched the grey skies overwhelmed by a degree of apprehension. His faith would be his anchor he vowed, his rock, which would give him the strength he would need.

He was unshaken in his ultimate mission. Everything he was about to undertake would be for this one aim and his determination to strike a blow for Jihad would know no bounds. He had not formed any definitive plan as yet; he was flexible and in no hurry. He needed to get to know his enemy, how he thinks, behaves, and reacts, his weaknesses and strengths. Only then will he be ready. Allah would guide him.

He reached the immigration desk and passed through with his student visa without any question. His one suitcase containing all his worldly possessions was opened by a customs inspector and his laptop examined, but within an hour or so, he was making his way to the Underground station that would take him into central London.

He read his notes again he had received from Jake. *'Take the Piccadilly line which will take you direct to Kings Cross – it will take about 45 minutes.'*

The hustle and bustle of the airport was mind-boggling, and Tariq had difficulty in taking it all in. People from all nationalities, all walks of life, aircrew, baggage, shops, restaurants, a far cry from his own background in Basra, even Baghdad was nothing like this. There was an excitement about the place but it was an alien and confusing experience.

He put his piece of paper back in his pocket and made his way to the Underground ticket desk and bought a single fare. He had two-hundred pounds in cash in his pocket courtesy of his father, which was to cover his travel and food. Further money would be sent out to him at regular intervals although there was a suggestion he could earn some money working with the boys in the Cash and Carry.

He viewed the map of the London Underground next to the ticket office window while he was waiting in the queue and looked with fascination at the names of the stations along the blue line he would be taking - Hammersmith, South Kensington, Knightsbridge, Piccadilly Circus. He had heard of Piccadilly Circus, of course, but none of the others.

He eventually got his ticket and he took a deep breath as he made his way to the platform. It was still light but cloudy; something he hadn't experienced for several months. The drop in temperature was noticeable, and he shivered as he waited for the train; his leather jacket was now going to be put to good use to keep warm.

The journey to Kings Cross took the time suggested by Jake in his email, and Tariq was strangely drawn by all the comings and goings; the diversity of the passengers was something he was not expecting. For some reason he thought that the country was predominantly populated by versions of Major Howard and his soldiers. He had no touchstone, his knowledge gleaned only by books, and very occasional television, but mostly the teachings of his tutors.

As he got closer to Central London, so the Tube train got busier and busier and by the time he reached Kings Cross, it was standing room only. Tariq felt claustrophobic and was pleased to see the sign for his destination. He followed the directions to the main-line station and the main concourse. Although past rush hour it was still frenetic, certainly compared with anything Tariq had experienced before.

He suddenly felt totally lost and doubts crept into his mind for the first time. He really wanted to be back with his family in Basra.

His boyish frame made him look a lot younger than he was, and to any outsider he would appear somewhat forlorn. He stood there in the middle of the concourse looking around, staring, trying to take in his surroundings, and with his small battered he resembled a Paddington Bear figure.

His priority was to buy a ticket. He took out his dog- eared piece of paper from his pocket with his email instructions from Jake and read it again. He was knocked twice by apologetic passengers rushing to catch their connections and he moved to a less crowded area.

'*You need to find the ticket office to get a ticket,*' it said, and Tariq scanned the bewildering array of notices. He eventually spotted what he was looking for and made his way to a large kiosk with several windows with queues at each. He joined the shortest line and after a few minutes bought his single fare.

Then it was back to the crowds around the destination boards. He was trying to take everything in; it was so different, culturally an anathema. He looked at a hoarding advertising women's underwear and repelled at the scantily clad model. In fact, he couldn't understand the behaviour of any of the women he had seen; their familiarity, their lack of respect; how could they allow themselves to be used in this way.

He checked the time; there was still twenty minutes before his train was due to leave. He had not eaten much during the day, just the meal he was provide on the plane, and he had left most of that. He could feel the pangs of hunger and spotted a sandwich bar. He walked up to the kiosk and viewed the fare. He chose a cheese baguette and a bottle of water.

"Six pounds fifty," said the coloured girl behind the counter. He looked at the confusing notes and coins in his purse; his money was not going to last long at this rate. He gave her a ten pound note which he thought would cover it, and avoid being embarrassed at his lack of knowledge of the strange currency.

She presented him with the change and Tariq put the money

into his purse, collected his meal and returned to the departures board.

He scanned the list of destinations to find the appropriate platform for his train to Leeds. The signs and directions had posed no problems and he could read them easily enough; his English was already at a proficient level.

He joined the hoard of other passengers who were also waiting for the trip north and when the gates opened followed them along the platform to board the train and find his seat.

He put his luggage on the overhead rack and settled down to eat his sandwich while he waited for the train to depart. The carriage was busy and after a couple of minutes a large man sat in the seat next to him. There was a commotion as he tried to stow his briefcase and jacket on the rack above which meant pushing Tariq's baggage to one side. The man took out a newspaper and made himself comfortable. He looked across at Tariq.

"Ah do," he said, which Tariq failed to translate, but to took it as some form of greeting. Tariq meekly nodded and went back to his Quran.

The train pulled away on time and he stared out of the window at the environs of North London, past a football ground, then on the left he noticed a large mosque which cheered him.

He'd eaten his sandwich, swilled down with the water, and it was now gone eight o'clock. As the train sped laboriously onwards, he was beginning to feel the effects of the long journey; his body clock had now turned eleven. Then, with the light fading, he gradually drifted into a deep slumber.

He wasn't sure how long he had been asleep, but he was rudely awakened by the ticket inspector.

"Tickets please," he said, in a gruff Yorkshire accent.

For a second Tariq was disorientated, but quickly attuned his senses. The man sat next to him had been to the buffet car and was consuming a large sausage roll; a cardboard cup of hot beverage was perched on the fold-down tray in front of him. Tariq rummaged in his purse and passed the ticket. The large man took it from him and gave it to the inspector who scribbled on it and handed it back. The man went back to his sausage roll.

The rest of the journey was uneventful. Tariq was deep in his own world, and every now and then, out of curiosity, he would view some of his fellow passengers. He noticed a vicar sitting diagonally opposite wearing a smart suit and 'dog-collar'. He was the first non-Islamic clergyman Tariq had seen, very different from the mullahs and Imams back in Iraq. The man smiled as he caught his gaze, but Tariq quickly looked away not wishing to maintain any eye-contact.

His large seat-companion left the train at Doncaster, and there was a further kerfuffle as he retrieved his belongings and binned his discarded rubbish. He put on his jacket and made no acknowledgement to Tariq as he walked up the compartment to the exit. Tariq felt more comfortable now his private space was not being invaded.

The train pulled into Leeds station only a couple of minutes late and Tariq followed his fellow passengers to the exit.

Jake's email had indicated they would be waiting for him outside the main entrance and Tariq looked around for any sign. He had no phone, so he had to rely on the original message.

Tariq again began to feel very alone. Although he had been away from home in the training camp, he had been with people of similar backgrounds. This was an alien experience.

The rest of the passengers had dispersed to their onward journeys leaving Tariq staring blankly at the signs and wondering how he would be able to contact his relatives.

Suddenly, there was a tap on his shoulder which made him jump. He turned around and saw a face that he vaguely recognised from his mother's photographs.

"Tariq?" asked the young man, casually dressed in a hoodie, jeans and trainers.

"Jamal?" said Tariq in response.

"Yes, but call me Jake, everybody does," and he held out his hand in greeting. They were quickly joined by another young man of a similar age and an older man.

"Tariq, my boy," said the elder man and embraced him warmly. Freddie joined in.

"Hello Uncle," said Tariq slightly overwhelmed at the generosity of the welcome.

"You must call me Abdul," said his uncle.

Tariq didn't know what to expect, but the genuine warmth expressed by the distant relatives had not been anticipated.

Abdul picked up Tariq's suitcase and Jake took the briefcase and the small group headed for the exit. He looked at his three relatives as they walked out of the station. Jake was a good thirty pounds heavier than his younger brother who was scrawny but a couple of inches taller. Abdul was an older version of Jake with thinning dark, greying hair which tapered to a widow's peak, his face showing signs of life's struggles, lined but full of character.

"How are you after your long journey?" asked Abdul. "What are things like in Iraq?" fired Freddie, before Tariq could answer the first question, then another and another.

"Now then boys, let Tariq alone, he has had a long journey," admonished the father.

The van was parked on the opposite side of the road next to

the taxi rank. The words 'Charma Cash & Carry, Batley' was painted on the side in big bold letters together with a telephone number and the website address.

"We were lucky to be able to park here, but nobody bothers this time of night," said Abdul, as they crossed the road.

He aimed his key fob at the van. The four indicators illuminated, and a clunking sound of the van's locks disengaging could be heard. Abdul slid back the door and the two lads got into the back and crouched behind the seats.

"You can sit in the front," said Abdul, as he handed Tariq's suitcase to Freddie.

The van pulled away and the two brothers continued to fire questions at their cousin despite remonstrations from Abdul.

Just over twenty-five minutes later the van pulled up outside the terraced house in Batley. Sabeen had heard the noise of the parking vehicle and had opened the door; she too was anxious to meet the new arrival.

"Come in, come in," she said excitedly, as Tariq approached the door. She kissed him on the cheek and led him into the front room.

"Would you like a cup of tea or coffee?" she asked as Tariq sat down.

"Just some water," he replied quietly.

He looked around the room, not large but space for a good size sofa, dining table with four chairs, coffee table and a large television which was switched off. The decor was plain but tasteful; this was not a house of ostentation which pleased Tariq. He also noticed there were no religious artifacts.

After answering further questions, Abdul suggested that Tariq should see his room and get some sleep, "There will be time enough for questions tomorrow," he had said.

Tariq was grateful, and Jake, who was the stronger character of the two brothers, led the way upstairs. There were three bedrooms and a bathroom on the second floor.

"We've just converted the loft," said Jake, as he noticed Tariq viewing another staircase leading upward.

"You were going to have Freddie's bedroom, but Dad decided to do up the attic instead to give us more space. It'll be your own room, I'll show you. Oh, the bathroom is just down there," he added pointing along the corridor.

Tariq tried to keep up with the excited barrage of words and strange accent from his cousin. Jake went up the next flight of stairs to a door immediately in front of them.

"This is yours," said Jake and opened the door.

Tariq went in and was amazed. Although the slope of the roof had made it feel slightly cramped it was still much bigger than his room in his Basra house and appeared to occupy most of the top floor. There was a three-quarter size bed, a bedside cabinet with reading light, a TV on another small table in the corner. Halfway down there were joists across to support the roof.

"You'll need to watch your head on that," said Jake as he ducked underneath the wooden beam and led Tariq to the other end of the room where there was a desk and chair. "So you can study," he added.

"We've had satellite put in and there is broadband as well, so you can get on the internet."

Tariq took a moment to compute the words; the local accent and speed of speech meant he was finding it difficult to follow, but he could not have wished for a warmer welcome.

"Thank you... you are very kind," he said, but with little energy; he was now exhausted.

Tariq slept well, the bed was comfortable, and it was quiet.

There were no sounds of military vehicles or the occasional gunfire which had provided the backdrop to the Basra residence for as long as he could remember.

Sabeen knocked on his door at eight-thirty and took him his first cup of real English tea. He had to readjust to his new surroundings as he heard the knock.

"Come in," he shouted drowsily.

"I have bought you a cup of tea... I thought you would like to lie in for a while and catch up on your sleep after your long journey."

"Thank you," he said taking the drink and placing it on a coaster on top of the bedside table.

"What time is it?" asked Tariq.

"Eight-thirty," replied Sabeen.

"No, no," he said in an anguished tone. "I have missed early prayers."

"Yes... but there's always the Dhuhr later."

"Yes, I must be there for that," he said feeling relieved. He had never allowed anything to get in the way of his prayer routine.

"We have little time for prayers, the boys are so busy at the Cash and Carry," said Sabeen.

"Not even Friday prayers?" asked Tariq, somewhat surprised.

"You will find things are different here," said Sabeen, ignoring the implied criticism.

Tariq pondered reflecting on that statement.

"Yes, I can see they are," he said, sipping at his hot drink.

Still drowsy, Tariq went downstairs to the bathroom where he was able to shower. He looked at his beard, which he had grown in the training camp, in the mirror, and realised he would need to make compromises if he was to integrate into the new world he had entered.

There was a razor in a container on the shelf over the sink. Concessions to the new culture were going to be required and he started the painful process of removing the facial hair.

His limited wardrobe meant that he was dressed in the same pair of jeans that he had worn the previous day, but had a different shirt as he went down the stairs to the living room. Sabeen came out from the kitchen hearing the footsteps.

"Tariq…? You look different."

"Yes, I have removed my beard. Now I am in England, it is probably best."

She made no comment.

"I have made you some breakfast and there are some cereals on the table," she said, and Tariq sat down and examined the box of Cornflakes.

"I wasn't sure whether you ate meat or not," said Sabeen from the kitchen. She entered the room with a plate of beans on toast. "Hope you like beans."

"I don't know, I have never eaten them," he replied and stared at the red offering piled over two slices of bread in front of him.

"I do eat meat, but not pork; sometimes we have lamb and chicken," he said, looking up at Sabeen.

He started eating his new cuisine.

"That was very good," he said after finishing his breakfast.

"Would you like some more tea?" asked Sabeen.

"Just water will be fine," he replied.

After he had eaten, he sat on the sofa with his Quran in his hand; Sabeen joined him.

"I can imagine this will seem very strange to you after Iraq. I was only little when I arrived here, and I have no memories of my homeland."

"I didn't know you were born in Iraq," replied Tariq.

"Yes, in the north…" There was a pause. "We will need to get some new clothes for you today. It is getting colder now, and you will freeze in those short sleeves."

"Thank you, I am comfortable," he replied.

"When the boys get in they want to take you to the Cash and Carry and show you around. Abdul will see to what you need."

"That is very kind," said Tariq. "How far away is the mosque?"

"Not far, I will show you," Sabeen replied.

Half an hour later, Tariq was walking through the back streets of Batley, following Sabeen's directions to the mosque. Despite his leather jacket, it was still cool by Basra standards, and he felt a chill as he made his way up the deserted street where his uncle lived. With a brisk walk, it took only ten minutes or so, and he took a great deal of interest at his new surroundings. The line of terraced-houses all looked very similar in this part of town. Most had cars parked outside but were clearly not new. The pavement was cracked providing trip-ups for any unsuspecting or less-than-careful walker. There was also dog mess at regular intervals which he had to dodge.

When he reached the building, he felt disappointed; it looked run down and in need of some serious attention. Although the design was of traditional construction, it had none of the lustre that his father's mosque had. He walked through the door.

There were few people about, but he managed to attract the attention of one of worshippers. He was dressed in a white gown and sandals, ready for prayer.

He introduced himself. "Hello, my name is Tariq Siddique and I have just arrived from Iraq..." Tariq bowed instinctively. "Who is the Imam here, please? I would like to meet him."

"Wait here," said the man, "I will see if he is around."

Tariq soaked in the atmosphere; this was still a place of

worship and, despite its exterior shortcomings, inside it had the same feel as his father's mosque. He looked down the corridor in front of him which appeared to lead to the entrance of the main prayer room; in between there were two doors on either side, one of which had the word 'toilet' in English and Arabic. He felt at home seeing the flowing script.

A few minutes later, a man in religious clothes came out from one of them and walked up to Tariq and introduced himself.

"Hello, I am Abu Ebeida El-Ladashiri, Imam of the Batley mosque." He held out his hand in greeting.

"I am Tariq Siddique; my father is Imam at Sa'ad Al Ibn Abi Waqas mosque in Basra City."

"You are most welcome, Tariq Siddique. I am honoured to greet you to our place of worship."

"I was hoping to attend Dhuhr prayers and maybe 'Asr and Magrib today," replied Tariq.

"Of course, you will be most welcome," replied the Imam, impressed by the level of diligence shown by Tariq. "Follow me and I will show you around… You speak very good English."

The Imam led the way down the corridor to the main prayer room.

"Thank you," replied Tariq, "It is not always so easy to understand the English here. It is not how I was taught… I only arrived yesterday. I am staying with my uncle Abdul." Tariq explained his domestic arrangements.

"Ah, Abdul… and the boys. Yes, I know them, Yusuf and Jamal?" the inflexion indicated a question, but he continued. "Good people… although we rarely see them here; always so busy in their store."

The Imam continued with the guided tour of the building and outlined some of the community projects with which he was involved. A few other faithful arrived and the Imam took Tariq back to the main hall. As with all mosques the floor was carpeted with prayer mats all pointing east to Mecca in one gigantic pattern. The Imam showed Tariq where to wash and handed him a white gown and cap. "We keep some spare for visitors," he explained.

Tariq changed in a communal changing room with other men.

Around twenty worshippers, many, Tariq discovered later, were taxi drivers, lined up and led by the Imam started the Dhuhr or midday prayer, the third prayer session of the day.

"Allah is the greatest, in the name of Allah, most gracious, most merciful, all praise is due to Allah, Lord of all that exists..."

Tariq was able to recite in perfect Arabic, whereas many of the small congregation, having been brought up locally, had learned it parrot-fashion as children.

After prayers, the Imam invited Tariq into his personal quarters for tea and was keen to learn more about the new arrival. Tariq gave the Imam more detail of his life in Basra and his father's role as head of the local community.

Later, Tariq was keen to talk about the wider topic of Islam and how it was interpreted in the UK. It would help him understand the challenges ahead. It was a subject which was of most interest to him. He switched from English and spoke in Arabic which the Mullah clearly understood.

After a broad conversation covering, amongst other things, prayer discipline, Tariq felt confident enough to broach the topic that was at the top of his agenda.

"What about the sixth Hadith...? Do you believe in it?"

It was an oblique reference, but understood by the Imam. The mullah was cautious in declaring any outward display of jihadist rhetoric. There were rumours that mosques were being infiltrated by special branch operatives disguised as possible activists to gain intelligence. He answered in a suitably indirect way.

"We tend to follow the Deobandi code here, as do many of the mosques in the UK."

This was music to his ears. Tariq was familiar with the hardline sect whose leading preacher loathed Western values and regularly called on Muslims to shed blood for Allah. The ultra-conservative movement, which gave birth to the Taliban in Afghanistan, also shared Tariq's views about armed jihad. It also preached contempt for Jews, Christians and Hindus.

"Insha'Allah," said Tariq.

"Insha'Allah," repeated the Imam.

Tariq stayed for most of the day and learned much about the mosque and the connection with the local community. He also gleaned more about the ideological leanings of the cleric who, as the dialogue developed, recognised that he could trust the new arrival. The conversation was mainly conducted in Arabic which made understanding so much easier for Tariq.

"There is so much distrust about our beliefs. You will always need to be cautious," the Imam counselled. "Things changed here after 9/11. Before then we were generally ignored, left alone. Then, immediately afterwards, there was so much hostility. We were fire-bombed here... much damage, now..." he looked in despair. "Now, there is just hatred.'

The Imam spoke in a measured way with a calm authority as befitting his status as leader of the local Muslim community. He would never show any outward resentment towards non-Muslims and now, Tariq gauged, was not the time to engage in any detailed discussions about Jihad. He was in no hurry.

Tariq stayed for the 'Asr and Magrib prayers before heading

back to the house at around four-thirty with the promise of returning the following day for Friday prayers. It was raining when he left the mosque and Tariq looked up to the sky at the dark clouds and let the falling drips of water splash on his face as if cleansing him. The last rain he had seen was early March.

On his return, Sabeen expressed her concern at his absence.

"Tariq, thank goodness. I was so worried; where have you been?"

"The masjid," he replied, and Tariq outlined his day and his discussions with the Imam.

For Sabeen listened to his account with a mixture of relief and some disappointed that all the time had been spent at the mosque.

At five o'clock, Tariq heard a van pulling up outside.

"That will be the boys coming back for some food. We can eat together. Abdul won't be back until later; he will get something in the office."

The front door opened, and Jake and Freddie came in, excited at seeing their cousin.

"Tariq," effused Jake. "How are you? What've you been up to?"

"He's been at the mosque all day," said Sabeen, before Tariq could answer; her demeanour appeared disapproving.

"That's cool," said Jake, without taking much notice. "After we've eaten, we're taking you to the C and C to get you some clothes. Dad's still there; he doesn't leave till gone nine most days."

Tariq had difficulty in keeping up after an afternoon speaking Arabic.

"C and C...? What is C and C? I don't understand."

"Cash and carry, we're going to get you some gear," replied

Jake.

"Gear?"

"Clothes, clobber, stuff to wear," he said becoming frustrated. "And a phone, you'll need to get a phone. Don't worry, Dad'll pay for it," he added, seeing a look of concern on Tariq's face.

Tariq understood.

"That is very kind, thank you."

The meal was spent with Freddie and Jake telling Sabeen of their day. Tariq sat deep in his own thoughts and ate quietly trying to understand the fast exchange of banter.

After they had finished eating, Tariq was ushered into the van. The two brothers exchanged ideas on suitable clothing he would need and other possible improvements to his wardrobe.

With Jake driving, it was only a ten-minute journey to the Cash and Carry on the edge of an industrial estate, close to the motorway. Tariq was amazed as they pulled up and parked in the extensive car park.

It was much bigger than he was expecting. There was space for probably sixty or seventy cars and it was busy with only a few vacant spaces. Customers were ferrying trolleys from the exit to the waiting vehicles.

It was a large brick building, with a neon sign 'Charma Cash and Carry', which shone like a beacon in the evening gloom.

The three got out of the van and walked towards the front entrance; Tariq was trying to take it all in.

Inside it was vast, with rows and rows of aisles containing just about any commodity you could need. It was split into sections – food, electrical goods and clothing. Everything was boxed or packaged with no thought of the fineries of display. Staff were busy stacking, labelling or on customer service duty; there were twelve tills available, but only half of those were open. Tariq stood there for a minute; he had seen nothing like it in Basra.

"Come on," said Jake. "You must come up and see Dad."

The boys led the way through the hangar-like interior to the far end of the store where a flight of stairs led to another floor. Here too it was a hive of industry with an administration room and finally, next door, Abdul's own office where he was speaking animatedly on the phone behind a desk in the corner. There were filing cabinets and a large desk with two telephones. Paper seemed to be everywhere.

Abdul saw the lads and beckoned them in, still engrossed in conversation. He terminated the call and went around the desk and greeted Tariq.

"How has your day been?" he asked.

"Fine," said Tariq.

Jake interrupted before Tariq could elaborate. "He's been at the mosque all day."

"That's very dedicated of you Tariq. Regrettably we don't get a lot of time for prayers," said Abdul.

Tariq looked disapprovingly, but kept his counsel.

"You've come to find some clothes, yes? I have asked Jake and Freddie to choose something suitable for you. You must be feeling the cold after Iraq."

"Yes, it is very cold here," he replied.

Jake grabbed Tariq's arm. "Come on let's get you kitted out," and the three youths went back down to the sales floor.

After an hour, Tariq had just about everything he could possibly need to keep him going until the spring. They even managed to get him a pay-as-you-go phone, which Jake was eager to demonstrate.

For the next few days Tariq became more acquainted with his hosts and the surrounding community. Most of Friday was spent at the mosque and he met many local Muslims who had joined for the ritual prayers. It was full for the early sessions and busy for the remainder. Tariq was happy to see the faithful dedicating themselves to God.

On Saturday, Jake and Freddie had taken the morning off work to take Tariq into Leeds on the train and prepare him for his first day at University on Monday. The journey took only twenty minutes and Tariq was amazed at how busy Leeds station was on Saturday morning. It was almost like Kings Cross, bustling and vibrant.

The shops and traffic were something new and it took Tariq some time to get use to the noise and commotion. As it happened, other students were arriving from across the country and beyond and there was an information desk on the station concourse run by students giving advice on accommodation and directions. Tariq made contact and was given details of where he would need to report. It was only about another twenty minutes from the station. So, after a restful Sunday, Monday morning seven thirty, Tariq stood at Batley station ready to catch the train to Leeds and a new chapter in his life was about to begin.

Chapter Eleven

October 2006. Petronix Off-Shore training facility, Aberdeen.

Rory Calderwood was sitting with a group of other offshore workers inside a twelve man life-raft floating in a huge purpose built pool at the company's Aberdeen training site.

"What's the second thing you do when you get into a life-raft on the open sea?" asked the instructor.

Calderwood of course knew the answer. This was the second renewal of his Survival Certificate which he had to have if he was to continue in his role as a senior engineer at the Petronix Delta Bravo oil and gas platform.

The course took three days, and this was Wednesday, the final day, having previously revisited some basic first aid, fire-fighting, health and safety. Today's programme would consist of a rescue drill, simulating the evacuation of a capsized helicopter and entering a life-raft. Although still demanding, the large aqua centre could hardly be compared with the North Sea and its freezing temperature and mountainous waves. He didn't want to be here, he had better things to do with his time and, the sooner he could get it over with, the better.

None of his six companions, who were all completing the Survival Course for the first time, had proffered a reply, so Calderwood provided the correct answer.

"Hand out the anti-sea-sickness pills."

"Well done, Woody," said the instructor.

The complement barely registered; after three Survival Courses and over ten years' experience, if he didn't know the answer now, he never would.

Kim Barnes was impressed though.

As the local HR Manager for Petronix, she was the only

woman on the course, and, having now completed her three novice visits to the rig, she was required to take the full Survival Certificate if she was to undertake further trips. She had met Calderwood on her most recent excursion to the platform when he had acted as her buddy. It had been a long time since Calderwood had had a minder.

The instructor gave more pearls of wisdom relating to survival in a life-r aft.Calderwood looked across at Kim, attractive even in her unflattering survival suit, and remembered that journey only four weeks earlier. He and Kim had struck up a rapport. He was quiet and seemed locked in his own world most of the time, detached even, but there was something about him which Kim found interesting. She had been intrigued by her enigmatic companion.

She was tough and forthright, conditioned by being a woman in a predominantly male environment, but also with a hint of vulnerability. He was pleased to meet up with her again.

"And the reason is?" asked the instructor.

Losing patience, Calderwood responded to speed things up. "Because of the motion of the sea you can get violently sick very quickly in a life raft which causes dehydration, as well as being very unpleasant for those on board."

"Correct again," said the instructor. "The first thing you do, in case you were wondering, is to take a role call to make sure no-one is left overboard." The instructor looked at the group with a grim expression. "Remember, even with your survival suits, life expectancy can be counted in minutes in the North Sea in mid-winter."

Calderwood had long since lost interest. Conditions in the dingy were cramped and he just wanted to get it over with, so he could leave and get home.

After a further briefing, the instructor dismissed the class. The seven students vacated the life raft and made their way to the changing rooms. Special provisions had to be made for Kim by way of a curtain, but to save everybody's blushes she showered in her swimsuit. There were no concessions for women at the Centre, or the rig for that matter; the oil and gas industry in that respect was still firmly entrenched in the 1970's.

Having a woman on the course had been an unusual event, and the coarse badinage that you would normally associate with such an environment had been replaced by a rather unnatural politically correct version. Not that Kim was averse to male banter; she had experienced enough of it in her time at Petronix. The reticence had come from the men not wishing to cause any offence that would hamper any potential conquest. It was of no consequence to Kim who was used to the attention, but didn't seek it; she had better things to do than to fight off horny oil workers.

Kim was new to the area having moved to Aberdeen two months earlier from Head Office in the Thames Valley. She felt that a spell at the 'sharp end' would enhance her career prospects. Single, early thirties, with some horror relationships behind her, now was the right time to spread her wings. So, having successfully applied for the position, she leased her flat in Henley-on-Thames, which would pay the mortgage, and moved into a rented two-bedroomed barn conversion not far from the airport and only twenty minutes away from where Rory Calderwood lived.

Leaving the training centre, Kim, now comfortably dressed in jeans and sweatshirt, caught up with Calderwood in the car park. The intensity of the course had meant they'd had little time for no more than pleasantries; Kim was keen to further the acquaintance.

"So, what did you think?" asked Kim, as she aimed her fob at a two-year-old Alpha Romeo and lifted the boot.

"What, the course?" replied Rory.

"Yes," said Kim, stowing her gear and shutting the boot lid.

"Fine, this is number three, so you get used to it."

"What, even the helicopter escape?"

"It's not so bad when you know what's coming," said Rory.

"I hope I don't ever have to get used to it," said Kim.

"Well, you will if you stay here for four years."

"Hmm, let's hope it doesn't come to that," replied Kim.

They exchanged goodbyes and as she reached to open the driver's door she leaned to Rory.

"You better have my number."

It was one of those spur-of-the-moment things, and she had no thoughts of the consequences. He made a note and keyed into his phonebook.

"Here, you can have mine," said Rory, and she did the same.

"Keep in touch," said Kim, looking at Calderwood directly in the eyes.

She got in and fired up the Alpha, then drove out of the car park.

Having successfully renewed his survival certificate for another four years, Rory too headed home. The journey from the Off-Shore Training Centre, just off the Aberdeen quayside, to Dunmore, about four miles north of the City Centre, took just over twenty minutes due to the busy afternoon traffic.

As he drove back to the house, his thoughts drifted back to that time, to his first course ten years earlier. He thought of his wife, Janie, and the chance meeting in the wine bar on his first leave. It had been a passionate relationship and, after only two months, Rory had moved in with her; they married in the spring of 1997.

Nine years and two children later, the fire was almost burned out, and, on recent visits, Rory found himself looking forward to returning to the rig, away from the constant arguing and fighting, and the indifference.

He pulled onto the drive, in front of the four-bedroomed detached house he shared with Janie and their two boys, Matt and Jason. He got out of his 4 x 4 to remove a bicycle and other child debris littering the path.

He knew the house would be empty; at two-thirty on a Wednesday, his wife would be at her Yoga class, and the lads would be at school. She would pick them up later, on her way back. He took his kit from the boot and went inside and made himself a coffee.

Rory had returned on-shore the previous Friday, and he would have another ten days or so leave before he would return to the rig. He had maintained his original shift pattern, returning every two weeks for ten years and it had not always been easy; but, as he had said, it paid the bills. This week was slightly different, having had to complete the Survival Course in what was effectively his own time, he would be entitled to three days extra holiday in lieu or three days additional pay. He had chosen the pay; time at home had not, over the last few months at least, become as attractive as it used to be.

While he sat drinking his coffee, he looked at the pictures of his family in what were happier times. Janie and the boys had meant everything to him, and, stuck out in the middle of the North Sea, his thoughts were always with them. He had a photograph of the three of them as a screensaver on his computer. In fact, family life had been his salvation; it had eased his constant retrospection and flashbacks to his army days, and the guilt. Why had so many been killed? Why did he survive? Questions he could never answer, or come to terms with.

His boys were now eight and six, growing up quickly and acquiring their own identities, but it was Janie who had changed. Rory stared into his coffee. Before they married, they did discuss his choice of vocation, the potential difficulties in managing the frequent separation. For Rory it was less of an issue, he was used to isolation and was mentally self-sufficient, but it was tough for Janie, particularly with the arrival of the boys. He offered to look for a shore-based job, but financial pressures meant that they had attained a standard of living that required the enhanced salary that he brought in.

In the early days, as the boys were growing up, he used to just live for that Friday feeling when he was due back to shore. He remembered the occasional times during the winter when the weather had meant they couldn't land the helicopter and he would be stranded, sometimes for days. The pain was unbearable. But now he found himself seeking the respite of the rig; the rows on a Sunday night as he prepared to pack his rucksack were now almost routine; he valued the solitude.

Janie was still working at the solicitors in town and was trying to carve out her own career path. She had taken maternity leave to have the children, but later returned to work four days a week. Looking back, the present situation was probably inevitable. She had met Rory on the rebound from the love of her life, Tony, the childhood sweetheart she had set her heart on marrying. There had been talk of an engagement, but then Tony said he was feeling trapped and wanted to take a breather from the relationship for a short while, which Janie reluctantly agreed. The next thing she knew he had got engaged to one of her best friends and she was devastated. Rory was unaware of this past relationship.

That night in the wine bar, ten years ago, Janie was very available and spotted an opportunity to equal the score on her former lover. Rory just happened to be in the right place at the right time. He was an attractive guy with an inner strength that gave Janie a sense of security; she had been a willing participant.

When, later, the discussion came around to the question of moving in together and then the subsequent marriage, she was more than happy. Rory, however, was not an easy person to live with. As well as the fortnightly separations, he was regularly consumed with moroseness that Janie found difficulty in penetrating. It clearly came from his time in the army, but he would never talk about it. When at home he would often mope about the house, incommunicative, unable to settle at anything or would take to heading out to the hills on his own. He loved the desolate countryside nearby and would spend hours locked in his own introspection. He would also push himself physically with a punishing keep fit routine of jogging or cycling.

Things did improve when the boys arrived, and Rory was a proud and dedicated father. They became used to his two weekly absences and would be as excited as Rory on his return, but as they got older and started school, they developed their own routines and friends, and their need for their father lessened. Rory gradually reverted to the solitude of his own thoughts.

The regular two-week separation was particularly difficult for Janie who would be left to cope with bringing up the children on her own which made the days drag. She was not intuitively maternal, and found motherhood hard. She loved the boys of course, but found herself with feelings of being stifled and mentally unchallenged. This was not the life she had envisaged. She had always pictured the high pace, cut and thrust of her own legal practice. Things improved for a while, once she had returned to work, but with her emotions in a perfect storm, the inevitable affair started just over three months ago when she took up tennis lessons.

She had had a number of hobbies over the years, which she would start with enthusiasm then they would quickly lose their appeal. Pilates, keep fit, she even had some golf lessons, but it was tennis that changed things.

The instructor, Geoff Delaney, was tall, athletic, slim and very good looking; consequently, he was never short of admirers. Janie was smitten particularly when he would hold her arms and take her through the serve position. She would flirt, giving him lingering glances and taking longer than was necessary when bending down to pick up the stray tennis balls. Janie had always looked after her figure and having two children had, if anything enhanced her body, and now she felt she was in her prime.

The classic equation, disillusionment plus opportunity, sealed the inevitable.

During one of Rory's away shifts, Janie had an evening lesson with Geoff on one of the floodlit tennis courts. Her mother, who lived a couple of miles away, had offered to babysit. She was always available to spend some time with her grandchildren.

The session finished at eight o'clock, and it was Janie who said suggested they went to the Black Swan for a drink. As luck would have it, Geoff's car was off the road for a minor repair, and he was intending to take the bus back to his place on the outskirts of town. So, Janie offered him a lift.

They didn't get to the pub. Although she had her jeans and tracksuit top in her kit bag, Janie hadn't changed, and was still in her short tennis skirt. Walking to her three-year-old BMW convertible, Janie felt a tingle of excitement that she hadn't felt since her days with Tony.

She opened the car boot and Geoff stowed his gear; Janie put her kit bag on top and got in the driver's seat. Geoff got into the passenger seat. The driving position on the BMW meant Janie was almost lying down and her skirt had ridden up even further as she drove away. Geoff was in his tracksuit and they had only gone a couple of miles before Janie's hands started wandering. There was no doubting her intentions for the night.

It took about ten minutes to reach Geoff's three-bedroomed semi in a smart district on the northern edge of the town. She parked outside and followed him up to the front door. They had barely made it through the door when they were pulling at their clothes. He led her upstairs to his bedroom and in no time at all they were both naked.

Since then, Janie had found the excitement addictive, she couldn't get enough, and took every opportunity to meet Geoff. When Rory was away it wasn't a problem. They would meet up either in the evening after his tennis lessons, or, on her day off, during the day at their house.

When Rory was at home, Janie missed Geoff badly and treasured the Wednesday afternoon 'Yoga lessons'. As her feelings for Geoff had grown, so her feelings for Rory was waning exponentially. She was riding on the crest of a wave, but deep down she knew that sooner or later she would crash onto the shore.

Rory was sat in his chair in front of the TV, deep in contemplation trying to rationalise events. He knew that, over the years, he had probably taken Janie for granted. She would always be there for him at the end of each shift to take his kit-bag with his washing whilst he went to play with the boys. Now, however, she was cold and unresponsive and made every excuse not to make love, headache, time of the month, busy day tomorrow, anything to avoid physical contact with her Rory.

The previous weekend had been worse than usual. On his return on Friday, Janie had virtually ignored him. He had made the usual fuss of the boys, but they too, after the initial excitement, were soon doing their own thing. She then suggested that because of his regular nightmares that he slept in the spare room to avoid waking her. Whilst he could see the logic, it still hurt.

Saturday and Sunday, things got so bad that after breakfast he drove out and walked the hills, not returning until the boys' bedtime. Any semblance of reasonable conversation with Janie had descended into sarcastic put-downs or barbed comments. Things had not improved on Monday and Tuesday after returning home from the day's training.

Rory couldn't understand why Janie had become so distant; the thought that she might be having an affair had not really entered his head.

As he watched the blank TV screen, he felt the wave of depression returning, starting to wash over him. He needed to be in the hills again alone with his own thoughts, but he had to wait until Janie returned with the boys. Perhaps he would go for a run later; that had always helped see off any melancholy.

He had continued his fitness regime and was a frequent visitor to the gym on the rig. He picked up the paper and started to read without really taking in the meaning of the words. His mind was elsewhere.

Suddenly he was jolted from his ruminations. Beep... It was his phone, a text.

'Would U like to go 4 a drink sometime?'

It was Kim's number. He viewed the screen and read it again then thought about the look that she had given him when she had got in her car.

Rory was not normally someone prone to impulsiveness. Having had to make life and death decisions in the Army, he had been conditioned to weigh up possibilities, probabilities, analyse the best outcome, but something clicked, and he texted back.

'Yes... when?'

Moments later his phone vibrated into life.

He suddenly felt exhilarated; his depression had disappeared; what an unexpected turn of events. Rory's heart began to race. He argued to himself that it would be just an innocent meet up to swap experiences from the course, but deep down he knew his motives were not entirely innocent. Starved of affection, his normal, disciplined self had been taken over by an alter-ego that he did not entirely recognise. He was being swept away on a tide of excitement.

He pressed 'return' and the blank box opened for him to send a message.

Text... *'Free 2night. U?'*

Buzz... Return... *'Yes'*

Text... *'Where? When?'*

Buzz... Return... *'8.00, white swan BOD?'*

BOD referred to Bridge of Don, a small village about four miles away. It would be close to where Kim lived, Rory recalled from an earlier conversation. Ideal, it was far enough from Rory's house to avoid any friends he had close to home.

Text... *'Yes'*

Buzz... Return... *'CU there Kim x'*

Former SAS sergeant Rory Calderwood's hands were shaking, not a recognised emotion in his experience. He began to question his decision; he was used to being in control. It was as though any choice he had in the matter had been wrested from him... too late to turn back; the deed was done.

A few minutes later, Janie's car pulled into the drive and the two boys scrambled from the back of the BMW and into the house. They ran to their father and Rory picked them up in turn, both anxious to swap their day's experience. They talked excitedly, and he listening to their urgent chatter. Janie walked to the kitchen virtually ignoring him and deposited some shopping on the work top. She had left her yoga gear in a hold-all in the boot; it hadn't been used. She would pick it up later.

"How was your course?" she eventually asked, as she came back in the room and pecked him on the cheek.

"Yeah, ok, much the same as the last one," he replied, engrossed in his newspaper. The boys had gone up to their room to change.

"Don't know why they make you go through it again, it isn't as though you need a refresher after all the years you've done," commented Janie.

"Has to be done, it makes sense. It's easy to get complacent... How was your Yoga?" asked Rory.

"Fine, just going to take a shower... Can you start the tea and look after the boys? There's a lasagne which just needs heating in the oven. I won't be long," said Janie.

"Will do," he said then rather nervously added, "I'm popping out later, meeting up with a couple of the lads from the course. If you've no plans."

He didn't think there would be any resistance to his arrangements; she was always encouraging him to get out more.

"No, not doing anything tonight. What time will you be in?"

Janie recognised it would mean another opportunity for more contact with Geoff, despite only leaving him less than an hour ago.

"Not sure, about eleven, half past, I guess, not late... I've nothing planned for tomorrow."

Janie went upstairs for her shower and Rory checked the boys, who were back in the lounge and watching TV. Then he went into the kitchen to start the dinner.

At just after six o'clock, the four of them sat together at the table and watched the news on the TV in the dining room whilst enjoying their lasagne. Rory noticed that Janie seemed reluctant to make any eye contact with him and directed all her conversation through the boys. He felt disappointed that she had taken only a cursory interest in his day; it wasn't every day you get to escape from a simulated capsized helicopter. Any possible guilt he was feeling was soon assuaged.

After tea, Rory loaded the dishes into the dishwasher while Janie got the boys washed ready for bed; although they would be watching TV or playing on their computers until at least eight o'clock. At seven-fifteen, Rory showered and changed into a smart short-sleeved shirt and his best jeans before kissing his boys goodnight.

"Where are you going, Dad?" asked Matt.

"Just for a drink with some friends," he replied.

Five minutes later, he was grabbing his jacket and making his way to his car.

"Have a good time," said Janie as he left, making no attempt to kiss him goodbye.

Having watched him pull away down the drive, she settled down to her laptop. She would be chatting to Geoff again shortly.

Rory arrived at the White Swan about ten-to-eight and found a seat in the corner of the lounge which was still quiet. From his vantage point he could see the car park and waited anxiously for Kim's Alfa. He checked his watch twice before he saw her car pull into the car park just after eight. He watched as she got out of the car and made her way to the pub entrance; she looked great. A light weight jacket over a white tee shirt and jeans, her fair hair flicked up at the back as the cool evening breeze caught it.

She entered the pub and looked round the lounge and smiled warmly as she recognised Rory sat in the corner. A couple of lads stood at the bar ogled as she walked to the adjacent corner seat next to Rory.

"Some guys have all the luck," said one to his mate.

"Hi," said Rory, trying to rise above the uncharacteristic apprehensiveness. "What would you like to drink?"

"Glass of red wine will be great, thanks," replied Kim.

"Won't be a sec," he said and made his way to the bar.

He returned to his seat a few minutes later with a glass of lager and Kim's wine and sat down next to her. She moved towards him, a lot closer than was comfortable, but he was not about to complain. She had taken off her jacket which was folded neatly on the seat next to her; Rory had difficulty in averting his eyes from the contours of her figure pressing against the fabric of her cotton top.

"Good to see you," said Kim.

"Good to see you," replied Rory. "I have to say it was a bit unexpected."

"I was thinking about you when I got back."

"Really?"

"Yes," said Kim.

Rory sipped his drink.

Kim could detect his anxiousness and moved the discussion to neutral ground.

"So, what did you think of the course?"

"Fine, I've done it before. I get a tee-shirt after the next one," replied Rory. She smiled at the humour.

"It certainly gets the adrenaline going."

"Yeah, that's for sure," said Rory, as he took a sip of his beer.

Kim knew about his wife and two children from conversations which would account for his unease.

"Come on tell me about you. What do you get up to when you're not on duty?" enquired Kim, trying to get Rory to relax.

He talked about his walking and how he loved the hills and the work he'd done renovating the house. She in turn recounted her hobbies, musical interests, which they shared, and her keep fit classes.

Gradually, the conversation became easier to the extent that they became oblivious to anyone else in the room, totally engrossed in each other. The spell was only briefly broken when Rory offered to get another round.

"No, my shout," said Kim, and she got up to fetch another round. This time they both had soft drinks, mindful of their cars in the car park.

As she passed his drink to him she brushed his hand with hers; to Rory it felt it like an electric shock. She sat down even closer to him and he could feel the warmth of her body. She slipped her hand in his and looked in his eyes, a lingering gaze.

"What time do you have to get back?" asked Kim, sipping her orange juice.

"I said I'd be back around elevenish, but there's no curfew."

"Do you fancy a coffee, I'm only five minutes away?" she said.

"Yeah, ok, yeah," he replied, and they got up leaving their drinks half consumed and walked hand in hand from the pub.

"Follow me," said Kim as they reached the cars. "It's not far." She got into her Alfa, started the engine and slowly drove out of the car park; she turned left. Rory followed her.

About half a mile away, they pulled into a yard which served a barn conversion. It had been tastefully transformed into three self-contained flats. Rory parked his car in the space next to Kim.

"This is nice," said Rory admiring the outside of the building.

"Yes, it's only three years old and the builders did a great job. You wait till you see inside."

She led him through the entrance lobby and up a flight of stairs to a small landing with two doors opposite each other. Kim went to the one on the right, number 3, and turned her key in the lock. Inside there was a small entrance hall leading to a large lounge which had been furnished with a big sofa, a couple of armchairs, dining table and an entertainment centre, TV, satellite, hi-fi and video. Kim walked through into the kitchen to the right to make the coffee.

"Make yourself at home. You can choose some music if you like," she shouted.

Rory perused the neatly stacked CD's in the rack next to the hi-fi and chose Marvin Gaye. As the strains of 'What's Going On' filled the room, Rory sat on the sofa taking in his surroundings. A couple of minutes later Kim returned with a tray with two mugs, milk and a cafetière of steaming coffee.

"Good choice," she said, as she sat next to him and started to pour the coffee. "Do you take sugar?"

"No, just milk is fine, thanks."

As they sipped their coffees the ritualistic small talk continued about the flat and the area, both of which neither of them really wanted.

"Can I use your loo?" asked Rory as he started to feel the effects of his earlier drinks.

"Of course, it's just through there on the right," said Kim, pointing to a door on the opposite side of the lounge to the kitchen.

He came back suitably refreshed, and as he got to the sofa Kim took his hand and pulled him towards her. Their lips met, tongues hungrily exploring, breathing getting heavier. Rory almost unconsciously moved his hands beneath Kim's tee-shirt and felt the softness of her bra in his hands. He lifted the cups and felt her breasts. She quickly lifted her top over her head. His mouth teased her nipples and she groaned in ecstasy. After a moment she got up and unzipped her jeans revealing matching sheer panties.

Rory stood up and undid his shirt; he was a fit guy from his running and regular workouts. She could see he had a great physique, defined pecs and a lean waist. Kim eagerly wrestled with the zip on his jeans, pushing them down to his ankles. She saw his hardness struggling to escape the confines of his boxers and she slid her hand downwards and started stroking it. They resumed the passionate kissing.

They broke away for a second as Rory gently eased Kim onto the sofa. Kim lay down and raised her hips and he pulled off her panties. He stripped off completely and was quickly into her. She nearly fainted with pleasure, her hips bucking to his thrusts. She gently rocked back and forth until, unable to hold any longer, he exploded inside her.

Silence.

They held onto each other, neither saying anything; there was nothing to be said.

Gradually, as their breathing slowed, Rory looked at Kim and unable to think of anything remotely suitable just said, "thank you, I needed that."

Kim kissed him again, slowly.

"My pleasure," she said, and she started to laugh.

"I'd forgotten how good it could be," he added.

She looked at the clock; it was eleven-fifteen.

"You'd better be off if you need to get back. Do you want to use the bathroom?'

"Please," said Rory, and he made his way down the corridor.

After a few minutes, he returned to the lounge looking more refreshed. Kim was still naked recovering on the sofa. He wanted to capture the moment in his head and could only gaze at her.

"You're absolutely beautiful," was all he could say.

Kim got up and kissed him passionately. He could feel her body in his hands. He cupped her bottom and pressed himself against her. She closed her eyes.

"Mmm, you better go, or I'll drag you to bed," she whispered.

"Yeah," said Rory. "I better had."

He let her go. Kim grabbed a dressing gown and wrapped it around her.

"I hope we can do that again... soon," she said, as she ushered him to the door.

"I'll ring you tomorrow," he said, and she kissed him again.

He walked down the stairs. The cold night air hit him as he left the building and reached his car. His mind was in a frenzy. He just wanted to go back to Kim.

It was almost midnight by the time he had garaged the car. The house was in darkness apart from the porch light, and he squinted as he put on the lights in the lounge. He went to the kitchen and poured himself a glass of water and sat on a stool at the breakfast bar trying to take in the night's events. He replayed them over and over in his mind; analysing, justifying. He went upstairs quietly trying not to disturb Janie who, he assumed, would be fast asleep. He made his way to the spare room.

The alarm went off at seven. Janie was working today, and she got out of bed to make some coffee. Rory had not slept well and was in a deep slumber in the spare room when she brought him a cup.

"Didn't hear you come in last night," she said, placing the mug on a coaster on the bedside table.

"It wasn't late," replied Rory, still trying to regain consciousness.

"Can you see to the boys while I get ready?"

She made no further enquiries into his previous evening's adventures.

"Yeah, sure," he said.

Rory got up and headed to the bathroom.

"Come on boys, time to get up," he shouted, as he went.

Chapter Twelve

Thursday morning. With Janie at work and the boys at school Rory had the house to himself again and was seated in the lounge with his coffee catching up with the breakfast news on the TV, but not really concentrating on the content. His mind was still going over events of the previous evening. He replayed everything in his mind. Through his years in the army he had always been able to detach himself emotionally from most situations, but this was different.

He thought about the early days with Janie when they couldn't keep their hands off one another; those days seemed a long time ago. How things had changed; had there been a tipping point he wondered, or had it been just a gradual decline to indifference. It was easy to blame the job, undoubtedly a contributing factor, but not the sole reason for the problems in the relationship. Other people cope with separation. He remembered his army days when guys went months without seeing their loved ones and they managed to handle it. Maybe they wanted different things. Rory hadn't really considered what he wanted; just took each day as it came and made the best of things.

Buzz... a text.

He picked his phone up from the worktop where it had been charging and looked at the screen.

'Thnx 4 last night Kim x'

Rory dialled the number, something else he would not normally do.

"Hi," said Rory.

"I didn't know whether to call or not. Wasn't sure if you would be on your own," she said.

"Yes, Janie's at work and the boys are at school. Aren't you going in?"

"No, taken today and tomorrow off. Thought it would give me time to recover from the course."

"Good move," said Rory. "Fancy doing something?"

"Yeah, that would be great. What've you got in mind?"

"Don't know. Could go for a walk, Corby Loch or across to the woods. It would be good to get some fresh air."

"Yeah, ok sounds good. What's the time now…? Nine -thirty, can you give me an hour or so?"

"Yeah, no problem. I'll pick you up about half-ten. See you then."

"Can you find it ok?"

"Yeah, no problem," he replied.

Rory rang off and went upstairs to get showered and changed and felt more than a twinge of excitement. His melancholia had disappeared.

It had been dark when Rory had followed Kim to her house, but he had no trouble in remembering the route and drew up in the courtyard of the barn conversion just after ten-thirty. He had put a pair of walking boots in the back of the Land Cruiser and was dressed in a lumberjack shirt, jeans with a denim jacket.

He got out of the car and looked at the building. It had been tastefully renovated using most of the original stonework. The grounds were pristine and the wooden posts and black railings that surrounding the property had not been weathered. The gravel was new and looked like it had been freshly brought up from the beach. There were security lights attached to the side of the property which, he could see from the car park, housed four apartments. There were two other cars parked on the drive, neither were Kim's.

He looked up at the sky; it was cloudy but with no threat of rain and it was quite mild for early October, ideal walking conditions.

He went to the front door and pressed the 'Flat 3' buzzer next to the intercom. The door buzzed then clicked and Rory pushed it open and retraced his steps. He reached the door and, before he could knock, Kim had opened it and almost dragged him inside. She shut the door and before he had chance to speak she had wrapped her arms around his neck and was kissing him.

Rory responded immediately; the kisses slow and passionate. Kim was just wearing a Kimono-style dressing gown and that was quickly discarded; she was totally naked. She wasn't thinking of walking, not just yet. She broke away for a second only to lead him to the bedroom. "More comfy," she said.

There was an intensity about it which swept Rory along. He quickly undressed and joined her on the bed. She lay there looking at him provocatively then was on him again exploring every part of his body. He responded in kind before entering her... slowly, teasing every sinew of her being. She bucked and twisted with every push as if draining his very lifeblood. Finally, she arched her back as she reached a crescendo before relaxing herself to his needs. He too climaxed seconds later and collapsed onto her.

They lay there; her body rising and falling with her breathing; he, totally in tune with her.

"Now that was better than walking," she said.

"Can't argue with that," he said as he held her tight.

Rory lay next to Kim savouring the moment and, for a split second, thought about Janie and the boys. but felt little emotion. Subliminally, he had already compartmentalised them into a parallel world. He was in a different place, a place where he felt wanted.

"So, what about that walk?" asked Kim, shaking Rory from his thoughts.

"Yeah, ok," said Rory and twenty minutes later they were heading up the A90 past the golf course at Murcar and down to the sea at Black Dog in Rory's 4 x 4.

They parked up and, as they made their way to the beach, arm in arm, the sun appeared, raising the temperature by a degree or so. The tide was out, and Kim let go of Rory and ran to the water's edge, excited, like a teenager, playing 'dodge the wave'. Rory, as most men were inclined to do, picked up a couple of stones and skimmed them across the relatively flat surface of the North Sea.

She stopped her dalliance with the incoming tide and joined him walking along the deserted beach.

"On a clear day you can see some of the rigs from here," he said, looking out across the grey brown water into the horizon.

Kim tugged his arm in an affectionate way acknowledging the comment, words somehow were superfluous.

Walking along the hard sand was easy and they ambled side by side for a good hour swapping experiences.

"What did you do in the army?" she asked at one point.

"Nothing very exciting," he replied, his stock answer to enquiries in this direction. His experiences in the army were off-limits to everyone; even Janie had little idea of his past career. He had never mentioned it again after that first night together.

Kim didn't pursue it further and just snuggled her head into his shoulder. Rory responded and wrapped his arm around her. He couldn't remember being this content for a long time.

He somehow had been transported back to a calmer joyous time, running through wheat fields in Herefordshire as a child, carefree and innocent. It was as though his nightmare in Iraq had been erased, the killings, the subterfuge, the letters to bereaved widows; in another box, packed away.

After another few minutes Rory noticed the clouds which were building from the west.

"We better get back," he said. "The winds picking up... could be in for some rain."

He looked at the sea, a swell had got up and waves were now crashing onto the pebbled beach.

"Good idea, I'm starving," said Kim, and they headed back towards the car; it was early afternoon.

At the car park there was a small hut which served hot drinks and a selection of sandwiches and cakes. They ordered two coffees and two cheese baguettes and took them to the car as the threatened rain began to fall.

"Just made it," said Kim as she opened the passenger door and got in. She took off her anorak and put it on the floor in front of her. Rory looked across at her; she looked good.

They sat there for a while finishing the sandwiches and drinking their coffees. Rory put the radio on to provide some background music as they stared out across the bleak ocean. The waves were now beating the shoreline with some ferocity. It was as if a giant had risen from its slumbers. This was more like the North Sea Rory knew, wild and uncompromising.

After they had finished, he made a dash from the car and deposited the rubbish into a bin.

"That's very eco of you," she joked; then leant across and kissed him. It was another urgent passionate kiss and as she broke away she said, "God I want you again."

"We better get going then," he replied, and he started the car and drove along the track towards the main road.

"Not sure I can wait that long," she giggled. "What about here?" she said, pointing to a turning to the left which seemed to lead into a small copse.

Rory took the turn and pulled up about fifty yards inside. It was still raining and totally deserted. Rory turned off the engine and Kim had already removed her shoes and jeans and was starting to pull down her panties. Rory followed her lead and she moved across and sat astride him, her back resting against the steering wheel. The rocking of the car would have been a giveaway to any bystander. It was as intense as their earlier couplings and afterwards Kim held onto Rory.

"Wow, now that was good," she said and kissed him slowly and longingly.

The car's windows were now completely steamed up.

"Just a minute, I've got some tissues in my bag," she said, as they attempted to disengage. Kim leant across and rummaged through her handbag.

They dressed themselves and Rory started the car and put the blower on full to demist the windscreen. Gradually the visibility improved sufficiently for him to be able to see to drive and he reversed the Land Cruiser and returned to the main road. It took fifteen minutes to get back to Kim's apartment.

"Would you like to come in for a coffee?" she asked as they pulled into the car park.

He checked his watch, three-fifteen.

"Better not, Janie will be back at four with the boys. I'll call you later if that's ok," he said.

"Yes, of course," and she leant across and kissed him. "Thanks for today… It's been special."

"Yeah, it has," he said, and she opened the door and got out. He watched her go to the front door and let herself in.

Rory's thoughts were all over the place as he drove back to his house. He still didn't feel any guilt. In fact, he wasn't sure what he did feel, but it was something he hadn't experienced for a long time.

He arrived back at the house and parked up. There were a couple of letters on the mat as he walked in, the electricity bill and a special offer on double glazing. He picked them up and put them on the kitchen table, then went upstairs to get changed.

He returned to the kitchen and made himself a cup of tea. He was in a reflective mood, and for a few minutes he just sat on a stool staring into his tea cup contemplating the day, trying to make some sense of it all.

Janie arrived just after four and the boys again ran in, anxious to see their father. They chattered excitedly as they downloaded their day to him.

"Come on boys, go and get changed," said Janie in authoritative tones and they raced each other up the stairs.

"How was your day?" asked Janie, matter-of-factly.

"Fine, went for a walk," he said.

"Anywhere nice?" she said as she put some shopping into the cupboards.

"The beach by Black Dog."

"Haven't been there for years," she said and left the kitchen to look after the boys.

The early evening was spent with Rory looking after the boys while Janie made the evening meal. There was a strange atmosphere, he sensed. Not t h e cold indifference, he had become used to over recent months, more a tension you could cut with a knife. It reminded him of the hours before a mission in the army; an expectation that something was about to happen.

After the boys had gone to bed, Janie joined Rory in the lounge where he was watching the TV.

There was an uneasy silence; the atmosphere, unbearable, and his senses knew that something was not right.

He tended to avoid any confrontation with Janie; he would go off on one of his walks if things became too bad, but he couldn't let this go something was up.

"What's the matter?" he asked. "You seem very on edge, tonight?"

Janie ignored him and went to the cupboard and took out a bottle of red wine and poured herself a drink. She drank a glassful in one gulp and poured another one before returning to the lounge. Her hands were shaking.

"Can you turn the TV off. We need to talk." There was an anxiousness in her tone.

Rory aimed the remote at the TV and pressed the on/off button. The TV went to 'stand-by'.

"This isn't easy, but it has to be done," said Janie, who was now sat opposite Rory on the other armchair; they were separated by the coffee table. She took another large gulp of red wine.

"I want a divorce. I've met someone else," she said and took another mouthful of wine.

Rory tried to take in this information. Somehow it was starting to make sense; the reason for her behaviour in recent weeks. She sat nervously waiting for his response, unsure of his reaction.

"Are you sure?" was all he said.

"Yes," she replied.

Rory looked down on the floor, knowing he was in no position to take any moral high-ground.

"Is this something we can work out?" he asked.

"No, it's too late for that."

"What about the boys?"

"You can have as much access as you want. I would never stop you from seeing our sons," she said quickly; a statement she had obviously rehearsed.

Rory sat totally emotionless; Janie was beginning to worry.

"Ok, if there is nothing left, there's not much I can do is there?" he said in measured tones.

"I'm sorry," said Janie, and she took another mouthful of wine.

She got up and went back to the kitchen for a refill and came back to the lounge. Rory was sat with his head in his hands trying to assimilate everything, thinking through the implications.

"So how do we do this then? How do we tell the boys, everyone?"

"I don't know," said Janie, "I've never done this before."

Rory got up and, for a split second, Janie thought he was going to hurt her, but he just walked past into the kitchen and poured himself the remainder of the bottle.

He returned to the lounge with his glass.

"So, what's going to happen, you moving in with him? I assume it's a 'him'."

"Tomorrow. I'll collect some things after the boys have gone to school," she replied, ignoring the snide innuendo.

"And what about the boys? You're just going to take them to a new home, just like that?"

"Unless you can think of a better idea… Geoff's got his own

place."

She paused, realising she had dropped in a name which she hadn't intended. She was waiting anxiously for a reaction; there was none.

"You can't look after them, not with your job."

Rory was still trying to take everything in. Despite the events of the last couple of days, this had hit him badly. His boys meant everything to him, but of course she was right.

"Geoff...? He's the one you've been with I assume."

"Yes," she replied.

"And he's going to take over looking after my boys... is that how it works...? Is that it?" he said, looking down at his hands.

"No... No, not in the way you're suggesting... You'll always be their Dad, and you'll be able to see them at the weekends when you're on-shore."

"You've got this all worked out, haven't you... you and... Geoff?" he said, making eye contact again.

"No, not really... no, just trying to be practical," she replied.

"Practical?" he cut her off, his voice raised for the first time.

"Yes, the boys have to come first. They need some stability... Let's face it you're never here."

"It's my job, it's what pays for all this," he said, looking around the room.

There was an uneasy silence.

Rory got up and went to the hallway and took his jacket from its peg from behind the door.

Janie stood up, but, with the wine having taken effect, she sat back down again. Her speech was slurred.

"That's it, run away. It's what you always do isn't it? You're always running away. I can't get through to you. You're like, like, like a... a tortoise. When something goes wrong you go into your shell and won't come out again until it's gone away. But not this time, we need to talk this through and make it work, for the boys."

Rory took his keys from the table by the front door and left; the door slammed behind him.

"Damn," said Janie.

Then she just sat in the armchair for a moment, took another sip of her wine before reaching in her handbag for her phone.

"Geoff?" she said.

Rory got in his car and headed out of the drive and onto the main road. He checked his petrol, the tank was half full, two hundred and three miles it said on the indicator. Enough to get to Edinburgh and back if he wanted.

He pulled into the pub car park just up the road from his house to take stock, not really sure of what he wanted to do. He was used to being in control and able to overcome any emotional turmoil; it had been part of his conditioning, but for the first time in his life he felt he needed help, someone to talk to. He took his phone from his jacket pocket; it needed charging but there was enough for this call.

"Kim...? Rory, are you free? Is it ok to come over...? Thanks... yeah, twenty minutes. I'll tell you when I get there." He left the car park and headed for Kim's.

It was turned eight o'clock when he pulled into the drive.

He pressed the buzzer on the front door and it clicked open. He made his way to Flat 3. Kim was dressed casually in jeans and a sloppy top.

"Whatever's the matter?" she said as she let him in. "I've been worried sick... Janie's not found out, has she?"

Rory ignored the question and sat down on the sofa.

"Are you ok? Do you want a drink?"

"In a minute... Look, sorry to show up like this, but I didn't know where else to turn."

"That's ok, what is it?" she said. "Hang on…"

She went into the kitchen and returned with a bottle of red wine and two glasses.

Rory was sat with his head in his hands trying to arrange his thoughts into some semblance of order. He looked up as she handed him a glass and he took it from her and started to speak.

"This may sound strange after today, but after Janie had put the boys to bed, she just calmly announced that she is leaving me for another guy."

It was Kim who was now wrestling with emotions.

"I'm sorry… I don't know what to say."

"There's nothing to say… Things haven't been good for some time, a couple of months probably. I knew something wasn't right. But I never suspected anything… It just goes to show… Then today and yesterday have been so…"

He tried to think of the right words but couldn't come close. "I don't know… unexpected, I suppose."

"Yes, I know what you mean," she said.

There was a long pause. Then Kim got up and sat on the sofa next to him. "What are you going to do?"

"I don't know… There's not much I can do. She's made her mind up and she's moving out tomorrow and taking the boys with her."

"I'm sorry," she repeated.

"That's the thing… I don't know whether I am. The truth is, over the last couple of days, I haven't been able to think about anything else but you… If I'm really honest, I don't feel anything. I'll just let her go… It's the boys I'm really worried about. I don't know how they'll take it."

Kim moved to Rory and held his hand.

"Boys tend to be pretty resilient, I'm sure they'll be ok. You'll get access, won't you?"

"Yeah, Janie says I'll be able see them when I'm on-shore… It makes sense; I couldn't look after them."

Kim watched him and could see he was in turmoil.

"Do you want to stay?" she asked.

This was a question that strangely he had not anticipated, and he paused before answering.

"No pressure," she said quickly, sensing his uncertainty.

"Oh, no, it's not that… Yeah, I want to stay, if that's ok… but my head's all over the fucking place."

"That's ok," she said.

"I'll need to text Janie. She may be concerned," he said.

"Yes, you should do that," she replied.

Kim went into the kitchen and opened another bottle of wine.

Rory checked his phone, three missed calls and a text. *"Just let me know U are ok,"* it said.

He texted back, "Staying with a friend will be back in morning."

"I don't have any stuff with me," he said.

"That's ok, I have a spare toothbrush somewhere," she said, handing him a glass of wine.

They sat up until gone midnight and consumed the rest of the bottle and half another before Kim suggested they turned in. The wine had made Rory more morose and there were long periods of silence as he mulled over his situation.

Kim, for the most part, listened as she had been trained to do; she had wide experience as acting as counsellor to members of staff with personal issues.

This time as they lay together there was no sex; drink and

general fatigue had taken its toll. Rory soon drifted into a deep sleep, but his demons which had lain dormant for a long time, resurfaced. Suddenly, he was transported back to Iraq. He could taste the cordite from his rifle, smell the stench of death. He woke sweating and panting heavily.

Kim also woke and gently stroked his head. "Sshhh, it's ok, it's ok," she said, and gradually he went back to sleep.

The following morning, Rory was awake early and was momentarily disorientated as he looked around the unfamiliar bedroom. The large mirrored wardrobe, the curtains, the duvet, even the bed itself were alien, and he had to readjust his senses to his new environment. Kim stirred and opened her eyes and saw Rory sat up in bed.

"You ok?" she said, sleepily and put her arms around his waist her head face down in her pillow.

"Yeah, just getting my head together. How much did we drink last night?"

"Too much… I'll make us some tea in a bit," and she tugged his arm to get him to lie back down.

She turned over and cuddled up to his back.

"You were having nightmares last night," she said. "Who's Lennie?"

"He was a buddy in Iraq, got killed," Rory replied.

"I'm sorry, didn't mean to pry."

"No, it's ok. I just don't tend to talk about it."

"In that case I'm going to get us a cup of tea. Can't have you maudlin about. You've got issues to sort out," and she pulled back the bedclothes.

He watched her wrap her kimono around her before making her way to the bathroom.

Rory liked her straightforwardness and it was an antidote to his self-pity and he snapped out of his ruminations.

There were certainly issues to sort out and after a cup of tea and slice of toast; he left Kim to go back to his house to face Janie.

Chapter Thirteen

Friday morning, Rory felt anxious as he made his way back to the house. Janie's car was parked in the drive; it was gone nine o'clock and the two boys, he assumed, had been dropped off at school. Rory parked up and noticed her car was full of boxes and cases.

Before he reached the door, Janie was there standing on the step.

"Where have you been...? I've worried sick?"

"Didn't you get my text?" he said sharply.

"Yes but..." she didn't finish the sentence.

He walked past her into the kitchen and put his keys on the work top, plugged in the kettle and turned it on. Janie was by the kitchen door watching.

"Are you ok?" she said.

Rory looked around. "Yeah... I guess," he replied, still with an edge.

Janie walked towards him and, for a moment, he thought she was going to hug him, but instead went past and took out two mugs from the cupboard.

"I'll join you, if you're making coffee."

Rory poured the water into the mugs and spooned in the instant then handed Janie a mug.

"Thanks," she said.

"So, when are you going?"

"Soon, I was waiting for you to come back."

"And you'll be picking the boys up and taking them with you after school."

"Yes," she said.

Rory stared into his coffee trying to come to terms with

everything.

"And there's nothing I can do to stop this?"

She was now staring into her mug of coffee.

"I'm sorry... it's too late for reconciliations. I just don't feel the same anymore. You've shut me out for too long."

Rory thought about this and realised she was right. "Why didn't you say something before?"

"Would it have made any difference...? You wouldn't have changed. You were, no, are, still locked in some sort of time warp. It's as though you never left the army. I don't think you're capable of giving affection."

He thought about this and could understand.

"Why are we having this conversation now? You could have said something before."

"I tried, lots of times I tried, but you were always preoccupied when you came home. It's as though your whole world is out there in the North Sea or back in the desert somewhere."

Rory drained the last of the coffee.

"So, what's the process? I assume you'll have worked out everything. How am I going to see my boys?"

Janie put her mug down on the worktop.

"You can ring me when you get back from the rig and we can discuss you picking them up."

Rory thought for a moment and took in the comment.

"What about the house...? I can't afford the mortgage and pay you maintenance... I assume you'll want maintenance?"

"Only for the boys. I intend to keep working." She paused and took a drink. "I suppose we'll need to sell it and split the equity... I'll need to speak to a solicitor."

"That's going to cost a fortune. It'll be better if we can sort out as much as possible without their interference."

"Yes, ok, as long as we can agree."

"I don't want to fight. I just need enough to start again and be able to live."

"I'll work out some figures and let you have them... Look, I'm going to have to go."

"What about the rest of the stuff?"

"I'll call in again tomorrow and collect some more... there are a lot of the boys' bits and bobs I'll need to get."

"Got a big house has he, this... Geoff?"

"It will do for now," she replied, without being drawn into a possible argument.

Janie picked up her car keys and went to the front door. She paused before opening it and looked at Rory who was looking quite forlorn in the kitchen doorway and for a moment she felt some sympathy and sadness.

"I'm sorry, Rory," she said and turned around and left the house. He heard the sound of her car leaving the drive.

Rory went into the lounge and sat in his armchair. He noticed a child's toy car by the side of the settee and felt an emptiness washing over him. It wasn't just the rejection, but the loss of his 'life', his way of life anyway, that hurt.

Questions going through his head... his boys, how would they cope? Then there were the financial implications. He was earning a good wage, but living up to their means meant there was never anything left for savings and the mortgage payments were high. As he had said, there was no way he could afford them and maintenance. The house, which represented years of investment in time and attention, would have to be sold. Where would he live? What about all the furniture? Only now was he beginning to take in the implications.

Beep... a text.

"How R things? Ring when you can K x"

He snapped out of his contemplation and phoned.

"Hi. Yeah, ok I guess... no, she's gone. Yeah, that would be good. I need to sort some stuff out here... I don't know, lunchtime...? Ok. I'll be there about one-ish," and he rang off.

He put his phone in his pocket and went upstairs. The wardrobe had been completely cleared and it was just his trousers, shirts and jackets that were hanging there. He went to the boys' room and all their clothes and favourite things had gone, but there were plenty of less-played-with toys in the bottom of their cupboard.

He looked at their bunk bed and the children's quilts, the picture of Aberdeen football club on the wall, which Mattie had just begun to follow with his best school pals. Rory had promised to take him to a game one day, but had been too busy; he always said that. Now things were different he would make sure he would take him to a game, maybe the next one. He would make enquiries.

The bathroom looked strange; no make-up or toothpaste tubes squeezed half-way down, lying on the edge of the bath, and no children's toothbrushes, empty. He walked back down stairs.

There were some practical things he would have to deal with. The bank, that would be ok; he and Janie had separate accounts, but, until the house was sold, he may need some financial support. He couldn't handle it at the moment; he would be ok this month; he would deal with it on his next shore leave.

By midday, he'd had enough of the house. Somehow it didn't feel like 'home' anymore; just bricks and mortar and 'stuff'. He locked up and headed to Kim's.

As he drove, he thought of Kim; she was not really in the equation, yet. Where was that going? Was that his exit route, his way forward? It had certainly cushioned the blow of the break-up of his marriage, but it was far too early. He had not thought of her as a permanent arrangement, in fact he'd just gone along for the ride. She was, or appeared to be at least, a free spirit, and he wasn't sure whether she was looking for anything other than a casual relationship.

She was waiting for him as he reached the door in her blue jeans and tee shirt; she let him in.

"Are you ok?" she said, and kissed him on the cheek in an affectionate way; then led him into the lounge.

"Yeah, I guess. Just trying to get my head round it all."

"Would you like a coffee, tea or something stronger?" she said, as she went into the kitchen.

"Tea will be fine, thanks."

He went to join her and sat on one of the stools at the breakfast bar and watched her as she boiled the kettle. She went to him and kissed him warmly.

"Thanks," he said.

"What for?"

"For being there," he said.

"That's ok. I was concerned."

"I know, and I owe you, big time."

"No, you don't," she said, as she poured the teas. "I'm just glad I was here for you."

She handed a mug to Rory, and looked at him with her blue eyes.

"And if it's any consolation, I really want you in my life... There I've said it."

Rory thought about that for a moment.

"Really?"

"Yes. These last two days have been amazing, very special...

I never want it to end."

Kim finished her tea.

"I know, let's go out. Come on, we can find a pub, get something to eat. It'll do you good."

Kim had a knack of saying the right things at the right time.

"Yeah, good call," he replied, and he finished his tea and put the mug on the draining-board.

Kim went to the bedroom and came back a few minutes later having freshened up and wearing a leather jacket.

"I'll drive," she said, and twenty minutes later they were sat at the bar of the Ship Inn down on the Esplanade on adjoining stools drinking an orange juice and mineral water. The journey had been relatively silent until they had found a suitable hostelry; Rory was still brooding.

Sitting there on neutral territory made the conversation easier somehow, and Kim recognised she needed to engage Rory if she was going to hold onto the fledgling relationship.

"When do you have to go back, off-shore I mean?"

Rory looked up from his drink. "A week on Monday."

"So, I think we need to make the most of that time, don't you?"

She looked at him and a frisson ran through his body like a reviving elixir. The magic had returned.

"Yeah, you're right. Time to move on."

She leant forward and took hold of his hand and smiled.

"Don't know about you, but I'm starving; fancy something to eat?" he said and picked up the bar menu.

"Yes, that would be good. What've they got?"

Rory read out the sandwich selection.

"Just a cheese salad on brown," she said.

Rory chose a tuna melt baguette and placed the order.

Ten minutes later they were tucking into their lunch; the conversation was more relaxed.

After they had eaten their food Kim looked at Rory.

"I tell you what," she said. "When we've finished here, you go back to yours and get some clothes, and I'll cook us something. You can stay over if you want."

"Yeah, ok, sounds great," he replied.

Later, Kim drove them back to her apartment for Rory to pick up his car.

Arriving back home, Rory was surprised to find a strange car on the drive; the front door of the house was open.

He walked up to the door just as a tall, youthful looking man appeared holding a box of his boys' things. He stopped in his tracks; Janie appeared and walked in front of him effectively blocking Rory from entering.

"Rory... I did try to call you. This is Geoff," she said.

Geoff looked suitably embarrassed and just nodded, not really knowing what to do or say. Rory just stared at him. Janie quickly intervened.

"Just came to pick up some of the boys' things. I did try to call," she repeated.

Rory just looked at them and barged past and went into the kitchen. Geoff continued to his car with the cardboard box and Janie joined Rory in the kitchen. He heard the car start up.

"Sorry about that, I didn't want a confrontation," said Janie.

Rory stood for a second pondering then looked at her.

"It's ok, just do what you have to do then get the fuck out," he said, and he walked into the kitchen.

The expletive came out of the blue, and unnerved Janie; she turned around, picked up two carrier bags which were by the front door and left the house without speaking.

Rory heard the car pull away. He sat at the kitchen table with his head in his hands.

He thought back to his time in the Regiment, and recalled one of the guys getting a 'dear John' letter from his wife while on duty in Basra. He went berserk, smashing up the canteen, throwing crockery and chairs around until a couple of the lads were able to subdue him, thankful that he wasn't near a rifle. He was put on charge then shipped back to the UK to sort 'his shit' out. He never returned to the Regiment.

Rory didn't feel like this. If he hadn't met Kim, though, things might have been very different.

He went upstairs to pack an overnight bag; how empty and quiet the house looked without the boys. They were always running around, so much energy. He went to the window and looked down at the goal net on the back lawn, the grass scuffed away in bare patches from all the activity. Most days when he was home he would kick a few balls at Mattie who would dramatically punch them away or dive on them like a real goalkeeper. Jason wanted to be a striker and loved scoring goals. Rory could see him running around with his arm raised excitedly when he had managed to get one past his brother. The next few weeks were going to be hard.

To keep busy he decided to do some washing, not his normal domain, but he'd looked after himself before and knew the routine. By five o'clock, he had finished the chores. He showered and changed, then headed back to Kim's apartment, pleased to be away.

He drew up to the drive and rang the buzzer. The door was open, Kim was waiting for him dressed in her Kimono with a glass of red wine.

"Thought you might need this," she said, holding it out to

him.

He took the glass and leant over and kissed her. He caught the fragrance of her perfume.

"Mmm, you smell nice."

He stood back and admired the view. "And you look even better."

"Come through. Dinner won't be long, drop your bag in the bedroom. I'll be in the kitchen."

Rory stowed his holdall then joined Kim.

He sat on one of the kitchen chairs watching her stir something in a wok which smelled delicious.

"Thai stir fry with chicken and ginger," she said lifting the spoon from the mix and taking a taste. She picked up her glass and joined Rory at the table.

"So, how's it been?"

Rory told her about Janie and her new boyfriend when he'd returned to the house.

"How did you feel about that?"

"I'm ok now... it was a bit of a shock at the time."

"Good," she said, 'Because I'm going to take your mind off things," and she gave him a look that said more than any words.

"Great," said Rory.

He got up to and wrapped his arms round her as she stirred the wok. She pulled away.

"No, you sit down, or you won't get any dinner," she admonished playfully.

"Look but don't touch," and she pulled open her Kimono to reveal a black lacy bra and panties.

Rory nearly spilt his wine; cooking was never this much fun. After a few minutes dinner was ready and Kim ushered Rory to the dining room table where a candle was burning.

"Hey, this looks good, thanks."

"As I said, I'm going to take your mind off things tonight," and she put the stir fry into a bowl and placed it in the centre of the table next to a bowl of boiled jasmine rice.

"Help yourself," she said, and Rory spooned a portion of chicken and ginger with some rice onto his plate. Kim watched in satisfaction. They chatted while they ate.

"That was fantastic," said Rory, after clearing his dish.

He finished his wine and Kim took the empty dishes to the kitchen then returned with two bowls of diced pineapple and a carton of fresh cream.

"Its ages since I've had pineapple," he said.

"I hoped you would like it," she said, and placed a bowl in front of him then kissed him passionately.

As she was stood over him her kimono gaped open revealing her lingerie. He rubbed his hand up the back of her legs and started to massage her bottom. She broke away.

"Not yet," she said.

Rory smiled at her. "You're cruel you know."

"It'll be worth it," she said.

They started eating their desert and Kim looked at Rory, a long, long look. She put down her spoon and dropped her kimono from her shoulders and unclipped then removed her bra, then draped her kimono back on.

"God, you're incredible," said Rory, her breasts seemingly trying to escape the confines of their covering; he was now struggling to finish his pineapple.

"Coffee?" she asked after the dessert was finished. "Or would you like another glass of wine?"

"A top up," said Rory offering his wine glass. "Coffee later," and she leant over him again refilling his glass with an

Australian Cabinet Sauvignon.

This time she made no attempt to escape as he ran his hands back up her legs and she grabbed his arm and took him to the sofa.

It was slow and sensual; Kim had called it just right. He was desperate for her; and she for him. She removed her kimono and the two of them revelled in each other's bodies until they were both spent.

As they lay together in the warm glow of the artificial coal fire, it was a reflective moment, each in their own thoughts. It was Rory who spoke first.

"What are you thinking?"

"I was just thinking how quickly things have moved. It's never been like this with anyone."

She rested her head on his shoulder and stared into the flickering light.

Rory too was struggling to come to terms with events; his marriage had broken down, his wife and children now with another man, but suddenly he found himself in a passionate, physical relationship which at the moment was all consuming. Kim had already taken away much of the hurt.

"I don't know what I would have done without you," he said.

"I'm just glad I was here."

That night curled up together Rory slept well; it was as though his ghosts had been exorcised.

The following morning, Rory left Kim's early, around nine o'clock. He needed to speak to Janie about seeing the boys. He let himself in. The house felt cold; he hadn't bothered turning on the central heating. He went upstairs and raised the thermostat on the heating to warm the house through and made a call to Janie's mobile.

"Janie? Rory, I'm phoning to see the boys." There was a pause. "What do you mean I can't see them? I'm their Dad. We agreed."

He listened to her reasoning.

"Not settling down? What do you expect?" he said, getting quite animated. "Well, when then? Next week...? But I'm back off-shore on the Monday... That means it'll be another fortnight before I can see them."

Janie kept apologising but was not backing down, and, of course, Rory didn't know where Geoff lived, so he couldn't turn up unannounced. After more heated exchanges Janie hung up.

The thought of not seeing his boys for another week was agony, but after he'd calmed down and thought about it rationally; she was probably right. She wasn't coming back, and it would be wrong to keep bouncing the boys backwards and forwards, they would never settle, and, for now at least, their welfare was priority.

He phoned Kim and explained what had happened. She listened closely.

"Fancy going out tonight...?" he said. "I don't know, get a bite to eat or something, my treat... Yeah, great. What time? Ok I'll see you at six, and I'll phone around and find somewhere nice."

Rory decided to have a clear out and took some bin bags from the kitchen drawer. He went upstairs and started rummaging through the cupboards and drawers and filled up two bags with Janie's stuff. He found an old photo album and flicked through; fading pictures of their wedding, the boys' christenings; pictures of Janie's parents and his mother, sadly deceased.

He felt angry for the first time and he threw the album across the room hitting the wall on the other side and dropping to the floor in pieces. His heart rate had increased and he realised that this was not a productive exercise; he was not in the right frame of mind for this duty. He wondered whether to call Janie's parents and sister, but he reasoned she would have already done this. He wouldn't know what to say, in any case.

A little later, around midday, Janie's father did ring to express his sadness. Rory didn't know what to say and just thanked him for calling.

As on the previous day, by four-thirty the house was closing in on him, and he was pleased that he had arranged to see Kim. He showered and changed then headed back to her apartment and she was waiting in her casual jacket and jeans. She had been waiting by the entrance. He thought how great she looked as she walked to the car. She got in and leaned over and kissed him.

"Italian ok?" he asked as he pulled away.

"Yeah great," she said putting on her seat belt.

"You look great, by the way."

"Thank you," she said.

Rory drove off into town to a Pizza chain.

It was another great night and Rory was learning more about his new girlfriend. In turn he was beginning to open up, and told Kim some of his, more light-hearted, experiences in the army. He did not of course reveal that he was in the Regiment or any details of the action he had seen. Mostly it was about the friendships he had made and what had happened to his former comrades.

The relationship continued to develop, and again he stayed the night. Sunday, he took Kim out to the hills, where he had regularly found solace in the bleak, windswept landscape. With

Kim working on Monday, Rory suggested he would return home, and offered to cook a meal for her that evening, if she fancied coming over to the house.

"I've a better idea," she said.

She went to her purse and produced a spare set of house keys.

"Here, have these... You can cook here if you like."

Rory was taken aback.

"Are you sure?" he said, looking at the keys.

"Yes, of course, if you don't mind getting the food in... I won't have time to get to the shops; it'll be pretty hectic having been a way for a week. It'll take me most of the morning to clear my emails."

"Yeah, ok, that'll be great."

Kim showed him where the various cooking utensils were and the code number for the front door. Rory eventually left for his house around ten o'clock.

He was beginning to realise that Kim was getting to him in a big way. She was interesting and importantly, interested in him, funny and very down to earth, and, despite the twelve years age difference, he was really in tune with her; he missed her already.

The house was empty and cold, devoid of any homeliness and he switched on the TV, for company as much as anything. He sat in his armchair and watched it until he eventually fell asleep in his chair.

He woke up around two o'clock, an old black and white film was playing. He turned off the TV, went to the kitchen to get a glass of water, then made his way to bed.

The following day, Rory received a text around eleven o'clock.

'Hi, miss you, hope you're ok. Work's manic. See you at 6

Kim xx'

He texted back. *"Everything is good, promise not to burn the place down. See you later."*

Rory went into town and did some shopping, not just for the meal, but for himself. He had cancelled the milk delivery and there were few provisions in; he needed to stock up. By late afternoon he had cleaned and showered. before he left for Kim's apartment, he called Janie on her mobile. It was gone four and he assumed she would have picked them up from school.

"It's Rory. Can I speak to the boys please...? Yes, I know they'll be busy, but I want to speak to them... please."

She relented, and it was Mattie who came to the phone.

"Dad! Dad! We're having a great time. Geoff took us to Pittodrie on Saturday. It was brilliant, he's got a season ticket. We won, one nil against St Mirren," he said excitedly.

Rory was devastated but tried to play down the hurt. Then Jason came on the phone equally effusive. They were obviously settling down just fine. After a couple of minutes, he couldn't take anymore, and told them he had to go. He had a brief word with Janie about further contact, then rang off.

The call had caused a lot of pain and he did not know whether he would phone again before the weekend or not; the hurt was too raw.

A few minutes later, he left the house and made his way back to Kim's apartment. He let himself in and went into the kitchen. The flat was warm and cosy, in contrast to the weather, which was wild and stormy; much like the way Rory felt.

The cooking proved to be a therapy; he remembered Kim's earlier offering and decided on an Italian chicken dish with pasta.

At just before six there was a rattling of keys and Kim walked in with her briefcase and laptop. She hung her coat up on the pegs by the door and went to the kitchen to join Rory. She was dressed in a smart business suit.

"Hi. How was your day?" he asked, as she walked over to him and kissed him.

"Hectic. Hmm, something smells good," she said, walking over and looking at the mixture in the pan.

"Ready in twenty minutes," he said, giving it another stir.

"I'll just take a shower and change," she said and went to the bedroom.

Refreshed and reinvigorated she returned to the kitchen just as Rory was straining the pasta.

"You find everything ok?"

"Yeah thanks, no problem. You're very well organised."

"Have to be, the only way I can cope."

She picked up the carrier bag she had brought with her and produced a bottle of wine.

"Here, I got us a bottle of red," she said, and went to the cupboard for two glasses.

"Great," he said.

Rory dished up the meal and they sat down opposite each other on the small table.

"So how was your day?"

"Busy, busy," she said, emphasising the point. "I've got a bit of news for you. There's a new graduate intern starting on the rig next week. I've suggested you could buddy him. What do you think?"

"Yeah, fine by me. What's his name?"

"Tariq, Tariq Siddique, he's on a gap year from Leeds University, comes from your old stomping grounds I think, Basra."

Chapter Fourteen

October 2004, British Military HQ, Basra Palace, Iraq.

Two weeks after Tariq started his further education at University in Leeds, two visitors, wearing the traditional simple hijab gowns, walked across the bridge that led to the heavily fortified main gates of the British Military HQ. The Basra Palace, which housed the military headquarters, was formerly a home of Saddam Hussein, and over five thousand, five hundred troops were based there. On the banks of the Shat al Arab River, it is an impressive building and ideally suited for its purpose. The men walked up to a guard post and asked to see the commanding officer.

"Who wants to know?" replied the guard, dressed in full Kevlar body armour and carrying a rifle. It was twenty-nine degrees and there were sweat stains under his arms.

One of the men spoke.

"I am Mohammed Al Baqir al-Hakim, this is Salim; his father was Ibn Hajar Al-asqulani who was killed by British soldiers two months ago. He has some information."

The two were thoroughly and roughly searched by two more guards who had joined their colleague.

"Wait here," said the soldier and he went into a guard house and picked up a telephone.

He returned moments later, and the two men were escorted deep inside the building where they were greeted by Major Howard and two uniformed Iraqi's. They were taken to an empty room, bare plaster walls with a single table in the middle surrounded by six chairs. There was a small window high up in the far wall which did not let in sufficient light to avoid using an artificial source; a solitary bulb hung from the ceiling casting a stark glare across the room. Flying insects immediately started buzzing around the light. The atmosphere was hot and stuffy, and an acrid smell hung in the air.

The sight of the two Iraqi's made the visitors anxious; memories of Saddam's henchmen were too recent. The major recognised this and attempted to put the two men at their ease.

"Sit down won't you," he said, pointing to the chairs on the opposite side of the table.

The Iraqi officers also sat down, but slightly behind the major. The wooden chairs made uncomfortable scraping noises   on the floor as they were dragged into place.

"I understand you have some information... Is this about the car bombings earlier this year?"

The major addressed the pair who looked anxiously at each other; one of them nodded.

The major continued. "I should mention the matter is now in the hands of the local police. This is Inspector Malik and Sergeant Uday… but we are of course supporting them in their investigations."

The introductions did nothing to ease the two men's concerns, and they were beginning to regret their decision to go to the British compound. Mohammed looked at Salim again and spoke to him in Arabic. "This is for your father remember, my friend," and his companion looked down and nodded.

Mohammed addressed the major. "This is Salim; his father was Ibn Hajar Al-asqulani."

The major showed no emotion, but encouraged the man to continue. "Go on."

"His father was shot in his house by British troops."

"Yes," replied the major, "I recall the incident."

"We know exactly what happened," said Mohammed, looking

at Salim.

"How do you know this?" asked the major.

Mohammed spoke to Salim in Arabic and he responded at length. Mohammed translated for the major. "Salim says he was there... He was sat at his table eating with his father when there was a phone call to warn him that soldiers were coming."

The major looked on, his interest total. "Go on," he said again.

Mohammed continued. "Salim says that the caller told his father not to be taken alive."

Salim spoke again to Mohammed. "He says his father ordered him leave the house... that the soldiers were coming."

The major looked at Salim. "What happened next?"

Mohammed continued his translation. "Salim says that instead of going outside, he went upstairs, and was hiding in the bedroom. He heard everything. When the soldiers came, his father fired at them then the soldiers fired back and killed him."

"We know all this," said the major.

Salim spoke again, and Mohammed translated.

"He says his father was betrayed by others who were far more involved than he was. He says his father was forced to hide the shuhada, the martyrs, who drove the trucks that killed the innocents. He says it has brought shame on his family."

The major looked at the policemen, then back at the visitors.

"Explain, why was he forced? Who forced him?" said the major.

Mohammed spoke to Salim again and Mohammed translated.

"He says it was the Mullah... He told Salim's father it was every Muslim's duty to support the Jihad and force the infidels from Iraq. It was he who called to warn my father."

To the untrained ear Arabic seems an urgent language which somehow added to the tension of the moment. Salim was now quite animated and spoke quickly to Mohammed who again translated.

"He says his father housed the martyrs for many weeks, Salim saw them hidden in a back room which he and his sisters were not allowed to enter, but the Mullah visited regularly to check on them and gave his father money to buy food for them. They left on a truck the day before the explosions."

"Who is this Mullah you keep referring to?" asked the major.

Salim understood and looked at the major and said, "Abu Hanifa."

The major put down his pen and looked at the two men in front of him.

"Abu Hanifa? From the Sa'ad Al Ibn Abi Waqas mosque?" he clarified.

"Yes," said Salim.

The major's eyes looked down appearing to focus on the table and his brow furrowed as he considered this information. He quizzed the visitors more closely.

"Tell me, why have you waited until now to say anything?" asked the major.

Mohammed spoke to Salim and then translated.

"He said he was too frightened. Abu Hanifa has some powerful and dangerous friends, but recently the Mullah, my friend says, has renounced violence, and now it seems as if Salim's father died for nothing."

Mohammed looked at Salim then at the major.

"He blames Abu Hanifa and wants to avenge his father's death."

The interrogation lasted another hour with Salim providing more information on the number of martyrs who were at his house, how they were fed, details of other visitors where they were housed and so on. When Salim mentioned the name Zarqawi it had everyone's attention.

"Zarqawi?" clarified the major.

Salim nodded, and the major made notes as details of the sighting were revealed. Zarqawi was by this time suspected of major atrocities across Iraq and was a wanted man by the UK, USA and Iraqi authorities.

When he had got all the information, the major thanked the men and led them from the room followed by the Iraqi officers.

As this was now ostensibly a police investigation, the major discussed the implications of the information with the two officers. It was agreed that the Mullah should be brought in for questioning. The major was keen to know more about the Zarqawi connection.

The next day a convoy of Iraqi police turned up at Abu Hanifa's house at six o'clock when the family was sleeping. It was still dark as they broke down the door and went through the house until they found the mullah and dragged him from his bed. His wife was screaming at them asking what did they want with him. He was handcuffed and man-handled into an awaiting car which sped off down the deserted streets in a cloud of dust, followed by a truck of armed officers.

Abu Hanifa was taken to the National Iraqi Intelligence Agency detention facility in central Basra, a place with an awesome reputation for cruelty under the Saddam regime.

He was bundled through a back entrance and immediately secured in a cell. What happened next is uncertain, but the official version was that when they came back later to interrogate him they found him dead on the floor; apparently, he had had a heart attack. Other, considered reliable, witnesses said he died under torture; the truth will never be known for certain.

His wife was informed, and his body released immediately for burial in accordance with Muslim practice.

October 2004, Batley, West Yorkshire.

It was Monday and just turned eight o'clock in the evening, the start of his third week at University and Tariq Siddique was at his uncle's house. He had taken a break from reading the Quran, and was in his room on his laptop 'chatting' on a website to a like-minded Muslim in Luton.

Tariq was finding it difficult to adapt to the different culture; in his own mind, everywhere there was corruption and violation of the laws of Allah. He needed to be around people with whom he could identify, share a common bond. Even his own family had deserted the faith, despite his warnings of eternal damnation. He had given up any hope of trying to convert his cousins; they were too far indoctrinated he had decided.

Since his arrival in the UK he had spent most of his spare time at the Masjid where he felt more comfortable and secure speaking to other Muslims and trading ideology with the Imam who had become his closest friend and confidante.

In the relatively short time he had been at the University, Tariq had found the course undemanding; each member of the twelve in his syndicate were at different stages of learning and experience, and the tutor was making sure that there was an equalisation before moving into new areas of study. The language had not been a problem; other members of his group were only too keen to help where any clarification was necessary.

It was a diverse group with one called Wang Li, who came from Wakefield, but was of Chinese extraction, and a West

Indian with the unusual name of Brenton Livingstone; the rest were English from various places across the UK. He was pleased initially to find he was not the only Muslim in his year. However the other, a girl from Bradford, had refused to wear the veil and Tariq would have nothing to do with her. Like Tariq, the students were on sandwich programmes, where the course would be a mix of study and work placement with their sponsoring company. A variety of organisations were involved, but Tariq was the only one supported by Petronix.

During his second week, he had been visited at the University by the Petronix graduate co-ordinator from the company's HQ. She was keen to know more about him, how he was settling in with accommodation and so on. She was also able to give him full details of the programme.

The four-year course would include a year working for the company, and he was given a number of options from which to choose. There was also the possibility of working during the long summer holiday to gain valuable experience.

The co-ordinator spelled out possible choices. There was a chemical division with a huge complex on Teesside, and also opportunities to work on projects at one of the refineries at Milford Haven, but he had already made up his mind; he was adamant that he wanted to work offshore on one of the rigs.

This was not a common request, and one welcomed by the graduate team; succession planning for offshore staff was always a challenge and good quality engineers were essential. She was sure they could arrange it. Tariq was more than happy; a plan was forming in his mind, and this opportunity was exactly what he was seeking.

He would commence his placement at the end of his second year.

Today was the start of the Ramadan festival, and Tariq had begun the as-suam, the fast. He had started the day by eating a pre-dawn meal, the suhoor, and then declaring his intention to fast. Tradition required him to declare the niyyah, or oath, before his fast if it was to be deemed valid. In addition to fasting, as he had been taught, he would read the entire Quran during the period, and his studies, such as they were, would come second. He had questioned the mullah at the mosque about using a computer during Ramadan, but there seemed to be no opinion on the matter providing he wasn't accessing gambling or pornography. Stimulation of any kind is not permitted during Ramadan to allow total concentration on the word of God.

In the relatively short time he had been with them, the relationship with his uncle and his family had become strained. He had declined their many attempts to integrate him into the family and spent most of his time either in his room or at the mosque; he did not want to become 'unclean' with their interpretation of Islam. The boys had tried to get him to join them on their Friday night trip into Leeds to 'do the clubs'.

He had been introduced to Jake's girlfriend who was not only a non-Muslim, but white. He thought of her as a slut and made no attempt to hide his contempt. He was grateful for their kindness, but basically, he was just using the house as a base.

During the three weeks, the local mullah at the mosque had come to like Tariq and had taken him under his wing as his adopted father had done in Basra. At Tariq's request, he had supplied him with some website addresses which were aligned to the more devout ideology to which Tariq subscribed. They were not readily accessible on the large search engines. Through these websites Tariq had managed to link up with several other potential jihadists.

He had taken a break from his Quran reading to 'speak' with his latest contact, Majid Iqbal.

Majid Iqbal was an IT engineer working for a major software company in Luton and had built a private network through a virtual hosting arrangement. To further secure the network he had linked it to other servers around the world. It was untraceable he had assured Tariq.

He told Tariq he was part of a small group who were intent on taking the struggle direct to the kafirs.

They were originally part of a small sleeper cell run by Muhammed Naeer Noor Khan, but after his arrest whilst on a trip to Pakistan in August, they had split up and gone their separate ways. There had been no subsequent arrests and Majid was happy that he was not under any surveillance or suspicion.

He told Tariq that he and two friends were planning on using chemicals to produce homemade bombs for an ongoing project which they hoped to launch in 2005. There were various websites that gave full details on how to do this, but Majid wanted Tariq's views on the subject.

Having first-hand experience in these matters, Tariq would be able to provide some useful advice on storage and execution, but, bearing in mind the mullah's warning about security, Tariq was not revealing anything just yet, certainly not over the internet. Gaining trust was a priority, and he suggested a meeting to discuss issues to avoid any possible compromise. Majid said he would arrange it.

Strictly speaking even these conversations were not allowed during Ramadan, as Tariq was required to show compassion, generosity and mercy to others, exercising patience, and controlling anger. He justified it to himself on the grounds they were engaged in 'God's work'.

Sabeen called him. "It is time to eat, Tariq."

Tariq logged off and made his way downstairs. He was disappointed to see his cousins and Uncle were still at the Cash and Carry. There had been a heated debate the previous evening when Tariq had discovered that the family ignored Ramadan. Abdul explained that his work was to the benefit of the community and he could not afford the time to be involved with prayer and fasting. He needed food to give him the strength to do his work.

It was now starting to get dark and Sabeen had set a place for Tariq; she had eaten earlier. Tariq started the Iftar, the evening meal after the daily fast, in the customary way by the eating of three dates and drinking a glass of water which Sabeen had supplied. This was followed by the Maghrib prayer, which Tariq recited to himself. Sabeen bought in Tariq's meal just as the phone rang. She gave the food to Tariq and answered the phone.

Sabeen had to concentrate hard, it was not a good line and the caller was speaking quickly in Arabic. She handed the phone to Tariq who had yet to start his meal.

"It's your mother," she said.

He listened intently to his mother's voice and Sabeen watched his face turn from joy into one of great anguish. "What? How? When?"

His mother outlined how the police had come for his father and taken him away to the detention centre where he had died at the hands of British interrogators. This was the rumour that had been spread by the Iraqi authorities to deflect any criticism. Abu Hanifa was a powerful man and not without influence, and there was concern that his death might cause a problem for the local administration. The funeral had already taken place in accordance with Islamic laws, and his mother said that there was a great outpouring of grief in the community. His father was much loved.

Sabeen listened to Tariq's conversation and understood the gist of what had happened. After a few minutes he hung up and sat in his chair with his head in his hands not able to take in the content of the call. Eventually he composed himself sufficiently to explain to Sabeen what had happened.

"Dragged from our house while he was sleeping and taken to the prison in Basra... Then he was murdered by the British," he spat.

"I'm so sorry, Tariq."

She sat down next to him and spoke gently.

"What will you do, will you return to Basra?".

"No, I cannot... It is too dangerous... I might get arrested also."

"But why...? You have done nothing wrong."

"No... That is true, but it won't matter... They take innocent people and kill them... many times, I have seen this."

"No, that can't be true," said Sabeen.

Tariq looked at her. "Your television here does not tell the truth, only what the British want to hear."

Sabeen got up and went back to the kitchen to leave him on his own.

Tariq was in turmoil and decided to walk to the mosque to seek solace in the final prayers of the day, and to think. His meal had been left untouched.

There was one problem that was immediately apparent. How was he going to manage financially? His uncle had set up a bank account for him to receive his father's remittance, but he would not now receive money from Iraq and, somehow, he would have to find other ways of supporting himself during studies.

He reached the mosque and Abu Ebeida El-Ladashiri was just leaving the washing area when he saw Tariq. He greeted him warmly.

"Tariq, it is good to see you. Have you come to join us for isha'a?"

"Yes, but I need your counsel also."

"Of course," replied the mullah.

After completing the final prayers of the day, Tariq joined the Imam in his office and told him of the death of his father and the circumstances.

"Do you think you might be in danger?" asked the mullah.

"I don't know. I do not think so... My mother knows nothing of my father's work and still doesn't know why he was taken."

"Do you know...? Why he was taken?"

"Yes, I think so," said Tariq, but did not elaborate.

"Allah will give you strength to get through this," said the Mullah, not pressing for any more detail.

"My heart aches for revenge. I have so much pain, so much anger," replied Tariq.

"I understand, it is natural for you to feel this way, but it is the will of Allah, Allāhu Akbar," replied the mullah.

"Allāhu Akbar," Tariq repeated, God is great.

The mullah continued, recognising the intensity of Tariq's feelings.

"I am not sure what you are going to do Tariq, my friend, but I must counsel great caution. You will need to tread very carefully, ever since the bomb in Spain everywhere is on high alert."

Tariq was not aware of the Madrid train bombings which

had happened in March. It had not been widely covered in the Basra newspapers; the mullah gave him an outline. Tariq also did not tell the mullah of his recent internet conversations with his friend Majid Iqbal.

"There are many here who are sympathetic to the cause," said the mullah. "Have you heard of Imam Anwar al-Awlaki?"

He went to a metal filing cabinet behind him.

"No," Tariq replied.

He took out a small set of keys from his pocket and unlocked it. Tariq watched the mullah as he rummaged through several files.

The mullah pulled out some small pamphlets in Arabic and handed them to Tariq.

"He is an American, but born in Yemen... quite outspoken and wanted by a number of countries. It is rumoured that the Mossad are interested in him... He was in England until earlier this year, but has gone back to Yemen. He is still active and lecturing at a University there. He has made many speeches; you might want to read these."

He handed Tariq a number of small booklets.

"They are transcripts of some of his more recent addresses at the Masjid al-Tawhid mosque; that's in London."

The mullah closed the drawer and relocked it.

"I will read them with interest," said Tariq, who was starting to come to terms with the initial shock of his father's death. All he could feel was this searing anger.

It was a dreary night with intermittent rain and for once he wished for the shimmering heat of Basra. The walk back to the house was a chance to reflect. He let himself in and found all the family sat around the table in the living room.

Abdul was the first to speak. He got up from his chair and

went to Tariq. "I am so sorry to hear of your father's death," he said and hugged him as a favoured son.

Jake and Freddie got up and joined their father in attempting to console Tariq.

"Yeah, bad news," said Freddie.

"Thank you," said Tariq forlornly and after accepting their condolences in good grace he excused himself and went up to his room.

It was gone eleven, and Tariq wasn't in the least bit interested in sleeping. He opened his laptop and linked into his recent contact. He fired off a message.

"Please arrange meeting, we have much to discuss, Tariq."

The following day Tariq continued his Ramadan ritual and set off for the train to Leeds with his Quran in his briefcase to read on the journey. He said nothing to his colleagues about the death of his father. but his reticence in college had been noticed and Brenton was the first to offer his concerns.

"Hey Tariq, my man. You ok today? You don't seem to be wiv us bro. Know what I mean?"

Tariq just shrugged his shoulders "I'm ok," he said, and the enquirer left it at that.

That evening as soon as he returned from college he was upstairs on his laptop. There was a message in his inbox from Majid Iqbal.

'Can meet this Saturday in Leeds. Outside Queens Hotel two o'clock. Confirm Majid.'

Tariq felt a degree of elation. He had someone who not only shared his passion, but was also willing to sacrifice himself as a sahid to the cause if necessary.

He replied. *'Yes, see you there, Tariq.'*

Tariq passed the Queens Hotel every day; it is a famous

landmark in the centre of Leeds and close to the station.

That evening after the Iftar, Tariq made his usual walk to the mosque for evening prayers. The Imam was pleased to see Tariq and keen to know how he was. After the formalities were completed, he joined the mullah in his office as had become customary in recent days. Tariq wanted to raise a sensitive question and after discussing various matters he chose the right time and raised the enquiry.

"I have heard much on the question of martyrdom but what is your view?"

The mullah thought for a moment before replying, then looked at Tariq.

"I am sure you know there are many schools of thought on this. Suicide is haraam in Islam, not permitted, but, put simply, martyrdom is not suicide."

Tariq nodded at the distinction. "That is what I have been told. I wanted your wisdom."

"There has been much publicity and debate in the newspapers, but I share the Takfiri view. In my mind, and I am clear on this, the term 'suicide bomber' is a derogatory term invented in the West to try and describe what in Islam we call a Fedayeen or Sahid, a martyr. The motivation of the sahid isn't suicide; it is to kill infidels in battle and is rewarded in heaven."

The mullah paused allowing Tariq to consider this; then continued.

"In the holy Quran, Mohammed says, '*Let those fight in the way of Allah who sell the life of this world for the other. Whoso fighteth in the way of Allah, be he slain or be he victorious, on him. We shall bestow a vast reward'.*"

The mullah looked at Tariq and could clearly see the pain he was still suffering at the news of the death of his beloved father. He was concerned and spoke wisely.

"If this is a route you are thinking, I must counsel great caution, Tariq. You must consider the wider implications of any actions you might want to take. The struggle should not be a personal crusade of revenge but in the name of Allah... Allāhu Akbar."

Tariq repeated, "Allāhu Akbar."

"It should be part of the wider Jihad."

"Yes, I understand. Thank you for your wisdom I will pray to Allah for guidance. He will be my light," said Tariq.

Tariq walked back to the house with the words of the mullah resonating in his head.

Chapter Fifteen

Saturday October 22nd 2004, Basra, Iraq.

The Arabic morning edition of the *Al Manarah* newspaper, page 5, the headline read *'Bodies of two men identified'*. The article expanded. *'The bodies of two men found on waste ground in Al Azamiyah have been identified as Mohammed Al Baqir al-Hakim and Salim Hajar Al-asqulani. They had been tortured and beaten to death. The authorities are investigating.'*

At his uncle's house in Batley, Tariq was making his plans to visit Leeds to meet Majid Iqbal. It was seven o'clock and the sixth day of Ramadan and, once again, the morning ritual was carried out. This time Abdul joined Tariq at the dining table; he needed to talk to him. Tariq was, as usual, being non-communicative; not rude; his beliefs, particularly at this time, would not allow that, but just not forth-coming. It was as though he was continually pre-occupied.

His uncle looked at him and spoke.

"Tariq, I know your visit here has not been easy for you, and it has been difficult for you to get use to the ways here. I also understand that your father's death has affected you greatly, but I want you to know that the family love you dearly and will do all we can to help you."

Tariq looked up at these words. "Thank you," was all he said.

Abdul continued. "It was the same when I first arrived here, but I was determined to do all I could to build a life here for my family. It has not been easy. We have had many trials along the way, but Allah has been kind to us."

"What do you know of Allah? You have abandoned him," said Tariq with more venom than he probably intended.

Abdul stood up. "I have not abandoned him. He is here," he said animatedly, placing his hand on his heart. "You have no responsibility, you have only yourself to consider and can do as you please." His voice was raised. "I have to provide for my family, and, yes, the community who rely on me to provide food and things cheaply, so they can live, and for that we have to make compromises." He paused then added, "I am at peace with God. He is all seeing, and he knows what is in my heart. Because I don't go to the mosque or observe the holy Ramadan does not make me a bad person. In your world everything is black, or it is white, but life is not like that. Life is grey with decisions that have to be made… all the time. I do not get them right always, but I do what I can with a clear conscience and good heart."

Tariq was taken aback by his uncle's response, not just the passion and vehemence, but the clarity of thought and reasoning.

"I am sorry, uncle," said Tariq. "I mean no disrespect. It is not me who will judge you."

"That is true," said Abdul. "But as long you are here with us, you must show some respect also. Sabeen worries about you as she does about Yusuf and Jamal."

There was a long pause having made his point before Abdul spoke again. "Anyway, I have said my piece, but I do have an important question I want to raise with you."

Tariq looked up from his food in acknowledgement.

"I assume you will not be getting any money from Iraq now your father will not be able to provide. Have you thought how you will manage your course... financially, I mean?"

Tariq shook his head and looked down at the table; it was something that was worrying him greatly and was intending to speak to the mullah, not wishing to burden his family who were already providing him with food and shelter.

Abdul continued. "Well, I may have a solution," he said and sat down opposite his nephew.

"We desperately need some help at the Cash and Carry. Not in the store, with the computers. Jamal tells me you have a lot of knowledge. I need a new system to manage the stock and also build a new website using the internet to manage the orders, invoicing, everything. It is beyond me and Yusuf and Jamal do not have the time, also I need someone I can trust. I will pay you for your time and for maintaining it."

He paused, waiting for a reaction. Then added, "I know, you could be my IT manager. How does that sound?"

Tariq thought for a moment, but suddenly there was a feeling of relief, as if a weight had been lifted from his shoulders.

"But what about prayers," he said, bringing back a perspective.

"Well, we can manage that. You will not be working all the time. You will still be able to go to the masjid," replied Abdul. "We could agree on so many hours a week, work around your college time, and at weekends. I will pay you enough to buy your books and cover your travel plus some spending money."

In reality, Tariq hardly spent anything on himself; virtually all his money so far had gone on college expenses and course fees.

He thought about his uncle's offer and reasoned it must be Allah's will; a divine intervention to redress the pain he had felt at his father's death.

"Yes, thank you… That is very kind. That will be good. I will work for you." Tariq looked at his uncle. "You are right it is something that has worried me greatly."

As Tariq got up from his seat Abdul also rose and went across to embrace his nephew. A new understanding had started.

Later that morning, as Tariq rode the train to meet Majid Iqbal, he considered the conversation with his uncle earlier and tried to give it some spiritual meaning, putting it into context of his own understanding. He found it hard to reconcile his uncle's family as true Muslims. They did not observe Ramadan and as far as he could tell did not engage in prayers, certainly not in any outward display; so, two of the obligatory pillars of Islam were not practiced. In effect the scriptures would dictate that it would make them infidels, but for all that, did that mean they were evil people? He would give that some further thought and maybe gain the views of the mullah who seemed wise in such matters.

The train pulled into Leeds station about twenty minutes after leaving Batley. It was packed with shoppers heading for the retail delights that the City Centre emporia famously held. Tariq looked at the people; different from the commuters he rode with on college days. They were casually dressed, some outrageously so, Tariq looked at them with a degree of disdain; he felt angry that he had to share a train with these people. The reality was, he would prefer not to share the same planet.

He was early for his meeting with Majid Iqbal. His contact had given Tariq a description but with mobile phone numbers swapped they would ring each other at two o'clock, to be on the safe side.

With five minutes to go Tariq waited outside the front entrance of the hotel.

The Queens Hotel is a large building, and enjoys a prominent place on City Square in the heart of Leeds. The main loop road passes directly in front of it and, particularly on Saturday lunchtime, the traffic was incessant. Tariq's phone vibrated, and he answered it while looking around. Then Tariq spotted someone only yards walking towards him, a mobile phone at his ear. He was similarly dressed in the traditional simple white smock with a jacket over the top. They rang off, immediately recognising one another.

"Tariq?" enquired Majid.

"Majid?' responded Tariq and they shook each other's hands warmly.

"Where should we go?" asked Majid, "I don't know Leeds that well, but somewhere where there are no CCTV cameras; we can't be too careful."

Both were observing Ramadan, so they could not go for a coffee.

"Down by the river," replied Tariq. "Follow me."

The River Aire runs through Leeds and, by tunnels, under the station and it was only a short walk to the footpath that runs alongside the river. Majid walked beside Tariq until they came to a bench just before a bridge carrying a main road over the water. They sat down.

"It is good to meet you, I have enjoyed our discussions," said Majid.

"You too," said Tariq and the two began talking like long- lost brothers, comfortable as kindred spirits.

Majid was the same age as Tariq, and described his background, poor family, racially abused at school, 'rescued' by a friendly Imam and deeply committed to the Jihad cause.

Almost twelve months earlier, through the local mosque in Luton, he had been introduced to Muhammed Naeer Noor Khan, whom he described as an inspiration. Other potential Jihadists had also been recruited, including his friend Shehzad Tanweer. It was a small group, six in all, and had been discussing ways to blow up trains on the London Underground which they believed would cause economic as well as political problems for the Government.

In the summer, Muhammed Khan had gone to Lahore to visit relatives, and was arrested by the Pakistani police. Majid was alerted by the Imam, and the group decided to split up. Three had moved to Leeds and were living in Beeston. Majid had remained in Luton, but would be staying with them overnight.

"Why don't you join us? The brothers would be pleased to meet you, I have told them all about you. Stay for Iftar, and the isha'a if you like. Someone will drive you back to Batley. It's not far I think."

Tariq thought for a moment. "Yes, that would be good, I'd like that. I will just have to call my Uncle and tell him I will not be home until later."

Tariq took his phone from his jacket and called Abdul's number at the Cash and Carry. A receptionist answered and eventually managed to locate his uncle. Tariq explained he was meeting up with some college friends and would be joining them for Iftar and would see them later.

Abdul was initially surprised at the message, Tariq was not one to socialise, but then thought their talk earlier might have made an impression on his nephew and was encouraged by the call.

"That's fine, Tariq, I hope you have a good time. I will let Sabeen know. We will see you later."

The bus stop to Beeston was at the back of the station, a short walk away and as they approached the stop they stared at a crowd of at least twenty football supporters waiting for the bus adorned in scarves, banners and other Leeds United attire.

Majid put his hand across Tariq's chest. "Wait...! Cross over the road, quickly."

Too late, they had been spotted by the group and it started.

"Pakki... Pakki...Pakki," one of them shouted.

"Get back to fucking Pakki land," shouted another.

"Blown up any fucking trains?" said another.

"Kill the Pakki bastards," cried another, and so it went on, menacingly.

Tariq and Majid were now across the road and walking away from them, but, then, a number sixty-four double-decker bus came around the corner and stopped. Although this was the bus they would need, they decided to hang back and wait for another. The mob got in and it pulled away. Majid and Tariq just stared as the bus went past, faces at the windows contorted in hate, shouting more abuse which they could not hear.

"Football supporters," said Majid, as they turned around and headed back towards the bus stop. "Leeds must be playing at home today... It is like this in Luton. They are like animals."

"What do we do?" asked Tariq.

Majid took his phone from his pocket and checked the time, two thirty-eight.

"We should be ok now. The match usually starts at three, so there shouldn't be any more."

Tariq was more stunned than frightened; it had been his first experience of racial abuse.

Ten minutes later, another number sixty-four arrived, and the pair got on. Tariq was able to use his travel pass to Beeston, Majid paid the driver, and they sat downstairs trying to be as inconspicuous as possible. Thankfully there were only two football supporters on board, elderly men dressed in tweed herringbone overcoats and flat caps, white scarves visible; they and the other passengers took little notice.

Tariq and his friend sat in silence as they watched the drab inner-city buildings go by; a massage parlour, that had seen better days, extolling pleasure, incongruously; numerous takeaways, run-down shops then the football ground with thousands of people milling round.

Tariq reflected on the abuse; the hatred it seemed was reciprocal, something he hadn't considered. Perhaps this really was a war.

Another ten minutes, and they had arrived at their destination. They got off in Old Lane and walked a short distance to a street of non-descript Edwardian terraced houses, many in need of repair. It looked like a picture of the slums from the 1920's. Majid led the way, and, after about a hundred yards, turned down an alley between two blocks into a back yard. It was littered with rubbish, an over-flowing dustbin, the skeleton of an old pram, bottles, broken glass, and numerous wet cardboard boxes. A dog barked as Majid knocked on the back door of the house to the right.

A young man of Asian origin opened the door and invited the pair in. Like Tariq and Majid, he was dressed in the Ramadan smock. The door opened directly into the kitchen which looked in a similar state to the back yard, plates unwashed in the sink, opened tins of soup and other food, stale bread and cutlery of all description. There was an unpleasant smell.

Tariq looked around the room. There was an ancient cooker with congealed food resting neatly among the gas rings, an old fridge with opened boxes of cereals on top, and a wooden table with, what looked like, someone's dried leftovers on a plate. The wall-paper was peeling and there were black damp marks of mould in the corner of the ceiling and other stains which looked like water had leaked from an upstairs room at some time.

"Hi," said the host. "You must be Tariq. I am Mohammed Hussein. Welcome, come through, there are some friends who would like to meet you... Majid said he would see if you could join us."

Tariq nodded rather nervously and followed Mohammed past a flight of stairs into what was the living room. There were three other men; two sat on an old thread-bare sofa in the middle of the room, and one sat at a table against the wall to the left; all dressed in Ramadan smocks. Hazy sunshine struggled through the net curtains which hung limply at the window. The decor was as dour as the kitchen, with wallpaper, old and scraped, pealing in places.

Mohammed made the introductions.

"This is Hasib Tanweer," a youth of about eighteen with bright eyes and even brighter teeth. He smiled from the sofa and nodded to Tariq.

"He is my friend Shehzad's brother," said Majid.

"This is Milton Azeri," said Mohammed, pointing to an older man in his late twenties of West Indian origin with a shaved head and full beard; he was sat next to Hasib, Tariq acknowledged.

"And this is Amir Ali, who has recently returned from Pakistan," he said, and a tall man in his early twenties got up from his chair and bowed his head to Tariq and gave the traditional Arab greeting, "as-salamu `alaykum."

"Wa alaykum e-salam," replied Tariq.

As everyone was observing Ramadan, there would be no refreshments. Majid took over hosting duties and was clearly viewed as leader by the other four.

"Have a seat," he said to Tariq, who chose the only armchair next to the sofa facing a dead gas fire. The seat was lower than

Tariq was expecting and momentarily he lost his balance as he sank into the upholstery, his legs lifting off the ground. No-one appeared to notice.

Majid pulled up the other chair from the table and the group were now sat in a circle anxious to hear what Tariq had to say. Majid had given them some of Tariq's background from the discussions they had had over the Internet; unknowingly Tariq had become somewhat of a celebrity.

Majid started. "I have asked Tariq to come today, so he can tell us about what he did in Iraq."

Tariq was anxious, unsure of his role; he had only come to meet Majid to say 'hi' and discuss Jihad in broader terms. He was not expecting to address a group who clearly had expectations of him. He sat forward in the chair to be more comfortable.

"What would you like to know?" asked Tariq, a sensible starting point.

"Tell us about the car bombs?" said Hasib.

"What was it like at the training camp?" asked Milton before he had chance to answer.

"One at a time," called Majid.

They listened intently as Tariq described his time in the training camp in Iran, the communications, the discipline and the eventual explosion.

"I am sure it was American… a cruise missile," said Tariq, who by this time had gone up in the group's estimation even higher following his revelations.

"Wow," said Amir.

"If you are thinking about Jihad, here, in England, you must have… er, security; it must be very good. In Iran the Americans were watching from the sky. Here it is not so, but they listen to your calls on your phones... and watch the Internet... I heard that. Do not underestimate the enemy... There are spies everywhere. My Imam has told me that brothers are being paid by people to go to the masjid to listen for any Jihad talk."

The room had gone quiet as Tariq delivered his message slowly and deliberately almost in a whisper ensuring his translation was accurate, his message clear.

"Can you help us make bombs?" asked Hasib.

"Yes, I can do that, but you must understand, I will not join you on any mission... I have a bigger destiny."

The group looked at each other baffled by this cryptic comment.

Tariq continued. "Making a bomb is not difficult, moving and storing, more so."

Tariq described his friend's demise in the workshop in Basra.

"Acetone peroxide, the mother of Satan, very... er, dangerous, but effective."

He continued to enlighten the group further.

"You must have a proper... er, plan and be organised, everything must be planned in every detail, particularly buying the things you need... You will need money, much money."

"That won't be a problem," said Majid, but did not elaborate.

Tariq continued. "The peroxide is the same that the, how you say? the... er... hair people, they use to colour the hair."

"Hairdressers," corrected Majid.

"Yes, that is it. But you will need to be careful, any big... er, amount will make... suspicion and would be checked."

He paused then added. "You can use, how you say...? fertiliser also... but peroxide is best, you do not need so much."

These words echoed around the room and they nodded to each other in satisfaction.

Majid suggested they take a break and engage in the Asr prayers to give them strength; they all agreed. Mohammed led the group from the living room and up the staircase that Tariq had passed earlier. There was a toilet immediately at the top of the stairs, to the right a bathroom and to the left two bedrooms. They entered the first room which was an average size for a bedroom comfortably accommodating a double bed. But there was no bed. On the wall was a large banner with the word 'Allah' in Arabic. It was the same background that Jihadists in Iraq had used when filming the beheading of kidnapped Western prisoners. Prayer mats were aligned on the floor all pointing in the same direction facing diagonally away from the window.

"This is our prayer room," Mohammed told Tariq, and the six knelt down and started the afternoon ritual. Tariq with his fluent Arabic led the session. He was impressed with the standard of language pronunciation by the group; they had practiced well.

After the prayers, Tariq discussed the bomb making in more detail and encouraged the group to take notes. Majid had brought in a laptop and he accessed an internet site which had a video describing the procedure which Tariq added commentary.

"Getting the things you need is going to be your problem," said Tariq.

"We could steal some," said Hasib.

"I don't think so... That would definitely draw attention." Majid berated him.

It was Milton who came up with a possible solution.

"My sister has a hairdresser's in Chapeltown. I could tell her someone, a mate or something, wants to start a business and needs some stuff."

"Yeah, that could work, and gradually increase the amounts.

That shouldn't cause any suspicion," enthused Amir.

Hasib was quiet following his earlier rebuke, but nodded in agreement.

"That is something you must work out, but take your time, do not be in a hurry. You are anxious to strike a blow, I know, but you must be careful... do nothing that will raise suspicion," reiterated Tariq, who had learned the art of patience from his own experience.

"The other problem will be how to make it... er, go off," said Tariq. "I found a way using a mobile phone... I know it works, we tried it. I will show you."

Tariq explained to the group the mechanics of the process and what they would need to do to make it work.

"It is up to you, but you can use a simple cord which may be easier if you are wearing... er, the vests. There is a website I will show you that explains how to load a vest and set up the detonators."

Tariq took Majid's laptop and loaded a ULR. The group watched closely at the ten-minute instruction from the screen, then looked at each other with an air of satisfaction.

Tariq then described the dynamics of explosions.

"Where you, er... set the bomb off is really important, for the best, you want... er, somewhere where the explosion cannot escape... a subway perhaps or underground train for instance. You can also add things to the explosives which will be like, like... er... I don't know the word."

"Shrapnel?" proffered Majid.

"Yes, I think," said Tariq.

More plans were drawn up, with each of the group given specific responsibilities. Milton was now in charge of peroxide.

"Don't forget you will need somewhere to store it, out of

sight," said Tariq.

Majid would be responsible for choosing possible targets. They had already decided it would have to be in London to have the biggest impact and as he lived the nearest he was the obvious choice for this role.

Amir would look after the detonators and vests aided by the recent instruction. Mohammed would lead the group, look after security and map out strategy. Hasib as the youngest would be used to help the others when necessary.

As it was starting to get dark Mohammed led the group back down stairs to prepare for iftar. Having seen the state of the kitchen, Tariq was not sure about the food but was reassured when he saw fresh bread and fruit being removed from the fridge.

After the post Ramadan ritual Tariq addressed the brothers one more time suggesting that they did not meet up as a group again for some time and that all communication should be via Majid's network.

"You must not use mobile phones to talk; they listen. It is about routine," said Tariq. "You must not do anything to cause problems. For instance, Asian men meeting in houses could cause the police to take notice. If you must meet, do so at the Masjid." The group looked at each other and nodded their agreement.

Tariq continued. "When I leave today I will not contact with any of you again nor will I be able to speak with you Majid." There was a look of dismay and Majid looked at Tariq with surprise.

"Why, my friend? If we are careful it will be ok to talk, surely?"

Tariq looked at him.

"Here, I see brave people who are willing to sacrifice themselves for Allah… Allāhu Akbar."

"Allāhu Akbar," responded the group."

"But I also see, how you say?"

Tariq spoke in Arabic and Amir translated.

"Naivety, yes, that is the word... You are like children, but this is not a game. People will die, I have seen it with my own eyes. Your families will suffer; they will not understand and will tell the authorities everything. I know this."

The group looked at each other; Tariq's words were registering and a quiet descended, as they considered the implications.

Majid was first to speak and looked at the group. "Tariq is right. This has been like a game but not now, not from today. We must think like our enemy and protect ourselves and let nothing get in the way."

He looked at Tariq. "Thank you, my friend, for being honest with us. We will take your words and they will become a sword to the infidels."

The group looked at each other; concerned faces were transformed into smiles.

"Allāhu Akbar," said Amir.

"Allāhu Akbar," replied the group, followed by excited chatter.

After iftar, Mohammed agreed to take Tariq back to Batley. It was around ten o'clock, and Tariq was warmly thanked by the group. Majid agreed to accompany Mohammed to take Tariq back to Batley. It was more for the return journey; an unaccompanied Asian was potentially vulnerable, he explained.

Tariq said his farewells and left the house with Majid and Mohammed through the back way. The lock on the front door was faulty and had yet to be repaired, Mohammed explained.

Tariq hadn't worked out who actually owned the house, but Mohammed was the only one who slept there; the others were based a walking distance away.

Cars were parked on both sides of the street, staking claims to their respective dwellings. There was a ten-year-old Nissan immediately outside Mohammed's. He unlocked the door with a key and leant across to open the passenger door from the inside. Majid folded the front seat down, allowing Tariq to get in the back and then sat next to Mohammed. The inside was untidy and littered with sweet wrappers and old parking slips. The exhaust manifold bracket rattled as the engine coughed into life. A touch on the accelerator and it sounded more like a Jumbo Jet. Mohammed navigated the vehicle out of its narrow confines and it juddered down the street to a main road at the bottom. There were speed bumps every twenty yards or so, which bounced the occupants in their seats and did nothing to improve the loose exhaust.

"Whereabouts in Batley do you live?" asked Mohammed as they turned left towards Elland Road.

Tariq was cautious, he had no intention of revealing his residence, just in case. "I can walk from the station… It's not far."

"I think I know where that is," said Mohammed and headed the car to the Motorway.

With a top speed of sixty miles an hour, the engine needed an overhaul, Mohammed explained; it took twenty minutes to reach the outskirts of Batley. A police car was parked at the first roundabout after leaving the motorway and as the Nissan went passed, it immediately started up in pursuit. Flashing blue lights lit up the car and Mohammed indicated he was pulling in.

The police car pulled up behind and the driver got out in his yellow Hi-Viz jacket.

"Don't worry," said Mohammed. "We're always getting stopped."

This did nothing to hide the nervousness of the two passengers.

Tariq's experience of police was from Basra and the thought of being taken into custody worried him greatly. He was concerned that he might be sent back to Iraq.

Mohammed opened the car door and met the officer walking towards him.

"Is this your car?"' asked the policeman.

"Yes," replied Mohammed.

"Any ID?" asked the man.

Mohammed opened the driver's door and rummaged round in the glove compartment and pulled out a wad of papers and shut the door. Tariq couldn't hear the conversation. A torch shone through the window like a search light and scanned the interior. Tariq blinked as the beam hit his eyes. He covered his face with his hands.

Two minutes later, Mohammed got back in the car and started it up.

"What did they want?" asked Tariq.

"Nothing... like I said, it's what they do. Harass the black kids, happens all the time. That's why I keep my documents in the car, saves time. If you don't give them any problem and be polite they just let you go."

Tariq knew he had made the right decision in not disclosing his whereabouts.

A few minutes later they arrived at the station and Majid got out of the car to let Tariq out from the back. They embraced warmly, and Tariq wished them well with their Jihad. Tariq bent down and spoke to Mohammed sat in the driver's seat.

"Thank you for the ride and your hospitality, good luck."

He watched as the old Nissan exited the station car park and head back to the motorway. Tariq started walking back to his Uncle's house, thinking about the day's events.

Chapter Sixteen

Abdul and Sabeen were watching TV when Tariq got in and were eager to hear how Tariq's day had gone.

"Fine," said Tariq and he went into the kitchen to get a glass of water. Abdul looked at Sabeen, their enquiry appearing to have been rebuffed.

Tariq returned to the room with his drink and spoke. "Yes, it was a good day. Thank you for asking."

He took a sip of water.

"I would like to start my job tomorrow?" he asked, looking at Abdul.

His uncle looked at Sabeen. "Of course, of course, Tariq, that would be fine. Yusuf and Jamal are working, so I will be able show you around the computers we have."

"Are they not in?" said Tariq.

"Oh no, it's still early for them, especially on a Saturday night. They've gone into Leeds. They'll be back on the last train I expect. It gets in at midnight," said Sabeen.

Tariq looked at the clock on the wall, it was eleven-fifteen.

He didn't have a watch; it was a vanity and against his faith.

"What time tomorrow?" asked Tariq.

"After suhoor," said Abdul, observing the tradition for Tariq's benefit.

"Thank you. I will say goodnight," and Tariq went to his room.

"Goodnight," shouted Sabeen.

The day had proved to have been a watershed for Tariq. There was Abdul's talk and offer of work, and then the meeting with Majid and the brothers in Beeston. That episode worried him;

he knew it would only be a matter of time before they came under surveillance or blew themselves up. They lacked the professionalism required to undertake such a difficult venture, but at the same time he admired their bravery and enthusiasm, and, who knows?

Tariq lay there reassessing his own mission, sleep eluded him.

His long-term goal was to strike a blow bigger than anyone had ever seen, bigger even than 9/11 perhaps. He wanted to be honoured by all Jihadists, a role model even. If he was to become a martyr it would have to be for something worthy of the sacrifice, not taken out by a sniper's rifle or getting blown up in some back-street kitchen. He was after all a talented engineer.

He realised he was going to have to compromise. This meant he would have to change his whole attitude, be accepted in the community, blending in. He could not fight it. He would mix more with Jamal and Yusuf, even call them their western names if that what it would take. Everything would have to change. He would still visit the Masjid, he would not give that up; tomorrow he would speak to the Imam and explain. Sleep overtook his thoughts.

The following morning he was eating his pre-fast meal with Abdul.

"Did you sleep well?" asked his uncle.

"Yes, thank you," replied Tariq. "Will Jamal and Yusuf be joining us?"

"Later, they don't start till ten o'clock on Sunday," replied Abdul; it was still dark outside. "But I can show you what needs to be done."

They finished their meal and left the house. The Cash and

Carry van was parked outside in front of a three-year-old Toyota.

"We'll take the van; Jamal will come later in the car," he said, nodding at the Corona.

The sky was getting lighter as the hazy dawn broke across the town. It was cloudy but not cold and a light breeze raised fast food debris and tossed them around the deserted streets. They arrived at the store just before seven-thirty; the car park was empty, and Abdul parked in the disabled bay outside the front doors.

Abdul opened up and reset the alarm.

"The staff will get here around nine-thirty; we don't open till ten so there will be plenty of time to show you around."

Tariq acknowledged.

They went up to Abdul's office where Tariq had been before on his only other visit just after his arrival. Abdul went inside and took off his coat, then led Tariq to another room at the end of the corridor which was locked by a security pad. Abdul keyed in four numbers and there was a click as the door opened.

"This is the office where we have the computer terminals."

Tariq remembered it. Abdul flicked the switch on the wall above the security pad and a row of neon illuminated the room in fluorescent light.

Tariq surveyed the room; it was larger than it looked from the outside. There were six four-drawer filing cabinets along the wall to the right and a large desk opposite the entrance with a small swivel office chair behind it. There was a computer monitor and two telephones on top.

"There's also a safe," Abdul said pointing to a large heavy-looking container in the corner against the left-hand wall, clearly load-bearing, to take the weight of the safe.

"We don't carry much cash on the premises. There are two collections by the security van every day."

Abdul was understandably proud of his life's endeavours and enjoyed showing it off to his latest recruit.

"These are the computer terminals," he said, unlocking a door in the opposite corner next to the desk.

It opened onto what looked to be a large cupboard. He turned on the light. Inside was a bank of black computer terminals behind a smoked glass front, clicking and humming, small red lights indicating their activeness; wires snaking about in all directions like plastic spaghetti. It was noticeably warm and there was a buzz of the blades of an extractor fan rattling in the small sky-light.

Tariq looked at it with knowing interest.

"IBM, excellent choice," said Tariq.

"Not cheap," said Abdul.

"No," said Tariq, looking almost lasciviously at the equipment. It took him back to his time at the camp.

"This is the server... All the counter terminals feed in here and Samira collates the information on her screen over there," he said, pointing to the monitor on the desk.

"Samira?" queried Tariq.

"She's our administrator. I don't know how we would manage without her," said Abdul. "She will be in later. I will introduce you to her."

They left admin and went back to Abdul's office and Tariq sat opposite his uncle at his desk. The phone rang, and Tariq sat patiently while Abdul took the call.

"Suppliers," he said, concluding the call after a couple of minutes. "Non-stop... Luckily, Jamal and Yusuf are able to deal with most of them. The sales reps are the worst, you can never get rid of them," and he smiled. Tariq smiled back.

Abdul was pleased. For the first time since arriving in Batley he felt he was starting to engage with his nephew.

At eight-thirty, other staff started to arrive. The sales area was about two-thirds of the building, but, adjoining the shop floor, was the warehouse where large stocks of produce were stored prior to being moved to the customer space. There was a loading bay at the far end of the building where supplies were delivered attracting a constant flow of trucks and vans.

Tariq, hearing other people about, was at the window watching them arrive.

"We will have some deliveries this morning; the roads are quieter, and it is easier for the trucks to get here," Abdul said noting Tariq's interest.

By half-past nine the whole building was a hive of activity. Cashiers were making their way to the staff room to get refreshments and change into their uniforms before opening time. Tariq noted that most were of Asian origin, some wearing traditional veils; others not, but there were also white people who appeared to be older than their counterparts. Abdul was taking yet another phone call when Tariq, who was back at the desk, heard a voice at the opened door.

"Hello."

Abdul waved, and Tariq looked round to see a smart looking woman in a business suit. She came in and introduced herself.

"Hi, I'm Samira," she said to Tariq, whispering so as not to disturb Abdul's call.

"Tariq," he replied in similar tones.

Abdul finished his call.

"Ah Samira. This is Tariq, my nephew. I mentioned last week that I was going to ask him to look at the computer systems and website for me."

"Yes, of course, I remember. Pleased to meet you Tariq," she said and offered her hand, which Tariq shook limply.

Tariq would not normally shake hands with a woman, personal contact with the opposite sex was not allowed, but, recognising he needed to adapt, he made an effort.

Abdul explained Tariq's brief to Samira and suggested that she show him around and explain the computer set up.

"I need to sort out a few things, before the boys get here," he said.

"Of course," said Samira. "We'll go to the office."

Tariq got up and followed her.

"See you later," said Abdul and Tariq acknowledged. His uncle was back on the telephone again.

They returned to the admin room, and Samira switched on the lights and keyed in the numbers. She put her handbag on the desk, took off her jacket and hung it on a coat stand behind the door.

Tariq was in a different world now. His life had been totally male-dominated, in fact, his only real female contact had been his mother and sisters and, more recently, Sabeen. Even at college, there was only one female on the course, and Tariq ignored her. It seemed strange watching Samira go to the desk and switch on the computer tower. This was not a female roll, in his experience. The screen sprang into life with the 'Charma Cash and Carry' logo.

"Oh, I'll need to find you something to sit on," she said and walked past Tariq and out into the corridor. A couple of minutes later she returned with an office chair.

"Here."

Tariq took it from her and sat down.

"I expect your uncle has told you what we need," she said, as she sat down. "I've been saying to him for ages that we need to upgrade our computer system. It can't cope with the volumes. Everything's so slow; the Internet takes forever, and, if we don't modernise, we'll grind to a halt."

"I see," said Tariq.

"You can do this?" she asked, not rudely but needing clarity. Tariq was taken aback by this directness.

"Yes," confirmed Tariq. "I have er... learned computer networks and web updating... I did some basic programming at college in Iraq."

Samira appeared satisfied at Tariq's competence.

"I'll be with you in a minute," she said, as she worked her keyboard with some dexterity.

Tariq was impressed. He watched her and tried to take in this new experience. Samira was clearly older than him, but not much. Her business-like approach matched her attire, a white blouse with a smart dark knee-length skirt, fashionable, like those worn by many of the female commuters travelling on the train into Leeds. Her hair was black shoulder length and not veiled.

She finished her log-in work and looked at Tariq.

"I was going to offer you a coffee, but I see you are observing Ramadan."

Tariq was in his smock.

"Do you mind if I get myself one? I need a lift after the drive in. You can wait here I won't be long."

She got up. "I know, come around here and have a look at the website... I've logged on," she added, before Tariq could reply.

He got up and sat on Samira's chair as she went out of the office. He looked at the screen and started to navigate the website.

Ten minutes later, Samira returned, and Tariq watched as she closed the door behind her. He suddenly realised he was staring and quickly averted his gaze back to the computer screen. She moved next to him, still standing, he could smell her perfume; not allowed under Islam. He went to get up and relinquish the seat.

"It's ok, stay there, I'll bring the other seat across and I'll explain what we want."

He noticed her eyes, so expressive, eyes that said, "I'm in control."

He quickly turned away again. He felt uncomfortable with eye contact.

For the next two hours they were at the monitor looking at the website and considering options. Samira was pleased with Tariq's knowledge; he clearly knew what he was doing.

Tariq had written some notes in Arabic, and an outline plan of what he would need to do, which they discussed and amended until they were both happy. It was turned midday.

"I could do with a break," she said. "Why don't you come down to the staff room, I'm sure there're others observing Ramadan. We do have a small prayer room if you would like."

"Thank you, I will."

Tariq logged off.

They made their way down the stairs; the store was busy with all the cashier positions open and queues at each one.

"Hi, Tariq, how's it going?" said a voice.

Tariq looked round to see Jamal helping out at one of the tills.

"Hello Jamal, fine, thank you," Tariq replied, and followed Samira through a door marked. 'Private Staff Only', which was again accessed via a security pad.

It was a reasonable sized room with a sink and drainer, large fridge and a long work top with a kettle and several mugs with cupboards above; unwashed crockery sat next to the sink. There were several round tables with chairs and more comfortable seats against the wall. A radio was playing tuned to a local radio station and a couple of newspapers were in a rack, crumpled from use. There was a TV in the corner, but it was not switched on.

"Toilets are over there," said Samira, pointing to the far end of the room. "The prayer room is over there." She indicated another room on the opposite side.

"Thank you," said Tariq and he made his way to the prayer room.

He opened the door and looked round; it was a converted store-room, probably a stationery cupboard, but he had been in worse and it was perfectly adequate for his purpose. He spent ten minutes in contemplation and saying the words of the Dhurh, the lunch-time prayer before returning to the staff room.

Samira was sat at one of the tables eating a sandwich, a steaming mug of coffee next to her plate.

"I'm sorry Tariq, I hope you don't mind me eating. You can go back to the office if you like."

"No, it is all right, I am used to it at college," he said, and sat opposite her at the table.

They struck up a conversation and Tariq learned that Samira had been with the firm for three years having achieved a Business Studies degree at Bradford University. Her father was a taxi driver and worked long hours; they lived in Bradford. Tariq wanted to discuss her beliefs, she appeared to understand Muslim culture, but was not, or appeared not, to be practicing

Islam.

"I was brought up a Muslim, but I started to question its relevance and its treatment of women when I got to college."

"But Islam worships women," argued Tariq before she had time to finish.

"By subjugating them?" retorted Samira. "That's not worshiping women."

Tariq had clearly met his match and did not want to get into an ideological debate. It was Ramadan and arguments were not allowed.

"I have never seen it that way," said Tariq.

Samira took another bight from her sandwich.

"Of course not, you're a man," she said, clearing the bread from her mouth. "Why would you? Women are conditioned to comply. They're not entitled to think for themselves."

"That is not true," said Tariq. "There are many women doctors, nurses, many, doing many things."

"A minority, and many will, like myself, have rejected the faith."

Tariq recognised that this was an argument he couldn't win and changed the subject to work related issues.

Having finished lunch, the pair returned to the office and the rest of the day Tariq spent trying to understand the intricacy of the various programmes and mapping out viable solutions and recommendations.

Yusuf appeared during the afternoon. "Tariq, man, how's it going."

"Hello Freddie, how's things?" replied Samira.

Tariq suddenly remembered his new approach, and acknowledged with a "Hi, Freddie," which Yusuf couldn't initially take in.

"See you, Tariq," was all he said, and went back to his duties on the shop floor, bemused at the use of his adopted name.

At four o'clock Samira started packing up.

"Are you staying?" she asked, as she started locking her desk drawers.

"I think I will speak to my uncle and talk to him about our discussions."

Samira took her jacket from the coat stand. Tariq unconsciously watched as she put on her jacket, her white blouse straining at the buttons by the curves of her breasts. Momentarily the glimpse of a black bra between the buttons was visible before Tariq could look away; a vision that would come back to haunt him later.

He said his goodbyes to Samira and she closed the office door and turned out the light. Tariq made his way to his uncle's office. Abdul was pleased to see him and wanted to know all about his ideas. He had never seen Tariq so animated as he outlined his conclusions and recommendations.

Just before five, Jamal knocked on his father's door, seeing him in conference with Tariq.

"Just heading back, do you want a lift Tariq?"

Abdul looked at his nephew.

"Go on and get yourself home; it's been a long day. I won't be long here."

Tariq said his goodbyes and joined Jamal and Yusuf who were chatting excitedly wanting to know what Tariq thought of the set up and the computer systems and his ideas for improvement, and how quickly he would be able to implement everything.

"It will be a long job, cost much money," Tariq replied.

That evening, he made his way to the mosque to join other worshippers for a communal iftar hosted by the Imam. On his walk he had much on his mind. He considered his discussion with Samira. She was a Kafir, no question, but Tariq was wrestling with the Quran and its interpretation of disbelievers. He wanted to raise the issue with the Imam.

After the formalities and prayers Tariq, again, was entertained by the Mullah. Tariq told the Imam of his new job at the Cash and Carry which would help him pay for the college course and explained that he would not be able to attend as many prayers as he had done previously. The Imam understood, and told Tariq he would always be welcome whenever his time allowed.

He then described his meeting with Samira and her apparent rejection of the faith; he needed some guidance. Why had she rejected the faith? Women were a cornerstone of Islam, worshiped, the provider of children and comfort for their husbands. He could not understand her motivation or what might lie in store for her in the after-life.

The Mullah listened to Tariq and replied.

"According to Tafseer ibn Katheer there are a number kufh or disbelieving's."

Tariq looked at him in awe at his intellect.

"The Quran uses the word kufr to describe a person who covers up or hides realities, one who refuses to accept the dominion and authority of Allah... Allāhu Akbar."

"Allāhu Akbar," responded Tariq, hanging on his every word.

"There is Kufrul-Juhood, disbelief out of rejection...This applies to someone who acknowledges the truth in his heart, but rejects it with his tongue. This kufr is applicable to those who call themselves Muslims, but who reject any necessary and accepted norms of Islam such as Salaat and Zakat." He paused then continued. "The Quran states: '*And they denied them, though their souls acknowledged them, for spite and arrogance. Then see the nature of the consequence for the wrong-doers'."*

That seemed to describe Samira, but the Imam continued. "Then there is Kufrul-Kurh, disbelief out of detesting any of Allah's commands... The Quran states: *'And those who disbelieve, perdition is for them, and He will make their actions vain; That is because they are averse to that which Allah hath revealed, therefore maketh He their actions fruitless'."*

Tariq considered this wisdom.

"Why do you ask these questions Tariq?" enquired the Mullah. Suddenly, Tariq realised that there was no real reason and that it had just come into his mind.

This concerned the Mullah. "Has this woman affected you in anyway?"

"What do you mean?" asked Tariq.

"Have you been visited by desires or unclean thoughts?"

Tariq thought about the question but couldn't answer it. "The Quran says, *'The person who performs marriage with his hands is cursed.'* You know what I am saying? It is *haraam*, forbidden. It is the work of the devil. He visits us in our darkest hour and tries to take our minds away from our beloved saviour."

"Yes, I know these things, and I have not been swayed, ever," replied Tariq.

The Mullah did not press it; he had made his point, but deep down he was troubled by Tariq's gradual change. It was Tariq who anticipated the question.

"I can see you are concerned, but I will say this, in my quest for Jihad against the infidels, I have come to realise I need to understand my enemy and adjust to his world, which will mean some changes. My mission will not be denied. I will one day enter paradise in the name of Allah... Allāhu Akbar."

"Allāhu Akbar," replied the Imam.

That night Tariq lay in bed mulling over the day; his mind racing. He was considering what needed to be done at the Cash and Carry, the computer configurations, the different software programmes, new hardware; how he would fit in his new role for his uncle around his college work, and his discussion with the Imam.

Suddenly, from nowhere, an image flashed into his mind and he couldn't shake it. Samira and her blouse, the flash of bra, the long legs, perfectly-shaped bottom. He felt a pain in his groin and he had become aroused, harder than he could ever remember. He berated himself. This could not happen; he had to resist the overwhelming temptation to relieve himself. The devil had visited, and he would fight the natural urges with every sinew.

He got out of bed and self-consciously walked downstairs to the bathroom; everyone was asleep, and run the cold tap until the wash basin was full. He stood on tip-toe and eased his swollen appendage over the rim of the sink into the water and started praying. After a few minutes his mind had refocused, and his 'problem' had eased.

Chapter Seventeen

Ramadan finished at the end of the lunar month, Sunday 14th November.

The end of Ramadan is celebrated in most Muslim countries by a holiday, Eid Al-Fitr. Naturally, the Cash and Carry continued without a break, but Abdul wanted to mark the occasion at home by laying on a special meal for Tariq.

Jake and Freddie (as Tariq now referred to them) suggested that they go into Leeds afterwards; they thought it would do him good.

Tariq of course declined; he would visit the mosque to join the faithful with the celebrations, but, after much persuasion, agreed to go the following Saturday after the Cash and Carry had closed. So, Tariq was rail-roaded into going to a night club.

On the day in question, he felt strangely apprehensive. He was working at the Cash and Carry and was ribbed mercilessly by Samira, which became a source of embarrassment. He had no idea what to expect, but from the description, it was nothing short of Jahannam itself; the fiery hell that awaited all non-believers.

The reality lived up to his expectations; worse if anything. They left Batley around ten o'clock in Jake's Toyota and his girlfriend Jasmine had tagged along, not wishing to allow Jake in a club unattached. She naturally sat in the front next to Jake and proceeded to rub his thigh for most of the journey; Freddie and Tariq were in the back.

Jasmine tried her hardest, but Tariq had already passed judgment on her; nothing more than a common whore, he thought, and conversation was naturally strained. It was Freddie who was doing his best to create some sort of party atmosphere and entertained the group with some inane chatter.

They arrived in the city centre and parked underneath one of the railway arches; there were several clubs in the vicinity. Jake and Freddie were seasoned clubbers, and knew the right one where they thought Tariq would enjoy himself; some chance, there was a definite air of sufferance.

They found the club, Mephistopheles, aptly named after the demon in the Faust legend, and went to the entrance which was guarded by two burley bouncers; Zabaaniyah Tariq wondered - the guards of hell.

They were eyed closely as they made their way to the pay desk, but were not stopped or hassled in any way. As they entered the club Tariq caught his breath; he had not experienced anything like this before; this was purgatory personified, the music pounding incessant, rhythmic; a vexation to the soul.

They made their way to the bar and having got their drinks Jasmine wanted to dance, leaving Tariq and Freddie standing both with orange juices watching the activity. It was packed with hardly room to breathe, and Tariq suddenly found himself feeling claustrophobic. He watched the girls gyrating with little attempt to hide their modesty. Tariq was regretting his weakness in being persuaded to visit such a place.

After about half an hour, Jake and Jasmine rejoined them and went back to the bar to replenish their drinks. With no money Tariq was excused paying for a round. Jasmine looked at him.

"Tariq, you've got a face like the middle of next week. Why don't you have a dance? You never know you might enjoy it. My friend Stacey's here, I can fix you up if you like; she'll go with anyone. Buy her a drink and you'll probably get a blow job."

"I'm ok," said Tariq not understanding a word of what she

was saying.

"Suit yourself," said Jasmine and proceeded to drape herself over the somewhat embarrassed Jake.

As an attempt to give Tariq a lift, the evening did nothing of the kind; he was in an alien world and wanted no part of it, and worse was to come. He spent most of the evening sat on one of the few chairs staring into his orange juice as if in a trance apparently meditating, trying to block out his surroundings.

Seeing their cousin was not entering into the spirit of the occasion, Jake and Freddie eventually decided it was time to return home; it was just before midnight. Jasmine had made a comment about Tariq's lack of sociability and her friends were beginning to talk.

Needless to say, Tariq was delighted when Jake approached him.

"We're heading back now," he said. Jasmine did not look too pleased.

They left the club and made their way back to the car park. After a couple of minutes, they came to a set of stone steps leading down to the access road, and at the bottom there was a group of about seven or eight white youths smoking and chatting. A couple of the lads were drinking from cans of lager. Jake initially stopped but Jasmine carried on. One of the lads turned around hearing the clomping of her shoes behind them.

"What have we got here?" said the lad, and the rest of the group were alerted to the four coming down the steps towards them.

"It's Pakis with an English girl," shouted one.

"What's the matter, can't get none of your own kind?"

"Paki whore," shouted another, and the group became more and more animated, taunting the four as they made their way past, trying to ignore the vile jibes. Freddie was bringing up the rear with Tariq just in front of him. Jake and Jasmine were holding each other with their heads down running the gauntlet at the front as they walked on.

Suddenly, Freddie felt a punch in the small of his back and the group ran off. He fell to the ground.

"Freddie!" shouted Jake and went back to his brother. He knelt down and lifted his head up his eyes seemed glazed.

"What's that?" shouted Jasmine.

Tariq stood looking at Freddie dazed and bewildered.

"He's bleeding!" she shouted.

"Quick, phone an ambulance," shouted Jake, as he cradled his brother's head.

Jasmine took out her mobile and dialed 999.

"Ambulance... quick... Someone's been stabbed," and she gave the details.

Within a matter of minutes, a police car arrived having been alerted by the call; the city centre was well-patrolled by police on a Saturday night.

Freddie was drifting in and out of consciousness as two officers approached.

"What happened, lad?" said the first policeman.

Jasmine was hysterical, and Jake was trying to calm her down; it was Tariq who was trying to keep Freddie awake. Paramedics arrived soon after and got Freddie comfortable and into an ambulance.

Whilst the medics were attending to Freddie, Tariq was nervously talking to the police, but they appeared sympathetic and merely wanted descriptions and statements of what had happened.

As Jake had the car, it was Tariq who rode with Freddie to the hospital. Jake went back to Batley to collect his parents; he had phoned ahead. They were in bed when they got the call.

Freddie was taken into the emergency ward. He had been stabbed with a small blade; a pen-knife or something similar.

It was almost an hour before Jake and his parents arrived at the hospital. Tariq was in the waiting area and they wanted to know what was happening. He was unable to give them a great deal of information, no-one seemed to know. Time dragged by as the concerned relatives speculated on what was happening. Tariq had again gone into his shell and appeared to be praying. Eventually a doctor approached them, and Abdul immediately got up.

"What is the news? How is my son?"

"It's good news," said the doctor. "He's not in danger. Luckily the knife missed any vital organs... another centimetre and it would have punctured his kidneys. He's under sedation and we'll be taking him up to a ward for observation, but he should be able to leave later tomorrow or Monday."

Sabeen burst into tears.

"Thank you, doctor, thank you," she said.

It was almost four o'clock before the family got back to Batley. At least they had been able to talk to Freddie, who was drowsy but seemed to be recovering from his ordeal, They left with the promise of an early return.

Back in his room, Tariq had no urge for sleep. He opened up his laptop and logged in.

He had not made any contact with his Luton and Beeston friends and had wiped out any reference to them from his computer. He had however found a new website and had created his own 'blog'. It was an encrypted extreme Jihadist site which, on its home page, paid homage to the nineteen martyrs of 9/11. There were pictures of each one in a black frame. The narrative was in Arabic and the feed originating in the Yemen, he concluded, judging by the various references. He was sure there were Al Qaeda links due to the informed comment that was posted which could only come from someone with inside knowledge of the movement. Anwar al- Awlaki was a regular contributor to the website and Tariq had received several messages of support on his blog from him which he had found inspirational.

As Tariq did not have an Arabic keyboard, he would post his comments in English and then used the translator software to upload. He had checked the script and was happy that the translation aptly described his views and feelings. So, whilst he appeared to everyone to be integrating into his new environment, he was posting his observations and thoughts at what he had seen. It did not make comfortable reading.

'Sunday morning, November 21st 2004. Last night I witnessed terrible things which confirms my worst fears; this place is really hell on earth,' it read.

He went on to describe the night club and the sexual displays by the women and of course the racial abuse, 'the intolerant society,' he described it. He made the translation and posted the comments and knew there would be some interest in his remarks.

There was support from all over the world, mainly Middle East, but Indonesia, with its large Muslim population had also provided several followers. Tariq went on to confirm his intention to take the struggle direct to the infidels with what he described as 'significant' force, but would not go into detail. It was not the right time and he no definite plan; just ideas in his head.

With Freddie convalescing, as soon as college had finished for the Christmas recess, Tariq worked full time at the Cash and Carry. Many of the staff, including his new family, did not celebrate the Christian festival, but the store was booming, and Abdul did a roaring trade. By that time, Tariq had managed to completely up-date the computer systems and, with his uncle's financial backing, had installed new hard-ware which was significantly faster and more flexible than the old set up. Everyone at the store was impressed at the speed of access and capacity, even Samira.

Tariq's relationship with her had developed into a professional arrangement, and his initial difficulties had been replaced by a mutual respect. He was no longer 'troubled' at night.

Freddie gradually recovered from his ordeal at the nightclub; a small scar on his back the only tangible evidence, but he had changed as a result of the experience. He would rarely venture out and had lost his 'joie de vivre' persona.

The police had visited a couple of times, much to Tariq's consternation, but the perpetrators were never found. Shortly after his return from hospital Tariq suggested that Freddie join him at the masjid, a place of solace and reflection, he said. Much to Tariq's surprise, he agreed.

This was the start of a different relationship for Tariq with his new family and by the New Year, Freddie had dropped his adopted name and reverted to 'Yusuf'. He grew a beard and became closer to his cousin and would regularly join Tariq at prayers. This change had caused a rift with Jake who had seen his best friend taken away from him, ostensibly by Tariq, and the two rarely spoke to each other. Abdul and Sabeen were caught in the middle and would regularly have to step in to maintain peace.

One evening the family were sat eating when an argument broke out. Jake asked Freddie (he still referred to him by that name) if he would come to Jasmine's birthday party the following weekend. Freddie declined saying he didn't want to go.

"I don't understand you, Freddie," he said. "You love parties."

Freddie stuck to his guns. but Jake suddenly turned on Tariq.

"This is all your fault! Why did you have to come over here and split up our family?"

Abdul intervened. "This is nobody's fault, Jamal. If anyone is to blame it is those animals that hurt your brother," he said, trying to calm the situation.

Jake put down his knife and fork, left the table and headed out the door. He didn't return that evening, and the next day he announced he was moving in with Jasmine and her parents.

Tariq watched the events unfold with little satisfaction. He derived no pleasure from seeing the family, who had taken him in and looked after him so well, in turmoil. It was more ammunition to his view that the society was broken and an example of what happens when you turn your back on the principles of Islam.

Over the next few months Tariq continued his routine. He continued to view with disdain the cultural differences, the TV, newspapers, magazines, advertising billboards in fact everywhere there were symbols of everything he had been brought up to detest. The contrast with Basra couldn't be greater, but, sadly, contact with his former family had waned as his new life took over. Phone calls to Iraq were expensive and therefore infrequent. It seemed a lifetime away.

Despite his differences with Jake, Tariq continued to work

at the Cash and Carry, which took up most of his spare time in the evenings, at weekends and during holidays. He needed the money. The work suited him; fortunately, he was left on his own most of the time, although, occasionally, he would have to report to Samira and explain a new process.

Jake also worked there and did eventually make up with his parents but still lived with Jasmine 'as man and wife', he told Sabeen. That had upset her deeply. He had abandoned all his principles and she wondered what would become of her son.

Tariq was still a frequent visitor to the mosque, often with Yusuf in tow, and would visit whenever his schedule would allow but always made Friday prayers; he would never miss his obligatory salāh.

His studies at University were progressing well, and, into the second term, the emphasis moved from basic engineering to electrical engineering, systems projects and computer programming; topics that interested him greatly. It was knowledge that would assist him in his future endeavours. His tutor had been complimentary about his progress, and indications were that, on his present form, he would be on course for a 2:1 or even a first.

The first-year term ended in the middle of June, and Abdul was happy to extend Tariq's hours at the store. The main requirement was to set up a new stock control system. Tariq had researched alternative options and found a process which would suit the business and set to work.

Early July Tariq was on his blog, as he was on most days, exchanging ideology and dogma with other fanatics. He noticed a number of posts from people saying that 'retribution was close at hand' and 'soon the infidels will feel the wrath of the sword'. Tariq had seen such messages before designed to motivate sympathisers. It was a display of defiance and intent, but promises had rarely been fulfilled, and he didn't take much notice, but, this time, things were about to change.

Thursday 7th July, 2005, an ordinary day in London, cloudy, but a mild 16°C. Tariq was in the staff room getting some water from the cooler. The TV was on showing the newsfeeds. A report interrupted the breakfast programme. *'Reports are coming in of an explosion on the London Underground.'*

Tariq stood for a moment and went to the TV and turned up the sound. Other staff stood up and went closer to the screen. The pictures showed emergency services in full flow; reports of more explosions, possibly gas; people rushing about, ambulances, police, fire engines, mayhem.

Tariq was transfixed; later another report, this time a bus in Tavistock Square; a newsreel camera showing the roof hanging off at a crazy angle. This was not a gas explosion and the newsfeed was updated; the words 'terrorist attack' went around the world. Tariq carried his laptop everywhere with him in a satchel and made his way to the admin office. Samira was on the phone and he walked passed her desk, nodding in acknowledgement, and into the computer control room. He opened his laptop and logged onto the office Wi-Fi, then to his blog. He updated his page describing the events in London as it was being reported but others were already commenting.

'Death to the kafirs, glory to Allah, martyrs in heaven,' he wrote.

Tariq continued to monitor the events of the day, and eventually the full facts started to emerge; four suicide bombers, one from Aylesbury, three from Leeds.

'It couldn't be,' he thought, but when the names were revealed it was clear that the four were not the people he had met in Beeston, although it was quite possible they were connected; it was too much of a coincidence. Initial reports said that the bombers had used plastic or fertilizer-based explosives, but later forensics would show that an 'organic peroxide-based' device was used which gave more credence to Tariq's theory.

He was right to be worried. There was an outpouring of anger following the 'massacre', as many of the newspapers were calling it. Fifty-six people dead, including the bombers; security was on high alert. The press covered the on-going investigations in minute detail, and for weeks Tariq thought he might be taken into custody, but nothing happened. The far-right parties gained popular support particularly when news reports showed so-called 'fanatical' Muslims ostentatiously showing support for their martyred brothers. In Batley, there were protests, and the mosque was daubed in graffiti. Even the Cash and Carry had seen takings fall as the white local population steer cleared of anything connected with Asian origin.

Abdul was concerned on several fronts. He read the newspapers and watched in horror at the back-lash; reports of white youths attacking Asian taxi drivers, buildings set on fire, protests and an increase in bigotry. With the sales at the store declining he wondered if he could maintain his workforce.

Abdul was in despair; he had no sympathy with the bombers or their cause.

"Look at the damage it has caused and for what?" he said at dinner one night. "All it has done is created more problems for the Muslim community, just when things were going ok."

"What about the **arkān-al-Islām**?' asked Tariq.

"There is no **arkān-al-Islām**?" replied Abdul.

Yusuf looked on, not understanding. "What's that?" he asked.

Abdul replied. "The so-called sixth Hadith, another pillar of Islam. Some Muslims believe that there is a sixth pillar that refers to Jihad, the taking of direct action against non-Muslims."

Yusuf looked at Tariq, but he was not about to be drawn on his views which were clearly at odds with his uncle.

At the mosque, there continued to be uncertainty, fear and anger. Some were angry; as Abdul was, about the disharmony the bombings had created in the community at a time when race relations generally were good. Others sympathised with the bombers referring to them as martyrs and calling on other Muslims to take action.

It was left to the Imam to bring some order and stability to the community and he was regularly seen at public meetings and on TV with other community leaders, calling for restraint on all sides. In private, he would discuss his own views with Tariq and recognised that the death toll although large, it was the deadliest bombing in London since the Second World War, it had not had any major impact... little had altered. Tariq recognised this fact; but he would change that, he vowed.

For days he continued to watch the news reports, trying to gauge reaction and importantly how the bombings had been carried out; there were lessons to be learned. It transpired that the shuhada had used white cord to detonate the bombs with vests filled with shrapnel; it bore all the hallmark of his master-class in Beeston.

One thing that had disappointed Tariq was the lack of economic and political impact. The value of the pound decreased slightly against the U.S. dollar. The 'Footsie' dropped 200 points during the morning but rallied to be only seventy-one points down on the day; and if anything, the government's position was marginally enhanced by showing effective leadership in dealing firmly with the situation. The country remained on high alert and, later that month, further arrests were made in Leeds and Luton and controlled explosions carried out when further bomb-making material was found. Tariq logged it all on his computer.

On 1st September, Al Jazeera released a tape that the ring-leader of the bombings had made to justify his reasons for becoming a 'soldier'. Tariq had already been aware of its content via the website and various Al Qaeda members including Ayman al-Zawahiri claimed involvement in the London bombings. The video commentary went as follows:

'I and thousands like me are forsaking everything for what we believe. Our drive and motivation doesn't come from tangible commodities that this world has to offer. Our religion is Islam, obedience to the one true God and following the footsteps of the final prophet messenger. Your democratically-elected governments continuously perpetuate atrocities against my people all over the world. And your support of them makes you directly responsible, just as I am directly responsible for protecting and avenging my Muslim brothers and sisters. Until we feel security you will be our targets and until you stop the bombing, gassing, imprisonment and torture of my people we will not stop this fight. We are at war and I am a soldier. Now you too will taste the reality of this situation.'

The following had been added later; it was presumed by Zarqawi.

'I myself, I myself, I make dua to Allah... to raise me amongst those whom I love like the prophets, the messengers, the martyrs and today's heroes like our beloved Sheikh Osama Bin

Laden, Dr. Ayman al-Zawahiri and Abu Musab al- Zarqawi and all the other brothers and sisters that are fighting in the... of this cause.'

By the start of the next University term, the media interest in the bombings had calmed down and Tariq continued with his studies. During the first week back at college he received another visit from the Petronix HR department. This time it was the Graduate Recruitment Manager, Kim Barnes, who had driven up from London for the meeting. They met in the university refectory and she was eager to hear how Tariq was progressing.

She was impressed with his academic achievements, 'clearly a bright young man' she said in her notes; although less taken with his personality, which, she noted, lacked spark and she wondered how he would fare with stronger characters. In her review she described his introvert demeanour and there was something about his eyes, she commented, which would not engage. In her meeting she was keen to clarify his intentions for his one-year attachment which was drawing closer.

"We find our interns regularly change their mind as they get into the course and gain a wider perspective," she said.

Tariq was quite certain, and told the manager he was looking forward to the attachment and was starting to research Oil and gas rigs. This was true, and he had accrued a lot of information and a great deal of knowledge on their workings. As well as the internet, the college reference library was an invaluable source. His tutors had noted his interest and were always ready to offer guidance and advice on technical matters.

Chapter Eighteen

For the rest of the academic year, Tariq's understanding of the workings of an oil rig increased considerably. He took particular interest in the Piper Alfa tragedy, the worst off- shore disaster in history.

Piper Alpha was only about fifty miles from Delta Bravo, some hundred and twenty miles north east of Aberdeen. It produced crude oil and natural gas. On the night of July 6th 1988, several explosions tore the rig apart costing the lives of one hundred and sixty-five men.

Tariq had been fascinated by this incident, not just the loss of life but by the potential economic impact such an event would have on the country; far more, he reasoned than blowing up tube trains or buses in London. It could be another 9/11.

The Cullen enquiry, which was set up subsequently to understand the reasons for the disaster, produced a large report cataloguing the events that took place that night and making recommendations to the industry to avoid future incidents. It was freely available and gave Tariq details of the circumstances that had triggered the disaster from a technical perspective. Now what if that scenario could be replicated deliberately, by sabotage?

This was what he had been waiting for, and, unconsciously, been working towards ever since he moved to England. He had considered the Milford Haven option, taking out a refinery but an oil rig had almost a mystique about it and the effect he believed would be far more dramatic. He felt a twinge of excitement every time he considered the possibilities. It was a sign. This would be his destiny.

It ticked all his boxes. Petronix was a bonus; the company

was despised in Iraq for stealing the country's natural resources and pocketing huge profits from the operation which should rightly belong to the local people. For the UK, the loss of gas and oil production for any length of time would have significant implications not just economically but politically as well, he reasoned. This would make the government sit up and take notice.

What made Tariq different from his counterparts in the struggle against the western forces was he was not motivated by any political doctrine, like many of those that had gone before; the Palestinian question, the occupation of Iraq and now Afghanistan were sideshows. His was religious ideology that dated back centuries, to the time of the Crusades and the mighty Muslim leaders, Saladin and Al-Kamil, which he had studied in Basra. He strongly believed in Jihad, and, with the moral support from those influences he had made via his Internet contacts, he was more committed to his objective than ever, believing his voyage to paradise would be guaranteed.

Back in December 2001, Richard Read was overpowered by passengers and crew on a Paris to Miami flight whilst trying to detonate explosives contained in his shoe. He was British and had been converted to Islamic fundamentalism and inspired by the rogue cleric Abu Qatada. Read claimed to be working for Al-Qaeda, but it later emerged he had carried out the operation alone. The biggest fear for British Intelligence at the time was a lone operative. Tariq was a lone operative. He had shared none of his plans to anyone and was not under any suspicion or 'watch lists'; a deadly combination.

Just before his University term ended in June 2006, disturbing headlines were hitting the BBC newsfeed on his laptop in the college refectory. He read in dismay.

'The US and UK have hailed news that Abu Musab al-Zarqawi, leader of al-Qaeda in Iraq, has died in a US air strike. Zarqawi died when US planes dropped two 500lb (230kg) bombs on a site near the city of Baquba. He was identified by fingerprints, tattoos and scars. The US struck after receiving specific tip-offs from within Zarqawi's organisation, officials said.'

Zarqawi had been an inspiration for Tariq in his formative years, and he had of course met him briefly. There was some significant traffic on the websites seeking vengeance for his 'murder'. Tariq felt the pain again of the injustice and his frustration at being able to do nothing about it, yet.

That night prayers were said for Zarqawi at the Masjid, but there had been no mention of it that evening at home when he returned from college. It was like an elephant in the room.

The following week, there was another visit to Leeds from a Petronix HR representative to finalise details of his work placement. She was able to confirm that he would be attached to an offshore rig for the twelve months period and he would need to report to the local headquarters in Aberdeen on Monday 21st August for a six-week induction period which would include his Survival course, before he would be allowed off-shore. Tariq was eager to get started and baulked at the delay, but realised he would need to go along with whatever protocol dictated. His patience would be rewarded, he reasoned.

Accommodation would not be a problem, he would have the use of a company flat for the duration of his work placement and could claim travel expenses to and from Leeds which would cover his airfare; in addition he would receive a very generous salary package enhanced to reflect offshore working. Everything was in place; it was just a matter of time.

August 15th 2006, British HQ, Basra.

A few days before Tariq was due to start in Aberdeen, Major Howard was clearing out his desk and cupboards ready for a new assignment; the regiment was being transferred to Afghanistan.

He looked at the sacks of waste paper, mostly classified files and correspondence that would be incinerated prior to departure. He was on his last cabinet, second drawer down, 'H-K'. His first file in that run was a familiar name and, as he pulled out the folder and opened it, he was touched with sadness at the course of events and wondered what the truth was. He couldn't believe the man was working for the insurgents. He had come to view Abu Hanifa with a great deal of respect, in fact he remembered he had offered him the opportunity of taking the role as Regional Governor in the days immediately after the war. He read the reports and then the witness statements of the two informants, then a copy of the death certificate from the Iraqi regime. 'Heart attack' it said in English after the Arabic script.

The next piece of paper was the letter he had received from Leeds University confirming the acceptance of Tariq Siddique as a student. He had forgotten all about him.

Suddenly, as he read the file again, a thought went through his mind, a chilling thought. 'What if?' he suddenly asked himself.

If the rumours were correct and the witnesses were right that the mullah had been supporting terrorists, there was a good chance that his son may also have been radicalised. He remembered him as being an intense young man, polite and certainly very bright. But it was his eyes, eyes that seemed to be assessing, almost furtive, not 'honest' eyes, he recalled.

He looked again at the placement, Leeds University; an Engineering degree sponsored by Petronix; what opportunities might that open up for someone with mal-intent?

He picked up the phone.

"Brian? Tim... Can you spare me a few minutes... your place...? Yes, I know you have better coffee... ok... be with you in about twenty minutes, no... just tidying a few loose ends."

Twenty minutes later Major Howard was pulling up outside a rather grand looking building in the so called 'green zone' about half a mile from the 'Palace'. The fact that there was a sentry on guard was the giveaway that this was a place of some significance. After the obligatory security check, the driver steered the armoured jeep through the double gates and into the courtyard in front of the building. Major Howard left the jeep carrying a file.

"Come back in an hour," he told the driver, and watched as he pulled away.

The building, which was partially hidden from the road by high walls, was even more impressive close up. Formerly a hotel, its two white marble columns which framed the entrance glistened in the blistering heat. The major looked up and, despite his sunglasses, blinked at the intensity of the sun's rays reflecting from the brilliant-white building. Inside it was refreshingly cool.

"Thank goodness for air-conditioning," the major said to the desk sergeant.

The man looked up at the major without acknowledging the remark, eyebrows raised with an air of expectation.

"Major Howard for Major Dickinson. He's expecting me,"

The sergeant picked up his phone and dialled numbers and spoke.

"He's on his way, sir, please take a seat," the sergeant replied.

The major thanked him and sat opposite the desk. He looked around the concourse with its fine domed ceiling, ornately decorated in Islamic motifs. Purposeful men and women in military uniform crisscrossed the open area reception. It was a hive of activity.

A voice came from behind him. "Tim?"

The major turned around and greeted the voice.

"Brian, good to see you," and the pair exchanged handshakes warmly.

Major Dickinson was a tall man around six-feet with light sandy coloured hair which was beginning to thin; he spoke with just a hint of his Orkney origin, a rather pleasant understated Scots accent.

"Come through to the office," and the two walked down one of the adjoining corridors.

"I've got Graham Guest with me. I don't think you've met him; he's a Commercial Attaché at the British Embassy, based here at the consulate."

"No," said Howard and they entered a room about halfway down with Major Dickinson's name attached on a nameplate.

Inside it looked like any other office with filing cabinets, a map on the wall, a large desk with two seats in front, and a more casual space by the window with a coffee table and four easy chairs. A grey-flecked, dark-haired man in his early forties wearing an expensive-looking, light-weight pale blue suit was sat on one of the chairs and immediately got up and walked towards Major Howard with his hand extended.

"Major Howard? Graham Guest, Commercial Attaché at the embassy. Brian's been telling me about your exploits, seems you've done a great job here."

"Thanks," he said humbly. "Team effort."

The three sat down; there was a cafetière on the table with three cups.

"I'll be mother," said the civilian.

"So, Tim, Why the cloak and dagger? You sounded quite mysterious on the phone," said Dickinson.

Major Howard looked at the civilian.

"It's ok. He's one of us," said Major Dickinson. It was an open secret that many of the so called 'commercial attachés' were employed by the secret service.

Major Howard took a sip of his drink. "You're right about the coffee, Brian, this is very good."

"Italian, shipped in from Venice, best in Basra," said Dickinson with a grin.

Major Howard opened the file on the table and pulled out the top note which had a grainy photograph attached to it. He handed it to Dickinson with Guest looking over his shoulder.

"Imam Abu Hanifa," said Major Howard. "A contact of mine, provided some useful intelligence for us on the April 2004 bombings."

He looked at his hosts in turn; Dickinson was engrossed in the file.

"We had some intelligence on a man called Ibn Hajar Al-asqulani who had housed the bombers before they carried out the attack. They were using his house as a safe-house, Hanifa told us where we could find him," he clarified.

"What happened?" asked Dickinson, looking at the file.

"We paid Al-asqulani a visit, but he was killed in a fire-fight. Seemed to have been waiting for us."

"I remember that," said Dickinson looking up and making eye contact.

Guest was still trying to read the narrative on the note.

"A few months later, I received some information from two informants, one of them was Al-Asqulani's son; he said that the Imam, Abu Hanifa was very much involved with the insurgency, helped finance and paid for the housing of the bombers, according to the source."

"Were they reliable?" asked Dickinson.

Guest had finished reading the note and was now listening to Howard's response.

"Well, they seemed very plausible."

He took another sip of coffee.

"In fact, so much so, the Iraqi's arrested Abu Hanifa."

"What happened? Did they find anything out?" asked Guest.

"No, unfortunately. Died in custody, heart attack according to the Iraqi's, but they are inclined to be, how shall I put this? Over-zealous," said Howard.

"What about the informants?" asked Dickinson.

"Turned up dead on some wasteland a few weeks later, tortured... horrific it was. That's what got me thinking at the time. Someone badly wanted revenge for Abu Hanifa's death, which means he must have had some importance. We'll never know for certain."

"So, what's this got to do with Army Intelligence? A cold case, surely?" said Guest.

"Not necessarily, which is why I'm here. He had a son, adopted if I recall. I met him a couple of times, very bright, spoke good English. Anyway, following Abu Hanifa's earlier help with the Al-Asqulani situation, we managed to get him a place on an Engineering course at Leeds University as part of the sponsorship programme," said Howard.

Dickinson looked at Guest.

"So, his son is in the UK?" clarified Guest.

"Yes," said Howard. "Been there almost two years."

Guest picked up the file from the table and started looking at the rest of the correspondence.

"Petronix?" said Guest. "Says here he's working with Petronix," he repeated with a look of concern.

"Well, they're sponsoring him. I don't know where or even whether he's actually working, probably still studying," replied Howard.

It was Guest who was mulling over the letter from the university who responded.

"Could be nothing of course. We sent several students to the UK as part of the regeneration effort," he said. He flicked through Abu Hanifa's file again, "On the other hand."

He paused, then said. "Can I keep this file, major? I need to make some calls."

"Of course, it was going to be incinerated. It was only by chance that I opened it," said Howard.

The file remained closed on the desk whilst the three finished their coffee.

"So, what do you think of England's chances on Thursday?" asked Dickinson, a great cricket fan.

"What, at the Oval? Well if they play as well as they did at Headingly they should be ok. I thought Pietersen's knock in the first innings was amazing," said Major Howard, who shared Dickinson's passion.

The civilian put down the empty cup and got up.

"I'll leave you two to it." He put the file under his arm. "Thanks for this," he said, tapping the folder. "I'll let you know if I dig anything up," he added and headed for the door.

Dickinson acknowledged his wave as he made his farewells,

leaving the two military men debating the merits of the Pakistani spin attack.

The British Consulate-General in Basra reports to the British Embassy in Baghdad. The base played an important part in the British intelligence community and MI6 operatives used various covers over time while operating from there; they also had cultivated a network of agents among the local community. Back at the Consulate, Intelligence Officer Guest picked up the phoned a dialled the UK.

"J-TAC," was the reply, Joint Terrorism Analysis Centre, MI6.

"Andy Brittain there? It's Graham Guest, Basra HQ." There was a pause for a few seconds.

"Brittain," was the assertive voice.

"Andy...? Graham Guest...Basra... yeah, fine thanks. Look, it may be nothing, but I'm going to scan a file across. Could be a problem... not sure... possibly a lone operative."

Guest described the background to his enquiry. "Sandwich course at Leeds University sponsored by Petronix... name of Tariq Siddique... yeah ok... will do... cheers."

The pair hung up and Andy Brittain, a seasoned field operative waited for the ping of the email. It was a large file and took several minutes for the material to be uploaded but eventually Major Howard's Hanifa file was on the MI6 database being scrutinised by Andy Brittain and his deputy, Emily Porter.

Like his Basra connection, Brittain was in his early forties, slim and fit the result of a gruelling regime of triathlons and regular gym work. He had served with some distinction in covert operations across the world, but specialised in the Middle East theatre. He was an expert on Al Qaeda, and worked closely with the CIA and Mossad in trying to prevent terrorist attacks.

He pinged the email to his colleague's laptop, so they could both read the correspondence.

"What do you think?" asked Brittain.

"Don't like it," said Ms Porter, a thirty-year-old, former Cambridge Mathematics Graduate and renown in the office for her analytical skills, looking at the open laptop.

"Me neither... Zarqawi's name worries me. If Hanifa was involved with him then it could mean trouble. There are many factions out there dying to avenge his death... literally," said Brittain.

They both continued to read the file.

"What are you going to do?" asked Porter after she finished her scrutiny.

"Have a word with the boss," said Brittain.

"Oh, by the way," said Porter. "That website we've been monitoring... Saladin's been very active over the last few days... talking about striking a decisive blow to the infidels."

Brittain looked up from his laptop. "He's been banging on about that for ages."

"Yes, I know, but this is a bit different. I've spoken to the language guys and the latest translations suggest that the messages are more threatening, more... imminent."

"Ok, I'll take a look, but first we need to track down this guy to be on the safe side. I've got an uneasy feeling about him."

Each department in MI6 is controlled by a director, and Brittain and Porter walked into his office at the other side of the room. James Mansfield was a career Intelligence officer, now in his early fifties; he was well known and well respected in the 'community'.

He looked up, but not annoyed at the interruption, informal briefings were part of the ethos.

"Problems?" he asked.

Brittain outlined the information he had received from Basra.

"Hmm," said Mansfield. "You could be right," having heard the officer's recommendation. "See if you can find out where he lives... and where he's working. As you say it may be nothing but I don't believe in coincidences and the Yorkshire connection is worrying."

He looked at Porter. "Where are we with Saladin, any progress?"

"No, we've got GCHQ and the techs all over it, but no trace I'm afraid. I was telling Andy, the latest messages, he appears to be upping his game."

"What do you mean?" asked the director.

Porter outlined the content of the last message. *"'Revenge is close brothers... 9/11 will be a mere pimple on the...'"* she paused. "Ahem... *'arse' of the infidels compared with the destruction I will wreak.'"*

"Strange language," said Mansfield.

"It was as close a translation they could make," said Porter.

"How long has Saladin been blogging now?" asked Mansfield.

"Well, we picked him up about a year ago... the site's encrypted. We were lucky to find it, but there have been all kinds of nasty people commenting on there, including Zarqawi and Anwar al-Awlaki; definitely Al Qaeda linked."

"I thought he was in Yemen... Al-Awlaki," clarified the Director.

"He is... The Americans are keeping an eye on him." Porter continued. "Since Zarqawi was taken out, Saladin has been particularly active, almost as though he had taken it personally."

"And we are definitely sure that the blog originates from the UK?" asked Mansfield.

"Yes… according to the techs."

The Director looked at his desk as though in deep concentration.

"We really need to find him. Pull out all the stops on this one. I want him found."

"What about Siddique?" asked Brittain to clarify priorities.

"Yes, find out what you can and report back," said the Director.

Saturday August 20th 2006, Batley.

Having considered all his options, Tariq had decided to remain in Aberdeen for the six-week induction period, making use of the Petronix accommodation and, depending on the situation, would stay there during his on-shore periods. This surprised his Batley family who thought he would return to them, at least at weekends, as he knew nobody in Aberdeen. He said he would visit from time to time, but did not want to continue to be a burden on them.

This day, therefore, would be his last at the Cash and Carry and, despite his somewhat distant demeanour, the staff there were genuinely sad that Tariq was leaving. As he did the rounds of the store everyone had commended him on the work he had done; the computer systems were fast, flexible and, importantly, they worked. Tariq had recommended a local firm to continue with routine maintenance in his absence.

Samira was particularly effusive in her praise and, giving a lie to her ice-maiden image, actually hugged Tariq as they said goodbye.

"It's only for a year and you'll be back during holidays, so it's not as though we won't see you again," she said, portentously.

Later that evening, he visited the mosque and had dinner with his great friend the Imam. He related his excitement at his new job, mixed with a little apprehension.

"Allah will guide me, Allāhu Akbar," he said.

"Allāhu Akbar," repeated the Imam.

The Imam was wise and recognised that Tariq was on some kind of mission and urged caution.

"Please be careful, my friend. The path of righteousness is paved with many obstacles… You will need to be constantly vigilant."

"'Inšā' Allāh, I will prevail," he said, God willing.

They embraced warmly as they said their goodbyes. The mullah was not certain he would see Tariq again.

Back in his room, Tariq opened up his laptop and signed into his blog. He typed his user name 'Saladin' and started to compose.

'My brothers, I have talked for many months about my will to avenge Zarqawi and the blessed 19. Please be clear, the time is near.'

The following day, Tariq was on the doorstep saying goodbye to Sabeen, Jake and Yusuf. He had much to thank them for; they had endured a great deal during his stay which had disrupted and almost split the family. That said, Abdul was grateful for his expertise at the Cash & Carry. So, it was with mixed emotions that they said their farewells. Jake had made up with Tariq, but was still living with Jasmine's parents. Yusuf, on the other hand, had become closer to Tariq since the attack and promised to continue his prayers and to visit the Masjid. For Sabeen it was a relief and a chance to get the family back to normal.

Abdul had agreed to take Tariq to the airport which was only half an hour away. As was customary, he travelled light, just a hold-all carrying his clothes and toiletries with his laptop in a shoulder bag. There was an emotional farewell at the airport;

Abdul had become fond of his nephew despite the difficulties. There was, however, something that bothered him; he couldn't put his finger on. It was the way Tariq was talking; a finality. It was as though he was not expecting to see them again; no mention of any future visit.

"Goodbye Uncle," was all he said, as he walked away to the airport terminal carrying his modest luggage.

Abdul pondered this as he drove back to Batley.

The journey to Aberdeen was uneventful, taking just over an hour and, being in the UK, there was no passport-control just a walk to the baggage carousel, wait for the luggage and then a taxi. It was noticeably colder than when he had left Leeds and he was glad of his jacket and long sleeve sweatshirt despite it being August.

He looked again at his instructions as he waited for his bags. It was on Petronix notepaper and gave the address of the hotel where he would stay overnight, a temporary situation until he could pick up the keys of the apartment. The note also included the details of the local head office where he was to report the following day at nine o'clock. He checked his wallet... fifty pounds, a final gift from his uncle in recognition of his work. His bank account was healthy enough to last him until he received a salary, thanks to the generosity of Abdul, who had already covered all his University fees and books. Money was not an ongoing necessity.

The hotel was within walking distance of the Company HQ in the old part of the city close to the University, ironically. The taxi took him to the door. Tariq had difficulty in making any conversation, it seemed a totally different language, and after an initial attempt at small-talk, the driver gave up and the journey was conducted in silence.

He checked in and took the lift to the third floor and his room for the night. It was seven o'clock and still broad daylight outside, but rain was starting to cast a greyness over the city. After settling in he left the room and headed out for the mosque with his prayer garments which he had packed. The rain had been replaced by heavy cloud.

He had checked the internet earlier and delighted to find that the Islamic Centre was only a few minutes' walk from the hotel. He had found out that there were over five thousand Muslims living in Aberdeen; some, students or undergraduates, others in the legal and medical profession and many in the oil industry. This was great news as his worst fear was that he might attract unnecessary attention being the only non-white worker off-shore, particularly as the country was still on high alert.

He stayed for the isha, the evening prayers, which were well attended, over a hundred people inside. After the formalities were completed, he made a point of seeking out the Imam and introducing himself.

"You are most welcome," said the mullah, Ibrahim Hasam.

It was a busy evening and there was little time for pleasantries, but Tariq made a promise to visit again when his work schedule allowed. The Imam thanked Tariq "You will always be welcome," he said.

Despite being in a strange city, the spiritual comfort he received from his visit to the mosque meant that he had no feeling of loneliness; he was with his kind and felt at peace. He returned to his hotel and used the hotel's Wi-Fi connection to log into his blog and started to write his observations of the day. He would not be naming any locations just the fact he was moving closer to his dream of paradise. Tomorrow would be different.

Chapter Nineteen

Monday 21st August, 2006. Leisure Inn Hotel, Aberdeen.

Tariq awoke around six-thirty in his hotel room and took out his prayer mat from his luggage.

The built-in compass gave him the direction of Mecca and he knelt down and recited the words of the Fajr.

He had slept well in his temporary accommodation and, after a light breakfast, headed to the Petronix offices, again within walking distance. He was wearing the required smart casual attire, a jacket, slacks and shirt. It was a bright morning and several degrees warmer than the previous day with a hint of blue sky. There was a fishy smell in the air. Tariq remembered that there was still a fishing industry in Aberdeen.

Tariq walked towards the impressive glass-fronted building; the company flag flying proudly from a staff on the roof. It was just before the nine o'clock deadline, and he went in and found reception.

"Take a seat," said the receptionist, and, five minutes later, an administrator approached him.

She spoke in an accent similar to the taxi driver from the previous evening and Tariq couldn't understand a word. She had to repeat herself several times.

She gave Tariq his identity badge, which he was to wear at all times whilst in the building; they controlled access doors she said; or that is what it sounded like. They headed for the lifts and went up two floors.

"This is the HR department."

They were in a bright office with four people engaged in paperwork at their desks. There was another desk in the corner with someone that he thought looked familiar concentrating intently on a computer screen. They approached, and the person looked up.

"Kim, this is Tariq; he's starting with us today."

The lady from admin left him with the HR Manager.

"Hi Tariq," she said and offered her hand in greeting. Tariq shook it limply. "Won't be a second just finishing this email."

Tariq looked around the open-plan office. There was a large window running the length of the room and in the distance, you could see the sea.

After a few pleasantries, Kim stood up.

"Right let's go into the meeting room and I'll explain everything."

Her accent was not local and the dialogue much easier to understand. She picked up a file and walked along a short corridor to a small empty room. Tariq followed.

There was a table with chairs either side and Kim sat down.

"Have a seat… Would you like a coffee?"

"I am ok, thank you," replied Tariq as he sat opposite.

Kim was suddenly reminded of his understated personality.

She started by asking about his course at University and how he was getting on then outlined the next six weeks activity. He would be attached to the rig on-shore team which dealt with a variety of engineering related projects.

"It'll give you a better understanding of what we do here… and what it's like on the rig. Several of the team are ex off-shore workers. You can ask them any questions… Your Survival Course has been booked for..." She checked her notes. "September 11th for three days, so you'll have a few weeks to get acclimatised and get used to us before you go off-shore."

"Which rig is it?" he asked. Petronix controlled six in the upper North Sea.

Kim looked at her notes. "Delta Bravo."

Tariq nodded with some satisfaction. It was one of the most important rigs in the North Sea, certainly in Petronix' portfolio and with oil and gas production would have significant economic value.

After about half an hour, Kim got up and led Tariq to the floor below and to a bustling open plan office.

"We have several departments in here," she said.

Tariq looked at the screens on the wall with various pieces of information being frequently updated; wholesale gas prices; Brent Crude, spot rates, exchange rates, stock prices and a feed from BBC News. At the far end of the room by the window there was an area separated from the rest of the office by a two-metre-high divider.

Kim headed for the segregated spot with Tariq following. It was a comfortable area with what looked like a break-out space and six desks, four of which occupied with people with their heads in computer screens; one of them looked up.

"Hi Kim," then looked at Tariq who was hovering anxiously behind her. "You must be Tariq. I'm Keith Cohen, Project Manager. Come in, welcome to the mad-house."

He smiled warmly and offered his hand which Tariq took with no more than a token gesture.

"I'll leave you with Keith, but don't believe everything he says, he's a great story-teller," she said and smiled at the manager before walking back to her office.

The other three in the pod had by this time broke away from their respective computers and were assessing their new arrival.

"Hi Tariq, come and sit down and I'll introduce you to the rest of the team."

Rather nervously, he made his way around the back of Keith's chair, to a vacant adjacent desk. Tariq was aware that the other members of the team were staring at him.

Keith made the introductions.

"This is Ted Foreman, metallurgist, Alan Farmer, mechanical engineer, Will Suggett, electrical engineer."

They stood in turn and shook hands with Tariq who nodded in acknowledgement.

It was not easy for Tariq to make a first impression; he was short, five feet three or so and, due to his diet, extremely thin. This slight frame and his rather nervous, boyish-looking disposition meant he lacked bearing and authority from an appearance perspective. He relied on his knowledge and pragmatism to earn respect. It didn't bother him at all; he wasn't out to impress.

Keith gave Tariq some background about what they did and the various projects they were involved on together with a snapshot of each member of the small team. As Kim had said they were all veterans of off-shore working and between them had many years' experience. Will Suggett was younger than the rest; mid-thirties, the other three were in their late forties.

"You can have this desk here," he said pointing to one of the free chairs across the table from Keith. "We'll fix you up with a laptop later. I've spoken to IT and they are popping one up about eleven."

Tariq was trying to take everything in but eventually Keith left him to settle in and the rest of the team went back to their computers.

August 26ᵗʰ 2006, Vauxhall Cross, London; MI6 Headquarters.

Emily Porter was on the phone; she fiddled with her dark hair which hung lankly below her ears, trying to make curls; she pushed her fashionable spectacles back up the bridge of her nose. With her long skirt and loose white peasant blouse she looked a throw-back to the 1960's.

"Thanks for your help," she said and hung up.

"What's the latest on Siddique... any joy?" asked Andy Brittain.

"That was Petronix, HR department. It seems our man is in Azerbaijan."

"Are you sure?" asked Brittain.

"That's what they said, twelve-month attachment."

"Well, that lets us off the hook for the moment. He won't be causing any problems out there. If he steps out of line in that place, they'll lock him up and throw away the key."

He went back to his screen and updated some notes then looked across at Porter who was similarly adding notes to her laptop.

"What about Saladin?"

"Interesting post last night, '... *the clock is ticking... soon the sword of Allah will be rising from the sea like a mighty serpent*'... whatever that means."

Andy Brittain looked up quizzically.

"Rising from the sea, rising from the sea," he repeated. "What does that mean?"

"A ship perhaps?" posed Porter.

"Yeah, possibly..."

Brittain thought for a moment. "Where's the Illustrious?"

"In the Med I think, been helping out with the evacuation," replied Porter.

"Lebanon?"

"Yeah," she replied.

"Get in touch with her and let the captain know what we

have," said Brittain.

"You think they plan to take out an aircraft carrier?"

"I don't know, but we can't take any chances," said Brittain.

"But if he's UK based, it would seem unlikely," said Porter.

"Unless he's directing suicide bombers," he replied.

"I'll get on to it," said Porter.

"We must find him, get whatever resources you need," said Brittain.

"Already have. GCHQ have it as A1 priority, anything on that website will come straight to us for analysis. We've got Scotland Yard and the CIA on board as well… They're taking a big interest, but they've had no joy either."

Andy Brittain went back to his computer for a few minutes, but couldn't settle. He kept asking himself if he'd missed anything. He walked across to the Director's office. Mansfield looked at him as he walked in.

"You look troubled Andy. Anything I can help with?"

Brittain told him about the latest blog from Saladin.

"Thought it might be the Illustrious. She's in the Med at the moment off the Lebanese coast helping with the evacuation. I've sent out an alert just in case, but something's bothering me. Can't put my finger on it, but it doesn't feel right somehow."

They went through the transcripts again which were detailed on the Director's computer; he had taken a special interest in Saladin since he came on line.

"I know what you mean," said the director who was examining his screen with some purpose.

"You know something. I think he's a loner," continued Brittain. "If you look, he never talks about 'we'. The narrative's always in the third party or first person singular. Look at this one from the other day, he refers to the destruction I will wreak," he emphasised the 'I'.

"Yes, I take your point. Now, that gives us real problems," said the director. "What about those we took in following the London bombings?"

"We've interviewed all the detainees, and our contacts, but nobody knows anything... Or if they do, they're not saying."

Mansfield was deep in thought.

"No, I think you're right; this is a lone operator... with a real grudge. We're just going to have to rely on the techs."

Brittain got up and started to walk out. Mansfield called to him.

"You better keep our friends across the pond informed as well. You never know they might be able to throw something up."

"Will do," said Brittain.

He stopped at the door and turned. "Oh, nearly forgot. That graduate with Petronix." The director looked up. "In Azerbaijan, twelve months attachment."

"That'll save you a trip to Yorkshire then," said the director with a smile.

"Every cloud," said Brittain, "every cloud."

Monday 9th October 2006. Aberdeen Airport 6.15a.m.

Rory made his way to the registration desk from the main building where he had been to collect his parking permit for the two weeks. As a senior technician, he qualified for a pass which would be paid for by the company. Brent Helicopters had their own mini terminal a short distance away from the normal passenger entrance specifically for handling the offshore traffic.

Little had changed in the ten years since his first visit; it was still hectic on team-change days. He knew the desk team well;

he was a regular traveller and a popular face.

"Hi Woody," said Len Forrest behind the departure desk, a stocky man in his fifties with a shock of grey hair and wearing a 'Brent Helicopters' navy woollen jumper.

He checked in his baggage and ticked Rory off the list of passengers.

"How many have we got, Len?" said Calderwood.

"Aye, it's a full flight. Should be a reasonable trip, weather's set fair, slight breeze from the North West," he replied in his strong local accent.

Len was almost obsessed with the weather, but then so much depended on it; the helicopters couldn't get off in adverse conditions and it caused disruption on a regular basis. Something of which Rory was only too well aware.

"Thanks Len. Have you seen anything of a guy called Tariq Siddique, first trip. I'm his buddy?"

Len checked the twelve names on the manifest.

"Aye, he's on the list. Not checked in yet, take a seat; I'll give you a shout when he turns up."

"I think I'll notice," said Rory with a grin and took one of the uncomfortable plastic and metal seats that were fixed to the floor in the reception area.

There were four others, so far, returning on-shift, also waiting. He knew them well and was soon in conversation swapping stories of their shore leave. Doug Smallbrook, the safety rep for over twelve years and one of the few staff still on the rig from the early days, returned from the vending machine with a paper cup of what was euphemistically called coffee and sat next to him.

"How're things Woody, had a good leave?"

Rory considered the question for a moment; it had certainly

been eventful, but for the moment he wasn't disclosing too much. He did however recount his Survival Course renewal.

He checked his watch for the third time, six forty; his buddy was cutting it a bit fine, but, just then, he noticed a lad of Middle Eastern appearance getting out of a taxi and walk towards the terminal with a rucksack.

Rory approached him as he came through the automatic doors.

"You Tariq?" he said.

"Yes," replied Tariq.

"Well, you better get a move on, they'll be calling us through in a minute."

There was no formal greeting, and Rory led Tariq to the registration desk and introduced him to Len.

"Any mobile phones, laptops, cigarette lighters?" asked Len.

Tariq delved into his pocket and pulled out his phone.

"Put it in the bag. You can pick it up when you return. Anything else?"

Tariq shook his head and secured the mobile in a transparent plastic bag, then signed over the seal. He had left his laptop, out of sight, in the corporate flat... just in case he returned.

He handed his luggage over the counter to be scanned and loaded. He would pick it up again on arrival.

"Follow me," said Rory lengthening his stride and they went into an adjoining room where the passengers were changing into their PPE. Rory summoned the officer in charge of departure.

"Have you got any kit for this lad?"

"What size?" came the reply.

"Not sure, tiny I guess; he's as skinny as a rake," and one or two of the men overheard and started laughing.

"You'll need to hang on tight to those handrails. You'll get blown away," commented one wag.

They found a suitable suit, but it was still at least two sizes too big and the sleeves hung below his hands.

"Smallest we've got," said the officer.

Rory explained to Tariq the workings of the equipment and his responsibility as buddy. They completed the preparation with the re-breather kit and life jacket; he resembled an astronaut preparing to go to the moon.

"You've done your survival course?" the statement was phrased as a question.

"Yes, three weeks ago," replied Tariq.

"Good, just remember what you were taught, and you'll be ok... here grab a seat," and the men gathered round the TV to watch the compulsory evacuation video. Rory had seen it that many times he could recite the dialogue in his sleep.

Once the formalities and checks were complete, the men were ushered outside where the helicopter was in final preparation.

"You'll need these," Rory said as they waited to be called aboard, and handed Tariq two brightly coloured earplugs from the vending machine. Tariq looked at them, they resembled children's sweets. Rory indicated to Tariq what he needed to do with them.

The twelve were led to the trusty Puma which was in final preparation, the blades sweeping round at incredible speed. Rory pointed to Tariq to get on board. As a novice he would be seated in the middle of one of the rows.

The Puma slowly taxied onto the runway then after a short run lifted off the ground, which provided the team with what was colloquially called 'stomach awareness'. That soon passed, and they were out over the sea heading for the platform.

It was impossible to speak on board, as the noise, mixed with ear plugs, meant no-one could hear. This was no bad thing on the first day of a shift as most men did not want to say much. The pilot did have a microphone to give instructions to the passengers which was loud and clearly audible.

As they sat back each in their own thoughts, Rory reflected on his two weeks leave which had changed his life, his three-day survival course, Janie leaving him... and Kim.

For the first time in a long while he felt empty as he said goodbye this morning. He had stayed over at Kim's and it had been another passionate encounter; he had never experienced such intensity. Getting up at five was a real wrench, but Kim had made him a coffee and some toast for breakfast while he showered and got his gear together. She too had found it difficult to say goodbye.

"Don't forget I'm coming out a week on Tuesday for an overnight," she said. "I can nip down the corridor to see you," she said with a grin.

"I don't think we'd get away with that," said Rory and smiled.

He thought of his boys, he had not seen them for over a week and was missing them badly. He couldn't gauge his feelings towards Janie; he didn't hate her or anything, just a blank where there used to be affection. He had tried to analyse where it had all gone wrong, but it was a pointless exercise; she had gone and that was that. He would have to move on.

He looked across at Tariq who had his eyes closed and appeared to be meditating; his hands were shaking.

His demeanour concerned Rory; it reminded him of the helicopter trips in Iraq to 'a job' where men would be contemplating going to war. He nudged him, and Tariq opened his eyes and looked at Rory.

"You ok?" he mouthed. Tariq nodded but there was no warmth

in the exchange. Rory couldn't believe he was babysitting a 'rag-head'.

Tariq was meditating again and considering the task that lay before him. It was also the third week of Ramadan and he needed to maintain his prayer routine.

Despite his earlier reticence, his induction period had proved to be a valuable part of his preparation. He had spent two weeks with each of the team learning about all aspects of the rig and had gathered a great deal of information that would help him in his quest for martyrdom. He quickly recognised that he wouldn't be able to exactly replicate the conditions that had caused the Piper Alpha disaster as he had, in retrospect, naively, hoped. The processes had been changed to prevent such circumstances. Everything was controlled electronically, and sensors would indicate any defects or faults and feed them back to the central control panel for investigation. The human element, including the permit process which had been an important factor in the tragedy, had been virtually eliminated.

Tariq also discovered that all servicing and repair work on the rig was carried out in pairs, no-one was allowed outside the accommodation area unaccompanied. All of this had created additional problems for Tariq in his plans.

It was his two weeks with Will Suggett, the Electronic Engineer, which proved to be most informative. Tariq was now an expert in circuitry diagrams and computer technology; the last module in his degree course before recess was computer science and programming which he had found fascinating. He already had a good understanding, but his studies had taken it another level. Will had commented on Tariq's expertise which was, he had said, on a par with his own.

The survival course he had found the most intimidating part

of his induction. He had lied when the group were asked the question if he could actually swim; which he couldn't, so when faced with the daunting prospect of walking twelve feet under water to use the re-breathing apparatus, it was a terrifying experience. He was told beforehand and in the initial briefing that anyone 'failing' the survival course would not be allowed to work off-shore and as swimming was an essential part of the course, he would have to manage. Staying afloat wasn't a problem, everyone wore life-jackets reflecting real conditions, but propulsion proved difficult. In fairness his fellow delegates had been very supportive and helped him get through. It had been one of the most traumatic events of his life, but he later reflected that it had been his strong faith which had enabled him to overcome the fear.

The company flat he had been allocated was clean and comfortable and in a convenient location; not too far from the hotel which made visiting the mosque a short walk. There was a launderette close by for his washing and a number of fast food outlets, although, uncertain of their Halal credentials, he had become a vegetarian.

He was a regular visitor at the mosque and had made new friends, although getting there during Ramadan, which had started on 23rd September, had proved to be a challenge due to his work commitments. He got on well with the Imam, although it was quickly obvious he did not share Tariq's version of the Quran and the sixth Pillar. He held the same view as his Uncle Abdul.

The Masjid played an active part in the Muslim community both as a social centre and educational facility, and Tariq was only too pleased to help out training some of the children in religious studies.

As he reflected back over the last six weeks or so from the noisy surrounds of the helicopter five hundred feet above the North Sea, it was his blog which had kept him going. He had received messages of support from across the world and some high ranking Al Qaeda officials were already heralding his posts of significant importance and giving strength to the cause of Jihad, inspiring others to 'take up the sword'. These messages from people he respected gave impetus to his mission.

The rig came into view. Tariq couldn't see clearly being in the middle of the helicopter but as they got closer he could get an idea of the scale of the structure. The enormous helipad with its letter 'H' to guide the pilot home was the aiming point. There was a large 'Delta Bravo' logo on the side of the main block. Tariq counted four derricks; crane-like constructions that rose from the rig like giant tentacles. One at the far end had a large flame billowing from it where surplus gas was being burned.

The helicopter hovered then gently settled down; the firefighters with their hoses at the ready looking like astronauts in their flame-resistant outfits. Tariq stared out of the window across Rory in amazement.

The door was opened and one by one the men peeled out and, bending to avoid the downdraft of the blades, made their way to the rear of the Puma to retrieve their luggage. Then it was down two flights of stairs to the accommodation block and control centre. Rory led Tariq to the changing area where they would store their PPE. Tariq had been allocated his own personal locker which had his name on it.

As was customary, Tariq was led to the control centre to meet the OIM, as Rory had been ten years earlier. Bill McCredie had retired in 2004 but it was another Scot, Hamish Ferguson, known, unsurprisingly, as 'Fergie' to everyone. Ferguson was a seasoned operator with over twenty years' service off-shore, with experience in Africa and the Gulf of Mexico. He was someone the men respected. He was in discussion with a couple of his managers when Rory knocked on the open door.

"Fergie, just delivering our latest recruit. This is Tariq," Rory said.

"Sid," said Tariq, looking at the man. "People call me Sid."

They didn't; but this was part of Tariq's plan to ensure integration, choose a western name like Jake and Freddie.

Rory left him and walked towards the galley to get a coffee.

The two officers turned around to look at the visitor, and the OIM got up from his desk and introduced himself. He offered his hand which seemed to engulf Tariq's. The OIM was a big man, archetypical of an oilman, John Wayne-like in appearance and dwarfed Tariq who for a moment felt like the young lost little boy that had been found wandering around the compound all those years earlier.

"Can you come back later, guys? I'll just spend a few minutes with young Sid here," he said, and the others left leaving Tariq alone with Ferguson.

Tariq looked around at the office; it might be important. It was not a large room, but functional, with charts and screens on the wall displaying various pieces of information. Tariq took in everything. He observed the view of the North Sea which appeared reasonably amenable today with just a three-foot swell. On the desk there was a two-way radio and a couple of phone handsets next to a computer monitor.

After the welcome briefing and introduction, Ferguson eventually took Tariq to the galley and handed him back to Rory who had finished his drink.

"Want a coffee, Sid?" asked Rory.

"I'm ok," Tariq replied, and Rory got up and continued a quick tour of the accommodation area including the cinema and recreational rooms. He was losing interest in his uncommunicative protégé and keen to get on with his work.

"Is there a prayer room?" asked Tariq. Rory viewed him with a look of disbelief.

"Not much call for a prayer room here."

"I'll manage," said Tariq.

"Come on, I'll show you to your suite," said Rory, with a hint of sarcasm, and the pair went back upstairs to the sleeping area. Rory hadn't warmed to him at all.

Half an hour later, Tariq was back in the control room and was introduced to his mentor, Dave Morrison, like Tariq, a young graduate, but with two years' service on Delta Bravo.

"I'm Dave," he said without any other formalities.

"Tariq, but people call me Sid," he said again.

Rory had had enough of wet-nursing; he had got work to do and left the pair to go back to his office. As a senior engineer he had the status of an office and a reporting team of six. Their main task was routine maintenance which was like painting the Forth Bridge someone had said; it never finished. There were schedules for every piece of equipment; every nut and bolt, every girder, joist and fitment had to be regularly checked against a strict timetable and signed off. Where potential failures were spotted, a detailed note was made, and replacements ordered; then the remedial work carried out. Some pieces of equipment were replaced as a matter of course as recommended by the manufacturer. As well as repair and maintenance, Rory, because of his experience, was also regularly called in to sort out breakdowns. The 'trouble- shooter', the OIM called him.

During the day he thought about the new recruit. Apart from

the fact he was Iraqi, which automatically put him on guard, he didn't trust any of them; he had taken a dislike to him. His whole persona was almost arrogant. Then there was his limp handshake; in his book that denoted a weak character, and, although he spoke little, his shifty eyes said a lot. They appeared to be assessing everything. He hadn't said anything to the OIM; he was going to keep a watching brief.

Elsewhere on the rig, 'Sid' was being shown around by Dave Morrison. Mid-twenties, with an engineering degree from Exeter, he was over six feet tall, well-built and a keen user of the gym; he was soon sharing his passion for Rugby in his West Country burr with the new recruit.

"Yes, play prop for my local club when I'm onshore. Do you play at all?" he asked, which given Tariq's stature, was a daft question. Tariq just shook his head.

Dave was given the task of mentoring Tariq during the first few weeks and would be on hand to answer any questions. He had given him a breakdown of his work schedule which had been allocated by the duty officer. Dave also detailed the permit system on the rig, a fundamental part of working in hazardous environments.

"It's a simple but effective process that requires a permit to be issued for any piece of work to be undertaken on site," he said rather formally; he was taking his coaching role seriously.

"I understand," said Tariq. "We covered it on my induction."

"Oh, good," said Dave. "To start with, you'll be based in the Control Room. You'll get an idea of the workings from there," he added, walking quickly towards the central stairwell.

Tariq followed trying to keep up with Dave.

"We'll pick up your laptop when we come back up for lunch."

Tariq did not respond verbally, but nodded in acknowledgement.

Dave would not have seen it.

They descended another two floors to the hub of the rig.

"Below here it's 300 feet to the North Sea," said Morrison, dramatically, stamping his feet on the floor.

This was more like it, Tariq thought, as he entered the room; banks of dials, switches, and screens all feeding data into the control desk monitoring the rig's performance. They were larger versions of the information being fed to the screens in the OIM's office, he recognised.

There was a computer room adjoining the control centre with a red sign saying, 'No admittance, Authorised Persons Only'.

There was a security pad to gain access.

Monday 16th October, MI6 headquarters; 4.45 pm.

Junior analyst, Dominic Vestry, walked up to his boss, Emily Porter.

"I think you should see this, Em."

"What am I looking at?" she asked scanning the two forms he had presented.

"This one is a copy of the immigration papers for Tariq Siddique, September 2004."

"So?" she said scanning the detail.

"These are the visa documents for Tariq Siddique for a twelve-month attachment to Petronix Oil and Gas Inc., Baku, Azerbaijan."

"So," said Porter.

"The photos," said Dominic. "They're not the same."

"Fuck!" exclaimed Porter.

Chapter Twenty

Porter and Vestry went across the room to Andy Brittain's desk. He was on a call. Emily Porter began pacing up and down, clearly agitated, and in a hurry. Brittain spotted the urgency.

"I'll call you back," he said, and put down the phone. He glanced up at the pair.

"What is it?" he said, recognising the anxiety on Porter's face.

"Andy, you need to see this," and she handed him the two pieces of paper.

Dominic was behind her watching for his reaction.

"The photos, Andy," said Dominic. "They're not the same."

Andy re-read the documents and stared closely at the photos.

"Even with the beard, they're not the same people," Dominic re-iterated.

"Shit, you're right. Well done, Dom... Em, get onto Petronix straightaway, and check again, would you."

Porter went back to her desk and picked up the phone. She opened her address book on her desktop; she looked at the clock, four fifty-five.

"What time do HR departments close, Dom?"

"About now, I expect," he replied.

"Shit." She said under her breath as she dialled the number. The phone rang out, five seconds, eight seconds, twelve seconds. She looked at Dom and raised her eyebrows.

"HR department, Becky speaking," came a bright voice.

"I need to speak to your manager, urgently, this is Emily Porter, Security Services. I spoke to her last month."

"She's left I'm afraid. She picks her daughter up at quarter to... I'm the only one in the office. Can I help at all?" said Becky.

"Yes… yes, you can. I need some information on one of your graduate trainees, a Tariq Siddique," said Porter.

"Sorry, Jessica's left as well. She's the Graduate Recruitment manager; she looks after all the graduates."

"Can you access your personnel database?" said Porter.

"The terminals are closed. I was just leaving," said Becky.

"Becky, this is very important. I need this information and I need it right now," said Porter, her frustration getting the better of her.

"I can't give out personal details over the phone."

Porter was exasperated.

"Becky, I need you to do this; it's very important."

She tried another tack. "OK, ok, ok, who is the Head of HR?"

"Giles King, but he doesn't work here, he's on the sixth floor."

"What's his number?"

"Just a minute."

Porter was about to explode; another minute.

"He's on extension 2789."

"Becky, turn on your computer and access your personnel database. I'm going to phone Mr. King and he will authorise the information. Don't leave... ok?"

"You won't be long will you, only I've got a bus at twenty past?"

"Just wait there and turn your computer on."

Porter put down the phone and looked at Dominic. "Arghhh!" she exclaimed, and started dialling again. The phone was answered after three rings.

"Giles King's extension."

"Can I speak to Giles King please?" said Porter.

"Sorry, he's in Dubai this week, can I help? Vicky Walters, I'm his PA."

"Vicky, listen," and Porter explained what she needed. "Can you ring down and speak to Becky in HR and get her to give me this information, it is extremely important. No, I know you don't usually give out personal details, but I haven't got time for a court order."

This seemed to have a resonance and two minutes later Porter was back on the phone with the unlucky Becky who was about to miss her bus.

"Becky, it's Emily Porter again. I need some information on one of your graduates called Tariq Siddique... that's S I D D I Q U E," she spelt it out. Have you got your personnel database up?" she said.

"Yes," said Becky.

"Siddique, you say...? Just a minute."

"Yes... ok."

There was a delay as Becky tried to find the information. Porter drummed her fingers on the desk anxiously. "Come on, come on," she said to no-one in particular.

"Which one do you want...? We've got two," said Becky.

"I just need to know where they are," said Porter.

"One's in Azerbaijan..." There was a pause. "The other is in... just a minute... Aberdeen... Yes, gone offshore it looks like, according to the notes."

"Thank you, Becky," she said.

"Anything else I can help you with?" said Becky.

"No that's fine, thank you," said Porter and she rang off.

Porter looked at Dominic.

"Aberdeen, gone offshore."

They went across to the Director's office where Andy Brittain was already briefing Mansfield.

They looked up as Porter entered the room.

"Aberdeen, James… gone off-shore, they think."

"Do we know which rig he's on?" asked Mansfield.

"No," said Porter.

"Right, get onto Petronix in Aberdeen, they'll know, and you and Andy get up there as soon as you can. You better take Dom as well, could be useful. Well done by the way," he added, looking at Dominic.

"Dom, can you get us booked on a flight to Aberdeen tonight?" asked Porter.

The three left the Director's office and started to make arrangements. All three were soon on the phone. They knew the drill; all three kept emergency kits on the premises for such occasions.

Dom was the first to come off the phone.

"British Airways, Heathrow eight twenty-five, last flight from London. I've booked three. I'll get a hotel sorted."

"Thanks Dom," said Brittain who had just come off the phone to his wife. He wouldn't be coming home tonight. It was not the first time; part of the job.

"Andy, I've just come off the phone from Petronix in Aberdeen… Siddique's on Delta Bravo," shouted Porter from her desk.

She joined him at his desk; he was already Googling the name. The search engine brought up a picture and details from Petronix website.

"Here it is, Oil and Gas. Wow look at that," he said, looking at the production output.

"Jesus, that could turn out a few lights if that lot goes up," said Porter.

The Director joined him at the desk.

"Andy, I've been on to Arbroath and put them on alert…"

"Ok, so, how do you want to play this?" said Brittain.

The Director looked at him and Porter.

"Well let's calm down for a moment and just think this through. We'll need to be very careful. Firstly, we should remember that we have no evidence, at this stage, that this guy is up to no good... he could be just another graduate trainee. We don't want another Menezes situation on our hands." He looked at them gravely.

Brittain and Porter looked at each other, only too aware of the innocent Brazilian who was shot not so long ago by armed police following inaccurate intelligence and poor decision making.

"And, if he is a threat, then we don't want to spook him in taking any precipitous action," continued the Director.

"But he could be active now, this minute," replied Porter.

"Yes, he could, but he hasn't made a move yet, which means either he hasn't had the opportunity or... he's not ready."

Porter and Brittain digested this thought.

"So, what do we do then?" asked Porter.

"Get up to Aberdeen, find where he's been living, see if there's anything to cause us concern, then we can act with more certainty. If we do need to call out the SBS, they can be there in under two hours by helicopter."

"Bit of a gamble, sir," said Porter.

"I know, but we need to be certain," said the Director. "I don't want to find myself in front of a Select Committee."

"Shit!" exclaimed Andy. "I've just had a thought... that message from Saladin... Allah rising from the sea?"

"Oh my God," said Porter.

"What's the latest on Saladin?" asked the Director.

"Nothing since last Sunday," said Porter.

"You mean a week yesterday?" asked Mansfield.

Porter nodded. "Yeah."

"Now that is worrying... Ok, find out when Siddique went offshore," said the Director.

A few minutes later, Porter was back in the Director's office.

"Just spoken to Petronix again. He went out last Monday."

"Where's Andy?"

"Gone to get his stuff together," replied Porter.

"Let him know. I'll speak to Arbroath again keep them in the loop," and the Director picked up his phone and dialled.

Twenty minutes later, three agents were on the Tube heading to Heathrow. It would take over an hour in the rush hour, the carriages packed like sardines until they got they got past Hammersmith when they were able to get a seat.

It was seven forty-five before they reached the check-in desk. The office had phoned ahead and explained the situation and the desk crew were waiting for them with their boarding cards.

The journey to Aberdeen took just over an hour and a quarter and they touched down about quarter-to-ten. Outside the terminal building they queued briefly for a taxi, then they were heading for the hotel, ironically the same one that Tariq had stayed at on his first night.

"Wind's getting up," said Andy, as they got out of the taxi and made their way to reception. Porter and Dominic were crossing the road with their heads bent to protect themselves.

"You can say that again," shouted Porter to make herself heard.

Tuesday 17th October, Aberdeen Airport 6.45 a.m.

Kim was at the check in desk and Len was giving her the latest weather information.

"Wind's dropped a bit since last night, but will increase again by midday, deep low pressure building from the west. Just as well you're staying over, we may not get you off later today. Could peak at force ten or severe storm force eleven by this evening; slight drop predicted for tomorrow," he said gravely.

"Stuck out on a gas rig with two hundred hunky men, a girl can't complain about that," she said with a grin.

Len laughed. "Hadn't seemed so attractive until you mentioned it."

It was a difficult trip, the wind tossing the helicopter like a sycamore seed floating to earth from the safety of its tree. Landing on the rig was a tribute to the skill and dexterity of the pilot; but uncomfortable and disconcerting for the passengers. The Puma had to make two attempts, but they eventually touched down, much to the relief of the passengers. Kim completed her disembarking procedures and headed for the changing area before reporting to the OIM.

Rory was hanging around his office wanting to make sure she had arrived safely.

They had managed to stay in touch; offshore, the men were allowed to use outgoing lines for personal use on a 'reasonable' basis, but seeing her as she came down the steps, still managing to look attractive even in her PPE, made Rory realise how much he had missed her.

"You ok?" he said, but wanted to hold her.

"Bit bumpy... I'll catch up in a minute... just get changed," and she went to stow her PPE.

Rory was waiting and with no one around managed to steal a kiss.

"Missed me then," she said with a smile.

"You'll never know," he replied.

"Catch you in the lounge later, better get down to some work," and she quickly pecked him on the cheek and headed for the OIM's office for her routine visit.

Ferguson was pleased to see her. As the only female on board she was used to the attention.

"Coffee?" he asked, as she came into the room. Before she answered, he was pouring two mugs from a filter coffee jug that had been stewing on its base for two hours.

"Thanks," she said, making herself comfortable at the table opposite Ferguson.

She took a sip from the mug and looked at the sludge staring back at her masquerading itself as coffee.

"'Urghhh!" she exclaimed as the liquid hit the back of her throat. "Good grief, Fergie, what on earth do you call this...? Much more and I'll be bouncing off the ceiling."

The OIM laughed. "Put hairs on your chest."

"Now that I don't need," she replied.

After a catch up, it was down to business and Kim discussed usual matters - headcount, training, succession planning, and performance issues. It took over an hour to cover their agenda.

She was putting her papers back in her briefcase, ready to get to her on-board desk. She looked across at Ferguson.

"How's that new graduate, Tariq, getting on?"

Ferguson had to stop and think for a moment.

"Oh, Sid you mean? Seems to be settling in alright, bit quiet, doesn't mix with any of the lads. Seems to know his stuff though. Davy Morrison's mentoring him, says he's a bright lad. He's off-shift at the moment."

"When's he due back on?"

The OIM checked the roster on his computer.

"Eight o'clock, started the nightshift yesterday... He

volunteered, which is a bit strange, we don't often get graduates volunteering for nights. He said it was so he could schedule his prayers. It's not a problem, I don't mind doing my bit for diversity… He'll be around later this afternoon… He doesn't seem to need much sleep, very keen. Wish we had more of them… I'll get Davy to send him to you when he surfaces; he won't mind."

"Thanks Fergie," she said and got up and went to the cafeteria for a more palatable injection of caffeine before heading to her work desk.

Tariq's first week had gone well; the rest of the first day was spent with his mentor. He had taken him through the various safety processes, evacuation procedures, and muster stations and then it was meeting people; he continued to introduce himself as 'Sid'.

There was some initial curiosity of having the first Muslim on board, not least from the new catering manager, George Stafford, who wanted to clarify any special needs. This was a token gesture, there was no provision for 'namby-pamby' diets.

It was clear that halal meat could not be guaranteed, so Tariq would continue his vegetarian regime, but with it still being Ramadan for another two weeks, food would not be a major issue. When Tariq explained about Ramadan he was surprised when George agreed to put a meal by for him to eat in the evening after sunset.

Tariq was delighted with the prospect of working in the Control Room; from here he hoped to be able to launch his plan. He was introduced to the Manager, Rob Cousins who was happy to be taking the new recruit under his wing.

After the introductions, Dave Morrison left them to it, leaving

Rob to explain the function of the control room with Tariq.

"Welcome to the brains... it's what makes this place tick," he said proudly.

Tariq was already very familiar with its workings and had studied the circuitry and schematics in some detail. He even had a mock up on his laptop which nobody knew about. Brian was impressed by the trainee's knowledge based on the intelligent questions Tariq was asking as he was explaining the flow diagrams. Tariq still needed to finalise information just in case of any adjustments to his plan.

On the second day, in a break from his duties in the control room, he received a guided tour of the production platforms by Dave Morrison. Tariq looked ridiculous in his full PPE; there was nothing that would fit properly. The hard hat was perched on top of his head at a strange angle and kept slipping; his goggles were three sizes too big and so were his boots.

"We're going to have to build you up a bit," said the quartermaster who issued the kit.

Luckily, for the immediate future, his work would be carried out inside, which would give enough time for appropriate clothing to be shipped in. An order would be requisitioned.

They left the confines of the accommodation and control module and headed outside. Tariq was trying to keep up as his boots slopped around his feet, his toes attempting to grip the leather soles. The wind at this time was not too bad, just force three according to the anemometer; a stiff breeze by North Sea standards, but the noise from the sea was unbelievable, even drowning out the sounds of the rig.

To get to the production area meant crossing the open walkway with the metal grill flooring. Tariq held onto the guide rail and looked straight ahead trying not to display the nervousness he felt; the crashing waves of the North Sea were clearly visible three hundred feet below. He said a silent prayer to give him strength. Spray splashed his face as the force of the waves on the rig sent water vapour soaring into the sky even reaching their narrow crossing, fifty feet of hell.

Through another door they entered an area resembling an aircraft hangar open at each end to allow wind to pass through the construction. Tariq looked on in amazement; seeing things in computer diagrams was one thing, seeing it live was something else, awe inspiring. The scale was immense. There was piping of every size and description everywhere, pumps, extraction units, and enormous vessels, metal cages, safety equipment. In fact, everything you would expect to see to enable the natural resources of the North Sea to be safely delivered to the UK consumer. There was the constant hum from the machinery and Dave had to shout to Tariq for him to hear.

He explained the inner workings of the rig and Tariq took particular interest in the incoming condensate pipes where gas in its natural liquid form is received from the wells before being processed and sent on its way through pipelines downstream to the shore. This was one of the most dangerous areas on the rig and where the initial Piper Alpha explosion had occurred.

There were numerous safety features built in, including an automatic shutdown system and hoses that had the capability of shooting sea water at high pressure which would, in theory at least, be able to extinguish most fires.

Tariq had also studied this area whilst on shore and was very familiar with their workings. Dave noticed his keen interest and was impressed by his detailed knowledge.

On the other side of the gas production site was another walkway which led to the final module which managed the oil production; Tariq could see the huge derrick hanging out from the far end of the rig, well away from the accommodation module, with the flame associated with oil rigs lighting up the grey sky at its top. The roaring noise of the flame was quite audible. Dave led the way across the gantry but it was to be a brief visit just a 'show around', he was due in a meeting, but Tariq knew the workings.

"A brilliant piece of engineering," he said later. All the time he had been taking everything in, particularly the positioning of the CCTV cameras and sensors. Back in the Control Room Tariq had much to think about and having seen the layout of the rig first hand he began fine-tuning his plans.

Tuesday 17th October. Petronix Headquarters, Aberdeen, 8.30 a.m.

Andy Brittain and his team were in discussion with the on-shore duty manager, Doug Earnshaw, getting some background information on Tariq's duties during his induction attachment. The answers did nothing to allay his fears. They left with the address of the caretaker who had keys to the corporate flat. The plan was to make a discreet entrance and take a look around.

Having acquired the keys, within half-an-hour they were in the back of a taxi heading for Tariq's flat. Brittain and Porter were in discussion outlining a plan of action. Dominic was on his laptop sending an update to the Director.

"From what I could gather, he's been working with one of the project teams and has had virtually unlimited access to information about the rig. They said he seemed very knowledgeable… They were actually pretty impressed with him," said Brittain.

"I bet they were," said Porter.

Ten minutes later, the three got out of the taxi at the address and headed to the front entrance.

"Wind's got up," said Porter as they crossed the road.

It was in a nice area, well maintained, a 1930's-style apartment block.

Tariq's accommodation was on the top floor, and they ascended the stairs. They reached the entrance and Dominic opened up; the search began.

"I'll say this, he's very tidy, for a man," said Porter.

Andy viewed the room.

"This is strange," he said. "Look at everything, nothing out of place."

They walked through the flat, just one bedroom; the bed was made. In the closet, what was left of Tariq's meagre wardrobe, was neatly washed and ironed.

"It's like no-one lives here," said Porter. She looked at Brittain.

"Laptop," he said, to bring focus to the visit. "If he's Saladin, then he must have a laptop... He won't be able to take it on the rig... so, it has to be here somewhere. That's our priority; we must find it."

A more systematic and detailed search took place, the sofa was tipped upside down; then replaced; the two armchairs, the wall unit, desk. Dominic was looking in less obvious places, the cistern on the toilet. "That's where all the villains hide their guns," he said.

"You've been watching too many gangster films," said Porter.

"Notice anything else missing?" asked Brittain.

"Like what?" replied Porter.

"There're no religious artefacts, pictures, symbols... nothing," replied Brittain.

"Probably taken them with him," said Porter.

"Yeah, possibly... but the son of an Imam. I would have expected something more demonstrative. I don't know, I may be reading more into this."

They went into the kitchen; it was small, but contained all the necessary requirements.

"The fridge is empty," said Porter.

"Probably would be, if you weren't coming back for two weeks," said Brittain.

"Or not at all," said Dominic. Brittain looked at him, then Porter.

"Here, Dom give me a hand," and the two of them moved the cooker back from the wall, nothing.

"It must be here somewhere," said Brittain.

"Just a minute," said Dominic. "What about...? Quick, pass me a chair."

Brittain pulled out one of the two chairs around the breakfast table and Dominic placed it by the cooker. He stood on it and examined the cooker hood closely.

"Either someone has changed the filters recently or...."

He released the two hooks on the side of the casing and pulled down sharply on the hood. There was a crash as a laptop slipped from its confines and hit the surface of the electric hob. There was a nasty crack running across it, caused by the impact.

"I hope that comes out of your expenses," said Dominic as he retrieved the computer.

He went to the breakfast table next to the door and opened up the laptop. It appeared non-the-worse for its fall.

"Password protected," said Dominic.

"Well it would be, said Brittain. "Can you sort it?"

"Possibly," and Dominic went to the lounge to retrieve his

hold-all, which had been inseparable from him since they left London.

Dominic returned to the kitchen with his tools and sat at the small table, the laptop open in front of him. He set to work providing a running commentary for his inquisitive colleagues.

"The initial login passwords on most computers are stored in an encrypted SAM file and in my box of tricks I just happen to have some software that will get me in there."

Brittain looked at Porter. "Let's hope it works," he said.

"While you are doing that, I'll pop out and get some sandwiches it could be a long afternoon," said Porter. "Any preferences?"

She took their orders and headed out.

"Won't be long," she said as she headed out of the flat. It was twelve-thirty.

Brittain watched Dominic insert a disc from his bag into the DVD drive; there was a whirring noise as it loaded up.

"Bingo," said Dominic, as the software wove its magic. "There it is."

"What's that?" asked Brittain.

"The user names for the laptop... Just Tariq Siddique, by the look of it. All I need to do is to choose the option, 'remove password',' he clicked the appropriate box. "Now we just reboot and we won't need a password, it'll have been over-ridden."

"That's impressive," said Brittain as he watched Dom at work.

"Don't worry, getting in is the easy part," said Dominic, as the laptop spring back into life.

Dominic opened up the web-browser.

"Now my guess is, he'll have deleted his browsing history...

if he hasn't, then we can find the websites he's been visiting…
If he is Saladin, then we can possibly get on the blog."

He tried the 'Browser history' button.

"No, it's empty, just as I thought. Never mind there are ways," and he went back in his bag and produced another CD.

As he loaded it, he explained to Brittain.

"The browsing history is normally stored on Index.DAT files," said Dom.

Brittain was none the wiser.

"Don't worry I can get in," and, once again, Dominic was able to retrieve the information.

"No porn sites," he said jokingly. "But… wait a minute, look at this," and several websites appeared in Arabic.

"Can you read it?" asked Brittain.

"No, but we know a man who can," and Dominic copied the information onto a memory stick.

Just then Porter returned, looking decidedly dishevelled, with some food.

"God, it's wild out there," she said. "Here you are guys."

She handed out packets of sandwiches and crisps. "Any joy?"

"Yes," said Brittain. "Dom's managed to get into the laptop and get his web browsing history. The websites are in Arabic."

"I'm going to email this to Malik in London. He'll be able to translate it and maybe we can access the blog if it's there," said Dominic.

He loaded the information to his own laptop and sent it down to Vauxhall House marked 'urgent'.

"Now, we just wait," said Brittain.

He started eating his chicken salad sandwich.

"Any tea?" he asked.

"No, and I'm not going back out there again," said Porter.

Chapter Twenty-One

The email reached Malik Shafiq's computer.

After more than ten years with the Service, he was an important member of the Middle East desk, a bilingual Arab speaker as well as an IT expert, an extremely valuable combination. Dominic hoped he had done enough for him to make sense of Tariq's websites.

Malik saved the data onto his desktop and opened the file. Using a standard browser, he was able to access the websites recently frequented by Tariq. There were several fundamentalist sites, but there was one in particular which recurred on a daily basis.

The literal Arabic translation was 'Sword of Allah', and the home page contained pictures of various 'martyrs' praising them for their sacrifice in the name of Islam. Malik scanned the pages which was full of the usual anti US, Israel, UK rhetoric proclaiming 'death to the infidels'.

Several speakers were featured on video links, calling on the faithful to take up arms; mostly repetition, nothing that hadn't been seen before. There was one page that Malik found interesting; a list of videos made by Jihadists prior to their final mission towards 'paradise'. There were postings stretching back over three years and it included the one shown on British TV made by Mohammad Sidique Khan from 2005, before the 7/7 bombings.

Malik called the Director,

"John, I think you ought to see this," and Mansfield left his desk and went over to Malik's pod.

"What have we got?" asked the Director.

"This just in from Andy. They've got Siddique's laptop and

managed to get hold of his browsing history," replied Malik.

"Anything to be concerned about?" asked Mansfield.

"Definite jihadist leanings that's for sure. This website is full of the usual diatribe from the zealots, but these videos are particularly interesting. They go back three years. I found this one more recent, just over a week ago."

Malik replayed the video. The backdrop looked like a bedroom. There was a flag behind the speaker which had the word 'Allah' in Arabic written on it. The words were chilling as Malik translated the dialogue.

"He's calling on all Muslims to join the… fight against the… er… repression of the faith, that it is a Holy War, and it is every believer's duty to take up arms against the kafirs. Soon I will strike a blow that the mighty Saladin would… er… honour. The sword of Allah will rise like a serpent from the sea and strike terror to the infidels," said Malik.

"A bit theatrical," said the Director. "Wait a minute... Pause it there," he said.

Malik complied.

The speaker was dressed in traditional Arab peasant gear with a keffiyeh, a head covering once favoured by Yasser Arafat, wrapped around his face so that only his eyes were visible.

"Run it frame by frame." The video ran slowly.

"Do you think it's our man?" asked Malik.

"Can't be absolutely certain, but I'm pretty positive it's Saladin... it's certainly his style, let me speak to Andy," and the director dialled Brittain's mobile.

"Andy, it's John... I'm with Malik looking at one of Siddique's websites... mostly Jihadists, but we've found one which looks like it could be the Saladin blog. Unfortunately, we can't access the blog itself, but there's a page with suicide bombers giving their final rant and one of them is recent, last Sunday. Have you checked if there any videos on the laptop which he may have made and uploaded? I assume that's how he would have done it... yeah, ok."

The director looked at Malik. "He'll call us back."

Back in Aberdeen, Andy Brittain was watching Dominic going through the files on the computer.

"Can you check for any videos?"

"I've checked his open files and there's nothing there. Let me check any deleted items see if I can resurrect them."

Dominic fingers flashed across the keyboard. Porter and Brittain looked on intently.

"Nothing I can see." He scanned the list of files.

"Hang on... what's this?" and he clicked one of the hidden programme files. "Now this is interesting."

He opened the folder. It was named 'Ayyūb'.

"Ayyūb is Saladin's surname," said Dominic. "Ṣalāḥ ad- Dīn Yūsuf ibn Ayyūb."

"How on earth do you know that?" asked Porter.

Dominic looked at her with a grin. "A first in Middle Eastern studies from Cambridge. It's surprising the amount of useless information you acquire."

"Oh no... look at this," and he ran the video. Brittain and Porter watched in horror as Dominic played the file.

"That's it. That's the key," said Brittain, and he was back on the phone to the Director.

"John, its Andy. It's here, the video, no doubts... Tariq Siddique is Saladin, and he's on one of our biggest oil and gas rigs."

"Shit!" exclaimed the Director.

"That doesn't come close," said Brittain.

"Right, you and the team get across to Petronix and see if they can get in touch with the Installation Manager to warn him. I'll get onto Arbroath and mobilise the SBS. Time could be critical here."

Brittain checked his watch; it was almost four o'clock.

Dominic was given charge of Tariq's laptop. He called a taxi from his mobile while the others packed the gear. Ten minutes later there was a sound of a horn outside and they left the flat.

"Jesus, where did this come from?" said Brittain, as he peered from the lobby. The rain appeared to be coming down sideways. Trees were being bent at crazy angles as they braced themselves against the deluge. Wheelie bins and other objects were being blown around like children's toys. The storm drains were failing to keep the water at bay, blocked with falling leaves and other ancillary rubbish.

"It feels like a hurricane," said Porter as she dashed to the waiting car.

"God, I'm soaked," said Dominic as he got in the back.

Brittain sat in the front and gave the driver the details. The windscreen wipers were making heavy weather of the torrential rain.

"Is it always like this in Aberdeen?" he said to the driver to make conversation.

"On a good day," he said laconically. "Sometimes it's worse."

As they went past the docks, it was an amazing sight; ships bouncing up and down at their anchor as if on a trampoline, waves crashing against the sea wall and showering the road with spray.

"I'll tell you what, I wouldn't want to be stuck out there in this weather," said Brittain.

"It's blowing force eleven in the Forties Field, gusting over ninety," said the driver, hearing the remark.

"Well, they certainly won't be getting any choppers off, that's for sure," said Brittain, grimly.

They reached the office in ten minutes, the weather causing chaos with the early evening traffic.

"We would have been quicker walking," said Porter.

"But a lot wetter," said Dominic.

Brittain paid the driver and they made a dash into reception.

"Doug Earnshaw, please," he said to the receptionist, shaking excess water onto the marble floor.

"Who should I say is calling?" Brittain showed her his identity card.

She dialled the number.

"He's on his way down," she replied.

A lift opened in the lobby a couple of minutes later and the duty manager appeared.

"How did you get on?" said the dour Scot, ushering them into an adjacent office. He shut the door.

"We have an update on the situation we discussed this morning," said Brittain, still standing.

The manager looked at him with concern. There was a table with six chairs around it and the four sat down.

"We have evidence that Tariq Siddique is a suspected terrorist and could be planning some act of sabotage on the rig. I need you to warn the Installation Manager," said Brittain.

The manager's worried look increased.

"We don't want him to take any action at this stage, but I assume you'll have emergency procedures for this eventuality."

"Yes, but that was geared to a boat attack, not someone working from within," said Earnshaw.

"Hmm, you'll need to improvise for the moment. The SBS

have been scrambled and will be on their way."

"Not by helicopter they won't, not in this weather, they'd never make it, nor by the fast crafts. It's swelling over sixty feet at the moment," said Earnshaw.

Brittain looked at Porter.

"If they can confine him to his quarters without alerting him, I don't know... say it's an exercise drill or something... would that be possible?" said Brittain.

"Mmm, possibly, but isn't that likely to look suspicious?" replied the manager.

There was a knock and head appeared.

"Sorry to disturb you Doug, something urgent," she said.

Doug got up and went to the door; whispers. He walked back to his chair, his face ashen, and looked at the three agents.

"We've lost contact with Delta Bravo... complete blackout... ship-to-shore, telephone, email... everything," said Earnshaw.

"How can that happen?" said Brittain.

"Well, it can't," said Earnshaw, "theoretically."

"Weather?" said Brittain.

"No... Not all three," said Earnshaw.

"Jesus!" said Brittain. "Right, Doug, you need to get back to your team. Can we use this room as a base?"

"Of course, anything you need. I'll get someone to get you some coffee," and he left the room.

Brittain was on his mobile.

"John? It's Andy... We've got a problem."

Earlier in the day Tariq was awake at eleven-thirty. He had finished his night shift at eight o'clock and had gone to bed, but his body was having difficulty in adjusting to the new sleep patterns. He turned on the TV and flicked the remote to the news channel and stared at the screen. In moments he was wide awake. He could feel the adrenaline flowing through his body; pictures of violent storms in the North Sea.

Flooding in Orkney and Shetland, the main railway line from Edinburgh to Inverness closed due to high winds, the road from Dundee to Forfar blocked by falling trees; these were the headlines that leapt from the screen. Edinburgh, Glasgow and Aberdeen airports shut. The Tay River at Perth was at record levels and there were flood alerts in several counties. The weather expert was giving a piece to camera with a backdrop of the storms, sixty feet waves he was saying with little change in the next twenty-four hours; storm force gusting force twelve, the worst storms in the UK since those in October 1987 which devastated the South of England.

Carrying out his mission was never going to be dictated by time, but by conditions. He was anxious to strike his blow for the cause and gain his rightful place in paradise but he was in no hurry; it had to be right.

He took out his prayer mat and placed it in the narrow space between the bed and the bulkhead, no more than eighteen inches but enough. Looking around the room he had compared it to his idea of an Iraqi prison; it was certainly no bigger. He checked the compass and started the ritual chanting of the Shuruq. He finished his prayers and laid out the prayer mat on top of his bunk. He picked at the loose piece of cotton around the compass and gently put his hand in the gap between the two layers of cloth that made up the mat and gently slid out a CD wallet. Tariq had deliberately hidden it under the compass which, he concluded, would escape the scrutiny of the on-shore scanner. He had been proved right. He looked at the shiny disk in its clear plastic sleeve. This was it.

As he changed into his jeans and sweatshirt he used for work, his mind momentarily turned to his adopted family. In fact, he had not spoken to them since the day he left Batley. It had been deliberate; he did not want to cause them any grief. He was also worried that any calls from his mobile could be traced to them and possibly implicate them in what he was about to do. It was God's work. He hoped they would understand.

He made his way from the accommodation area on the second floor, down the wide-open staircase to the admin area where the OIM had his office on the next floor. It was like a gorge running down the centre of the structure with, what looked like, blue Formica walling incongruously decorated with patterns of sea creatures. He made his way downwards he could feel the rig moving in the wind, a disconcerting experience.

He walked past the staff notice board with its details of rosters, special safety notices and flyers for films showing on the in house cinema, surprisingly current, courtesy of George Stafford's contacts. He passed the short corridor that led to the OIM's office; the door was shut, he noticed, the morning briefing, and into the cafeteria where he poured a paper cup of water from a cooler. Although it was still Ramadan, given his shift patterns, he was 'allowed' to take a drink. He would be in danger of dehydrating without it. In any case, he rationalised, his pending sacrifice would more than make up for any minor indiscretions concerning the Ramadan ritual.

He looked around; lunch time, the galley area was heaving with very few seats free. Dave Morrison saw him and went over.

"What's the matter Sid, can't you sleep?" he said.

"Getting used to working nights," he replied weakly.

Dave noticed him looking around at all the men milling about.

"No maintenance work today, emergency crews only... too

dangerous outside," he explained.

On the rig during extreme weather conditions the men would be confined to the accommodation block for safety and only essential repairs carried out. Today there would be only eight men in the oil module and four in the gas. Even they would be called in if the weather deteriorated further, production could be safely managed from the control room; essentially a lock-down.

Tariq looked at the rows of tables. The nightshift, around sixty men, would be sleeping but most of the remaining two hundred would be eating, watching TV or playing pool in the games room/ lounge, or covering for their colleagues at lunch. The managers were still in the briefing meeting with the OIM.

Davy left Tariq who was still standing by the water cooler, and went back to his seat to finish his lunch. Watching people eating during Ramadan would normally have been difficult for Tariq, but he had no appetite. The door at the back of the galley opened and Ferguson with three of his managers and Kim Barnes walked in and sat at the end of one of the tables taking the remaining spaces. Tariq watched the comings and goings. Rory joined them a couple of minutes later and sat next to Kim. Tariq decided to leave before his presence was noticed further and he made his way back to the staircase and went down two more floors to the Control Room.

Tariq keyed in his security number and the door clicked open. The duty manager and three other engineers were busy watching the flow rates on the screens, checking for any abnormalities, any glitches; they knew every nuance of the rig and all its peculiar traits through many years' experience. Tariq watched the illuminated gauges bouncing up and down on the monitors; everything looked as it should.

"What are you doing up, Sid?"

It was Rob Cousins, who was duty manager again, one of the few Welshmen on board, a veteran of the Ebbw Vale Steel Works.

It was one o'clock. The three other engineers got up as Tariq walked towards the manager's desk, and headed off to the canteen without any acknowledgement of Tariq's presence.

"Couldn't sleep. Thought I would finish off my project from yesterday," he replied.

Tariq had been clever; Rob Cousins was not the duty manager on the nightshift and would have no reason to doubt Tariq's words. The handover document passed between managers at the end of each shift would have no mention of his project, but, given his trainee status, that was not a surprise.

"Yeah, fine, but you'll still be needed at eight o'clock, mind. I should try to get some sleep; you'll be knackered by the end of the shift."

"Yeah, I know but I'm ok at the moment. I'll give it an hour or so and then get my head down," he said, using one of the colloquialisms he had learned.

"Suit yourself," said Cousins.

"What was it, Sid...?" asked the manager. "Your project?"

"I was working in the computer room checking some circuit connectors. My laptop is in there."

This was true. He had not been allowed in the computer room since his arrival, but the previous evening, being quiet, he had asked if he could have look at the set-up and had been shown around by Jed McLaren, the night shift manager. He had managed to plant it in there when he wasn't looking.

Rob went to the security door to the computer centre and keyed in the four magic numbers that would allow access. The door clicked open.

"Is it ok to go in?" asked Tariq, playing it cool. Supervision in the computer centre was always required; but just then the phone rang.

"Cousins," he said, picking up the phone. Tariq was stood at the open door of the computer room and watched the manager's face change expression. He put the phone down.

"What's up?" asked Tariq.

"That was Brian, weather's worsened, blowing force eleven, gusting twelve, that's hurricane levels," he said gravely. "They're bringing everyone in."

The Beaufort scale describes a force eleven wind as a severe storm. 'Extensive widespread damage; large waves (9-14 metres), white foam, visibility further reduced (from force 10).'

He viewed the large screens with concern, like a mother hen protecting its brood.

"Is it ok if I get my laptop?" asked Tariq, momentarily breaking his thought patterns

"What…? Oh... yeah... but don't be long," said Cousins, not really concentrating. "Where is everybody?" he added looking around.

"Lunch," said Tariq.

The other three engineers had left the control centre before their cover had returned. It was just the two of them.

"You carry on Sid," he restated, seeing Tariq still waiting.

The phone went again; it was Ferguson.

Tariq went inside and quickly found his laptop where he had left it earlier and went to work. Quickly he removed the plastic wallet from the pocket of his jeans and took out the shiny disc. There were dozens of computer towers, probably ten times the size of the Cash and Carry computer system. He checked them one by one; he knew exactly what he was looking for. One of the computers had a DVD drive to enable software updates to be loaded from time to time. This one would be slightly different.

"This one," he said to himself, as he found the appropriate disc drive. He pushed the control button and the DVD drawer moved gently forward. He loaded the disc and pressed the button again and the drawer slid gracefully back in place. It was automatically set to 'RUN' and he waited until the contents had been transferred. The drive drawer opened again and Tariq removed the disc and put it back in the wallet. No trace.

He picked up his laptop, left the computer room and closed the door behind him with Cousins none the wiser for his escapade; he was still on the phone. Tariq hovered for a moment at his desk pretending to look through some files.

Cousins concluded the call just as the remainder of the team returned from lunch and the manager quickly briefed them on the latest news.

"Think I'll take your advice, Rob, and get my head down," Tariq said, interrupting the briefing.

Rob acknowledged without taking much notice; he was giving his team the emergency arrangements, and Tariq left the office with his laptop under his arm.

He climbed the five floors to the accommodation block, back to his room and took out his prayer mat again and recited the Dhurh; the omens were good. Allah was definitely with him conducting the winds outside to Tariq's tune. It was a waiting game; the time delay was deliberate to give him the chance to be well away from the chaos that was about to reign.

He went to the small cabinet next to his bunk and took out his meagre collection of boxer shorts, remnants of his Cash and Carry days, which had been neatly folded; three pairs, his only ones. He opened them out and three heavy items dropped onto the bed, a pair of bolt cutters, a screw driver and spanner. Such was the routine on the rig everyone was responsible for the upkeep of their own room; there was no external cleaning company. There were, however, spot checks as part of internal security; stealing things from the canteen was not unheard of.

His hiding place was not ideal, but he took the view that a spot check in the present weather conditions was unlikely. Collecting the items on his visit to the other modules had not proved difficult. Surprisingly, there were plenty of tools lying around and he just picked up what he needed and dropped them into the pockets of his PPE before transferring them to his jeans in the changing area.

The next part of his mission would be his most dangerous so far, and he knew he would be vulnerable. He would need some luck. He hoped Allah would protect him.

He couldn't collect his PPE from the changing room; it would look suspicious with everyone locked down, but he needed to go outside. If he was spotted he would be off the rig permanently, and would lose his sponsorship. He would almost certainly be sent back to Iraq.

He checked the time on the TV; it had been an hour since he loaded the virus. Things would start happening soon; he would wait for the tell-tale signs, and then make his move. Half an hour to go...

Tariq was restless, anxious to get on with his mission. He watched the latest on the weather; a ship had run aground near Peterhead and the Fraserburgh lifeboat had been battling against ferocious weather to reach it, according to the latest newscast. There were pictures of storm-lashed sea fronts, motorists braving the elements, some unsuccessfully, trees crushing their vehicles; three dead so far.

Three forty-five, the TV suddenly went off; the lights flickered, then returned, but dimly as the emergency generators kicked in. It was time.

In the Control Room there was momentary panic as the screens went dead, then relief as slowly they sprang back to life. Rob Cousin checked the readings; the screens had lost some luminosity as they went into power-saving mode, but everything appeared normal.

In his operation centre, Hamish Ferguson was checking readouts and was in touch by telephone with the control room. He was reassured by Cousins that the main power supply had tripped and two of his team were already checking the cause. All gauges working at normal safe levels, pumps were fine, flow rates level.

"Could be the weather," said Cousins to reassure the OIM. "Water in one of the control boxes, most likely."

Tariq's plan was in two parts; the first to trip the main power feed and cause the backup generators to kick in. This would put out all non-emergency circuits, including CCTV.

The second part was much more ingenious, and serious. He had switched the readings on the condensate pumps, so the gauges had reversed. There were four pumps controlling the inflow of gas, numbered $C1 - C4$. Shortly, the gauges would show a fault on $C1$, which would mean it would automatically shut down. This was not a major problem, as normal flows were possible from just three pumps to allow for regular routine maintenance. The problem for Cousins and the team was that $C1$ was showing as being shut down, but, having reversed the readings, it was $C4$ that was now really about to close down.

Cousins informed Ferguson, "Fergie, C1 Condensate pump shut down. There's an error message showing, I'm checking it out."

"Keep me advised," replied the OIM.

An emergency meeting had already been convened. Rory, as a senior engineer was included. He had left Kim who was on her way to one of the hot-desks in the admin area to send some emails back to the office.

Ferguson briefed his team. "We have an electrical fault on the main power circuit, Rob Cousin's team are checking it out. Backup generators are handling it on emergency power, probably weather conditions. We will know more after Rob has investigated."

There were six of the senior team around the table and they looked at each other. Although not unheard of this was not a routine situation, but emergency procedures were in place and the contingency plan was known by all.

"Hopefully temporary, but can you advise your teams I'm not proposing sending anyone outside for the moment, but that depends on what Rob advises."

The team dispersed.

Back in his cabin, Tariq picked up his tools and headed to the emergency exit which would normally been under the watchful eyes of the CCTV monitors. He pushed the door open. The force against him was immense as he battled against the power of the wind. He managed to squeeze through and immediately Tariq was confronted by the might of the storm.

The door slammed shut behind him. Fortunately, he was on the leeward side, sheltered from the worst of the tumult, but rain lashed at Tariq's face as he made the dangerous trip up the three flights of stairs to the helicopter deck.

Below the pad there was a gantry, a walkway which led beneath the landing stage. It was a metal construction resembling that of a lighting rig seen at rock concerts. The tread was about two feet wide, open metal mesh, the headroom about four feet which would mean a crawl or a definite stoop. There was a handrail on each side which ran the length with holding stays every two feet, not quite wide enough to prevent a man from falling through if he wasn't vigilant. Tariq held his breath and bent double to make himself as small as possible and crawled the fifty yards or so towards the middle of the rig. He looked down at the sea far below; it looked like a cauldron from hell; the waves crashing at the piles holding the structure and firing white foam upwards, like spitting demons trying to knock him from his precarious perch.

Tariq could feel the spray, but it was the noise; deafening, frightening, the girders creaking to withstand the strain from the mighty forces of nature; he could sense the giant rig actually swaying.

He found what he was looking for; the inspection box, which would enable him access to the main communication system. He opened the cover. Being regularly maintained, the bolts moved easily. It was dryer under the canopy of the helipad but every few seconds a stream of spray shot upwards soaking him to the skin. He took his bolt cutters and cut the three cables, disabling telephones, satellite communications and the radio antenna.

He replaced the cover and tightened the bolts with his fingers; then quickly crawled back to the main stairway. He reached the emergency exit which he used earlier, but gasped in horror as he realised that it was a one-way door; there was no entry. He stood for a moment, thinking. There was only one alternative, the main entrance to the reception area where everyone had to report following landing. It would be manned.

Tariq moved slowly to the door and peered through the small window. There was an almighty crash as another huge wave hit the rig drenching Tariq in a cloud of sea water. He turned the ball handle. As with all doors on the rig, they opened outwards, requiring Tariq to pull. The weight of the air pressure was acting against him, but gradually he was able to open it sufficiently to gain access. It slammed shut behind him with a huge bang. He quickly went through and entered the airlock which prevented the office from being blasted by winds when the outer door was opened.

Tariq looked through the glass but couldn't see anything. It was a fairly small area with a few seats to allow transit passengers to sit whilst waiting for their flight and next to them a small space where mail and other packages would be stored prior to transfer to the helicopter. On one of the pillars there was a vending machine which dispensed ear plugs. There was a small TV screen on the wall above the seats where passengers would watch the security video and opposite, the reception desk, where normally the attendant would log in all arrivals and exits.

Tariq slowly opened the second door and went through. Then froze; the duty desk attendant, Gordon Whittaker, came through from the entrance door to the main stairway on the other side of reception carrying a bag of mail. Gordon was in his late fifties with over thirty years' service and doted on his three children and five grandchildren. He was well liked by everyone, a bit of a character, always ready with the odd joke to calm the anxious passenger.

He saw Tariq straight away.

"Sid? What are you up to…? You're not allowed outside. I'll need to call this in."

Before he could move, Tariq pulled the spanner from his pocket and crashed it down on the man's skull. Gordon fell to the floor and lay there prostrate; blood started to seep from his head.

Tariq grabbed his legs and dragged the unconscious man backwards, through the exit door, into the airlock and closed the inner door behind him. He pushed open the second door. It swung outwards and crashed against the bulkhead by the force of the wind. Quickly, he pulled the stricken Gordon Whittaker through and onto the main walkway. He managed to man-handle him onto his feet and manoeuvre him into a standing position. The man gave a groan as he started to come around. Tariq grabbed his feet and tipped him over the safety rail and he fell the three-hundred feet to the waiting waves below.

Swiftly back into the airlock, Tariq wrestled with the outside door, but managed to pull it shut; then into the reception area. No-one was about, but there was blood on the floor which had smudged in the direction of the door where he had dragged Gordon Whittaker.

Above the pedal bin in the corner there was a kitchen roll on a spindle which men could use to dry their hands if coming in from wet weather. He pulled off a couple of sheets and cleaned the blood from the floor and disposed of the paper in the bin.

He looked around the room; the post bag was on the floor in the corner; he would leave it there; it wouldn't matter. Then he opened the door to the inner walkway, and walked down the stairs back to the accommodation block as fast as he could, then, into his room unseen. He lay on his bunk, his chest heaving from the exertion. He was soaking wet.

After a few minutes his breathing got back to normal and he changed out of his 'work' trousers and into his jeans. He had another shirt on the hanger in his clothes space and replaced his drenched top. He dropped back onto the bunk trying not to think about his recent actions. He liked Gordon; he had made a fuss of Tariq when he first arrived and made him feel like one of the team.

It was too late for sentiment; he had more work to do yet. He took stock. The virus would have caused the necessary diversion and disabled the main power; it would also have switched the pump gauges. Now, with communications down, there would be an immediate investigation and a maintenance team would eventually be dispatched to the control box under the helipad and the sabotage discovered. It would however take some while to repair. Now it was just a question of time.

Chapter Twenty-Two

SBS Northern Area HQ, Arbroath. Four thirty-five pm.

Although based in Poole, a unit of the SBS, the Special Boat Service, is stationed in Arbroath with specific responsibility for Oil Platform protection and Maritime Counter Terrorism.

Station Commander, Major Guy Redmond, came off the phone from MI6 HQ in London and put in some calls. Within five minutes the team was assembled in one of the briefing rooms.

"Right lads, listen up... I've just come of the phone with the Director of Operations, looks like we have a potential terrorist threat on one of the rigs."

"Which one?" asked Sergeant Pete Spearman.

"Delta Bravo," he replied and walked towards the large map of the North Sea on the wall.

All the gas and oil rigs were depicted, colour-coded in order of importance and giving details of their function.

Redmond spoke in serious tones. "This is a top priority installation. We're talking about eight per cent UK production of oil and ten percent gas. It's a biggy."

The men looked at each other.

"What about the weather?" asked another of the team. The rain was hammering at the window.

"This is going to be a major problem. No chance of a chopper at the moment, sea twenty metres, gusting force eleven, although we are keeping an eye on that. Our only chance at the moment is by VSV."

The SBS had one VSV in Arbroath, specifically for this purpose. The VT Halmatic, VSV 16 (very slender vessel) is sixteen metres long, and just over 3 metres wide, and powered by two 750hp engines. The exact composition of the VSV 16 is classified although it is thought to include carbon fibre and Kevlar. The angled design of the VSV16 gives the boats a low radar profile and reduced wake production. This design, combined with radar-absorbent materials and paint, make the boat highly stealthy, perfect for the SBS.

Because of its design, it has a top speed in excess of sixty knots. The other aspect of a VSV is they are a planing craft and spend their time on the surface of the water. This enables crews to travel at high speeds in adverse sea conditions in relative comfort and safety. They would be severely tested today.

"How far is it, sir?" asked Sergeant Jackson, one of the elite crew who had been trained on a VSV.

"Best part of a hundred and eighty miles," said Redmond.

"Three hours," observed Jackson.

"Quite," said Redmond, "No time to lose. Jackson, you drive. Huntley, Davies, and Spearman, you've got the job. Tool up and let's move out."

Petronix Headquarters Aberdeen 5.00pm

Andy Brittain was just finishing a call to the Director.

"What's the latest?" asked Porter.

"The Home Secretary's been advised. It's not looking brilliant. We have a blind gas rig and a potential terrorist on board. We can't be certain if the communication failure is down to sabotage, but we can't rule it out. As Doug Earnshaw said, the chances of satellite, telecoms and ship-to-shore all failing at the same time is remote, they're all on separate circuits to stop that happening."

"What's the plan?" asked Dom.

"Well, with the weather the way it is, there's no chance of a helicopter assault, nothing is taking off. The SBS have been mobilised and, the last I heard was, they were going to attempt a VSV approach, but that will take them at least three hours. It's the fastest thing they've got, but I don't fancy their chances. The other possibility is a drop from a Hercules. They would have no difficulty in getting off, but with the sea swell at over twenty metres… Well, let's put it this way; I wouldn't want to do it," said Brittain.

"So where does that leave us?" asked Porter.

Brittain didn't reply.

"What about the support vessel?" asked Dominic.

MS Pericles, the Delta Bravo's stand-by ship, a converted trawler, would be capable of taking off all the staff on board the rig; it also carries a fast rescue craft.

Before anyone could answer, Doug Earnshaw knocked on the door.

"Come in,' said Brittain, who was now on his third cup of coffee since they arrived.

"Just to give you an update. We still haven't been able to make contact, all the systems are down," said Earnshaw.

"We were just saying, what about the stand-by vessel?" asked Brittain.

"We've been in touch with Pericles, but they can't get anywhere near. They've had to pull back to almost a mile to avoid crashing into the platform and at the moment, they can't get a rescue craft off. Captain says it's the worst conditions he's seen in thirty years," said Earnshaw.

"Well, that answers that," said Porter.

"What about signalling?" asked Dominic.

"What, Morse you mean…? Unfortunately, not. I don't think anyone could read it on the rig anyway."

Brittain glanced at Porter with look of resignation.

"I feel so helpless," he said, banging his hand on the desk which made his mug jump off the table. He caught it before it hit the floor.

Delta Bravo Oil and Gas Platform 6.00pm.

Hamish Ferguson was in conference with his executive team; Rory, as duty senior engineer; Rob Cousins, Operations; Brian Kirkpatrick, Health and Safety; James Gilroy, Chief Technician; and Dave Brewster, Head of Production, who had been with Rory since the early days. Between them they had almost eighty years' experience on rigs.

"Where are we with the electrics Rob?" said Ferguson.

"Checked all the circuits and they're all reading normal," said Cousins.

"So, nothing to indicate a short or overload anywhere?" said the OIM.

"That's the weird thing. To trip the main feed would normally mean a power surge or short circuit. We thought it might be the weather, you know, rain getting into a junction box that sort of thing, but the readings seem ok. The only way to make sure is to go outside to check each one individually. It's possible one of the boxes has blown and not activated the sensor."

"How long will the stand-by generator last?" asked Ferguson.

"On reserve power? About six hours, but we could shut down more rooms and extend that," said Cousins.

Ferguson thought for a moment. "We'll give it a while longer."

"What about production, Dave?" said Ferguson.

"No problem, the pumps are fine apart from C1, flow rates are normal," Dave replied.

"Well at least that's one problem we don't need to worry

about," said Ferguson. "But it's the comms that concern me. Have you known all three systems fail, Woody?"

"No, never; in fact, I would go as far as to say it's impossible, in theory at least. Someone would have to cut them deliberately for that to happen. If you ask me we need to go outside and take a proper look. The junction box under the helipad would be my guess. If I was going to cause the three systems to fail that's what I would do."

"But you're suggesting... sabotage?" half question, half exclamation, said Ferguson.

"Unless anyone has any better ideas," said Rory.

There was a knock on the door.

"Come," shouted Ferguson.

"We can't find Gordon," said the messenger, Dodie Cameron, one of the day shift engineers and a close friend of the reception supervisor.

"What do you mean, can't find him?" said Ferguson.

"He's gone. We've looked everywhere. I went up to see him about half an hour ago to take a bit of post and the reception desk was empty."

"Well there're no flights today, so it wouldn't necessarily be manned," said Ferguson.

"No, but I was chatting to him at lunch and he said he would be tied up all afternoon catching up with some admin and he would have collected the post from the post room about four," replied Cameron.

"Not without a flight due, surely," said Ferguson.

"Yeah, he liked routine; he would have collected the post as usual and stored it in order till the next flight. We found the post bag. It was just on the floor in the corner. Gordon would never just leave it lying around. He was a stickler for health and safety," said Cameron.

"I'll vouch for that," said Kirkpatrick.

Ferguson was a worried man and turned to his team.

"I think as a priority we need to get the comms up and running. Woody, I want you to check the main junction box under the helipad. You'll need to take someone with you. No- one works solo is that clear, everyone?"

The team nodded.

"Brian, you go with Dodie and see if you can find Gordon; pass the word round, but stay inside for now. I don't want to lose anyone over the side... Rob, you get back to the Control Room, see if you can get the power restored. Everyone meet back here for an update in an hour," said Ferguson.

The team got up and after they had left, Ferguson wrote up his log defining the situation as he saw it and the actions he had taken.

Rory went to the staff lounge and there was a strange atmosphere. People were reading newspapers or books; a couple of lads were playing pool on the table in the middle of the room, but it was unusually quiet.

With the lack of alcohol, it was never rowdy, but it was as if everyone was lost in their own thoughts. With no TV there weren't so many people in their rooms as usual, and with the nightshift ready to take over at eight this was normally a busy time for catching up and socialising; tonight, few were making conversation.

Rory saw Kim in the corner reading some papers and he went over to see her. She looked up as he approached and smiled. "You ok?" she said.

"Yeah, got to go outside and check the main junction box on the top deck."

A look of concern spread over her face.

"Why you? Can't someone else do it?"

"Not really, it's my shift. Someone has to do it," he replied.

"Please be careful," she said, and mouthed a kiss; he smiled.

"See you when I get back," he said and left her to her work.

Rory spotted Dave Morrison in the corner. "Hey Scruff-bag, get your gear on, I've got a job for you," he said and headed towards the changing area.

Morrison put down his paper and caught up with Rory. "Where're we going? I thought we was on lockdown."

"We are," said Rory.

"Oh," said Morrison. "Shit."

They got their PPE from their lockers.

"Full kit and roped," said Rory.

It took ten minutes to get geared up. Rory went to another locker and pulled out a length of climbing rope and harnesses.

SBS Northern Area HQ, Arbroath 6.00pm.

The team were back in the assembly area with Redmond re-briefing; the four men were still dressed in their combat gear

"As you will have heard we can't launch the VSV, there's a boat capsized across the slipway and we're going to need a crane to move it." There were groans of frustration from the group.

"I have however just come off the phone with the Met guys and we may be in luck. They're telling me that the storm is peaking about now and is expected to back off to gale 8 within the next half hour. In the circumstances we are going for a drop," he said.

The 'drop' refers to SBS officers being carried to a destination, normally by helicopter, and literally being dropped into the sea some distance from the target and then swimming to their objective. A very dangerous task, but one the SBS train for regularly.

"How are we going to reach the target, sir?" said Spearman.

"I've just spoken to Ops and they can lay on a Chinook in about twenty minutes which can just about handle the weather if the wind backs as predicted. Jackson, you and your team be ready with your equipment and assemble here at 18.20 hours."

Major Redmond left the group and walked back to his office and phoned Director Mansfield at MI6.

Petronix Headquarters Aberdeen 6.15pm

Andy Brittain was just finishing another call from the Director.

"What's the latest?" asked Porter, as Brittain finished the call.

"SBS are going to try again. They couldn't launch the VSV," he said.

There was a look of expectancy on his colleague's faces.

"They're going to try a drop by a Chinook," said Brittain.

"Rather them than me," said Dominic.

"Aye, you're right there. However, the good news is the wind is expected to veer south west and back to force seven or eight in the next half an hour."

"Still a big swell though," said Porter.

"About thirty-five, forty feet. They train for that," replied Brittain.

"How long will it take?" asked Dominic.

"Max speed's about a hundred and seventy knots, so we're talking the best part of an hour. Then of course they'll have to swim. Can't risk dropping them too close in case they hit the rig, also we don't want to alert our friend and we don't know what he might do; so, they'll move in up wind to cut down the noise, my guess? Two hundred metres."

Porter looked at Dominic as Brittain phoned Earnshaw to update him.

SBS Northern Area HQ, Arbroath 6.20pm.

Sergeant Ted Jackson and his team were making final equipment checks. Major Redmond approached.

"Everything set?"

"Ready to go, sir," he replied and the four made their way to the exit at the corner of the hanger to the helipad where the twin rotors of the Chinook were battling against the rain.

"Eased off a bit, Ted," shouted Spearman trying to be heard over the noise of the chopper.

He got a thumbs-up reply.

Delta Bravo Oil & Gas Platform, 6.20pm.

Rory had checked his rope and clipped his connector to Dave's harness.

Climbing ropes are typically of 'kernmantle' construction, consisting of a core (kern) of long twisted fibres, and an outer sheath (mantle) of woven coloured fibres. They are extremely strong and would comfortably take the weight of a man.

Linked together, with full PPE, Rory and Dave made their way to the outer exit resembling two mountaineers. Rory went first and opened the door. The force of the wind almost knocked him off his feet; it was incredible. The door flung open, wrenched from his grasp and smashed against the side wall. Rain was still lashing down. Although still daylight, it might have well been night, such was the visibility. Dave Morrison followed through the opening five feet behind, and pulled the door from its resting point; it flew from his hand slamming shut with a crash.

Slowly, the two made their way to the metal stairway that would take them the three stories to the heli-deck. It took them ten minutes inching their way as close to the outside wall as they could, one step... stop... one step... stop. The roar of the waves below was drowning out any semblance of conversation. Rory gripped the handrail to the stairway; it was wet and slippery; his gloves were already soaked. Visibility was further impeded by the rain on his goggles mixed with the spray from the sea; every few seconds he had to wipe them with the back of his sleeve.

Eventually they came to the gantry which led to the gangway under the helipad; the same one Tariq had traversed a while earlier.

Rory ducked down and started to crawl; Dave was behind him, his plastic umbilical cord still connected to his buddy like a baby elephant to its mother. Rory was used to danger; he had been in many challenging situations, but this was different. It was the lack of control.

Inch by inch, he crawled closer along the two feet ledge to the junction box, followed by his buddy. The metal hand rail was three feet in height, but totally open to the elements. Rory wondered whether the stays supporting the rail would hold them if they lost their footing. He tried to look straight ahead, but it was hard; he was crawling along an open metal walkway; below him... a long way below him, the North Sea beckoned, its white horses continuing their assault on the fabric of the rig.

The steel cross girders moved, relentless in their complaint as they took the strain of the incredible forces being thrown at them; grating, screeching, whining as the wind howled like swirling zephyrs from the hand of the mighty Zeus. It took almost another ten minutes to reach the box, an eternity.

He stopped and waited for Dave to join him to act as a wind break and shelter him from the elements. He removed his gloves and took out a wrench from the zip pocket of his PPE trousers; then unscrewed the four bolts which held the inspection panel in place. He gave Dave the bolts and pulled the metal plate away from the housing.

Normally, it would take some strength to remove the housing, but it came away remarkable easily, which, straightaway, gave Rory cause for concern. He passed the plate to Dave and examined the damage. Dave watched and Rory looked at him and nodded.

"They've been cut," he shouted.

He replaced the plate and screwed back the bolts finger tight. He did not have the tools to affect a repair, but would report in and get a maintenance crew back up there as soon as possible.

Turning in the narrow space to reverse their journey proved difficult; Rory, having the lead, had to ease himself past his buddy. To give his partner enough room, Dave half stood up, but in doing so overbalanced coinciding with a vicious gust which howled under the helipad.

He gave out a piercing scream as the momentum took him over the safety barrier.

Dave was dangling in mid-air five feet below the gantry and three hundred feet above the foaming cauldron below, held only by the thin rope. The sudden jerk immediately pulled Rory against the safety rail, but it held firm and he was able to take the strain. Without any means of support, Dave was a dead weight, and it took all of Rory's muscle to pull the six feet, fifteen-stone Rugby player, upwards to safety, inch by inch, centimetre by centimetre... pull... take the weight... pull... take the weight.

Rory was bent backwards to provide leverage, his face contorted with the effort, as slowly his buddy edged upwards. Within touching distance, Dave made a grab for the gantry, and was able to use his own strength to get himself back on the walkway. The pair sat for a moment regaining their breath. Rory slapped Dave on the back in relief. He smiled in acknowledgment.

The return journey was made easier with the wind behind them, and it took just over five minutes to get back to the safety of the accommodation block. Through the door, which again slammed behind them, they both collapsed momentarily, totally spent from the effort of their ordeal. Without the luxury of time, they quickly recovered, and uncoupled the rope that had saved Dave's life, and made their way to Ferguson's office.

Rory walked in, still in his PPE and goggles, which immediately began to steam up. Ferguson was sat at the head of the eight-seater table with three of the maintenance team.

"The cables have been cut... all three... definitely sabotage," he said. There was a look of incredulousness among the group.

Rory took off his hard-hat and misted eye-protectors as the team digested the implications

"But who would do that?" asked Kirkpatrick who, with Health and Safety responsibility, was more than concerned.

"And why?" asked James Gilroy.

More looks of astonishment.

"Where's Dave?" asked Ferguson.

"Told him to get changed. He's done enough for today," and Rory told them of his narrow escape.

"Is he ok?" asked Ferguson.

"Yeah, bit shaken, but he'll be fine," said Rory.

There was a knock on the door and Dodie Cameron walked in.

Ferguson looked up at him and could see by his look that it was not good news.

"No sign?" he said.

Dodie shook his head. "We've looked everywhere. He's just vanished."

"Could he be outside?" asked Ferguson.

Dodie looked at Kirkpatrick who had made the enquiry. "Why would he? In this weather? Not for a moment, can't even get him outside for routine drills."

"Thanks Dodie. Let me know if he turns up," said Ferguson and Dodie left the room.

"You don't think…" said Ferguson.

"No, it couldn't be Gordon," said Gilroy. "He lived and breathed the rig."

"We need to keep an open mind for the moment," said Ferguson. He turned to Rory. "What do you need Woody?"

"We'll need a maintenance team up on the gantry to repair the breaks, but it's not going to be easy, the wind's swirling around under the pad. It's a fucking nightmare."

"Ok Woody... James, can you get one of the maintenance teams up there as soon as you can. Four men to be on the safe side. Get them tooled up and roped. Woody can you brief them on what they're going to need? If we can get the comms back working that's going to make a big difference; we can discuss the situation with the beach."

The 'beach' was the slang term for the onshore HQ.

"Will do," he replied, and went outside with the chief technician to discuss logistics. It was just before seven o'clock.

Petronix HQ, Aberdeen 7.00.

Andy Brittain was downing yet another coffee which hadn't gone unnoticed by his colleagues.

"You won't sleep tonight," said Porter.

"It's just the waiting and feeling... helpless. I don't do helpless," he said, and Porter smiled.

"What time are the SBS expected to drop?" she asked in an attempt to regain focus.

"About seven-twenty... then the swim. They're not going to get up there quickly that's for sure."

Delta Bravo Oil & Gas Platform 7.15pm.

Rory had been called back to the OIM's office where Rob Cousins was in conversation with Ferguson. There was another manager at the table, Kim. Rory looked at her in surprise.

"Woody, sit down a moment. I've asked Kim to join us to get her opinion on something."

Rory sat next to Kim and opposite Rob and Ferguson.

"It's about Gordon. I've been given some thought to what was said earlier... It's not common knowledge, Gordon didn't want to broadcast it, but he was due to retire at the end of the year; he's sixty next month." They listened to the OIM closely. "He asked me to apply for an extension, but unfortunately it was declined, and it was one of the things Kim was here for today. Kim, tell Rob and Woody what you told me."

Kim responded. "I saw Gordon this morning and told him that his request for extension of service had been declined and he didn't take it well. He was angry, abusive even, blaming Fergie and Petronix for not looking after the staff and then he became very upset."

Rob looked at Rory concerned. "Well that doesn't mean he

would do anything, surely?"

"It does happen," said Kim. "One of my old University colleagues is HR Manager for a company in Suffolk and a couple of years ago they announced some redundancies and one of the warehousemen came in and set fire to the factory."

The concern grew.

"I still don't think he would do anything against the rig, though. He loved his job... and the blokes. No, not possible," said Rob.

Rory hadn't commented, he was trying to think things through.

"Well someone's done it, that's a certainty, someone on board," he said, looking at Kim then his colleagues across the table.

He looked at Ferguson. "And there's still no sign of him?" asked Rory.

"No nothing, vanished into thin air," said Ferguson.

"You don't think he would have gone over the side, do you?" asked Rory. "You know, cut the comms and then jumped?"

"Suicide, you mean?" asked Kim.

The thought hung in the air.

"Well I don't buy it," said Cousins. "As I said, he's got too many mates here, he'd never have put them in danger, they are like his family, doted on them. No never."

"I guess," said Rory, but no-one at this stage was ruling out the possibility.

The group dispersed and Rory escorted Kim back to the lounge area.

"I need a coffee, but I would murder a drink right now."

Kim smiled and seeing no-one was watching leant over and kissed him on the cheek. Kim was going back to the recreation room and, just as she walked away, turned to Rory.

"You haven't seen Tariq have you, Tariq Siddique?"

Rory thought for a moment, "Oh, Sid you mean. No, why?"

"I was going to have a quick word with him, see how he was getting on."

"No, haven't seen him," Rory checked the time. "He'll be on shift in half an hour. He'll be about then," he said, and he went to check on how Dave Morrison was getting on.

Seven-thirty and back in his cabin Tariq was saying his prayers and mentally preparing himself for the final part of his plan. He retrieved his mini toolkit and put the spanner and screwdriver in his pocket. It was all he would need.

He walked out of the accommodation block onto the stairwell. It was empty; most staff were either in their cabins or in the admin block. He made his way up the two flights to the emergency exit he had used earlier. He wasn't dressed in PPE, just his shirt and jeans and a pair of trainers. He looked just like any other student about to go to a lecture; but his mission was altogether more sinister.

He found the emergency exit and opened the outside door again. He caught his breath as he entered the teeth of the gale; perhaps not as bad as his previous excursion; the wind had dropped a fraction. He needed to traverse halfway around the rig on the open side to get to the walkway that led to the gas module.

He reached the gangway and held his breath. Slowly he made his way across the abyss. Being of slight build was actually an advantage in making the crossing; less wind resistance. He glanced down and could see the giant piles of the rig being battered by the storm, the sea appearing to ride halfway up the supports as if trying to reach the top and then dropping down twenty, thirty metres even, revealing the giant legs that went all the way to the sea bed half a mile down. At this moment he wanted to be sick, but having not eaten for almost twenty-four hours there was little to bring up. He steeled himself and repeated one of his favourite prayers that would give him the strength to go on.

He reached the other side and entered the gas platform, then headed for the centre of the building to the condensate pumps.

The pumps were large, around thirty inches in diameter and connected to the risers that dropped to the sea bed and the drill hole. They were covered by a metal cage about six feet tall which protected them from flying debris. They were clearly numbered, C1-C4.

He opened the gate to the cage and checked the numbers and found the one he was looking for, C4. His computer virus had closed this one down, but was showing as 'working' in the control room. He used the spanner to remove the inspection plate. Pressure in the risers bringing the gas from the sea bed would be normally around two-thousand pounds per square inch and dropping to around two-hundred and fifty psi through the condensate pumps.

It would be impossible to remove this plate without the flow being shut off. Tariq's plan was quite simple. He would loosen the bolts to the maintenance plate to finger tight so that when the pump was restarted it would create a gas leak at considerable pressure.

Chapter Twenty-Three

7.30pm Chinook Helicopter, one mile from Delta Bravo platform, North Sea.

Sergeant Ted Jackson and his three colleagues were sat in the disposal bay waiting for the green light. It had been a laborious but bumpy ride. Jackson hated this time; adrenaline and nerves were at their peak and he tapped his feet anxiously. He looked at his team, all experienced operatives and each in their own world. He checked his Heckler & Koch HK53 carbine, safely stowed in his water-tight kit bag attached to the lanyard which was fastened by rope to his waste-band. The black frogman's outfit was made of special thermal protective material which would negate the icy waters of the North Sea. A mask and flippers made up the rest of his equipment. The noise from inside the Chinook made conversation impossible and commands were given by hand- signals.

The green light flashed, and a crew member walked towards the exit door. He attached himself to the frame of the door with a harness and swung it open. The wind swirled into the open door nearly knocking him off his feet, but he recovered and called the four men forward.

Jackson, as leader, would go first and he watched the rolling waves below him at one point no more than twenty feet from the Chinook then a trough where it dipped to nearer fifty. Foam sprayed from the tops of the surf as he waited for the right moment, then dropped holding his kit-bag in his arms. He threw his lanyard out moments before he hit the sea; then he was in. Breaking through the waves, he went down about ten feet before his buoyancy aid took the strain and brought him to the surface. It was like riding a roller coaster. He watched his three colleagues enter safely and pointed to the rig, a massive and foreboding black outline through the spray about five hundred metres away to the North-East. He received acknowledgement from his buddies and started the swim. Although they originally planned to drop against the wind to maintain a stealth approach, time was of the essence. It was decided therefore to make the entry from the South-West so that the wind and tide was with them. It made the going easier, but it was still going to be tough.

Delta Bravo Oil & Gas Platform 7.45pm.

The Exec team were back in the OIM's office for another update.

Rob Cousins explained that there was no news on the electrical situation, but the stand-by generators would provide sufficient power to maintain production and life support for another five hours according to the latest read-outs.

"Well, that's the good news," said Ferguson. "Any news from Jim and his team, Woody?"

"Not yet. Could be some time connecting all three cables in this weather. I told them to concentrate on getting the phone feed first. At least that will give us chance to speak to the beach."

"Thanks Woody. No news on Gordon I suppose?"

"Not heard a thing," said Rory.

"Oh, nearly forgot, have you seen anything of Sid, Rob? Kim was asking. Wanted a quick word before he went on shift, you know, see how he was settling in."

"Not seen him since lunch time," said Rob.

"Lunch time?" queried Rory. "You mean <u>our</u> lunch time."

"Yeah, he came down to the Control Room about one-ish to

collect his laptop. Said he couldn't sleep…. Wanted to do some work on his project."

"What project was that?" pushed Rory.

"Don't know, didn't say. Something he was doing on the nightshift I presume," replied Cousins.

"What did he do… when he came to the Control Room, I mean?" asked Rory.

Rob looked at Ferguson slightly uneasy at the questioning. "Nothing… he went into the computer room, collected his laptop and left."

"Did you go with him, into the computer room?" asked Rory.

Rob looked a bit sheepish.

"Well, not exactly. I was on the phone, and the guys were not back from lunch," he squirmed uncomfortably, recognising his error. "He was only in there for a couple of minutes."

Rory looked at Ferguson.

"So, Sid was in the computer room unsupervised?" he repeated.

"Yes, but only for a second or two," he exaggerated.

"When did the power go off?" asked Rory.

"About four," he replied.

"What about the pumps, when did C1 fail?" asked Rory.

"At the same time," said Rob, beginning to make the connection.

"What are you saying?" asked Ferguson.

"I don't know," said Rory. "But I don't believe in coincidences. Power off, condensate pump failure and comms down, which we know is sabotage…" He didn't finish the sentence.

"I think we need to have a word if nothing else," said Ferguson.

"Rob can you get someone to go to his room and see if he's there?" and Cousins got up and walked out.

"I hope you're wrong in what you are thinking, Woody," said Ferguson, then added. "Would he have the knowledge to do all that?"

"He's a bright lad; he's surprised a few of the engineers here that's for sure," said Rory.

A few minutes later Cousins returned.

"Not in his room and no-one's seen him… But I found this."

He put Tariq's laptop on the table in front of him. "And this. It was on his bed," he opened up the green blanket with the Arabic writing on it in yellow. "Don't know what it says," said Cousins.

Rory looked at the cloth. "Allah is great," he said, and the team looked at him and then at each other.

"I've opened up the laptop, there's nothing on it," said Cousins.

"What do you mean 'nothing on it'?" said Rory.

"It's been wiped clean, even XP. Certainly, no project," said Cousins, now really worried. "There was also a broken CD in his waste paper bin."

"Right, this puts a slightly different complexion on things... Can you get Kim in, Rory?"

Rory left the office and returned a couple of minutes later with the HR Manager.

"Have a seat Kim," said Ferguson. "Have you got Sid's file with you?"

She rummaged in her brief case and pulled out a manila folder.

"It's here," she said.

"What's his background?" asked Ferguson.

Kim read out the information.

"From Basra, part of the regeneration project, accepted onto the overseas Graduate Scheme by Petronix, recommendation from a Major Howard. Excellent academic qualifications, done well this year at Leeds. That's about it."

"What's he studying... at University?" asked Ferguson. Kim skim read the latest note.

"Engineering and computer science."

"Shit," said Rory. "I don't like the sound of this at all. I'm going to have to go outside."

Kim looked worried.

"What are you thinking?" asked Ferguson.

"Well, if you wanted to seriously damage the rig, what would you do?"

Ferguson looked at him. "The condensate pumps."

"Yep... and we have one that's failed and closed," Rory said.

"That's what the gauges say," replied Cousins.

"And which one is shut down?" asked Rory.

"C1... that's what the read-out says," replied Cousins.

"C1... right let's go and see, shall we?" said Rory.

"Not on your own, Woody. You'll need to take someone with you," said Ferguson.

"I'll be fine, I'm not putting anyone else in danger. We could have lost one crew member today already."

Kim looked at Rory. "Be careful," she said.

"Ok, but I don't like it. Just check it out and get back here as soon as you can," replied Ferguson. "And full PPE, right?"

"Got it," replied Rory. "Oh, and you might want to think about shutting down production. If he has rigged the condensate pumps we don't want any gas going through, do we?"

"No, you're right." He looked at Cousins. "Rob, I'm

authorising a full shutdown of Delta Bravo production. Can you get down to the Control Room and sort it? I'll write it up."

Rob Cousins and Rory left the room and went their separate ways. Kim was still with Ferguson who was trying unsuccessfully to persuade her to have one of his filter coffees.

A few minutes later Rory appeared in full PPE. He checked his watch, seven fifty-five.

He retraced his steps to the exit and braced himself for the wind. Surprisingly the door opened without too much difficulty and he was able to close it without it slamming.

The noise from the sea was still deafening and relentless. Rory reached the walkway to the gas platform and walked slowly across trying not to look down. The wind here was different, like in a tunnel and much stronger as a result, making it difficult to stand. The spray from the sea reached his face and the taste of salt permeated into his mouth. It wasn't rain. He reached the door to the gas module and pulled hard. It required all his strength, but it opened. The noise of the machinery replaced the sound of the wind; a cacophony from hell.

He walked directly to the pumps and straight away could see something wasn't right. The cage door was open. He was about to enter, but he would never have heard the footsteps from behind him. Flashing lights... then... nothing. The blow to the back of the head with a heavy wrench just below the protection of the hard-hat rendered him unconscious. Wearing the head-gear meant that a normal strike to the skull wasn't possible but the result was the same.

Tariq started to pull Rory's comatose form away from the cage towards the safety rail on the far side of the module. With full PPE kit Rory was heavy and Tariq found hauling him was not easy. He stopped every couple of yards. Then he remembered something he needed to do. He left Rory and went to one of the rig lights that lit the inside of the platform close to the condensate cage and opened the cover. It was a standard hundred-watt light bulb, the same you see in any household. He took the end of the wrench and smashed the glass bulb but left it in place without replacing the cover.

"Just to make sure," he said to himself, "Just to make sure."

Petronix Headquarters, Aberdeen 7.30pm.

Doug Earnshaw knocked on the door of the MI6 Ops room, as it had now become.

"Just had a message from Pericles, they've spotted a Chinook and what looked like divers... Thought you would like to know."

"Thanks Doug, keep me posted," said Brittain.

"Well, it looks like something's happening at least. Hope they make it. It's a hell of a risk," he said. Porter and Dominic looked at each other. The strain was beginning to show.

7.50pm the base of the Delta Bravo platform, North Sea

It had taken Sergeant Jackson and the team twenty minutes to swim the half kilometre to the rig with the tide behind them, but their troubles were far from over. The force of the waves was making it impossible to be able to cling to any hand-hold.

Each of the enormous legs had metal ladders that were enclosed by steel stays designed to prevent crew being swept off by waves. They were mostly used by divers when carrying out maintenance, but also provided a safe evacuation route to waiting boats in the event of an emergency. They went down well-below the normal sea level.

The roller-coaster analogy was apposite. Floating on waves that rose to the height of a three-story house, and then falling the same distance, made accurate swimming impossible. They were being carried along, literally, on the crest of a wave. Conditions were the worst the team had ever experienced in years of service and training; the noise, an incessant roar, like the gates of hell; then the spray, cutting visibility to next to nothing at sea level.

Jackson had managed to rendezvous with his team, so the four servicemen were together bobbing up and down like corks. They were now directly under the rig having missed their entry point and, realistically, had one last chance before being swept out the other side and away from the rig. The strength of the tide would mean a very arduous swim back; if their strength held out.

Jackson indicated to his team by hand signals what he wanted them to do. One by one he wanted them to aim at the last supporting leg of the rig and bounce their way on the swell using their arms to steer themselves. They had done this many times in training, but not in such severe weather.

The three held back, paddling their arms to try to hold their position, and Jackson went for it. He waited for the next surge like a surfer might do, and the force of the tide took him forward thirty or forty feet at least, before the next wave came. He was close now... the next one should do it, and sure enough the water rose ten feet, fifteen feet, twenty feet... rising... rising; then he felt it start to fall away. This was it; he was being forced at tremendous speed towards the giant leg of the rig. He could see the stairwell.

Now.

He made a grab. He had no idea how fast he was travelling, but it was like trying to grasp a handrail of a moving bus. The force of the water nearly pulled his shoulder out of its joint, but he held on until the waves had dropped back down leaving him high and dry.

He pulled himself through the protection stays and onto the steps. His lanyard, with his kitbag attached, was now hanging in the air below him twenty feet above the sea; he reeled it in like a plump salmon.

He signalled the others to repeat the process. Jackson needed to climb as fast as possible; the next surge would hit a good ten feet above where he was standing. He quickly moved upwards taking the metal rungs two at a time. He looked down as Spearman grabbed the steps, then Davies and finally Huntley. All safe.

There was no time to congratulate themselves; there was a job to do and they scrambled up the ladder, over two hundred and fifty feet, to the bottom of the rig. They had removed their flippers and were wearing rubber plimsolls specifically designed to grip on virtually any surface. Each member of the team was carrying his kitbag on his shoulder and holding the side of the ladder with the other. It was exhausting work.

It was five-past eight before they reached the bottom of the rig accommodation area. At the top of the ladder there was a circular metal escape hatch with a wheel on the bottom. Jackson turned the wheel and pushed hard. It was heavy. The door opened upwards enabling the team to crawl out onto the lower walkway. They would need to climb further to get to the accommodation deck and the gangway that led to the gas platform. Their orders were to secure the gas and oil modules before entering the accommodation area.

The team knew the layout of the rig off by heart and quickly found the steps they would need to take to reach the crossing point, a further three floors up. Onwards and upwards, they eventually reached their destination and regrouped. Before crossing they opened their kit bags to retrieve their weapons. They disconnected the lanyards and stowed their baggage in a recess in the wall of the platform used to allow people to pass each other along the narrow causeway.

The wind was stronger at this height, and they bent forward to cross the chasm to the entrance on the other side. Jackson went to the door; his three colleagues either side of the frame. He slowly turned the huge lever that controlled the opening mechanism, then pulled the door towards him. Slowly, he went through. The team followed and quickly assumed positions left and right.

They made their way across the production platform. It was the size of two soccer pitches from one side to the other. In the distance Jackson spotted a figure that appeared to be dragging something. Slowly they moved forward to get a better view. As they got closer they could see that the smaller figure was trying to manhandle someone in PPE to a standing position against the guardrail. They were over fifty metres away. Suddenly Jackson realised what was happening.

"Armed Special Forces," he shouted. "On your knees... Now!"

Tariq turned around and let go of the still-unconscious Rory and raised his wrench like a triumphant warrior with a spear. Four red dots appeared, dancing over his body and Tariq yelled defiantly in Arabic, "Allāhu Akbar, Allāhu Akbar".

His fate was sealed, and four shots rang out, three to the body, one to the head. The momentum of the hits sent him backwards and the force of the wind seemed to just pick him up and he disappeared backwards over the safety rail.

The team ran to Rory who was slumped on the ground, but

leant against the rail. He was starting to come around.

Jackson read the name tag on the PPE and removed Rory's goggles. He looked at his face then suddenly, recognition.

"Rory Calderwood, you old bastard, what on earth are you doing on this piece of rusting junk?"

Rory's eyes opened and looked at his rescuer. Dressed in his black frogman's kit; it could have been the angel of death.

"It's Ted Jackson," said the officer.

Jackson had worked with Rory briefly, just before he left the Regiment in 1993.

Rory smiled. "Getting a bit old for playing fucking Neptune aren't we, Jacko?"

Spearman, Davies and Huntley joined his colleague.

"Can you stand?" asked the sergeant, and two of them helped Rory to his feet.

"Come on, let's get you inside... Pete, can you take Davies and check the oil module, then report back to the accommodation block; we'll be there."

Spearman left Jackson and Huntley helping Rory to walk towards the exit door to the gangway and headed to the next platform.

Across the walkway then to the accommodation block, Rory was now just about walking on his own steam. The two officers stopped to pick up their kitbags and then entered the accommodation block still holding their rifles.

Rory led them down the wide stairway still supported by Jackson with Huntley just behind; then along the corridor to the OIM's office. Other staff were about, and were initially shocked to see the shadowy figures with Rory walking along the corridor; then concerned seeing him clearly in distress.

"Woody, you ok? What's happened?" questions being fired

off which he ignored.

They turned into the short corridor to Ferguson's office and opened the door.

Ferguson was in his usual seat at the top of the table and was talking to Kim who was sat next to him. James Gilroy, Chief Technician and Dave Brewster were also present; the only absentee was Rob Cousins who was still in the Control Room.

"Rory!" exclaimed Kim, as the still recovering Calderwood entered the room being held by a sinister looking black figure.

She got up and helped him into a chair and Ferguson was on his feet.

"What's happened?" he said.

"You the OIM?" asked the lead figure. Before Fergie could answer, the man continued. "Ted Jackson, Special Forces; this is Dave Huntley. I've two more officers checking the oil platform; the gas is secure."

Kim was holding Rory's head, his eyes still not properly focussing.

"Jim, quick, get the doc," said Ferguson.

Gilroy got up and opened the door just as the medic was approaching; he had already been alerted by concerned colleagues.

He went to Rory who was still being held by Kim. The officers and exec team looked on.

"What happened?" asked Mark French, the rig's medical officer.

"Not sure, someone hit me, back of my head," said Rory.

"He was unconscious when we found him," said Jackson.

"Sorry, Doc... Ted Jackson, Special Forces."

The doc nodded in acknowledgement.

Kim removed Rory's hard-hat to reveal a nasty gash just

above the hairline at the base of his skull.

"You need to get to the sick bay, Rory. We'll keep you under observation till we can get you off to a hospital," said the Doc.

"Sorry Doc, not yet... This thing isn't over."

"Rory, please listen to him," said Kim.

"I will, I am, just a few minutes; we need to sort out what's happening here, we could still be in danger," said Rory.

"It's ok, I'll stay here and keep an eye on him," said the Doc.

The door opened, and Spearman and Davies entered. "Oil platform secure," said Spearman.

It was getting crowded in the room. Kim was still holding Rory who was now fully focused.

Ferguson looked at his Production manager.

"Dave, can you take Sergeant Jackson and his men to the galley and get them some coffee and something to eat?"

"In a moment, I need to report in. What's your status?" asked Jackson.

Ferguson looked at his colleagues and replied.

"Well, we managed to repair the phone line about five minutes ago. I've spoken to the Beach and brought them up to speed. The electrics are still out so I've authorised a full shut down."

Ferguson stopped in his tracks. "That's funny, it's still running," he said, looking at the flow rates on the wall gauge. "I gave the authorisation a while ago."

Just then Rob Cousins opened the door; he was out of breath having run up the stairs from the Control Room.

"It won't shut down... All the switches have been compromised. I don't know what controls what," he said, in an air of despair. "We've been trying to work it out, but it doesn't make any sense."

"What about the over-ride?" asked Ferguson.

"The same," replied Cousins. "It's like a runaway train."

"Jesus! What about the flows?" said Ferguson.

"Well, if we can believe the gauges... They're all showing normal apart from C1, that's been off for some time."

"Where are we with the electrics?' asked Rory.

"Still on emergency power. The lads are looking into it, but so far we've not been able to sort it" said Cousins.

Rory looked at Ferguson. "Siddique?"

"Looks like it. The Beach confirmed he's a suspected terrorist. They've got MI6 in the office at the moment investigating," said Ferguson.

Rory was trying to take in the information. His intuition had proved right, but it was too late to do anything.

Rob Cousins left the office to return to the Control Room.

"Keep me updated," said Ferguson as he left.

Jackson was on his Sat phone to Arbroath.

"Yes, confirm that... rig secure, one male believed to be Tariq Siddique, neutralised and went over the side, presumed dead. We have one casualty with what looks like concussion needs emergency evac."

Ferguson was listening and interrupted. "We have one man missing."

Jackson passed it on. "One man missing," he said and listened. "Right ok... copy that."

He looked at Ferguson.

"Helicopters should be able to make a landing in the morning."

Petronix Headquarters, Aberdeen 8.50pm.

Back in his temporary HQ, Andy Brittain was on the phone to the Director.

"Confirmed message from Arbroath... rig is secure...

Siddique...? No, it appears he went over the side, shot by Special Forces. There's one man missing on board and search parties will resume when the wind drops... There's one injury, not thought critical, who'll need airlifting as soon as we can get a helicopter down... No, no news on electrics but they have managed to get the phone lines back... yes... sabotage. Looks like Siddique cut them. No... No news on production... seems to have been unaffected... still running apparently. According to the manager here, one of the gas pumps was mal- functioning and they're still on emergency power, otherwise everything seems ok...Yes, I agree we've been very lucky...Yes, I'm sure there will be an enquiry, but I've been thinking about that... If we broadcast it that we've allowed a terrorist to be employed on a major asset... well, let's just say questions will be asked. But there's something else; it'll be a huge coup for Al Qaeda and all the Jihadists. I think we need to manage this in a different way." He continued his explanation and idea to Mansfield.

Delta Bravo Oil & Gas Platform 9.05pm.

Back in the OIM's office, there was a flurry of activity. Ferguson was directing activity, clarifying priorities and distributing resources. With the wind starting to ease, he discussed action plans with his team.

"Priority's going to be getting power restored and the remaining comms systems repaired. James can you get a team out at twenty-one thirty? You'll need to set up some emergency lighting."

"Will do," said Gilroy.

"We need to check those pumps, Fergie, urgently," said Rory, still being held by Kim and being watched over by the Doctor.

"I don't think we're out of the woods yet. We don't know what he might've done."

"Well, you can't go, Woody. Dave, you take three men as soon as you can and do a manual check of the pumps and sensors," said Ferguson.

"Aye," said Dave.

Suddenly everyone looked at each other as the lights flickered... went out... then came back on again.

"What was that?" asked Kim.

Ferguson was already on the phone; "I see, what all of them?" queried Ferguson, the discussion continued. The group looked at him in anticipation.

He put the phone down.

"That was Rob, power's been restored, just came back on. Everything's working fine, back to normal."

"What about the pumps?" asked Rory.

"That's the strange thing, they're all showing normal flows," said Ferguson.

"What, all of them?" asked Rory.

"That's what he said," said Ferguson.

"Jesus no! Fergie, get onto Rob, tell him to shut everything down. Now!!"

Ferguson was back on the phone. Rob can you..."

He never finished the sentence.

There was a loud 'crumphh' and the whole of the accommodation block seemed to lift upwards from its base. The side wall appeared to buckle inwards from the force of the explosion. The digital clock on the wall stopped; it said 9.11!! Emergency sirens were automatically engaged and were screaming their warning across the accommodation area.

"Muster stations," said Ferguson.

He picked up the phone and called Aberdeen.

Gilroy led the team from the room. Rory tried to get up, but his legs went, and he immediately sat down. Kim and the doctor took an arm each and moved him.

Outside the corridor there was in chaos as men tried to get to their PPE; an evacuation would be extremely dangerous even in the improving weather conditions.

Ferguson phoned Cousins in the control room. "What's the status, Rob?"

"Looks like a blow out on C4 condensate pump... It ignited, but deluge systems are working normally, and we should have it under control very soon."

Ferguson got onto the internal tannoy, and addressed the crew.

"We've had an explosion on one of the condensate pumps, but the deluge system has activated which should seal it... I need the duty technical team to report to me, the rest of you, don PPE and report to the Temporary Safety Refuge."

There was no panic, people were well-trained and knew exactly what was expected of them.

In the galley all stoves and hotplates were switched off. In the lounges where the electricity had momentarily been restored all TV's and other electrical appliances were also turned off.

James Gilroy, as Chief Technical Officer, assembled a team of six and reported to the OIM in full PPE. A fire team was put on standby waiting for the team to report back.

Kim was having a battle with Rory. "I need to go with them," he was saying.

"I think you've done more than enough, don't you," she said, and together they made their way with the Doctor to the TSR.

The Temporary Safety Refuge was just one of the many improvements that the industry had to action following the

Cullen report into Piper Alpha. Additional blast proof walls had been added and potential explosive areas isolated from the main accommodation block. Delta Bravo had been completely renovated in the early 90's and all the safety recommendations had been implemented.

The phone rang in Ferguson's office as the technical team assembled.

"Rob, what's the latest? You have... thank goodness. Yes, stay there until I get back to you. I'm sending a team out to inspect the damage," said Ferguson.

He looked at the six men in front of him.

"That was Rob. He's managed to shut down all the gas pumps and he's also stopped the oil production as a precaution. We may have had a bit of luck. For the moment, just check and report."

The team left and crossed the bridge to the gas module and managed to prise the door open; the heat had welded it to the bulkhead. They went through and, for a moment, just stared unable to take in the scene.

It was carnage, total devastation. The force of the explosion had pushed out the side of the platform like some almighty fist. Pipes and metal were twisted, bent out of shape. The cage which had surrounded the pumps had disintegrated; there were bits of metal everywhere. Water was gushing under pressure from the deluge pumps drenching everything, but they had done their job and extinguished the resultant fire. The additional blast proofing had saved a major disaster.

Unfortunately, with the Piper Alpha disaster, the whole of the accommodation block was taken out by the first explosion resulting in many casualties and the complete breakdown of command and control. Here, the deluge system had kicked in as soon as the explosion had happened and suffocated the fire. With production shut down, there was no immediate danger.

The team went back to the office and reported their findings. Gilroy spoke. "It looks like everything is secure, but there is considerable damage to the gas platform and pumps. Repairs are going to take some time."

Ferguson was back on the tannoy, standing everyone down and asking them to return to their normal duties. The emergency was over.

The rig would remain shut down for the moment until the full extent of the damage could be assessed; a team would fly out from Aberdeen first thing, weather permitting.

By seven o'clock the next morning the wind had dropped to force four, within helicopter tolerance, and the first of the emergency teams started to arrive.

Rory was the first to be airlifted accompanied by Kim. She had stayed with him all night on doctor's orders.

"Just keep an eye on him," he had said. "He shouldn't be left on his own."

Rory reported to the doctor for a final check before they left, and he was happy with his progress. He re-dressed the wound which had swollen to the size of an egg.

"I've phoned the E.D. at Aberdeen they'll do a scan just to make sure there are no fractures, but it seems ok... You'll probably have a hell a headache for a few days and some bruising for a while."

The Puma lifted off. Rory had packed his gear and as he watched the helipad disappear below him he knew that would be the last he would see of the rig.

Epilogue

The fall-out from the incident on Delta Bravo was interesting in as much as there was very little.

Although gas production was halted for over a month whilst repairs to the damage was carried out, there was a certain amount of back-slapping at Petronix that a major catastrophe had been averted due to the investment and improvements carried out in the mid 90's following the recommendations of Cullen. Training and good leadership had also played its part, not to mention the bravery of the crew.

It was the security forces who had most to lose, and there was a significant amount of damage limitation going on.

Andy Brittain's recommendation was put into action. The headlines in the Daily Telegraph the following day read as follows:

'Two die in blaze on oil rig.'

'Two men are feared dead following a fire on a North Sea gas rig. The installation is owned by Petronix, but has not been identified. In a statement the company confirmed that two men have been unaccounted for following a small fire on one of their gas platforms. The severe weather is believed to have been a contributing factor. Their names are being withheld until their next of kin have been informed. Full report, page 6. Lessons from Piper Alpha learned, page 10.'

Back in London, Andy Brittain was discussing the fall-out with the Director.

"It is vital that we give nothing to the jihadists that would give them a rallying call. I'm not having Siddique as a martyr."

"No, you're right. I've spoken to Petronix, and the story will be kept very low key... minor fire, severe weather, no tragedy, a credit to the design changes following Piper Alpha; the Telegraph have already picked up on that... Regret loss of life etc., etc. I think we can head off any public enquiry on the grounds of national security. Petronix have contacted Gordon Whittaker's family, they told them he went overboard in the storm. Siddique didn't have anyone that we can find, seems to have been our worst nightmare, a real lone operative."

"I wonder what really happened?" posed Brittain.

"We'll never know," replied the Director, "It seems most likely that Siddique threw Whittaker overboard to enable him to get to the junction box to cut the comms, but we'll never know for certain."

"But the knowledge and skill to take down a gas rig... well, all I can say, what a waste of talent," continued Brittain.

"Yes, you're right there. We'll certainly need to vet our students from the Middle East more closely. They might try again," said the Director.

The ensuing weeks were difficult for Rory. After a short spell in hospital, he made a gradual recovery from his injury; but it was not the physical scars which were the problem. The trauma had caused a recurrence of flash-backs from his SAS days.

Kim took two weeks' leave to look after him and he stayed at her flat, only returning to the house to pick up the mail. Once she had returned to work however, he would be back walking in the hills where he found some solace. Kim had suggested counselling which had been made available to him, but he had never subscribed to the talking treatment theory; he needed to 'sort his own shit out' he said.

The house had been put up for sale as part of the on-going divorce proceedings from Janie, but he had no qualms about this; too many memories. He had said nothing to her about his experience and didn't contact her until he had left hospital, an accident, he had said; he didn't want her sympathy.

His divorce to Janie eventually went through and, although he was given unlimited access to the boys, he was unable to maintain any relationship with them. Seeing his sons was just too painful. He stopped calling; the formal separation had been dealt with through lawyers.

His relationship with Kim also began to suffer; she had found it difficult to penetrate the emotional wall which he had built around himself. She had done everything she could to support him, but his mood swings and moroseness became too much and after two months, she applied to return to London, leaving Rory to fend for himself. "I can't do this anymore," she told him.

He moved back to the house temporarily, until it was sold, and then rented a small flat. He was officially on sick leave, but, after Kim left, he fell into a deep depression. Even running in the hills had lost its therapeutic effect. His days were spent in isolation; old friends and relatives were shunned until they finally stopped calling.

Surprisingly, he resisted the temptation to seek solace in drink or drugs, determined to beat it on his own terms without artificial crutches.

As part of their absence management procedure, he was eventually contacted by a welfare officer from Petronix, and it was she who was able to make some progress. After several meetings, he made the decision to start over and accepted a pay-off. He left Petronix and moved back to his spiritual roots in rural Midlands. He would never know his connection with Tariq Siddique.

In Batley a few weeks after the incident, Abdul Hussein was reading a short article about the initial inquest into the Delta Bravo fire and subsequent deaths. He was taken aback; the two missing men had been named; Gordon Whittaker, and... Tariq Siddique.

The family hadn't heard from Tariq for almost three months and they had been extremely worried. There had been some coverage of the fire on the rig the day after the event, but having no idea where Tariq was, Abdul and the family had not associated it with their nephew. However, seeing his name as one of the fatalities caused him to pick up the phone.

He dialled an Aberdeen number.

"Hello... is that Petronix? My name is Abdul Hussein... I am enquiring about my nephew, Tariq... Tariq Siddique."

The End

Alan Reynolds

"**...story left me with a racing pulse, jangling nerves and a real want for a follow up book.**"
- *Jacque Gerrard*

"**This book has everything.** The characters really come to life and I cannot wait for the next in the series!"
-Sara Seastron

"**Brilliant read, thoroughly enjoyed it**. Just waiting for your next publication"
- *Sarah Knight*

"**...one of those books you cannot put down... gripping tale**."
- *Anna-Marie Dreyfus*

"...currently reading Flying with Kites **CAN'T WAIT TO GET HOME TO READ MORE!**"
- *Keeley Edge*

"**...David is raving about Flying with Kites. He's half way thru and already sees it's potential for a film...**"
- *William and Victoria Restaurant - Harrogate / book club*

"... It will make you gasp, sigh and laugh out loud... Alan Reynolds has the ability to make this happen all on one page, absolutely superb... **a definite five stars!**"
- *Lynette Machin*

"**A Brilliant Read...** I'm never normally gripped so much by storylines but this kept me in suspense throughout. Just couldn't put it down!"
- *Anita Flowers*

"**Gripping stuff...** This story had me hooked from the outset. I'm sure that my pulse rate must have increased as I progressed through it and circumstances, decisions and fate all began to take effect. I recommend this book to fans of Ruth Rendell and I don't think for one moment they will be disappointed."
- *Anne Ulah*

"**Awesome read...** I don't read very much at all and it's not the type of story I would have chosen but I could not put this book down. The whole story is totally believable. Towards the end I just could not leave it and sat all night reading to find out what happened."
- *Claire Setchel*

"**I recommend it as a must read book...** Having read Flying with Kites I was eagerly waiting for Reynolds next book to be published. It was well worth the wait. Psychological thrillers are my favourite genre and this is one the best I've read for some time."
- *'Snow Leopard'*

"**I couldn't turn the pages fast enough to find out what was going to happen...** After reading Flying With Kites I was excited to read Alan Reynolds new novel, Taskers End, and I wasn't disappointed.
- *Heather McLaren*

"**...recommended.** Having worked in the banking system I can relate to the background culture that was prevalent in 1990s / 2000s, and in other sectors, and I feel I have met the characters. ...a roller coaster of emotion, excitement and despair, hedonistic fun and shattering sadness."
- *Richard King*

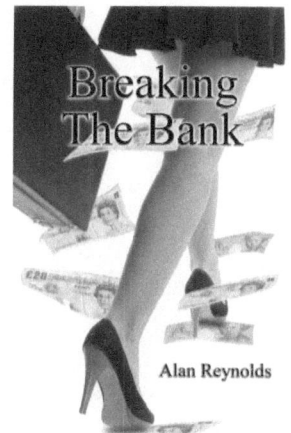

"**A riveting read...** Alan's writing is very engaging and keeps you enthralled from start to finish. Would definitely recommend for anyone with a curiosity about the inner workings of branch banking."
- *Sally Turgoose*

"**I couldn't put the book down...** Larger than life" characters are portrayed set in a ruthless and stressful environment; but are there elements of truth here? One is left wondering, particularly in the light of the recent banking crisis and recession! This book would lead to an interesting discussion in any book club."
- *CBL*

"**Brilliant and insightful...** It would probably have been less risky to have taken our money to the casino than to the bank. Brilliant and insightful into just what was going on from the government downwards. No wonder we finished up in the mess we did."
- *John Leach*

"**This book is one I could not put down...** As the title suggests, the storyline is set within a banking background. By the time I had finished, the reason the banks hit a crisis sending us into economic free fall became much clearer!"
- *Kate Goddard*

www.ingramcontent.com/pod-product-compliance
Lightning Source LLC
Chambersburg PA
CBHW020637020726
47494CB00001B/228